Dear Reader,

This month we're delighted to welcome best selling author Patricia Wilson to the *Scarlet* list. With over 40 romance novels to her credit, we are sure that Patricia's new book will delight her existing fans and win her many new readers. You can also read *Resolutions*, the conclusion of Maxine Barry's enthralling 'All His Prey' duet. And we are proud to bring you books by two talented new authors: Judy Jackson who hails from Canada and Tiffany Bond who is based in England.

You will possibly have noticed that some of the *Scarlet* novels we publish are quite sexy, while others are warmer and more family oriented. Do you like this mix of styles and the different levels of sensuality? And how about locations: is it important to you *where* an author sets her *Scarlet* book?

If you have written to me about *Scarlet*, please accept my thanks. I read each and every one of your letters and I certainly refer to your comments and suggestions when I am thinking about our schedules.

Till next month,

Sally Cooper

SALLY COOPER,
Editor-in-Chief – *Scarlet*

MAXINE BARRY

RESOLUTIONS

Part Two of **All His Prey**

SCARLET

Enquiries to:
Robinson Publishing Ltd
7 Kensington Church Court
London W8 4SP

First published in the UK by Scarlet, 1997

A copy of the British Library Cataloguing in
Publication data is available from the British Library

ISBN 1-85487-903–0

Printed and bound in the EC

10 9 8 7 6 5 4 3 2 1

CHAPTER 1

New York, 1975

Veronica Coltrane paused outside Ohrbach's to study the fascinating window display before hurrying on to Nibbits Department Store on 68th and West.

It was a freezing January morning, and as she waited by the crossing for the 'Walk' sign she blew into her hands to try and warm them. Without much success. She had thought her native home of England could get cold in winter, but this was new to her.

Not that she regretted coming to America, of course. No, she would never, *never* feel regret. She had needed to escape from England, and all the hideous memories it still held for her, with a passion that she knew was not healthy. The knowledge of her own vulnerability, even after all this time, still lurked uneasily at the back of her mind.

She still had so much to do. And keeping her job was, at the moment, top of her list. Travis was relying on her. But on a cold January morning her responsibilities seemed to lie all the more heavily on her shoulders. It sometimes felt as if she was carrying around her own personal iceberg. It made life so cold sometimes.

And so many people, kind, good people, had had to pull so many strings just to get her an entry visa and work permit to this new country that she simply *had* to make a go of it. She couldn't let them down. Not when they'd taken such chances for her. And she knew, more than anyone, how hard it must have been for them to trust her. Considering . . .

The 'Walk' sign flashed on, and her unhappy thoughts were suddenly jostled out of her. She found herself abruptly carried along by a human tide as thirty people made a mad dash across the road. Once on the other side, she glanced at her inexpensive watch and gave a sigh of relief. She was not as late as she'd thought.

But Travis had had to start a new school today, and he'd been scared, poor mite. She'd had to walk him to school and introduce him to his teachers, just to settle him down. His English accent would no doubt let him in for a lot of teasing by his fellow classmates, but Veronica was confident he'd soon make friends. Her son was a very open and lovable five-year-old, even if she did say so herself. Everyone said he was full of fun and a charming kind of cheek. Everybody commented on his warm and generous nature.

If only they'd known who his father was . . .

No! Veronica quickly cut the thought off. She would not think of . . . *him*. Never again would

2

she let that man so much as cross her thoughts. He'd been told that his son had died at birth and had not even bothered to check it out. No doubt he'd been only too happy to believe it was true. The shame of having a son born in . . . such a place . . . had probably curled Wayne D'Arville's fastidious lip. The thought was enough to make her want to scream or burst into tears. Quickly, she thrust the past away from her.

Instead, Veronica conjured up the sight of her son as he'd been on the plane coming over – cherub-cheeked and dark-haired, with big blue eyes that had stared out at their new home. America. No doubt he'd soon be inviting his new-made little friends over for tea, and looking forward to going to school in the mornings, instead of anxiously clinging to her legs.

No, she had no worries on her son's behalf. She couldn't help but be grateful that he'd inherited only his father's eyes, not his cold, ruthless heart.

Running part of the way saved her more time, and as she pushed open the swing doors of the gigantic shopping precinct it was just coming up to nine a.m.

She had worked at Nibbits for the past two months, and she quickly made her way across the grey-flecked carpet that lined the vast acreages of floorspace. Her own little niche in the giant store was on the cosmetics/pharmacy floor, and as she approached the colourful counter, lined with exquisite crystal perfume bottles, she pulled off her warm brown serge coat. She'd found it at a rummage sale just two days after arriving in New York, and

3

although it was old it was of an elegant cut and just about passed muster on the Nibbits Dress Code for employees. But she wasn't sure how much longer it would last, and the thought of the expense of a new coat was enough to push her heart into her boots. She was managing her budget on a precarious shoestring as it was.

'You're cutting it fine, aren't you?' Julie Preston, her ever-cheerful fellow worker, said with a knowing wink as Veronica lifted the wooden bar on the counter and closed it behind her.

'I know. I was up all night; Travis had a restless night. I only hope he behaves himself at school today. The last thing I need is a phone call asking me to come and pick him up. Old man Howard would have a fit if I had to have so much as an hour off.'

Julie gave a sympathetic shrug, then groaned as the two-minute warning bell sounded. Soon they'd be inundated with matrons looking for something 'different', teenage girls trying to sneak samples of Joy perfume, and the inevitable light-fingered professional shoplifter or two. 'You have to have eyes in the back of your head to work in this place,' Julie had told her the first day she'd started, and Veronica had soon understood what she meant.

Now, Veronica quickly turned to one of the large mirrors that Nibbits supplied for its customers and checked her appearance.

The rather elegant and capable-looking Veronica Coltrane who looked back at her was very different from the defeated woman who had served six months

4

at Nottinghamshire Open Prison for Women and a further six months at Holloway.

Had it really been five years ago? It seemed as if it were only yesterday . . .

She could still hear the bell ringing at six o'clock in the morning, and the muttering sounds of discontented voices. In her dreams, the sound of keys turning in endless locks chased her through restless nights. She could still remember queueing to 'slop out'. And queueing for breakfast. And queueing in work lines. Her whole world had consisted of queueing in a relentless place that existed in shades of grey.

It was not surprising that she had lost weight so drastically in prison after giving birth to Travis.

She'd suffered badly from post-natal depression and had quickly slipped down to a dangerous six stones. Even though she had regained a few pounds during the five years she'd lived with her father in their Reading semi, her figure was still pencil-slim. But her breasts were well-rounded, no doubt as a legacy of breast-feeding her son.

Veronica felt guilty at lying to the recruiting officer at Nibbits, but she knew she'd never be hired if she was honest about her past. And she didn't think the store had been the loser by it. She was now the top saleswoman on the floor.

Anxiously, she turned to a side view in the mirror. The dress she wore was also second-hand, for money was perpetually tight, but it was simple, black, and suited her.

Her cap of sleek black hair gave her a distinctly

Parisian elegance, always handy when selling trifles to rich women, and her small, piquant face needed the barest amount of make-up, which was just as well. Veronica had spent the last of her woefully pitiful savings on getting to New York, and now only her wages at Nibbits kept herself and her son from poverty's door.

Sebastien, being Sebastien, had offered to lend her a substantial amount, of course, but she had firmly refused. He'd done quite enough for her already in managing to get her into America at all. With a criminal record, she was still not sure how he had managed to secure her a work permit and visa, but she knew better than anyone that Sebastien Teale could move mountains when he wanted to.

Besides, as ungrateful as she knew it was, she didn't want to have anything to do with anyone who was friends with . . . *him*. Not that Sebastien was Wayne's friend, exactly. Were psychiatrists allowed to be friends with their patients? She wasn't sure, and cared even less.

When she'd asked him how he'd managed to get her the necessary documentation, he'd just smiled at her with that devastating smile of his. 'Let's just say I've got friends over there,' he'd murmured, his eyes crinkling at the corners as he smiled, his boyish grin flashing his usual gentle charm.

Sebastien had written to her the day after her trial had ended, telling her he believed in her innocence and always would. It had been the only ray of sunshine in a world turned unbearably bleak, and

6

she had immediately written back. A long and life-saving correspondence had resulted, with every two days of her sentence seeing her receive a long, cheerful and chatty letter. Those letters had enabled her to keep a grip on reality in that grim and awful place.

Even now, whenever a door opened or closed, Veronica could still hear the echo of the clanging of heavy doors. Every time she saw a picture of a particularly luxurious bathroom in a magazine, she remembered the ignominty of 'slopping out'. Every morning, whether her chamber pot was empty or not, she had to queue up outside the toilets with the others, the stench of human waste making her feel sick. She never ate breakfast, yearning only for the relative peace and sanctuary of the pitiful library where her past employment experience had allowed her to get the top prison job. Regular visits from her father and Sebastien had kept her sane, but even so, after her time was up, she had left a changed woman.

Trust was completely gone. You learned not to trust anyone in that place. Her things were stolen with almost monotonous regularity – stupid things like her toothpaste, the emery board with which she used to shape her fingernails, her hair grips. She had not realized how precious freedom was until it was taken away from her.

You could wear no make-up or perfume. You could have only one letter a day, and those were read, both incoming and outgoing. Any parcels sent in by friends or relatives were searched, and no food parcels were allowed. Looking back, Veronica wondered how she had survived it all.

'Excuse me, young woman, how much is this?'

Veronica blinked, shaking off the memories, and focused on the woman in front of her. She was one of what Julie called the 'blue rinse brigade', for her hair was silver-blue and her face, aged and lined, pinched in perpetual ill-humour. Veronica checked the pot of moisturizer, and said, 'That is four dollars sixty-seven, madam.'

'What? For this tiny thing? Preposterous! What else do you have?'

Veronica reached behind her for the wooden box of creams, catching Julie rolling her eyes at her. She grinned, quickly wiped off the smile, turned and began to explain the uses and prices of the creams. After half an hour the woman left, a small tube of cream costing sixty cents clutched triumphantly in her gloved hand.

The woman's white silk gloves alone, Veronica thought grimly, would have paid her rent at Mrs Williams's boarding house for a whole month.

Life was so screamingly unfair sometimes that it still managed to catch Veronica on the raw. And because she knew how quickly bitterness could destroy a person, she forced herself to think of something good.

She had been so lucky to find Mrs Williams, her landlady, for instance. She had stumbled upon the decaying but once elegant house opposite Central Park almost by accident.

8

Mrs Williams was a sixty-six-year-old widow who took boarders more for company than for the money. All her tenants were women, for the thought of a man in the house filled the tiny four-foot-eight woman with quivering trepidation.

Veronica had spent three miserable days trying to find a place that she could afford that also allowed young children. It had just been getting dark when her last attempt at finding a room had failed, forcing her to contemplate paying for yet another night at the YWCA.

But the porter of the modern apartment block she had just tried had taken pity on her and given her Mrs Williams' name and address. It was raining hard by the time she got there, and Travis, snug and dry in his padded anorak, was chatting happily to a stray cat, who was sniffing his chubby hands in search of titbits.

She walked up the broken steps of the house, hardly paying attention to the scrubby plot of land that was supposed to be a garden, too tired, weary and despondent to care about the flaking paint or the haphazard roof of the ancient house. Looking back on that interview, Veronica supposed that it was her too-slender appearance and the dull, hopeless expression in her eyes that had been the deciding factor in making Mrs Williams abandon her strict 'no children' policy.

That, and the fact that, when the old woman looked down at him, Travis had with miraculous timing decided to bestow on the old lady one of his dazzling, happy smiles.

Since then, Mrs Williams and Travis had developed a bond that had allowed Veronica to leave him in the landlady's care without having to pay the cost of a childminder.

That alone had probably kept her from starving.

It was approaching lunchtime and Veronica and Julie were swamped. The January sales were just winding down, and last-minute panic-buying had brought out the housewives in hordes.

Her feet were killing her, her face ached from wearing its customer-smile, and the counter was a mess.

''Allo. I'm lookin' for a perfume, luv. What'ya got?'

The voice was loud, male, and easily rose above the rest of the babbling female crowd. And its broad cockney accent had Veronica swinging around in amazement, her eyes picking out the voice's owner in an instant.

He was six feet or so, with brown, longish hair, deep-set, cheerful brown eyes and a narrow, boyish face that was as full of cheek as his voice.

Veronica, aware that she was staring, pulled herself together with a snap. 'Certainly, sir. What price range did you have in mind?'

The man's face broke into a huge grin. 'Luv-a-duck,' he said outrageously, his accent deliberately exaggerated. 'A bloody Englisher, as I live an' breave. What'ya doing over 'ere?'

Veronica's smile suddenly changed from her

customer variety to a very different kind. 'Working. Hard. And you're holding up the traffic,' she all but growled. She had been a virgin when she had met Wayne D'Arville, a young and foolish woman who didn't know enough to get out of the kitchen when it caught fire. The result was a severe burning, and she was not about to get burned again. Every instinct in her screamed at her to get rid of this . . . this . . . outrageous stranger.

The stranger in question barely glanced around him, noting the shoving feminine crowd as if for the first time. 'Don't worry about them. I promise I'm gonna buy somefink expensive. Nibbits is the same as all the other shops in this country.' He paused just long enough to rub his fingers and thumbs together in an expressive gesture. 'Money talks, luv.'

He noted her flashing brown eyes, with just a tiny tigerish glint deep in their depths, and grinned widely. 'Just shut yer eyes and fink of your commission.'

Veronica looked him up and down with quick, jaundiced eyes. On his feet were dirty sneakers with a hole in one upper, allowing his big toe to squeeze through. His jeans were faded at the knees and frayed at the ankles, and the shirt he wore had its buttons done up in the wrong order, so that the white cotton sat on his thin frame at an awkward ankle. On top of that, he wore a fur coat of dubious pedigree. It even . . .

She leaned forward slowly and gave a delicate sniff, her prettily shaped nostrils flaring as she did so.

Yes. Just as she thought. It actually *smelled*.

11

She met his eyes, which were by now twinkling with laughter, and slowly shook her head.

'I am the genuine article, luv, 'onest. You'll be getting a humungous commission from me. I'm after the biggest and most expensive bottle of smelly stuff yer got.'

'Uh-huh,' she said without the merest hint of expression of any kind. Keeping her feet firmly on the ground, both physically and metaphorically, she turned at the waist to reach for a gigantic bottle of Joy, the most expensive perfume available, in a real silver and crystal flacon.

The stranger's eyes nearly popped out of his head. Rapidly he ran his eyes over her slender curves, his eyes lingering at the angle of her shoulders, the teasing thrust of her breasts, and the very shapely length of her legs.

As her fingers fastened around the bottle, and she prayed that old man Howard wouldn't choose that moment to come on the floor to see her humouring a tramp, she caught a rapid movement out of the corner of her eye. Quickly, she turned her head to look at Julie, who was waving her hands frantically about below the level of the counter, and mouthing something at her that she couldn't quite lip-read. She had no idea that her unusual pose had made the stranger's appreciative smile turn oddly intense.

The man began to positively stare at her profile. With her body twisted one way, and her head another, she should have looked awkward, ridiculous even. But she didn't. She looked . . .

'Gorgeous,' he muttered.

Veronica, still wearing a puzzled frown, turned back to the cockney who reminded her so much of a Victorian barrow-boy for looks and cheek. She smiled stiffly. 'Did you say something, sir?' she gritted through her teeth.

'I said you looked gorgeous,' the stranger confirmed helpfully.

Veronica attempted to freeze her eyes. She did it remarkably well. In fact her whole face seemed to change, without really changing at all. It was a trick very few women could manage, as the stranger knew only too well.

He could feel his whole body begin to tremble. She was perfect.

'This is a thousand dollars, sir. But it's guaranteed to make the lady smile.' Veronica held out the bottle. Let's see how quickly *that* took the wind out of his arrogant sails!

'I'll bet. But is it guaranteed to make her forgive me?' The brown eyes widened in mute appeal, but the grin he gave her was strictly dastardly.

'That depends,' Veronica snapped. She was aware that she was enjoying herself enormously, and the feeling was more frightening than reassuring. She didn't want a man, any man, to make her feel anything. Not ever again. And certainly not a dirty, scruffy, too-cheeky-for-words cockney!

She turned her smile to one of plastic. It was her best I-have-to-serve-you-whether-I-feel-like-it-or-not smile that was designed to make even princes feel abashed.

13

The stranger's grin widened. 'Magnificent,' he muttered.

Veronica sighed. Hard. It made her breasts rise and fall, and she was not surprised to see the stranger's eyes fall to that area of her anatomy.

Men. They were so predictable.

She had to get rid of this clown, and now. She felt guilty at leaving Julie to cope with all the backlog he was causing.

'It depends on what, me luvverly?' the stranger responded to her taunt at last, and she just managed to stop herself from crowning him with the bottle. It would have been such a waste of good perfume to smash it over his ugly head.

'On what you've done, sir.' She smiled ever-so-sweetly.

'Oh. I've done just about everyfink,' he admitted, shaking his head sadly.

'In that case, sir,' she said, reaching under the counter to bring out a beautiful cosmetics case, 'perhaps the perfume *and* this would be in order.'

The box was of cream leather with an enamelled top in jade, turquoise and rose-pink. She opened it out to reveal an interior of tiers lined in rose-pink silk that housed everything from blusher to eyeliner, from moisturizer cream to the latest shade of nail varnish. 'This model is four hundred and seventy-nine dollars ninety-nine, sir.'

'You don't say? I'll take it. And the perfume. In fact . . .' he paused and thought about it for a moment '. . . I'd better take two of each. I somehow double-dated meself into one 'ell of a nasty pickle last night. So I've got two sets of ruffled feathers to soothe down.'

'Two of each?' she echoed stupidly. Did this idiot not know when enough was enough? Then she all but groaned as she saw Mrs Fitzpatrick, the floor manager, bearing down on them from a great height, no doubt attracted by the large queue. She was an extremely tall redheaded woman, with imperious eyes and a voice to match. 'Oh, no!' Veronica muttered, her face dropping to such a crestfallen low that her pain-in-the-neck customer turned his head curiously to follow her line of vision.

He gave a long, low whistle from between his teeth. 'Oh-oh,' he said. 'The dragon lady approacheth.'

Veronica closed her eyes briefly then opened them again, stiffening her backbone and so missing the expression in the brown eyes that watched her like a hawk.

The kid looked really scared. Did she really need this dead-hole job so much? A kid who looked like *she* did? Never. The stranger knew she could get a job anywhere. Doing anything . . .

As Mrs Fitzpatrick approached, her eyes fell at once on the disreputable-looking man hogging the counter, and Veronica tensed, just waiting for the disdainful look to plaster itself across her supercilious face.

Instead, to her utter astonishment, the dragon lady beamed a smile of almost fawning adulation across the remaining few yards. Her hands came out in a supplication of toadying welcome.

15

Veronica felt her jaw drop. Literally.

'Ahh, Mr Copeland.' The floor manager all but sang the name. 'I can't *tell* you how honoured Nibbits is to have you.' Her white teeth flashed into a perfect public-relations smile.

Veronica had noticed before that the supervisor tended to refer to the shop as if it were a person, not a pile of bricks. It was always 'Nibbits prefers its employees to wear heeled shoes,' or 'Nibbits is very good to its employees if they work hard.'

Now Veronica stood and gaped as she watched several of the women who had been queueing impatiently suddenly begin to whisper among themselves. Like one animal, all their eyes swivelled to watch the tall, beaming man. Lashes fluttered.

Incredible! Veronica thought. One minute they were elbowing and muttering about queue-hogs, the next, even the oldest of them were blushing like schoolgirls.

What the hell was going on?

'Well, now, I can only say I'm right sorry I never came before.' Was it her imagination, or had the cockney accent broadened again? 'I can only say that if I knew you always employed such helpful and pretty staff . . .' he turned to blow the still open-mouthed Veronica a hearty kiss '. . . I'd've come before, so I would, and that's the 'onest truth.'

Mrs Fitzpatrick blushed as if the compliment were directed at her personally.

Veronica looked from the scruffy man in front of

16

her to her beaming boss, feeling like someone who'd come in during the middle of a play. She knew she was the only one who was not in on the plot, and it worried her.

'Catchin' flies, luv?'

Veronica turned her head once more to her customer, like a spectator at a tennis match, and then, when the meaning behind his words finally filtered into her befuddled brain, she snapped her teeth shut with an audible click.

'Can I be of help, Mr Copeland?' Mrs Fitzpatrick asked, and Veronica nearly fainted. Mrs Fitzpatrick, offering to serve, to actually manually serve, a customer? Veronica wished she could sit down. Her legs had gone quite watery.

'Ah, that's a luvverly thought, but this young lady was just showing me all this luvverly stuff. I only came in to buy a tube of toothpaste. I must say, you certainly know how to pick your salesladies.'

Veronica opened her mouth to deny the outrageous lie, then quickly snapped it shut again.

His eyes met hers and twinkled. Damn him.

'I tell yer what,' he said cheerfully. 'I'll have three of these . . .' he tapped the flacon of perfume '. . . and three of these.' He indicated the cosmetics case.

Veronica's mind began to spin as she thought of the commission, and without another word, and not giving him so much as half a second in which to change his mind, she practically flew to the till and rang up the purchases while she still had witnesses to back her claim.

'Would you like them gift-wrapped, sir?' she asked, her voice now very Nibbits-best-customer in tone.

The brown eyes crinkled at the sides, attractive crow's feet making her reassess her earlier estimation of his age that had put him in his late twenties. He must be thirty-five if he was a day. The faker!

'Only two sets of 'em,' he said. 'This and this . . .' he pushed forward one box of cosmetics and one bottle of perfume '. . . are for you, luv.'

Veronica stared at him, blinked, then looked to Mrs Fitzpatrick for help. The dragon lady, however, couldn't make up her mind whether to smile graciously at Mr Whoever-the-hell-he-was or scowl at her.

'I'm not sure if I can accept, sir,' she eventually said, and smiled through her gritted teeth so sweetly that she was sure her face must crack.

'Oh? Well, now, if you don't, I won't pay yer a penny. Eh, ladies? Ain't that right?' He suddenly turned and appealed to the avid audience, who began to titter and nod their heads as he folded his arms stubbornly across his narrow chest.

Veronica glanced at her boss helplessly, and shrugged. 'Very well . . . sir . . . Er . . . thank you very much.' She forced the words out with a great deal of effort. He noticed her hesitation over the polite 'sir' and grinned even more widely.

'My name is Valentine Copeland,' he said. And gave a bow. 'Use it, why don't ya, luv?'

'Certainly, Mr Copeland. What colour paper

18

would you prefer? We have pink, silver-green or navy blue with gold poppies.'

For the first time he looked genuinely disconcerted. 'Er – the pink's fine,' he said, and then he began to smile in earnest as he watched her professionally giftwrap the four purchases. 'Ta ever so,' he said, took the parcels from her, and turned and kissed Mrs Fitzpatrick's cheek.

The woman blushed scarlet.

From his pocket he produced a small white square of paper and presented it to the flustered woman. 'A ticket for my show. You will come, won't ya, luv?'

'Oh, indeed, Mr Copeland. Indeed. Thank you so much. Nibbits is honoured.'

The man kissed her cheek again, but as his lips touched the perfumed skin of the delighted redhead, his eyes slewed over to Veronica and he dropped one eyelid in a slow, audacious wink.

Then he turned, and, whistling loudly and excruciatingly out of tune, sauntered off.

Veronica let out a long, slow breath. Mrs Fitzpatrick, clutching her ticket as if it were gold, floated away. 'Bloody hell,' Veronica said softly, but had a chance to say no more as the female deluge, after craning their necks for the last glimpse of the apparently famous Mr Copeland, once more besieged the desk.

19

CHAPTER 2

It wasn't until the store closed at five-thirty that Julie at last had a chance to speak to her.

Veronica had noticed that her friend had been straining at the bit ever since the incident with the cockney had happened, and she sank down wearily on to a stool and slipped off her shoes, preparing herself for an explanation of the morning's extraordinary events.

'Well, you're a bright spark and no mistake,' was Julie's opening gambit, her blonde hair tumbling around her shoulders as she pulled it free from the chignon she habitually wore. 'Did you see his face when you pretended not to recognize his name?'

'I wasn't pretending,' Veronica said drolly. 'Just who *is* he?' She couldn't deny, even to herself, that the man had thoroughly bamboozled her. He acted the tramp but was obviously nothing of the sort. He made her want to thump him, at the same time as she wanted to laugh at him.

And, worst of all, he was so damned attractive. And Veronica knew all about the devastation attractive men could cause. Which meant she would have nothing to do with him again.

Even so, she was naturally curious. 'I've no idea what all the fuss is about,' she added crossly, and wondered, with a lance of panic, just who she was trying to kid.

This time it was Julie's turn to gape at her, then she began to laugh helplessly. 'Oh, Ver, honestly. He's only the hottest hot-shot fashion designer of them all. Nobody's more "in". Everyone's wearing Valentine.'

'A dressmaker?' Veronica squeaked. 'Him?'

It was not only the raggedness of his own clothes that made his profession surprising, but the character of the man himself. There was something raw about him, something so openly virile and masculine and . . . sexy . . . that she just couldn't picture him creating women's clothes.

Julie gave her a quick run-down on the meteoric rise of the Valentine fashion comet, and repeatedly wished aloud that she could own just one, *just one* of his creations.

At last she wound down about how fabulous Valentine was, and muttered more incomprehensible grumbles about the floor manager as they prepared to leave. Collecting coats and bags – and in Veronica's case her unexpected presents – they walked wearily on sore feet through the mall to the outer door.

'Oh, hell,' Julie moaned, looking out. 'It's pouring. Doesn't that just beat all?'

It was indeed raining as if it meant it – a cold

January downpour. The two girls shrugged and glanced at each other in silent resignation. 'Oh, well,' Veronica said, and then they each made a dash for it in opposite directions.

But Veronica had only gone a yard or so in the direction of the subway when a nifty little black sports car, an E-type Jag no less, with wired wheels and a silver racing stripe, suddenly pulled up at the kerb, and the door was thrust open.

'Get in, luvverly lady. I wanta talk to you.'

Veronica knew the voice instantly. Could there be any forgetting it?

She hesitated, nearly got her eye poked out by an umbrella, and then shrugged. She quickly dipped into the small and cramped interior and slammed the door shut behind her.

'Hello again,' she said, a little nervously, smoothing down her dress over her knees and rearranging herself more decorously in the bucket seat.

Valentine Copeland watched her with avid brown eyes.

'You can forget that for a start,' she snapped, and he blinked.

'What?'

Veronica didn't bother to reply, but gave him a speaking glance instead. He grinned and gunned the engine. She gave him her address and then sat back and sighed, utterly exhausted. What a day!

His next words, however, had her eyes snapping open with a vengeance. 'How d'ya fancy bein' a model?'

'What?'

22

'I said,' he repeated patiently, 'that you should be a model. I mean, just look at yah. Biggish boobs, slender as a whippet everywhere else, and with that 'airdo – you look like a fancy French trollop already.'

'Gee, thanks.'

'Don't mention it. With a little work, you could look halfway decent. Do I turn here?'

'Next left.'

He pulled into the narrow street, stared up at the decrepit building, and sorrowfully shook his head.

'Thanks for the lift, Mr Copeland,' she said crisply. Bloody nerve! Did he really think she would tumble into his bed just because he spun her some old chestnut about getting her into showbusiness, or the fashion-world equivalent? Hah! She wasn't born yesterday. She had been naïve once, but now she was a thousand years old. Way too wise for one of his clumsy attempts, at any rate.

The man was a rank beginner. She'd been taught about male perfidy by the best. For an instant, a look of such bleakness crossed her face that Valentine Copeland felt his heart do a funny kind of lurch in his chest.

Then she was opening the door, without so much as a goodbye, and making a mad dash up the steps. She fumbled in her bag for the key, the wet rain managing to drip, as cold rain always did, down the back of her collar. She shuddered, opened the door and turned.

'Oomph,' she grunted as he cannoned straight into her.

'Shut the door, for Pete's sake. It's bleedin' perishin' out there.'

She snapped the door shut and glowered at him in the dingy hall. She opened her mouth, about to enjoy the experience of chucking him out on his ear, when her anticipated pleasures were interrupted.

'Is that you, Veronica? Ah . . . oh, I didn't realize you had a young man with you.' Mrs Williams's gentle voice took on a flustered tone.

Veronica opened her mouth again, but was too late.

Valentine spun on his heel, looked way down into the wide watery blue eyes of the silver-haired Mrs Williams and grinned. He bent, took her withered hand gently in his, and kissed it.

Actually *kissed* it?

Just who does he think he is now? Veronica fumed. Don bloody Juan?

Veronica closed her eyes, groaned silently, counted up to a hundred and listened in disgusted silence as he charmed the little lace knickers off her landlady.

'Oh, but you must stay for dinner, Mr Copeland,' she heard her landlady twitter a few minutes later. 'I've never entertained a famous gentleman before,' the old woman went on making Veronica blink. Good grief! He really was famous, if even Mrs Williams knew all about him.

Giving her a 'I-told-you-so' look, mixed with the clear message, 'it's-pointless-to-resist', he followed the gushing woman into her cosy little kitchen.

Mrs Williams didn't often cook for her guests, and as she began to lay the table Veronica was worried that they were putting her out. She watched Valentine shrug himself out of the tatty coat, revealing a long and skinny chest, and then felt a small tug of something dangerous pull at her stomach as he rolled up his sleeves and said, 'You'll need some extra spuds done. Where they at, luv?'

To her surprise, Mrs Williams didn't demur, but pointed under the sink. She watched, totally nonplussed, as he poured water into a bowl, hunted about for a knife and then began to peel potatoes as if he'd done it every day of his life.

Veronica, knowing when she was beaten, shrugged and left them to it, going to her room to change and let Travis know she was home. As she expected, he was full of school, and what they'd done in art class, and all about his new best friend, Ira, who was a Jew, and what was a Jew anyway?

Veronica patiently explained about Judaism, and gave him a thorough lecture on the evils of antiSemitism, and then stood, looking at her son thoughtfully.

A slow smile spread over her face.

It was time to launch a counter-offensive against the cocky Mr Valentine Copeland. It was time, she thought, taking her son by the hand, to bring on her secret weapon.

Valentine glanced up from the sink as she paused dramatically in the doorway, his eyes going straight to the dark-haired boy she was holding a little awkwardly on one hip.

Travis was getting a little old to carry around like a

baby, but she was anxious to create the right effect.

Across the top of the boy's head, her eyes met his, and she smiled grimly.

Now what are you going to do about *this*, Mr Fashion Guru?

Travis looked around him keenly, spotting the stranger instantly, of course, his blue eyes widening warily. He turned his head shyly into his mother's shoulder. Then he chanced another peep. Men were rare in his life. His grandpapa had stayed behind in England.

Having a man in the kitchen was something new.

Val met the boy's curious gaze and gave him a jaunty grin, which was instantly returned by the toddler, and looked back at his mother. His eyes dropped to her left hand. Seeing no ring there, he gave her an even jauntier grin and turned back to shelling some peas. Then his loud, tuneless whistle once more filled the kitchen.

Veronica felt oddly unnerved. It was not the reaction she had expected. Or been hoping for. There was supposed to have been a look of horror across his face, quickly followed by some sort of sickly grin and an excuse to leave.

No man wanted a woman with a child. A single, unmarried woman with a child . . . So why the hell couldn't he act true to form with the rest of the male kind? she wondered furiously.

Nervously she guided Travis to the table. It was as if a whirlwind had come into her life, turning it upside down. And it scared her. She'd had enough of whirlwinds; the last one had almost killed her.

They sat down to eat an hour later. Valentine had wolfed down almost half of the pile on his plate by the time Veronica had unfolded her napkin, put it on her lap and poured a glass of orange juice. She gave him a vicious 'you-pig' look and speared a piece of lamb.

Mrs Williams looked from one to the other, her blue eyes twinkling. She suddenly felt years younger.

Turning to the old woman, Valentine said, 'Don't you think Veronica – ' he said her name for the first time, savouring it as if it were an exquisite wine ' – would make a good model for my spring collection next week, Mrs W.?'

'Oh, yes!' The old face lit up like a Christmas tree. 'Yes, I thought the first moment I laid eyes on her what a pretty little thing she was,' Mrs Williams admitted, the two of them quite happily talking about her as if she weren't there.

'Stop it,' Veronica hissed at him. 'Mrs W. . . . I mean, Mrs Williams,' she corrected herself sharply, 'he's just teasing you. I couldn't possibly be a model. I don't even know how to walk.'

'You just put one foot in front of the other, darlin'.'

'Shut up!'

'See how she treats me, Mrs W.?' he whined. 'An' all I wanta do is make her a star!'

The old lady tut-tutted, and then broke out the best cream sherry for an after-dinner nightcap. Veronica glanced pointedly at her watch, and then went upstairs to put her son to bed.

But for once Travis was reluctant to leave the

company of adults. Several times he looked over his shoulder at the stranger as they left the room, and each time Valentine winked at him.

Travis had said suspiciously very little at the table, but Veronica suspected it was only shyness. Now, as he more or less co-operated with getting into his pyjamas, he looked at her with a curiously adult look.

'I like that man, Mummy,' he said sleepily.

She winced and kissed his newly washed face. 'Do you, puss?' She pushed his hair off his face and straightened, her face thoughtful and just a little scared. She knew a boy needed a father, but . . . she just couldn't let a man into her life again.

She just couldn't risk it. Love was too dangerous. Love could betray you. Love could leave you in prison, pregnant and in despair. Love was a killer.

She lingered for ten minutes in her son's room, just to make sure he was asleep, but when she came back down she was not at all surprised to see that Val was still sitting in the same chintzy armchair looking as if he were set for the night.

'It's getting late, Mr Copeland,' she said, smiling calmly and glancing at the old lady, who was trying valiantly not to nod off in her own armchair.

'So it is. I'll pick yer up tomorrow, about ten and show you round the House of Valentine. After all, my star model must know about the ins and outs of the trade.'

Veronica sighed sharply. 'I've told you. I'm not taking the bait.'

Val glanced at her. She was nervous, no doubt

28

about it. It wasn't hard to see why. A single lady with a gorgeous son had to have had a few knocks in life.

So she was wary. That was all right with him.

He settled back and crossed his arms across his chest. 'I ain't movin' till you agree to come and be my new Venus.'

'I have to work tomorrow,' she lied, and then wanted to scream in frustration as he slowly shook his head.

'Oh, what porky-pies you do tell,' he said sorrowfully. 'It's your day off tomorrow – I checked.' He used the cockney rhyming slang for 'lies' on purpose, she was sure. In fact, she wouldn't have been surprised to learn that the faker actually came from upper-crust Cheltenham or some other such place.

'Oh, all right,' she snapped ungraciously. She was obviously not going to get rid of him unless she placated him. 'Ten o'clock, you say? But I'm only going to look around the place, mind.'

By nine-fifteen the next morning she'd taken Travis to school and returned. She was just putting on her coat to go out again. After sleeping on the matter, she'd awoken that morning with a screaming determination to be out when Mr Valentine Copeland called. A trip to the park, then the zoo was called for, so that when the pest called in she'd be long gone.

She simply couldn't risk it. She knew it was cowardly, but there was something about Valentine that scared her. He was so different from Wayne D'Arville, for one thing.

She must remember that threats came in all shapes and sizes.

She said goodbye to Mrs Williams, opened the door, slipped her handbag over her arm and, keeping a wary eye on the wet and slippery steps, walked down the path, straight into his waiting arms.

'Oh, I do like a lady who's always punctual,' he said, bundling her into his waiting car before she could draw breath. He was wearing the exact same outfit as yesterday, and she wouldn't have put it past him to have slept in it, either.

'You're early,' she accused, then met his knowing eyes for a brief second before he started the car. A tingle started deep in her stomach and she swallowed hard. 'Why, you dirty, no-good, sneaky . . .'

He pulled away from the kerb, her insults loud in his ear. When he pulled up outside a large warehouse looking over a dirty, sluggish stretch of the East River, she was still at it.

'. . . low-down, uncouth, arrogant, pig-headed . . .'

The warehouse was huge, warm, and full of fabric, people, chatter and girls in underwear.

'This is the manufacturing floor,' Valentine said, taking a huge and unmistakably heavy roll of white silk under one arm and carrying as if it were a suitcase.

Veronica had practically to run to keep up with him. 'These magnificent ladies with their sewing machines –' with his free hand he swept a gesture through the air that encompassed at least ten women,

30

all busily sewing, hand-stitching or cutting fabric –
'are the backbone of the House of Valentine.'

'Too right,' somebody's harassed voice piped up
from the back, causing a wave of laughter to ripple
across the floor.

'Girls, this is our new model for next week. Since
Darlene left in spitting fury and vowing never to
come back, I had to work fast. Do you think she'll
do?'

Veronica blushed red as she suddenly became the
focus of all eyes. She wished she'd put on a different
coat, then shrugged angrily. What did it matter? She
wasn't really going to model in his damned show!

'I'll take that resounding silence for a yes,' Valentine said, and juggled the enormous roll of silk more
firmly under his armpit, before setting off once more.

'Now, you've got to grasp some basics of fashion
styles,' he said, then stopped abruptly to look closely
at her. 'You do have a fairly good brain, don't yah?'

'Yes, I have. A damned good brain, in fact!' she
snapped back. 'I wrote a book on . . .' she began,
then stopped, so abruptly, he gave her a quick glance.
But she had gone so pale that he knew better than to
push it.

There was something nasty lurking in this girl's
brain, he thought grimly. And it had no place being
in there. He'd have to hoik it out.

'Good. In that case,' he began, 'take a gander at
this.'

An hour later her brain was awash with new facts,
figures and jargon. She knew now that fasteners came

in all sorts besides zips and buttons – there were press studs, button-down tabs, lacing, Velcro, braces and snap-fasteners, not to mention rouleau fastenings. She also knew that collars were not merely collars – they were either Funnel, Bertha, Gladstone, Quaker, Poet, Sailor, Eton, Pierrot or Mandarin. And dresses, according to Valentine, were not dresses at all unless they were appliquéd, riddled with bias-cuts, draped, embroidered, gathered or smocked. And that was not to mention the insertions, jabots, shirring or quilting.

They were back among the sewing machines again when he seemed to run out of steam. Veronica watched a woman with a big press putting pleats into a dress. 'That's a bonded silk organza sprayed fabric with a cutwork edge. She's putting box pleats into it,' he explained, catching the direction of her look.

'I know,' she lied. 'There are at least four sorts of pleats, right?'

Valentine tut-tutted, then finally put down the silk roll. In the same spot where he had picked it up.

He put both hands on his narrow hips and looked at her, shaking his head. 'Coltrane, Coltrane, Coltrane,' he said sadly. 'There are knife pleats . . .' he ticked them off on his fingers '. . . unpressed pleats, inverted, accordion and anchored knife pleats. Then there are crystal pleats and . . .'

'If you don't shut up,' Veronica screamed, totally at the end of her tether, 'I'm going to murder you!'

The silence was complete for a few seconds, then

the same harassed voice of over an hour ago said tiredly, 'You're going to fit right on in, I can see. Welcome to the wonderful House of Valentine.'

This time the laughter came louder, while Valentine grinned and Veronica glowered.

'Well, now you know summat about how they make the stuff you're gonna wear, let's get one of the gals to sort you out for the actual catwalk. By the way, I've always thought they named the catwalk very well. Put in your claws and behave yourself. Here, Chrissie, luv, will you show Veronica the ropes? You've got a week to get her right.'

'A week!' The skinny blonde woman who approached, covered in pins, tape-measures and ribbons, looked almost dead on her feet, but the sharp hazel eyes she turned on Veronica were as alert as a bird's. 'Walk over there,' she said, pointing imperiously to a far-flung table.

Veronica, caught on the hop, did so, then stopped and stalked back. 'Look here, I'm not . . .'

'She walks well enough already. She's got natural style,' the tired blonde said, both of them ignoring Veronica completely. 'She just needs to sway her hips more. I'll give her some exercises to do. She's had a kid?' she suddenly asked.

Veronica began to look like a thundercloud.

Valentine nodded complacently. 'Yep. You can tell, yeah?'

The washed-out blonde nodded. 'Babies do good things for the hips, funnily enough.'

Veronica stamped her foot, but the blonde had

33

already been called away to deal with a recalcitrant bra strap giving a tall big-breasted brunette some trouble, and nobody else paid the slightest attention to her tantrum.

'Look, once and for all, I'm not doing this damned show. I have to work, for a start,' she yelled, feeling as if she was being steamrollered by an out-of-control maniac.

'Nah, yah don't.' Valentine shook his craggy head, his longish hair flying about all over the place. 'I called them up today and handed in yer notice. They was none too pleased, until I told them what you were doin' instead, and then they rubbed their hands in glee. Great publicity for them, you see. ''Valentine model found in Nibbits''.' He held his hands up as if at an imaginary billboard. 'Good headline, that, don't yah think?'

Veronica stared at him, opened her mouth, closed it, then opened it again.

'I hate you,' she finally muttered.

'Oh, good. Beats indifference every time. Anyway, I 'ear it's usual for married couples to 'ate each other.'

Veronica sat down abruptly, Valentine only just managing to yank a chair under her in time to save her from falling flat on her behind.

'You're mad,' she said at last.

Was it only yesterday that she'd been crossing the road in the rain, pursued by the demons of her past, determined never to have anything to do with another man again?

Where was that angry, bitter girl now, when she needed her, dammit?

'You don't know anything about me,' she said at last.

'Not yet, nah,' he admitted cheerfully. 'But I dare say it'll be fun learnin'.'

She looked into those deep, dark eyes of his and swallowed hard. She had to stop it. She had to. This was madness. She was falling, and they both knew it.

For a long moment their eyes met, his for once totally serious and determined. Then she said the one thing that she knew would save her.

'I've been in prison,' she said, her voice flat.

'Really?' Valentine said, fascinated. 'So've I. What were you in for?'

CHAPTER 3

Two years later

Duncan Somerville turned and glanced from the window of the descending plane and surreptitiously watched the man beside him. Ben Levi, the Israeli Mossad agent, looked perfectly at ease, but Duncan knew, from having read his file, that Ben had lost both his parents and an older sister at a concentration camp that he himself had barely survived.

Duncan smiled at a passing stewardess, who nodded and smiled back automatically. Duncan was always a favourite of stewardesses wherever he flew.

It was not his looks, nor the fact that he had money. It was his manners that made him the darling of everybody, but especially those in public service. For Duncan was that rare commodity that was becoming more and more extinct with every passing year.

Duncan Somerville was a gentlemen.

Somewhere in his sixties, he looked like everybody's idea of a favourite uncle. His suit was impeccable but not showy. His only jewellery was a pair of plain gold cufflinks. He had ordered only one whisky and soda on the flight, and had glanced angrily at the young couple across the way who had been determined to get drunk – and succeeded.

And when he spoke, feminine hearts began to flutter. He might be slightly portly, slightly balding and just a little florid of face. But his voice was pure syrup. Southern syrup.

Having been raised in Atlanta all his life, on a plantation that could have been used in a *Gone with the Wind* remake, his whole demeanour screamed gentle, southern class.

The stewardess would have been astounded to know that Duncan Somerville was a first-class Nazi-hunter.

He'd been in the Diplomatic Service during the war, stationed in Switzerland. He'd had a beautiful wife, who had left him for a younger man, but not before giving him a beautiful daughter. That daughter was now married to a world-famous Hollywood director, and had made him a grandpa three times over. There was nothing about him that would have made anyone guess at his lifelong quest.

But since the war he, and a small group of people like him, had been responsible for bringing no less than five top-ranking Nazis to trial in Israel.

'Is your seatbelt secure, Mr Somerville?' the stewardess asked him, and her eyes fell to the belt in question, her eyes crinkling in a near-maternal smile.

The Israeli agent beside him hid a smile. He too understood the effect his gentrified friend had on people. When he had first met Somerville, over twenty years ago now, he had been expecting a loud-mouthed, know-it-all American. But he'd been prepared to put up with it, just because Duncan Somerville had proved himself a dedicated man.

Instead, the Mossad agent had been introduced to a man who could have played Santa Claus at a Christmas pantomime and not been out of place. It had taken him a long time to figure out a very simple truth.

Duncan had lost no relatives to the concentration camps, for he and his whole family for generations had been Anglo-Protestants. He had lost no money in Germany. He had, in fact, no reason at all to be so dedicated in the pursuit of Nazis. Except for one thing. Duncan Somerville was a passionate believer in what was *right*. Oh, he was also a profoundly compassionate man, who had been horrified right to the core of his soul when he'd first learned of the atrocities that had been perpetrated in Nazi Germany. And he also had this fear that some rich men had, of being useless in life. But it was his sense of justice that kept him on the track of Nazi criminals when most others had given up.

It had been his sheer dogged persistence that was bringing them now to France.

Wolfgang Mueller had been a Commandant for two years, towards the end of the war, in a particularly obscure camp on the borders of Poland. For years Duncan had been sure that Mueller now lived in Monte Carlo, under the name of D'Arville. Through Duncan's meticulous research, which was his great speciality, he had learned all about Mueller/ D'Arville.

The man had suddenly appeared in Monte Carlo after the war, with a wife and two sons, claiming to be second-generation American/German.

And, indeed, Duncan had been able to find paper traces of the D'Arville family in Kentucky. Too much paper. But nobody he'd questioned over the years in Kentucky could actually *remember* the D'Arvilles.

Patience had always been one of Duncan's strongest virtues. For years he had collated a dossier on D'Arville that was now complete enough to convince the Israelis that D'Arville was Mueller. When he had escaped Germany during the dying days of the war, one of his lieutenants had disappeared. Duncan suspected that Mueller had intended to use the lieutenant as a scapegoat. Many fleeing Nazis had killed aides, put their papers on them and then defaced the corpse in some way, thus leading the Allies to believe that many more Nazis had perished than really had. The fact that neither the lieutenant nor the supposed 'body' of Commandant Mueller had ever shown up had convinced Duncan that the lieutenant had got wise, and left before Mueller could complete his plans. If they could find him, they would have iron proof of Mueller's identity.

The plane landed smoothly in the bright French

sunlight, and Duncan checked his briefcase, then glanced at his friend. 'What if Mueller's already gone?'

His drawling southern accent, as ever, had the power to make his companion smile before he shrugged his massive shoulders. At six feet two, Duncan noticed, Ben had a great zest for life: he laughed a lot, ate a lot, and had a riveting habit of running his fingers through his bushy brown beard. Now, as he turned, snapping brown eyes on him, Duncan was once again flustered to see that they were full of good humour. 'He's already under surveillance. We owe you and the committee a great vote of thanks, Duncan.'

Ben found his eyes running over the smaller man, taking in every detail of his friend's appearance. It was a habit of his that he had no intention of breaking. In Duncan's case, his observations were hardly surprising, for he knew his friend well. Duncan's nails were manicured, and Ben's sensitive nose picked up the scent of his Dior cologne. The briefcase he was now clasping nervously to his English-made suit was of the finest hand-tooled Italian leather.

But inside it were documents that would make your hair stand on end.

Duncan had, for a start, a complete dossier on D'Arville. Some of it made interesting reading. He was the owner of the Droit de Seigneur casino, and had been for many years. His wife, Marlene, who now called herself Mary, was a very discreet drunk.

His younger son, Hans, had died in a tragic diving accident when he was only a boy. Apparently he had dived off some cliffs, hit the water at a bad angle, and drowned.

His elder son, Helmut, who had taken on the very un-German name of Wayne, was a very different kettle of fish, however.

He had lived and prospered, although Duncan was convinced that there had been a massive rift between father and son at some point in their past. In his teens, Wayne had worked at the casino, when he was not earning a first-class degree in economics at the Sorbonne. But suddenly Wayne D'Arville had left Monte Carlo and moved to England.

There, Duncan had been interested to learn, he had joined the ultra-conservative, ultra-reputable financial firm of Platts. Platts, headed by the late Sir Mortimer Platt, gave financial advice to the British aristocracy. The richer you were, the more you employed the agents of Platts. But on Sir Mortimer's death the private company did not come into the hands of Toby Platt, Sir Mortimer's only son, but into those of one Wayne D'Arville.

It probably wasn't as surprising as it sounded. Toby had caused a scandal in the past, and was out of his father's favour. And Wayne D'Arville had written a book on modern economics that was still, years after its publication, *the* book to read. It was a work of undoubted genius, and had changed money management not only at Platts but on a worldwide scale.

All of which meant that Wayne D'Arville, son of a Nazi, was now one of the wealthiest and most socially powerful men in England. Not that Duncan was interested in Wayne. He was not a vindictive man, and did not believe the sins of the fathers should be visited on the sons. Wayne had been a boy of four or so when the war had started. What possible guilt could be attached to him? Children could not choose their parents, but had to make the best of what they were given.

If anything, Duncan felt sorry for the man.

But what had really captured Duncan's interest was what had happened just before Wayne had left Monte Carlo.

In another document, this time a medical file, it detailed the extraordinary fact that Wolfgang Mueller was now blind. And, try as he might, Duncan had been unable to find a doctor who could tell him why or *how* Mueller had been blinded.

The plane slowly began to disembark, leaving only Duncan, Ben and three others seated. To Duncan's mind at least, the rest of their team were an odd assortment.

One was tall, slim and dark and so movie-star handsome that he reminded the Georgian of an Italian playboy prince. Only the glint of steel in the dark, melting eyes warned him that the illusion was dangerous. The second of the team, by contrast, looked like a ruffled salesman, with short frizzy hair and a tendency to sweat that left dark patches under his armpits. He ate toffees as if they were going out of fashion, and kept a blue duffel bag cradled posses-sively on his lap. The third man Duncan had diffi-culty remembering, simply because, wherever he went, he seemed to fade into the wallpaper.

Medium height, medium weight, medium hair colour and medium everything else; Duncan had trouble realizing he was even there.

But all were dedicated men. All had lost relatives to the camps. All were devoted to Israel. It was a good team to have on your side when you were fighting evil.

And Mueller was evil.

'Right – let's get going.' Ben's hearty voice was the signal for all of them to leave at intervals, mingling with the crowds in the airport and making their individual ways to the hotel that was their rendevous point. They took no chances. Ever.

Duncan took a taxi, but he noticed the handsome member of their team take a bus. The others he didn't spot at all.

The hotel was in Cannes, in the old part of town the locals called Le Suquet. On the road to Mande-lieu, only five minutes' walk from the port, it was a family-run small hotel, situated above a restaurant.

Duncan checked in, nose twitching to the scent of food. His room was square, airy and possessed a single bed, washbasin and wardrobe. He didn't bother to unpack, but walked instead to the window and looked out to sea, where a ferry was steaming across the Îles de Lérins, St Honorat and Ste Marguerite.

He sighed, aware he was deliberately letting his

43

mind wander to avoid facing the question they were all here to answer. Namely – if Marcus D'Arville really was Wolfgang Mueller, how did they get him out of France and to Israel to stand trial? He knew Ben was as convinced of D'Arville's true identity as he was, but Duncan was still afraid. Oh, not afraid of being too close to a man who had been responsible for the death of hundreds, but that he *might* have made a mistake. That he was stalking an innocent quarry – and a blind man to boot. It was Duncan's only recurring nightmare: that he might be responsible for the trial and execution of an innocent man.

A discreet tap on the door had him quickly crossing the room. Over the next fifteen minutes all four men arrived at his small, inconspicuous room, the cloak-and-dagger aspect of it never failing to give Duncan a schoolboyish thrill.

Ben and the others watched in bland silence as Duncan dialled the combination on his suitcase and extracted the papers from within. Spreading them out on the bed, the four men inspected them in silence. The pictures were of a stoop-shouldered, blind old man, taken mainly in front of his casino.

'Did you have any luck finding out how he came to be blind?' Duncan asked, knowing that Mossad had also been intrigued by the man's disability. After all, if it was due to some kind of genetic disease, conceived at his birth, there was no way he could be Mueller, for extensive research had showed that no such genetic disorder was prevalent in the Mueller medical history. But D'Arville had not been blind when he had first arrived in Monte Carlo, that much had been easy to ascertain.

'No,' Ben admitted shortly. 'We found the doctor who treated him, but neither money nor threats could open his mouth.' Ben smiled at the American's wince of distaste, and winked at the scruffiest member of the team, who winked back.

'And that's what makes it so interesting,' he added slowly. As expected, Darren's sharp eyes glanced questioningly up at him.

'How so? I thought doctors were supposed to be discreet?'

Ben smiled, showing massive white teeth. The southern gentleman's naïveté and innate goodness went a long way to soothing his battered soul, and he clasped a large hand on Duncan's shoulder, squeezing gently. 'It means, my friend, that the doctor is more afraid of D'Arville than of us. Now why should he be afraid of a mere blind casino owner?'

'Oh,' Duncan said, feeling stupid.

Ben squeezed his shoulder a little harder, then let him go, and, picking up a folder, began to read in concentrated earnest. The family history was vague – too vague. By the time he'd read through the newest findings, he was even more sure that D'Arville was their man. Eye-contact with the rest of his companions confirmed that it was unanimous.

'What now?' Duncan asked.

'We go to Monaco, of course. You have rented a villa?'

Duncan nodded, and handed over a set of keys.

'Good. And you my friend . . .' Ben slapped Duncan's back with his meaty paw '. . . will have the time of your life in D'Arville's casino. Who knows, you might even win another fortune to go with the one you already have!'

The Corniche road to Monte Carlo was notorious. Its serpentine coastal route was full of hairpin bends and skirted towering cliffs that looked down on wave-washed, jagged rocks. Duncan was glad to sit sandwiched between rock-solid Ben and the handsome playboy, who, Duncan noticed nervously, never kept his eyes in one place for more than a moment.

Two miles from the Monaco border, a black French Citroën stood parked on a grassy knoll opposite a cliff. With tinted black windows that reflected the sun, Wolfgang Mueller waited in anonymous impatience.

His hands were gnarled with rheumatism and constantly ached, but he hardly noticed the pain any more. Through the sunroof he could hear the screaming of the gulls and the hollow, echoing boom of the waves below. He could smell the sea air and beside him he could hear the slow, regular breathing of Gustave Landro, a Frenchman who had been a collaborator during the war and had made a living as an expensive 'odd job' man ever since.

'When did Waldo say they left the hotel?' he barked, his voice making the man by his side jump.

'They'll be here soon, Monsieur D'Arville. Try to relax.'

'I am relaxed,' Wolfgang lied, keeping his temper with an ease that spoke of long practice. For Wolfgang Mueller had changed in recent years. Ever since he'd been blinded, in fact.

He had lain on the floor of his study for what had seemed like hours after his bastard son had left, his head on fire with pain, his hands cupped in silent horror over his mutilated, useless eyes. Then the doctor had come, and a needle sliding into his arm had brought temporary relief. But the next morning he had awoken to the same hideous darkness as before.

For months afterwards he had stayed in his luxurious villa, utterly depressed. Not even the call he'd made to his son's would-be father-in-law, a rich and aristocratic vineyard owner, had helped ease his rage. Oh, Wayne's precious little fiancée had chucked him instantly, but Mueller knew that would not be much of a set-back for his poisonous offspring for long. Nor had it. The devil-spawn had quickly moved to England, and out of his father's reach.

Now his frustrated desire for revenge was instilled in him like a festering thorn. Marlene, his own wife, had been relegated to only a voice. After a while he could not even remember what she had once looked like.

But, eventually, and with an immense effort of will, he had forced himself up and out of the mire of his living death, and over the ensuing years found his remaining senses sharpening acutely. He heard things others did not, could interpret scent in a way that others found impossible. Food was now his main sensory pleasure, and three chefs worked in his kitchens.

'There! Jacques has given the signal.' The sudden excited words of his companion dragged Wolfgang from his thoughts, and he stiffened in his seat, a smile of satisfaction pulling at his thin and bloodless lips.

Mossad. Did they really think that they and their American lackey could dig into his past without him knowing? Fools! They were still all fools. The Fatherland knew how to produce men who would always rise to the top, like the cream of the human crop they truly were.

He heard the sound of a heavier motor starting just behind his car, and he let out his breath in a slow, satisfied whoosh. 'You are sure the lorry driver is legitimate?' he asked for the second time.

'Positive. Jean was hailed as a hero of the Résistance. No one will suspect either him or the genuine tragedy of the accident.'

Wolfgang grunted. 'He'd better be a saint. They'll investigate him until Doomsday. The lorry is just as I ordered?' he added sharply.

'Yes, sir. We had to search fifty transport firms before finding one with just the right amout of metal fatigue. The brake failure will be perfectly genuine – and if you could see the rust-bucket Jean is driving . . .' Wolfgang felt him give a lift of his shoulders '. . . you wouldn't worry. There is no one who can equal Jean in this kind of thing.'

The lorry rumbled away. Wolfgang nodded, and

slowly leant back in his seat. So be it. The die was cast now. And he trusted his luck to hold . . .

'Wind the window down, Ben,' Duncan said. 'It's getting hot in here.'

Ben did as he was asked, then breathed in gustily. 'Ah, God knew what he was doing when he created the earth. Just smell that air!'

The rumpled salesman was driving, the duffel bag still on his lap, and Duncan smiled as he leaned forward, eager to catch his first glimpse of Monte Carlo, and only wishing that the circumstances were different. 'What's the first thing we do when . . .?' he began, then broke off in surprise as the driver began to shout something in high-pitched Yiddish.

He felt Ben stiffen beside him, and then his own eyes widened in terror as a lorry lurched around the bend in front of them, its overbalanced load of fruit already beginning to topple the vehicle on to its side. The salesman tugged frantically on the wheel, desperately trying to steer the car clear, but it was already too late.

Duncan felt his throat close tight in fear, his stomach and heart rising up to choke him as the squealing sound of the brakes and the scent of burning rubber filled the air.

He cried out as the car hit the solid rock that skirted one side of the road, and then gripped Ben's knee in mute terror as the car was catapulted back over the opposite side of the road, to where a flimsy crash barrier awaited them. Beside him, he heard the

49

handsome member of the team begin to chant a Hebrew prayer as the car mounted the barrier, paused like an ungainly eagle for a split second, and then began to plummet down the hundreds-of-feet drop on the other side.

Duncan was not spared the obscene sensation of falling, and he closed his eyes on a terrified groan. Just before the car hit the bottom, he felt Ben's huge hand curl around his own, warm and human and strangely comforting.

Wolfgang Mueller listened to the sounds, cataloguing them in his mind: the squeal of brakes, the crunch of metal, the sudden silence, and the final groan of the dying car and the dying men.

Slowly he nodded. 'Well done. We said a hundred thousand francs, I believe?'

Far away, in a mental hospital in England, Dr Sebastien Teale looked up as his last patient of the day was brought in.

The girl was so pitifully young. She looked no more than fifteen, but was in fact in her twenties. Years of anorexia had reduced her to skin and bone. As she sat down, she fiddled with her long, mousy-coloured hair with hands missing several fingers.

She also had a long history of self-mutilation.

Sebastien smiled at her. The girl smiled back. 'Hello, Dr Teale,' she said nervously, but happily. Although she usually hated talking to the doctors, she loved Sebastien. He was her greatest friend in all the world.

Sebastien stood, slowly walking forward and sitting on the edge of the desk. He kept his sherry-coloured eyes alert for any signs of distress at his proximity, and was relieved to see none. That was a good sign. People with Selena's problems usually saw any physical closeness as a threat.

'Now, Selena. What's all this I hear about you not eating your vegetables?'

The girl looked up at him pitifully, and Sebastien felt his heart crack just a little more, deep inside him. He'd been working in mental hospitals and asylums for the criminally insane for all of his career. He had only one 'private' patient. If Wayne could be called that.

For a man still only in his late thirties, Sebastien's reputation was second to none. His late mentor, Sir Julius, had been a lion in British psychiatry, and although Sebastien Teale was an American, he'd never felt the desire to return to his native land.

His life was here now. With his patients.

Patients who were slowly, unknowingly, breaking his heart.

An hour later, Sebastien left the hospital, trudged across the full car park, and climbed wearily into his car. He didn't notice two nurses watching him with eyes filled with a mixture of admiration, respect and desire.

Every nurse in the hospital knew that Sebastien Teale was the best. And not because of the books he had written, or the lectures that he gave regularly at Oxford and Cambridge either. Sebastien Teale was,

51

quite simply, the nearest thing to a saint that any of them had ever seen. He was of medium height, but had hair the colour of conkers, which caught any stray gleam of light going. His eyes, too, were warm and sherry-coloured, and so kind that they could break down the hardiest barriers with just one look. His voice could soothe the most terrified of patients into healing sleep.

And there was something so . . . so . . . *human* about him that made him the favourite of every patient in the place. Nurses had caught him rocking a terrified seventy-year-old man in his arms. They had seen him stroke a patient in a straitjacket into a calm, nearly lucid human being. He was not detached, as all the other doctors were. And he paid the price for it.

Every single nurse, and some married ones too, longed to take him as a lover. And not only because of his looks. Or his innocence, as appealing as both were.

No, they knew that Sebastien Teale was a prize any woman would want. He would never patronize them. Never cheat on them. And would always understand a woman's point of view. Men like that were like gold.

But so far, no woman had been noted in the great man's life, and many jealous female eyes kept a sharp lookout. It was the nurses' sad but respectful conclusion that the man was just too dedicated. But now, as he climbed into his car, his face was drawn, pale and exhausted. The job was killing him.

He drove carefully through the rush-hour traffic and pulled up at his flat, feeling like a washed-out dishrag. He let himself in, yanked off his tie and slumped down on the sofa in utter exhaustion. A movement caught his eye and he looked across the short expanse of his living room, not at all surprised to see a six-foot-four Frenchman seated in the chair opposite him. The man was one of the richest in the country. He was handsome, powerful and quite, quite insane.

'Sebastien,' Wayne D'Arville said, his voice soft and chiding. 'You look like death warmed up. I wish you'd leave that place. You could go into private practice and make a fortune. Besides, I need you more than they do.' It was a simple statement of fact, but it had taken Sebastien over ten years to make the man understand as much.

Sebastien leaned back, and breathed slowly and deeply. He knew how dangerous this man was. He knew what he had done to Veronica Coltrane, although she was safe enough in America now, and he doubted if Wayne even gave her a thought.

He also knew that he was the only chance Wayne had.

He said softly, 'Why don't you tell me what kind of day you've had?'

CHAPTER 4

France

In the Château de Montigny in southern France, a single gunshot shattered the peaceful autumnal air. Gardeners ran in from the rose gardens, and outside the study door three maids hovered, none of them daring to go in. It fell to Jules, the sixty-seven-year-old major-domo, to knock timidly on the door.

'Monsieur le Duc? Can you hear me?' A Louis XIV carriage clock chimed the hour of four, making everyone in the hall jump.

Jules knocked and called again. When he received no answer for the second time he pushed down on the gilt-handled door, surprised to find it opening silently and obediently beneath his hand, and looked inside.

The study was a classic of its kind. French tomes lined ancient wooden shelves, while the scent of dusty books, cigars, fine old leather and Napoleon brandy wafted around on the meagre air currents. Sitting behind a fine seventeenth-century writing bureau was the slumped figure of the Duc de Montigny. Jules and the others could plainly see the shining dome of the Duc's head reflected in the sunlight filtering in through the open French windows. The door of the cabinet that housed his set of ancient duelling pistols hung open, and a fine eighteenth-century pistol hand-tooled in heavy silver was missing from its place.

Slowly, feeling suddenly much older than his years, Jules walked across the Savonière carpet to approach his master. Jules' family had worked for the Duc de Montigny's since before the days of Bonaparte, and he felt tears begin to burn in the back of his gentle grey eyes. The silver pistol lay a scant inch from the Duc's limp left hand, and he slowly dragged his eyes away from the functional but beautiful instrument of death. A deep, dark red hole in the Duc's temple had him shuddering, and he half-turned, glancing behind him to his pale-faced staff. 'Call the police,' he instructed no one in particular, hardly aware when one of the gardeners turned away to do his bidding.

The desk was empty except for the Duc's usual items. Cream, stiff paper of premier quality, bearing the Montigny crest and printed address, was stacked in a neat pile on the left, together with a silver rack of matching envelopes. Fine gold-plated pens with old-fashioned nibs stood in ebony and ivory holders, ready to be used. Jules eyes scanned the desk, but could see no suicide note, only a single typewritten sheet. Unable to withstand his curiosity, Jules picked

55

it up and read it, holding it gingerly by the very topmost corners.

His old, sad face barely altered in expression as he read to the end. It was just as he had feared. The vineyards had had a bad four years. Early frosts and heavy rainfall had ruined the last two harvests, and their back-up supply of grapes was sadly depleted. The Duc had borrowed heavily from the banks last year, and this year there had been a rumour circulating in the town that they had insisted on the Montigny castle's being mortgaged for collateral before giving a second, massive loan.

As he read the words, Jules frowned, recalling the name of Wayne D'Arville. Wasn't that the upstart of a casino-owner's son, who had once, many years ago, been set to marry the Duc's only daughter and heir?

Of course, the Duc had put a stop to that. If Jules remembered correctly, the casino owner had disowned his son, and told the Duc so. Fortunately, the Duc's daughter was a sensible girl who knew her duty well. She had jilted this D'Arville character, and had since married into an old and respected aristrocatic family from the north.

Now why, Jules wondered, did Wayne D'Arville buy the options for the vineyard and castle from the bank? Surely it could only be for revenge. And after all these years . . .

He shook his head sadly and put the paper back. Whatever the reasons, this man had called in the loan, knowing the Duc could not possibly pay it. And so he had taken the only way out left to a beaten old man who had only his proud name left to call his own.

Jules turned away, and walked slowly back to the door where the women were sniffing quietly into their aprons. He didn't have the heart to tell them that the castle was no longer owned by a Montigny. The news would spread soon enough.

Poor Monsieur le Duc. To lose the family home, business *and* honour had been more than he could stand. As he closed the door on the dead man, Jules wondered what the Englishman would do with the castle now.

He would probably sell it. After all, it had not been the business he'd been after. Jules shuddered at the thought of a man who could hold such a grievous grudge, and for so long.

His soul must be as black as midnight.

Wayne received official notice of the Duc's death two days later, via the bank. The château, so he was informed, was now all his. The Duc's daughter had been informed, but had not taken it well. Her husband's family was rich in social status, heritage and history, but not much else. Both families had been relying on the Montigny estates to provide for their future.

The bank's manager also wrote that she had collapsed on hearing the name of the man who now owned the château and vineyards. Wayne sent back a short and simple message stating that the vineyards were to be sold to the highest bidder, which would undoubtedly be the house of Villiers,

Montigny's oldest rivals. The château, he informed the bank, had already been promised to a hotelier of Wayne's acquaintance, who was anxious to turn the family home into a showpiece hotel for the rich and famous.

Wayne had forgotten about the Duc and his poverty-stricken daughter by the following Friday. After spending a few days in France sorting out the paperwork, he was strangely glad to get back to England. He was very much aware that his father, Wolfgang Mueller, still lived in Monte Carlo. And, although it galled him to admit it, he didn't feel totally safe in France.

Once home, he drove his Ferrari to Platts with quick and efficient skill, pulling into the new underground car park. The car park was only one of the changes Wayne had made since inheriting Platts. He had had the cellars ripped out and the underground car park put in, his own space indicated by a huge placard that read 'President: Wayne D'Arville'. His own name appeared often throughout the firm. The stationery bore his name, the boardroom door bore it, his own office, the advertising literature and even the financial statements to their myriad clients played host to it.

He wanted no one to forget who was boss here.

He walked into a building that bore no resemblance to the old Platts. Gone were the dark, antique rooms, the old-world ambience, the cosy, cheerful family atmosphere that had so reassured the firm's older, more stick-in-the-mud clientele. Instead he walked into a foyer where huge windows let light flood over the muted grey carpet, functional furniture and modern switchboard and reception desk. The receptionist was young, pretty and up-to-date, and smiled at him with wide wanting eyes and big white teeth. Wayne walked past her to the express lift with electronically operated doors, not even noticing that she was alive.

The offices that he walked past were doorless; the days of individual, cosy little rooms had totally gone. Wayne kept a sharp eye on his employees. In their place stood open-plan offices, full of light, modern typewriters and messenger systems. Most of the old directors were gone and in their place were new men, only a few of them from Oxford or Cambridge. The movers and shakers that Wayne employed were of the new schools: economists, forecasters with an eye for the flashy, the trendy, the money deal that sold.

Over the past few years, Wayne had become rich. Not wealthy, not well-off, but rich, and mainly because Platts was totally his and he could do what he liked without consulting shareholders, directors or board members. Toby Platt, Sir Mortimer's homosexual son, and his wife Amanda had filed a law suit against him, contesting Sir Mortimer's will and claiming undue influence. Their case had been thrown out almost at once, but they were doggedly filing an appeal.

Wayne routinely received correspondence threatening more legal action, as well as a regular influx of hate-mail from Toby's friends and some of Platts' ex-directors. It all went into the bin. Now, as he stepped into his office that was unrecognizable as Sir Mortimer

Platt's, he worked solidly for two hours, clearing his desk of messages and returning phone calls.

At last, he pressed the button on his newly installed intercom, and his young, attractive secretary quickly responded.

'Miss Forsythe, call a meeting of the research division, will you? Monday morning, ten o'clock.'

'Yes, Mr D'Arville,' Judith Forsythe said, pencilling in the appointment, and then typing out the memo. So, the rumours about the research division being phased out were true. She was not surprised. It was the least profitable of all. That meant more redundancies. Judith sighed as she typed, glad that she was not a researcher. But Platts was a non-union shop, and she glanced at the closed door and shivered. Like all the female staff, she found Wayne D'Arville a fascinating mix; she couldn't stop herself from wanting him, while being simultaneously terrified of him. And although she wore her blouses with the top two buttons undone and her skirts to just above her knees, she knew deep down that he hardly noticed her presence.

But Wayne D'Arville was six foot four, with copper-coloured hair, a lantern-jawed face and the most beautiful blue eyes she'd ever seen, so she was not about to give up trying to attract his notice. Especially as he was still, unbelievably, single.

Unaware of his secretary's aspirations, Wayne folded away his papers and drew out the blueprints of a planned new office complex, but found he could not concentrate.

He'd have to start looking around for a wife soon.

An Englishwoman, with a hereditary title. One as unlike that bitch de Montigny as he could find.

He frowned, then rubbed his hand tiredly across his forehead. He felt restless and in need of his regular 'fix'. Lifting the telephone receiver, he dialled a five-figure number.

'Hello?'

Wayne took a deep breath, the familiar voice immediately affecting him. Slowly he leaned back in his chair, the nasty taste of France and Platts and everything else leaving him for a few wonderful minutes.

'Hello, Seb. It's me.' Ever since meeting the American psychiatrist, many years ago now, Wayne had felt himself being pulled inexorably closer into the man's orbit. It was where he yearned to be, and yet he fought against the magnetism furiously.

'Oh, hi. When did you get back from France?'

'Yesterday. I was wondering if you're free for dinner tonight.'

Sebastien twirled the telephone wire in his fingers and sighed. He just couldn't face Wayne tonight. He said quietly, 'No, I can't make it this time.'

Wayne sat up straight abruptly, the rotten taste of the world once more flooding into his mouth. 'Why not?'

Sebastien felt the man's need bite into him. It was no use – he just couldn't deny somebody who was in so much pain. He swallowed hard and ran his hand through his hair. 'Look, why don't I come to your place for lunch tomorrow?' he said softly, his voice soothing, even over a telephone line.

61

Wayne smiled, unutterably relieved, and leaned back in his chair. 'That's even better. I'll order in from Le Grille.'

'Don't bother, I'll cook. I'll bring some groceries with me.'

'OK. I'll give you a hand.'

'Fine. See you tomorrow, then.' Sebastien hung up, putting the phone back on its hook slowly, then took a deep breath and straightened his shoulders.

Sebastien left just after ten o'clock, driving the small Mini he had purchased second-hand just a month ago, and headed for the open-air market. Money meant little to him. He knew he could earn a fortune in private practice, but it was not what he wanted. And, in truth, he never envied his more wealthy colleagues, a fact that had not gone unnoticed.

At the market he bought fresh fruit and vegetables, a crusty loaf, beef and some crabmeat.

Wayne had moved into a house in Belgravia six months ago. It was a two-storeyed, yellow-stone building with black railings surrounding the square gardens at the front and rear. Sebastien was let in by Wayne himself, who took the groceries from him then followed him through elegant rooms, decorated by the latest interior designer, to the kitchen. Wayne always dismissed his servants whenever Sebastien was due. Wayne wanted nothing and no one to spoil these precious times.

Sebastien didn't comment on the rooms decorated in the minimalist style. He knew Wayne barely registered the house in which he lived, which was why the place had a curiously unlived-in feel to it. There was not an ornament out of place or one personal item to interrupt the harmonious colour-scheme. He thought of his own flat, with its untidy bookshelves crammed with all sorts of titles, the throw cushions that clashed with the curtains, and felt so utterly sorry for the tall Frenchman. To an outsider he seemed to have everything anybody could ever want, but Sebastien knew he had, in reality, nothing at all.

Over the years, he had carefully picked his way across the minefield that was Wayne D'Arville's tortured mind, picking up the barest scraps of information. It was a strange game they played, Sebastien trying to find clues to the man's paranoia and pain, while Wayne errected barriers to deny him. Half-truths, evasions, downright lies. Sebastien saw through them all. Wayne was both terrified of the psychiatrist and utterly dependent on him. Sebastien was the only friend he had ever had. Sebastien was the only man he trusted not to betray him. Sebastien was so dangerous, Wayne always came out in a cold sweat whenever he was around.

And yet, without him, Wayne knew he would perish.

Yes, it was a very strange game they played. But Wayne could not not stop it, and Sebastien wouldn't.

And so it went on.

In the kitchen, Wayne put on the kettle, and heaped coffee into the percolator.

'How's work nowadays?' Sebastien asked, checking the man for any overt signs of disintegration since their last 'session' but unable to find any. He knew Wayne had been excited over his 'business deal' in France. Too excited for it to be mere business. But Sebastien knew he would have to tread carefully.

'I didn't know you were interested in wine,' he said mildly.

Wayne stiffened. He always knew when Sebastien was on a hunting mission.

'I'm not. I'm selling the vineyard business.'

Sebastien looked at the tense, wide shoulders thoughtfully. 'Perhaps you've just always wanted to own a castle?' he mused quietly.

Wayne shrugged. He didn't know what kind of a mental 'symbol' a castle represented. And with Sebastien it didn't pay to take any chances.

'That's not it,' he said easily, turning to give him a careful smile. 'I've already got plans to sell it to a hotelier.'

Sebastien nodded. He knew how hard it was to get any kind of clues from a man as tightly controlled as Wayne. But even so, over the years, he'd learned an awful lot about the Frenchman. He knew he harboured intense guilt over the death of his younger brother, and Sebastien suspected he had been present at the diving accident. He knew he loathed his father, but not why. In fact, if Wayne had an inkling of just how much Sebastien had garnered on him, Sebastien might have been in much more danger than he already was.

'I'm glad business is doing so well,' Sebastien

changed tack. 'Power means a lot to you, doesn't it?'

Wayne smiled. 'It means a lot to everyone. Except you, of course,' he added softly. Sebastien's uniqueness was just one of the many things that added to Wayne's fascination for the soft-voiced, soft-hearted American.

Wayne quickly began to tell him all about the plans for the new office block. That was safer. The routine was familiar, and he talked unguardedly. 'I should have another ten million by the time I'm fifty,' he concluded with such grim satisfaction that the psychiatrist's antennae were immediately set twitching.

Sebastien put down the knife he'd been using to chop meat and wiped his hands on a towel. 'You need it for something, don't you?'

Wayne looked across the table, silently cursing, telling himself for the thousandth time that he was a fool to keep up this friendship, but knowing that he could not stop now. Sebastien was the friend he'd needed all his life, the friend he'd craved so badly during those dark days after the hideous fight with his father had pushed him over the edge.

Quite simply, Sebastien kept the pain at bay for a few glorious hours, and was the only man Wayne could ever hope to regard as an equal. Even though, of course, he could destroy Sebastien whenever he wanted . . . He shrugged idly and bundled some tomatoes into a dish. 'Who doesn't need money?' he asked glibly.

'I don't,' Sebastien said softly. 'Money isn't everything.'

'Oh, I know that,' Wayne said grimly, watching

with only half an eye as Sebastien crumbled a meat stock cube into some water. He began pouring it over the dish of meat and vegetables, then abruptly stopped as he caught the look on Wayne's face.

'What wrong?' Sebastien asked quietly, keeping the urgency out of his voice. 'You know you can tell me.'

'Nothing,' Wayne said quickly, trying to fight off the urge to confess everything without much success. 'I just . . . I think, you know, it's time I got married. I want a family.'

'Ahh. You miss your brother, don't you?'

'Yes,' Wayne said before he had time to think, and then glanced at Sebastien quickly. For a moment his blue eyes blazed in anger, then he managed to smile. 'I keep forgetting about you,' he said simply and without venom. Talking to Sebastien was like taking a narcotic. Exciting, dangerous, soothing, wonderful but potentially lethal . . .

Sebastien put the casserole in the oven and turned on the heat, scraped some potatoes and prepared the French beans. He was wearing plain jeans and a simple cheap white shirt. His hair was brushed casually back from his forehead and shone with the exact colour of conkers that littered the English countryside at this time of year, and Wayne felt a familiar peacefulness settle over his shoulders like a mantle. It was always like this when Sebastien was around. That was what made him so addictive.

'OK,' Sebastien said with satisfaction. 'Now all we have to do is wait two hours.'

'Fine. Come and have a drink.'

In the living room, with its pink, grey and cream colour-coded elegance, Sebastien watched him pour two Scotches. He took his but didn't bother to drink it, instead sinking down into a chair. There he watched the Frenchman drink mechanically and without any evidence of pleasure.

Slowly Sebastien put his drink down on to the cream leather armrest of his padded chair. 'So, tell me about your new vineyards. What do they look like at this time of year?'

Wayne shrugged and yawned. 'I don't know. I never looked. I just signed the papers over to the vintners who bought them.'

'What about the château? Are French castles as romantic as popular fiction would have us believe?'

Again Wayne shrugged. 'I stayed in a hotel at Nouvion. What?' he added, catching the sherry eyes on him with their usual mix of pity and strength.

Sebastien shrugged helplessly. 'Doesn't it seem odd to you that you went to France but didn't even look at what you own? That you didn't take time out to enjoy the sights, even?'

Wayne smiled grimly. 'I looked at the grave,' he said, then snarled in anger at himself and tossed back the last of his drink.

'Whose grave?' The questioning, as usual, was gentle but persistent. Like the exquisite probing of a needle, after a thorn in the thumb. Wayne got up and made himself a refill. When he came back to his chair, he crossed his legs at the ankles and looked the young American straight in the eye.

'You know, in your own way, you're almost as ruthless as I am.'

Sebastien nodded, not at all confounded. 'I guess I am,' he acknowledged simply. 'So, whose grave did you visit? Your brother's?'

'No!' Wayne said sharply, then slowly shook his head. Pleasure and pain, that was Sebastien. 'I should get rid of you,' he said softly.

'But you won't.'

'No. I won't. I don't think I can now. But you already know that, don't you? You always knew that. Right from the beginning. Didn't you?' Wayne pressed, his desire to punish himself so obvious that Sebastien wondered how the man himself could be so unaware of it.

'Yes. I knew. So, whose grave was it?'

Wayne smiled a brief hard smile, a mere acknowledgement of his adversary's persistence, and took another gulp of liquor. 'The Duc de Montigny. Once I was engaged to his daughter.'

'Oh? Tell me about her.'

Wayne shook his head. 'You're barking up the wrong tree. The old man didn't want me to marry his daughter when I . . . So I waited until I was rich enough to buy the notice papers from the bank. He committed suicide,' he added defiantly.

Sebastien reached for his drink and took a slow sip, taking time to make sense of the disjointed sentences. The fact that Wayne felt no remorse for driving a man to suicide was the strongest indication yet of his true mental condition.

But Sebastien knew he did not have enough yet to enable him to have Wayne committed. Wayne was a rich and powerful man. An influential man. To have a man committed, you had to go through certain channels, and be very sure of your diagnosis. Sebastian knew his word as a psychiatrist would be hard to shake, but he also had no illusions as to what Wayne would do if he got to hear of any moves against him before the committal papers were signed. Sebastien wasn't so much afraid for himself as he was for others. Wayne had all but destroyed Veronica Coltrane, one of life's innocents. Who knew what damage he could do if he, Sebastian, tried to have him committed, and failed.

Sebastien knew it was imperative, if he was to save Wayne, to learn more about what drove him. So he swallowed his own sense of outrage, and forced himself to concentrate on the problem at hand. 'So he was punished for going against you?' He kept his voice deliberately expressionless. 'How did Mortimer Platt go against you?' He knew that Wayne's takeover of Platts had been a hostile one.

Wayne shook his head. 'He didn't. He just had something I needed.'

Sebastien knew what that was without being told. 'So, now you have money, and your revenge on the Duc. What next?'

Wayne smiled so savagely that for a moment Sebastien felt a cold shiver shudder its way up his spine.

'Oh, I still have things to do,' Wayne assured him softly.

'I'm sure you have. Tell me about your father.'

Wayne shifted on his chair and took another gulp of Scotch. He was dressed in pressed white cotton trousers and a turquoise shirt. He looked cool and elegant, in perfect harmony with the room, and yet Sebastien knew that there lurked beneath the handsome exterior a personality so labyrinthine, so tortured, and so full of self-directed hate that he wondered how Wayne had survived it.

'I've already told you about him.'

'No, you haven't. You've told me lies.'

Wayne looked from the rich amber colour of the liquid in the glass to the man opposite him, his eyes narrowing. 'I could crush you,' he said softly. 'Ruin everything you have. I could destroy you and not even know I'd done it.'

Sebastien smiled, totally unafraid. 'I know. So it won't matter if you tell me the truth about your father, will it?'

Wayne smiled, almost glad that Sebastien was not afraid, that he was not like all the others. He knew, in a sudden, shocking flash of self-knowledge, that he'd die if Sebastien turned out to be like all the others. He looked Sebastien in the eye for a long, long second, not sure whether to be glad or sorry when Sebastien refused to back down, then sneered, 'OK. You asked for it. Here it is. He was a Nazi. For a time he was the chief officer at a concentration camp. He killed and tortured people for a living.'

Sebastien paled, but had no doubt at all that, this time, he was telling the truth. 'And your brother?

The one who drowned? Tell me about him.'

'I killed him.'

'You said he drowned.'

'He did. I was on the beach when his dive went wrong. I could have swum out and saved him, but I didn't.' Wayne was proud of his voice. It was level and strong. He might have been discussing the weather.

Sebastien heard only the pain. The so obvious pain. He knew that later, much later, he would think about a drowning boy who need not have died. He knew he would probably even shed tears over him. But he would not sit on judgement on Wayne. He could not help a boy who had been dead for years. He *could* help a man whose life was a living hell. 'He was your father's favourite, wasn't he?' he said, knowing he was on the right track even before asking the question.

Wayne blinked, then shook his head, shaking off the numb feeling of apathy that had allowed him to blurt it all out the way he had. 'You know,' he said, 'I've often wondered how easy it would be to lie to shrinks like you. Now I know. My father is a French winemaker. That's all. Now, hadn't we better fix some dessert?'

Sebastien nodded, knowing Wayne had had enough for one day. But they'd made some giant leaps. It was enough. Together the two men walked into the kitchen.

CHAPTER 5

New York, ten years later

Veronica Copeland nodded to Francis, the dour doorman, who grinned back and gave a cheerful wave. It said a lot about her long-time standing in the thirty-storey luxury apartment complex that she even received acknowledgement from the man, let alone such a conspicuously friendly greeting.

At nearly sixty, Francis had been in the building since its completion twelve years ago. The place, full of luxury, flair, interior designs and every modern convenience known to man, simply would not be the same without the grumpy, sour face of the doorman, who did his job well but with such a totally grudging reluctance that his fame had spread throughout the whole quarter. Once, Veronica knew, several tenants with no sense of class had tried to have him fired. When Francis, looking even more glum than usual, had told anybody and everybody who lived in the building that he was being sacked, there had been uproar.

Now Veronica winked back at him as she walked to one of the twelve sets of lifts, all of which were carpeted, with pot plants in two corners and awash with pleasant music, and pushed the button for the thirteenth floor. As she did so, she had to smile. Trust Val to select an apartment on the thirteenth floor. It was totally typical of him, and as usual he was right. Thirteen might be unlucky for some, but it hadn't done either of them any harm over the years.

As the quiet elevator whizzed her up, she checked in her handbag for the keys. Their apartment was at the end of the corridor, and, like all those similarly situated, was one of the largest in the building. Suites ranged from two-roomed large expanses for the modern bachelor to the twelve-roomed apartments like hers.

There was no doubt about it. Valentine Inc. had done well over the years. Very well. Valentine designed, and Veronica invested. It was a match that had made them both very rich, and very happy.

Against all of Veronica's gloomy predictions!

She opened the door and stepped inside, looking around at the wide expanse of living room, as they both still called it, much to Travis's more American-ized disgust, noting with familiar appreciation the muted and elegant peach-tinted walls, lightly stuccoed brilliant white ceiling, and peachy/beige expanse of carpet that seemed to stretch as far as the eye could see. The furniture was dark walnut, the couches and sofas a mixture of black and white leather. A few Picassos hung on the walls, and towering pot plants festooned greenery in every alcove.

Veronica walked briefly to a smoked-glass-topped coffee table and slung down her handbag, kicked off her shoes and went to the space-age kitchen. Done out in steel greys, blues, silvers and whites, it was sparse, functional and strangely elegant. There she put on the coffee percolator, then walked into the bathroom, slipping off her tailored three-piece navy-blue suit as she did so.

The bathroom was a gothic mixture of black, gold and red, with one wall entirely lined with mirrored tiles. She watched herself as she stripped, trying to gauge her face and figure with unprejudiced eyes. She was nearly forty, but didn't think she looked it. Her black hair was still lush and thick, the lines at the corners of her eyes were very fine and not visible under a light dusting of make-up, and her skin looked as youthful and firm as ever.

Her slender body, slowly being revealed as she pulled off the expensive suit to reveal a lacy teddy and pure silk stockings, looked as firm and curvaceous as ever. Val loved her to wear sexy lingerie, and although she had felt a little self-conscious about it at first, now she was quite at home in the satin teddies her husband still liked to design.

She sighed contentedly, turned away from her reflection and stepped into the shower, turning on the gold taps and murmuring in pleasure as the warm water cascaded on to her head and over her shoulders.

She had come a long way since that first fashion show of Val's. How he had ever managed to bully her into it, she still didn't know. She felt her lips curve into a smile of remembrance as she let the years slip back . . .

The venue was the Plaza hotel. The huge conference room had been transformed into a lush harem with cleverly draped red velvet and layers and layers of gauze. The theme was Turkish, from the ornate drinking vessels that served guests with the finest of champagnes to the menu.

Val had refused to serve them an actual meal, stating with his usual combination of brash arrogance and faultless logic that they had come to see a fashion show – *his* fashion show – and not to stuff their faces.

But the entrées and titbits served with the finest of Turkish coffees were strictly oriental and the real thing. Imported Turkish delight and traditional nibbles from that country had been flown in the day before on a specially chartered plane, and looked good on ornate beaten silver dishes, served with finger-bowls in which floated a single blossom. The whole layout was set on banquet tables festooned with tropical fruit and set against a mural backcloth that depicted belly dancers and lounging, obese sultans.

'If they want to nosh, they should go to a soddin' restaurant,' Val had muttered around a mouthful of pins as he readjusted a double-breasted jacket (sticking her with the pins more often than not) as they had worked together in the warehouses just two days before the showing.

'Stand still, for gawd's sake,' he'd gone on to snap as she jiggled and tried to dodge the pins, and she'd glowered at him, hating every lovely hair on his head.

Right up until this very morning, when he'd called to take her to the venue, she was still denying that she was going to walk out on that catwalk with all the others.

'Don't worry so much,' Val told her now, dressed in ragged jeans and a loose shirt. 'The other girls are the stars – Patrice and Jasmine. Everyone will be looking at them, not at your recalcitrant mug. You're just in there to fill in for some second-rater who threw a wobbly. Relax.'

Veronica, not at all sure whether she should feel reassured or insulted, glared at him, crossed her arms savagely over her breasts and sulked all the way to the Plaza. Once there, however, she began to sweat in earnest.

The famous hotel was as impressive as she'd always suspected it might be. And so was the guest list. Senators, TV stars, even pop stars were filing through the famous doors, flashing golden invitation cards and causing a backlog of black stretch limos, pink Rolls-Royces and nifty Italian sports cars.

In contrast to the splendour of the hotel, the changing room that Val breezed into, oblivious to naked female bodies, reminded Veronica of a cramped rabbit hutch. Hung up beside the mirrors

76

that lined one wall were costume jewellery, garters, stockings, even newspaper clippings. The room was chaos – the wardrobe girls each had their own model to look after, and everyone was talking at once. Hairdressers added last-minute changes to glossy curls, toenails were being painted, and make-up girls fixed faces on the run as models dashed from one costume to another, arguing, groaning, grinning.

Veronica took one look, turned around, and almost made it to the door. Almost.

Valentine's strong hand on her arm swung her about in mid-stride and he firmly frogmarched her back to an empty chair, set beside a washbasin. She felt his strong hands on her shoulder forcing her down, and as her knees already felt weak as water it didn't take much pressure to make her buckle.

Her face in the mirror looked white, scared and angry. Her dark eyes were huge, and as she met his smiling face in the mirror she could cheerfully have committed murder.

'Here's Carrie,' he said as a harassed-looking brunette, fifty if she was a day, swooped down on her. 'See if you can make this sow's ear into a silk purse, luvvie, eh?' He gave the unimpressed and hardly listening Carrie a peck on the cheek and then sauntered off, his sharp eyes on the lookout for badly hanging skirts.

Veronica stared after him then jumped as the touch of a make-up brush slid across her cheek. 'I've gone mad,' she said forlornly. 'I think I've gone totally out of my mind.'

'It does help, duckie,' Carrie said, her droll, tired voice sparking off a memory inside Veronica's head. Then she grinned. Carrie was none other than the droll voice that had so amused everybody on her first visit to the warehouse. She had an immediately calming effect, as he must have known she would. Bless Valentine for assigning Carrie to her.

The rotten dirty bastard.

'I don't have any idea what I'm doing,' Veronica wailed, watching Carrie's lined and bored-looking face carefully for signs of her own unease. After all, what Val was doing – assigning a complete unknown to a place on his prestigious show – must have caused a few shock-waves. But washed-out blue eyes met hers calmly in the mirror and the older face smiled, suddenly looking lovely. 'Don't let that worry you too much. There's a first time for everything, duckie, just remember that. Now, do you remember the order of costume change?'

Veronica nodded. 'Val's done nothing but drum it into me until it's coming out of my ears.'

'Good. But it'll probably be changed anyway. The girl who goes on before you will suddenly find a zipper gets stuck, or there's a run in her stockings and she'll have to change, and you'll have to go on instead. By the time the show's over the schedule will be in pieces. Just don't worry about it. I don't.'

Veronica stared at her, swallowed hard, and then, when Carrie ordered her, raised her arms above her head and let herself be stripped down to the skin. Literally.

Nobody took the slightest bit of notice.

The other girls, who'd gradually been sorted into names – Jasmine, Debbie, Gayle, Patrice, Grace, Connie – were all like obedient dolls, letting the hairdressers, make-up girls, wardrobe mistresses and other assorted personnel daub, paint, brush and work on them as if they were marble statues instead of flesh and blood.

Veronica glanced around, her hands hovering modestly and nervously over her breasts. Her gaze quickly found Valentine, who was on his knees, his head stuck up Gayle's skirt.

Veronica gaped.

Then he crawled backwards and emerged, a trifle flushed, his mouth still full of pins, around which he angrily shouted. 'Who the hell did the tambour beading on your underskirt?'

Veronica looked away. 'I'll kill him,' she said, making Carrie glance at her, and then shrug with a knowing twist of her lips. 'I will. I'll bloody well kill him.'

Her first costume was a tiered skirt and lace blouse, the picot-edged cotton organdie frills a bright scarlet, while the rest of the costume was brilliant white. When the make-up girl had finished with her, she turned to the mirror and gasped.

What she saw was somebody else, some glamorous model strayed from the front pages of *Vogue*, with her chic Vidal Sassoon short cap of black hair, and huge, dark eyes. Whenever she moved, the rippled tiers of the skirt seemed to shimmer and move like

79

waves around her knees and slim calves, and the stark contrast of white, scarlet and black fairly dazzled her.

'Oh, my giddy aunt,' she said, her voice little more than a rasp, and behind her Valentine's face appeared, reflected in the mirror. His eyes were thoughtful as they ran over her. Today his look was almost mechanical, and so unlike his usual hot, lazy, threatening gaze that she actually shivered.

She felt so cold suddenly. As if he'd turned off the sun. It was not her first taste of his professionalism, but it was the first time she'd realized for herself how very 'great' the 'great Valentine' really was.

'You'll do, luv. Just don't tip arse over tit down the catwalk, and I think we'll get away with springing you on 'em.'

All of Veronica's new-found respect for the man took a nose-dive. She dragged in a harsh, growling breath. 'You slimy, miserable, low-down . . .'

Val had already turned away by the time she'd run out of names, and was busy adjusting a lacy camisole top that barely covered Debbie's large breasts. The sight made Veronica turn away with a gasp that some would have sworn was a mixture of pain and jealousy.

Outside she could hear the soft wail of thick-bodied flutes that she'd heard played a thousand times in the movies whenever the hero found himself deep in the mysterious Orient. Tambourines softly shimmered, and the level of human chatter slowly ceased.

Veronica felt her insides turn to jelly. Panic attacked her, and she quickly looked around for

Val, who was gone. Damn him! The girls clustered around the door, which one of them pulled ajar, and, straining her ears, she could just hear Val's deep cockney voice welcoming the audience to his show.

It was real! It was happening. Now! She was the fourth one on . . .

The first three girls walked quickly out of the door with no trace of panic, their perfectly made-up faces calm and blank. Calm and blank, she thought as she stood shivering just inside the door, then forced herself to step nervously out into a small alcove waiting for Connie to finish her turn. The model was wearing a slinky blue turquoise wrap-over day dress with a rakish turban to match. She walked like an undulating snake, every curve of her oozing sex.

I can't do *that*, Veronica thought, feeling suddenly wobbly on her three-inch scarlet heels. Her throat was so dry that she rattled as she breathed. I'm an economist. I'm supposed to work in a office, for crying out loud, with a calculator and a secretary! If I go out there I'll fall flat on my face. I know I will. I'll freeze, I'll forget everything . . .

'And now we have Veronica, in a romantic but dashing day ensemble . . .' She heard his words, but from where she was behind the corner she couldn't see his face. Suddenly she grinned. Wouldn't it serve him right, she thought with panicky bravado, if I just didn't show up? Wouldn't he look a right Charlie?

She ought to have known he would think of such a contingency. She should have known that Carrie was as devoted to Val as anybody.

Suddenly she felt Carrie give a firm push in the middle of back, just enough to make her stagger into view, and then she had no choice.

Her legs moved automatically as the flashlights suddenly blazed, dazzling her for a moment. She walked on to the catwalk totally blind, her brain buzzing. Suddenly her vision cleared. A cool voice, oddly cockney in accent, began coaching her in the back of her mind.

Walk to the end slowly, turning left and right in slow circles. At the end turn three times, holding out the skirt, spinning to show the way it flies into the air. Then walk straight back. Smile. Always smile. Her face felt stiff, as if all the make-up on it would crack like fine plaster. She twirled, feeling dizzy. She was going to faint. She *was*.

The sea of faces became one blur. The hum of appreciation was like a faint droning in her ears. She found herself at the end, turning, her hands on her skirts. Then she found herself walking back.

As she passed the rostrum where Val stood, still in his baggy shirt and jeans, she threw him a speaking look. If looks could kill, he'd be dead in an instant, burned to a cinder.

He winked at her, and launched into the next description as Jasmine sashayed past her in a dress of tie-dyed rough-looking sacking that nevertheless managed to look unbelievably sexy. She got past the curtain and collapsed into her chair, then had to stand up again as Carrie hissed at her to get out of the dress and into the next one.

'You mean I have to do all that again?' she wailed, as Carrie shot her a funny look.

'Weren't you listening?' she asked, reaching for a sequinned evening gown of glittering ruby brilliance. 'I thought all you models had the ear.'

In Carrie's mind there was now no doubt. Veronica Coltrane was a model.

Veronica, however, missed the sudden change in Carrie's attitude. Instead she cocked a puzzled head on to one side. 'The ear?'

'Yeah, the ear,' Carrie muttered, using moisturizer on Veronica's eyelids and repainting on them a deep maroon eyeshadow. 'Every girl who goes out there has her ears tuned to the audience reaction. And you got a big one.'

'It was the outfit,' she mumbled. Even though she hated – literally detested – to admit it, Val had produced some stunning designs.

'That as well,' Carrie corrected, 'but the fuss was about you. You have to understand . . .' Carrie paused as she began some delicate work on Veronica's lashes, then carried on when she'd finished '. . . that this is a small business. Every model is known, every face keenly inspected. New faces have an advantage over the old ones to begin with, but still . . .' she daubed on some deep ruby lipstick over Veronica's quivering lips '. . . every girl who goes out there listens for the gasps. And boy, did you get some! Val was right about you,' she added with satisfaction.

This time Veronica didn't miss the awe in the woman's voice and her eyes snapped open.

'Watch the mascara. It isn't dry yet!' Carrie wailed.

'Sod the mascara,' Veronica bit back inelegantly, erupting on to her feet. Really, being around Val so much was having an atrocious effect on her manners. 'Just what did Val say?' she added more politely.

'That you were a winner, of course. Why else would you be in his show? Now sit down.'

'He put me in to fill in for that other girl,' Veronica said, then saw the flash of irony in the blue eyes and felt suddenly foolish and way out of her depth. 'Well, that's what he said.'

'You think Val would put just any girl in his show?' Carrie asked, obviously not taking Veronica's stunned look seriously. 'Look, kid, I don't blame you for working so hard to get a break. Every girl who wants to make it in this business has to pull some dirty tricks to get to the top. And in your case it's justified. You'll see – tomorrow you'll be inundated with offers from Ford and every other modelling agency. You'll have mags fawning all over you.'

This time Veronica did sit down. Hard.

'I thought he only wanted . . .' She stopped abruptly, going red, but Carrie laughed, her world-weary eyes missing nothing.

'You thought he just wanted to get you into the sack, hum?' she finished the thought for her with a twinkling eye and slightly bawdy laugh. 'Hell, I know he does. But Val is *the* Valentine. He wouldn't risk his show no matter how hot he was for a girl. Oh, grow up, for heaven's sake,' Carrie snapped as Veronica continued to stare at her dumbly.

'But I didn't want to do this!' she wailed, then promptly shut up as Carrie grunted in total disbelief.

'Sure – whatever you say. Now – slide into this.'

Veronica did indeed have to 'slide' into the gown, which was so tight it fitted her like a second skin. Any imperfection in her body would be instantly visible, Carrie knew, and she studied Veronica with minute precision until she was finally satisfied.

'OK. You're on.'

Veronica walked stiffly to the curtains and then stepped on to the catwalk, this time listening properly. She went hot, then cold, as she realized Carrie was right. The hum of voices and the flash of bulbs were far greater for herself than for any of the others. She walked down the catwalk, this time without turning, forgetting completely about the half-turns and teasing movements for the photographers, she was so stunned.

Watching her, Val realized that her apparently haughty unconcern for the photographers was egging them on, building her prestige and mystique more fully than any of the usual flirting tricks of the other models could ever have done.

When she walked past him, looking perfectly calm and cool, he grinned. He felt his loins harden in sudden animal reaction and was glad that part of his anatomy was hidden behind the stand.

As she passed him she turned eyes on him that were deadly. For a second his slick commentary faltered, and then he smoothly picked it up again. What a woman! A tigress had nothing on her! She was going to kill him in bed, he just knew it.

The thought was not unpleasing.

The rest of the show was faultless, but Veronica hardly noticed. She felt utterly depressed and couldn't understand why. When it was all over, the models had to change into their after-show party dresses and mingle with the guests and photographers.

Veronica's own outfit was a deep emerald dress with a V neck that plunged to her navel, and a similar plunge at the back that reached to the bottom of the spine. The other girls changed quickly, but she was aware of a shift in the atmosphere. She was no longer a rank amateur, a fancy of Val's to be petted or ignored.

Now she was a threat, a success, the girl who had stolen the show. She could feel the hate all around her.

The make-up girls, wardrobe mistresses and other personnel were busy packing away the scattered clothes. Accessories alone would fill several trunks – all the handbags, hats, gloves, costume jewellery, umbrellas and parasols, shoes, fans, shawls, scarves and stoles.

Still dressed in her last costume, she was told smartly to take it off, which she did, sitting back down again, totally exhausted and dressed only in a fine silk half-slip. Her last costume had not allowed her to wear a bra, but such was the atmosphere of the room that she sat bare-breasted without feeling the slightest bit of embarrassment.

She was aware of the noise in the other room rising

continuously as the champagne flowed more fully and the celebratory party got into full swing. For there was no doubt about it. Valentine had pulled off another success.

Slowly she leaned her arms on the cold top of the Formica table and leaned her forehead on her wrists. She felt tears, warm and hot, slide down her cheeks on to her skin, and took a deep, shaking breath. With only half an ear she heard the door open, and then Val's voice ordering the backstage women out.

Val stared down at her shaking shoulders and listened in an awkward silence for a few minutes as she sobbed with a quiet desperation that scared him.

Eventually he shuffled up to her, put a gentle hand on her naked back and said softly, 'You OK, darlin'?'

Veronica's head snapped up, her mascara-streaked face glaring at him in the mirror. 'Of course I'm not OK, you bastard,' she snapped, unaware that her pert, rose-tipped breasts quivered with every harsh breath she took. 'I wish I had a gun so I could shoot you straight between your lying eyes.'

Val grinned. 'That's better. I can't stand to see a grown woman cry.'

'You knew what would happen out there, didn't you?' she squawked, standing up and spinning around, arms akimbo, oblivious to the fact that she was naked except for the half-slip, lacy briefs, garter and white stockings. Her expression was tight and furious.

Val leaned back against the Formica surround and

nodded. 'Course I did. I told you from the start you should be a model. You were sensational, sen-bloody-sational.' He threw his arms wide and gave a shout of triumph.

Part of her knew that it was just the usual end-of-show euphoria. He had spent months working on his designs, and the critics out there could have destroyed him, his reputation and his company with just a few vitriolic sentences. But he had wowed them again, and the relief must have been enormous. Part of her knew and understood that.

Another part of her screamed out for blood.

His!

Vercnica stared at him for one long moment, then picked up the nearest hairbrush and slapped it at his face. It hit the side of his cheekbone with a dull thud that made her hand tingle.

'Owww!' he yelped loudly, standing up to put a hand to his stinging face. 'That hurt, you rotten bitch.'

'It was meant to!' she screamed back.

Val stared at her, his eyes changing and going as hard as black coal. She flinched when he snatched the brush from her hand, and for a moment she thought he was going to hit her back with it. Then he threw it away and grabbed her, hauling her into him so hard than she felt the breath slam from her body.

Then, before she could drag more air into her depleted lungs, his mouth was on hers, hard and hurting.

She struggled briefly, aware of her head pounding

and funny lights flashing before her eyes. Just as her knees began to buckle he suddenly snapped his head back. She had time to see an ugly red bruise beginning to form on his cheek, and then the room spun as he pushed her back on to the centre table, scattering ribbons, lace and pins in all directions.

'Val,' she groaned, then said no more as his head dipped and his lips began to savage her neck, her throat, her ears, her sternum and then her breasts.

His hands, so nimble with garments, had her naked in moments. It had been so long, so very, very long since a man had touched her this way.

And for a moment she forgot who that man had been.

Then she remembered. The visage of Wayne D'Arville flitted across her mind. So tall and broad, not at all like Val's more wiry body. His hair was copper and sleek, not the unruly brown mop that was Val's. His eyes had been piercing and blue. Val's were warm and brown.

And, slowly, the image of the handsome Frenchman was defeated. His face was pushed back, swamped and superseded by Val's.

She gasped as his hands splayed across her flat stomach. Instead of remembering a soft, purring French accent, she heard only harsh, guttural cockney words.

'It's about time you learned you can't go waving 'airbrushes about without some retaliation, my gal,' Val warned her, but his voice was thick and heavy, and shook with too many short, panting breaths.

And suddenly she knew.

She was free? The past, Wayne, the bleak months in prison – it was all gone.

She had a future once more.

And with this man.

She laughed, almost giddy with delight, and stretched back on the hard cold table, her head falling over the side to hang loosely as he knelt above her, his hands pushing aside her thighs.

She jerked and moaned, the room at an upside-down angle pulsing in time to her heartbeats that pumped blood to her head as he began to suck and nibble on the pulsing button of flesh he found there.

She felt herself began to jerk in spasms of reaction, and closed her eyes.

'Yes,' she said. 'Yes, Val, yes!'

This was what she'd always wanted. From the moment he'd stepped into her life and turned it upside down. She'd wanted a champion, a knight in shining armour to rescue her.

Thus encouraged, he stepped back on the floor and pulled down his jeans, his manhood springing proudly to attention. His hands reached for her knees, pulling her back more squarely on to the table, and when he moved between her parted legs and slid fully into her, her eyes watched him, every bit as hot and eager as his own.

This was where he belonged, and they both knew it.

Val's brown eyes seemed to melt and darken.

She moaned, her fingers clutching his shoulders, which were still covered by the old and shabby shirt.

Eagerly she thrust it from him and ran her hands across his collarbone. Her legs twitched and jerked over the edge of the table as he began to slide in and out of her, faster, harder, almost savage, almost brutal, and yet never actually hurting her.

His power and passion were so far removed from Wayne's more practised lovemaking that she was catapulted into ecstasy almost at once. Veronica held nothing back. It was too noisy outside for anyone to hear her, and she moaned and cried out with every thrust of his hard, hot member inside her.

Val winced and gasped as her strong vaginal muscles clenched him, and when finally his hot seed gushed forth into her, he yelled triumphantly and collapsed on top of her, his weight pinning her firmly to the table.

For long, long minutes their ragged breathing shuddered into the untidy room, and then, slowly, Val straightened up, his legs feeling like water beneath him as he stared down at her, so much love in his eyes that Veronica felt drunk with it.

Her body was bathed in sweat, her face, mascara-streaked, flushed and sweating, her hair soaked.

'So when will yer make an 'onest man of me an' marry me?' he asked, zipping up his trousers but never taking his eyes from her.

'How about tomorrow?'

CHAPTER 6

Veronica was still smiling at her memories as she turned off the shower. It had all been so long ago, and yet it seemed like only yesterday.

Since then, of course, a lot had happened . . .

She had been his top model for only two years, at her own insistence. It had been the mid to late seventies, and she was well aware of the reputations established by Twiggy and Jean 'the Shrimp' Shrimpton, who had come to the States on a huge tide of English sixties fever.

'But you can compete with them. All that's needed is a change of image, that's all,' Val had reassured her, and although she knew he right, she still shook her head.

'No. I've had enough. Besides . . .'

'Besides?'

From all those years ago, the words of her young cellmate had came back to her, and she'd repeated them with soft irony. 'You won't be new for long, then they won't know you're here.'

They were in Val's warehouse conversion (where

they had lived after their marriage) lying in bed at the time, at about five o'clock in the morning. Val sat up and turned on a light. 'That sounds suspiciously like a quote to me,' he commented, curiously.

Although they had been husband and wife for just over two years, he still knew very little about her background. He had not liked to pry, sensing her reticence on the subject.

'It was,' she admitted, and turned on to her pillow to face him and smile whimsically. 'Come on, Val. The eighties are coming. You want new faces for it. Don't forget, this is an English wave, and you'll be riding it high, being from the smoke yourself.'

'Ahh, good ol' London,' he said sentimentally. 'But don't change the subject. Are you tryin' to back out on me?'

'I'm trying to save you the embarrassment of having to sack your old lady. Besides, I have . . . something else I want to do.'

'Oh?' He turned to look at her curiously. Veronica watched him in silence for several minutes, almost hearing the wheels turning in his head.

'OK,' he finally said, as if *he* were doing *her* a favour. 'You don't have to do any more modelling. So what is it you have in mind now that you won't be on half the magazine covers in the good ol' US of A?'

Veronica smiled, and lay on her back, staring at the ceiling pensively. 'Did I ever tell you about a book I once wrote?' she asked softly, and by her side she felt him tense.

Val sensed that the time had come for confessions,

and although he knew he would never stop loving her no matter what, he was only human.

'Nah,' he said softly. 'I can't say as you ever did. What kind of book was it?'

'It was a book about money,' she said finally. 'How to make it, how to move it around, how to invest it, and, most importantly of all, how to make it grow. It also predicted that computers would change the world, and that the smart money would make full use of them. It was a . . . brilliant book.'

She waited, expecting a shocked laugh, a grinning, teasing reaction, but instead Val continued to watch her carefully.

'OK.'

Just that. Nothing more.

She turned to look at him, surprised at his bland reaction. Then she saw it was not blandness but trust in her that kept him so calm, and she felt tears prick her eyes.

'I wrote it when I worked for a company called Platts.'

'I 'eard of that place,' Val said. 'Go on.'

'I was only a junior member. I wrote the book as an exercise really. I didn't tell anybody. It was so ambitious I thought they'd laugh at me. But a . . . man . . . at the company read it. He must have known how good it was . . .' she laughed hollowly '. . . because he stole it. Put his name on it and told Sir Mortimer Platt that he had written it. There was only one copy, in the company safe, and when I found out what . . . this man . . . had done, I tried to get the book back.'

Val felt his muscles stiffen and forced himself to relax.

'And you were caught, I suppose?' he said softly.

Veronica gasped. 'How did you know?'

'I remembered you told me once you'd been to prison. I didn't think it was for armed robbery, luv.'

Veronica, unbelievably, found herself smiling. She had thought bringing the past back to life would be much more painful. Trust Val to be able to deaden even that pain.

'I though you didn't believe me,' she said at last. 'About being in prison.'

'Well, I did,' he said. 'Like I told you – I'd been in the clink too. Well, Borstal actually. My mate picked me up from school once in a car – a nicked motor, as it turned out.'

'Oh, poor baby,' Veronica crooned. 'Aren't we a hard-done-by pair?'

'Too right,' Val grinned, then sobered. 'This . . . man . . .' he echoed her own hesitation over the words. 'He's Trav's biological father, ain't he?'

Veronica nodded.

Val whistled. 'I'm glad I didn't know all about this when we first met,' he said, then saw her go white and cast a stricken glance his way.

'Nah,' he said, quickly taking her into his arms, not needing words. 'I didn't mean *that*. It's just that when we met, I knew some bloke had given you a hard time, and I was determined to give his memory a good kick in the old goolies. But at the time, I thought it was just the usual story. You know, the stupid sod had found someone else. If I'd known you

95

were so prickly because of all this book and prison business goin' down, I wouldn't have been so cocky about winning you over to me.'

Veronica almost wilted in relief. 'Oh,' she said, then laughed. 'But you wouldn't have hesitated, even if you had known,' she predicted. 'You'd still have come traipsing into my life with your clod-hopping boots and walked all over me.'

'True,' Val said. 'Now, about this book. It was good, huh?'

'A bestseller,' Veronica said, a touch bitterly. She hadn't had the heart to buy a copy for many years, but she could hardly live in England and not know that the book had been a smash. 'Which brings me to my not-so-new career,' she said, running a finger beguilingly around his nipple.

'Oh, ye-eah?' Val said, knowing when he was being set up for something.

'Val,' she coaxed, nipping his nipple between thumb and finger and hearing him gasp with pleasure. 'How do you feel about giving all your money to me and letting me play with it?'

Veronica's thoughts suddenly snapped back to the present as she heard the apartment door open, and she hastily pulled on a white cashmere sweater and black trousers and opened the bathroom door. 'That you, Val?'

'Nope, it's me,' a younger voice called back. 'How did it go this afternoon?'

As she closed the door behind her, she glanced

96

across the room at her son, and smiled. Travis, her son, was now, unbelievably, seventeen years old. He was a tall teenager, at six feet, with dark hair, wide blue eyes and a handsome square face that made him a natural target for all girls.

'It went fine. Valentine Inc. now owns the Trendy Boutique Range. I'm signing the papers next month.'

For Val, of course, had agreed to hand over to his wife whatever she wanted providing she went on tweaking his nipples, and over the years she had turned a one-man fashion show into a multinational corporation.

Travis grinned, showing wide white teeth. 'That's great!' He was dressed in a baggy T-shirt and oil-stained jeans, having learned his careless dress sense from Val. 'Where is Dad, anyhow?' he asked, uncannily echoing her thoughts of only a moment ago.

'I'm not sure. Probably still caught up with his French friends.'

'He's determined to hold a show in Paris, then?'

'Totally. And you know your dad once he's made up his mind.'

Travis grinned and launched himself on to the settee, where he bounced a few times and then came to rest, his head buried in a paper. 'How was school?' she asked, walking to the kitchen and pouring them both a cup of coffee.

'Great. I've been made editor of the college rag. Voted in, sixteen to two. It was probably Smith and Cann who voted against me. Neither of them knows a good rag from the *Inquirer*.'

'That's slander,' she said, handing him the cup.

'You have to watch out for libel and that sort of thing in the newspaper business.' Ever since he was ten, when Travis had informed them oh, so seriously that he wanted to be a 'newspaper man', he had worked steadily towards this goal.

Now, neither Val or Veronica doubted he would one day realize his dream to own his own newspaper.

'Publish and be damned,' Travis drawled in response to his mother's teasing, his eyes twinkling as they rested on her. 'I've got a summer job on the *NY Sentinel*. Nothing flash, just a gofer, but it'll be great experience for me. That OK with you?'

'So long as your schoolwork doesn't suffer.'

'It won't. I need the grades to get into a good journalism school.'

Veronica nodded. His determination was awesome. When he'd told his father – both Travis and Veronica considered Val as such – that he wasn't going to go into the 'frock' business, neither of them had dreamed of trying to change his mind.

They were behind him one hundred per cent in whatever he wanted to do.

Veronica was ecstatic to admit that Val was a wonderful father. From the very start, after they were married in a civil ceremony two days after the fashion show, he'd taken on the role of father with an ease that was, nevertheless, serious. He had given Travis his first 'birds and bees' talk. He'd taken him to baseball and football games. Together they went to PTA meetings, and together they disciplined him, although Val had only given their son's backside a well-deserved tanning on one occasion. Travis, at the age of nine, had been goaded into taking a swipe at a girl at school who insisted on tormenting him. Val had very promptly told him that no man ever hit a woman. It was the lowest of the low.

Now, at seventeen, Travis was showing every sign of turning out wonderfully, much to Veronica's immense relief. He was not on drugs, didn't drink anything stronger than beer, had not, so far, got any girl into trouble, and always let her know if he was going to be late. He showed none of his natural father's ruthlessness.

Veronica knew she had good reason to be so well pleased with her life.

Val had teased her unmercifully about her success with money, demanding that she pay to take them on a world cruise when she'd made them their first million. They had compromised on a tour of the Caribbean, and since then she'd made them three more million.

Val had been able to expand his fashion houses, which now encompassed New York, Milan and London. He would soon add Paris to its collection.

As she watched her son read every single word on all twenty national and local newspapers, she felt relaxed, contented, happy and sure that her world would always be as perfect as it was at that moment.

She was wrong, of course.

Thousands of miles away, Sebastien Teale closed the dossier he had been keeping on Wayne D'Arville and leaned slowly back in his chair.

He was still living in the same modest apartment. He still worked at the same mental institutions, although he was now head of the mental hospital's governing body.

But the passing years had done more than merely elevate his career. His deep russet head now had just a few touches of grey at the temples that, as so often happened with men, only made him look more handsome than ever.

He'd taken to 'working out' over the years, and his simple but effective excercise regimen had toned his body into a lean, lightly muscled machine that made him move with eye-catching grace.

His face was thinner too, though it showed little trace of the intervening years of heartbreaking work. A few crow's feet had appeared at the corners of his sherry-coloured eyes, which crinkled attractively whenever he smiled, and his cheeks were more gaunt, but that was all.

He was still single.

Now, as he put the dossier aside and pulled on his jogging shoes, he tried to thrust all thoughts of his most elusive patient away. Jogging to Hyde Park, he let his mind roam freely, but it always came stubbornly back to the big Frenchman.

Since learning of Wayne's horrific past, he'd at last began to make some progress with him, giving him mental exercises to do in times of stress and helping him control his more destructive impulses, but it was slow and hard work.

Now, with the sun shining and the birds singing, he

was suddenly made aware that spring was once more rampant in England. He found himself admiring the daffodils as he jogged past, and he breathed deeply as the strain slowly began to ease out of his shoulders.

With his head down, he was just breaking into a more energetic run when, from out of the blue, a black and brown furry body suddenly wrapped itself around his ankles.

The little dog yapped, enjoying the fun, as Sebastien faltered, desperately trying not to step on the little animal. It was hopeless, of course, and with a sense of the inevitable he felt the dog's tail under his foot as he began to fall.

The dog let out a blood-curdling yelp.

Sebastien felt instant guilt hit him, even as his knees hit the grass. He put out a hand to try and save himself, saw in dismay that the little dog was right underneath him and would be crushed, and heard a wailing female voice, somewhere over his right ear, cry out, all in the same instant.

'Jackson, you stupid little mutt. Get *out* of there!'

The stupid little mutt, Sebastien thought with a sudden flash of humour, didn't stand a chance. Time seemed to coalesce into a long-drawn-out sigh. Reaching for the small furry body, Sebastien lifted it high up into the air, at the same time twisting his body. Consequently, his ribs hit the floor with a breath-robbing crack.

His other hand, still holding the wriggling dog, shot out comically and catapulted the dog safely out of the way.

Sebastien's head hit the dirt with a star-making thud.

'Ooomph,' he grunted, and closed his eyes.

Jackson, of course, promptly showed his gratitude by standing at his head and yapping ear-piercingly into his ear.

'You shouldn't be telling him off, you ungrateful cur,' the same female voice suddenly said, and Sebastien opened his eyes in time to see a strong pair of pink-nailed hands reach down and snatch the dog up. 'He was saving your hide, you ingrate! Honestly. Dogs!'

The ungrateful Jack Russell was set down, and suddenly a face appeared in Sebastien's view. Since he was lying sprawled flat out on the grass, he blinked in surprise.

A woman was on her hands and knees in front of him. Sparkling green eyes dropped on to a level with his as the woman dipped down to him, so close that their noses were almost touching. He could feel her breath, sweet and cool, on his cheek, and felt something flutter in his chest.

'Are you all right?' she asked, then laughed at her own stupidity. 'Sorry, of course you're not all right. You were brought down in mid-run by a Jack Russell. Let me rephrase that. Do you think your ribs are still intact?'

Sebastien was feeling dazed, but he wasn't sure it had anything to do with his fall. He blinked his eyes, and focused them on a mane of thick, sable hair.

'Huh.' He forced himself to his elbow. 'It's not my

102

ribs that worry me,' he finally managed to mumble, and rubbed the back of his smarting head ruefully.

'Oh, no!' The woman scrambled around him. It was an amazing sight – she was dressed in a very expensive cream leather coat, which was now badly grass-stained. Gentle hands went to the back of his head.

Sebastien winced.

'You've got a bump there the size of a quail's egg,' the woman said, reluctant laughter in her voice. 'Sorry I couldn't be more dramatic and say it was the size of a duck's egg. Or an ostrich egg, to get into the realms of melodrama!'

Sebastien was about to say that a quail's-egg-sized bump was quite enough to be going on with when he felt warm, strong hands on his shoulders, pulling him back.

He let out a startled gasp, all his muscles instinctively clenching, but found himself being drawn back on to a cradling lap. Where he'd never felt safer. His head touched soft thighs, and his body began to tremble.

It was not, he knew, due to delayed shock.

He looked up and found himself looking up into the most arresting face he'd ever seen.

The woman was not as young as he'd first thought. Her face was sharp and angular, like a cat's. Her skin had a series of fine lines that put her age on a par with his own, but Sebastien found those very lines so attractive. They gave her face a character that younger women never had.

Her eyes were like emeralds, and right now they were laughing down at him. Her hair was so long it brushed his face. He could smell a delicious peachy smell coming from it. The desire to run his hand through it was so strong that he reached up for it.

Mistaking his intention, and thinking it was annoying him, the woman brushed it back. 'Sorry about that. I keep threatening to have it cut, but my ex threatened to stop my alimony cheques if I did.'

Sebastien felt his heart trip. So she was married – no. Divorced!

He smiled, then realized how ridiculous they must look. He struggled to sit up and the woman, with some signs of reluctance, helped him.

'Think you can get to your feet?' she asked, with that mixture of concern and humour that soon had him laughing too.

Sebastien struggled to his feet, chuckling and a little embarrassed. 'I hope your dog's all right,' he said at last, wondering where all his powers of urbane and clever speech had gone. Talking to people had never been a problem for Sebastien Teale. Now, as he looked at this stranger with the cat's face and cat's eyes, he found himself, for the first time ever, tongue-tied.

'Oh, it's not mine,' the woman said. 'I'm looking after him for a friend while she's on holiday. Oh, I'm Lilas Glendower, by the way,' she said, and thrust out a hand.

Sebastien blinked at her for a moment, and then jumped, aware that she was raising one eyebrow slowly as her hand remained, untouched, thrust out between them.

'Oh, er . . . Sebastien Teale,' he said, for a moment having trouble remembering his own name.

It must be the bump on his head, he thought ruefully. Then, as his hand closed around hers and he felt a current of electricity shoot up his arm and lodge unerring in his heart, he knew that it was nothing of the kind.

Lilas Glendower watched the most handsome man she'd ever seen blush like a beetroot, and smiled.

It had suddenly turned into a very good day.

'Right, Mr Teale, I think I owe you a drink. Don't you?'

CHAPTER 7

Hollywood

Bethany Harcourt turned the last page on the Kafka
novel she had been reading, her pale oval face creased
in concentration until the very last word had been
read. With a soft sigh she snapped shut the leather-
bound book and rolled on to her back, the huge
Queen Anne bed barely bending under her slight
weight. At twenty, she was filling out and turning
into a rather voluptuous figure.

Outside she heard the 'pop, pop' of tennis balls
hitting two pairs of racquets, and got off the bed,
stretching luxuriously as she did so before walking to
the wide double windows that led to her balcony. She
was dressed casually in blue cotton shorts and white
blouse, the outfit showing off her long, sun-tanned
legs and arms.

The Harcourt mansion was sixty acres of luxury,
but to Bethany's pale blue eyes it was simply home.
She knew every fountain, and had traced the stories
behind every statue and sculpture that sprinkled

water in the vast gardens. At only six she had read the Greek and Roman mythology that explained the fountain of Eros, near the white wooden pagoda on the east boundary of the estate. At seven she had read the English story of Beowulf, which had sparked in her fertile brain a lifelong interest in ancient English history, and at eight she had made a catalogue of all the art treasures lovingly collected by her mother over the years.

The Harcourt residence, set in the most exclusive tract of Bel Air real estate, boasted six tennis courts, two outdoor pools and one indoor one, sculpted landscaped gardens, rockeries, two greenhouses where tropical flowers were grown all year round to decorate the twenty-foot-long dining table whenever they were entertaining, numerous fountains, gazebos, summer-houses and a two-acre lake where huge fish swam unimpeded among flowering lilies and trailing river weeds.

It was not surprising. Kier Harcourt, her father, was the most successful movie director of his generation. He had yet to make a film that was not a solid gold hit. Her mother, Oriel, had once been a Somerville of Atlanta. She had been raised in luxury, although her marriage to Kier had brought about a temporary rift between Oriel and her mother, Clarissa.

Bethany liked her grandmother, even if she had caused a scandal all those years ago by divorcing her first husband, Duncan Somerville, and marrying a mere garage mechanic many years her junior.

Her grandfather, Duncan, had been killed some years ago in a traffic accident in the south of France. Bethany wished she had been able to have her grandfather around for much longer. Bethany admired and respected her grandfather, who had spent the latter years of his life in a dedicated pursuit of war criminals. A pity that such a good man had had to die so comparatively young.

Bethany forced the sad thoughts away and smiled in contentment as she let her gaze roam across the landscaped grounds and beautiful gardens – her mother's pride and joy. But Bethany's true domain was the Harcourt library, which she had all but taken over at the age of twelve. Gemma, her younger sister by two years, made an almost daily habit of moaning about the size of Bethany's allowance as compared to her own, her stubborn mind rejecting as irrelevant the argument that Bethany spent the money on improving the family library.

'Who the hell cares about three-hundred-year-old books of poetry, for crying out loud?' she'd snapped on more than one occasion, her ferocious scowl smoothing out to reluctant laughter, as it always did, on interpreting the amused look that passed between her parents.

Nobody doubted that if Gemma were let loose with such a generous amount of money there wouldn't be a boutique, beauty parlour, jewellery shop or car showroom safe in all of Beverly Hills!

Bethany leaned on the black wrought-iron railing that surrounded the second floor of the three-storeyed white edifice in which she lived, her eyes narrowing against the sun as she watched her little sister on the number one tennis court.

Bethany smiled wryly. Number one. Would Gemma ever play on anything else?

From where she stood the figures were small but unmistakable. Gemma, five feet six, with short but carefully styled dark brown hair, was dressed in a white tennis skirt that barely covered her thighs, and her top was little more than a white bikini bra exposing her midrift and a generous cleavage.

Bethany looked to the man on the opposite side of the net, her mind grappling to come up with the name of the tennis coach, but failing. She shrugged and turned, walking barefoot across the thick-pile blue carpet and retrieving a huge, floppy straw hat from off the hat-stand in one corner.

Hats were Bethany's one extravagance. She seldom wore make-up, much to Gemma's amazement, didn't give a hoot about what she wore by way of clothes and could take or leave perfume and jewellery. But hats were different. Their shade from the hot California sun was the reason why her narrow and thoughtful face was always so pale. In a state full of tanned people, it set Bethany Harcourt apart, but other things accomplished that as well. In a town of frantic paranoia, she had an inner peace and harmony that drew people to her, people from all walks of life who found relief in her intelligent, kind and quiet company.

The number of female friends she had was the one

thing her sister truly envied her. Gemma, who needed to be liked by everyone, found it much easier to relate to men.

Bethany skipped down the wide, semi-circular marble staircase, her bare feet slapping noisily against the cold black and white tiled hall as she walked past a Louis XIV *bergère*, on which resided a huge floral display of gladioli. She barely noticed the high-ceilinged elegance of the rooms she walked through before she found herself on the patio. There the warm flagstones heated the soles of her feet before she moved across to the grass, heading for the tennis courts. Once there, she slipped on to one of the sun-loungers that lined the court, glancing at her dozing brother, Gemma's twin, who was bare-chested and wearing only a brief black pair of swimming trunks.

'Who's winning?' she asked idly, and Paris, named after the city where he and Gemma were born, opened one brown eye and looked lazily across the court.

'From the look on her face it must be Carl,' he said, his voice already deep and rich and highly amused. At eighteen, Paris was almost as tall as his father. Like Kier, he had rich earthy brown hair and eyes, a tanned, handsome face, a wide mouth that was always curled into an easygoing smile, and his obsession with swimming was shaping up his body nicely.

The Harcourt family had it all – success, money, fame, looks and a tight-knit family unit. On that warm summer's afternoon, none of them could have known that the entire family would soon be thrust into the midst of a battle with a man they'd never even heard of before. A battle that was as deadly and dangerous as any fought in a war.

But the dark presence of Wayne D'Arville was still hidden from them in the mists of the future, and when Bethany looked at her sister's scowling face as Gemma whacked a ball back with more viciousness than precision, she grinned in happy ignorance.

'As usual, Paris, you're right,' she murmured.

'Out,' the tennis pro called the shot.

'What? No way. I saw the chalk dust fly into the air. It was in!' Gemma stood, arms akimbo, her flashing eyes fixed aggressively on the six-foot-tall man with the mop of blond hair, deeply tanned face and piercing grey eyes.

'Oh-oh,' Paris drawled, still with his eyes shut. 'I think that was the cue for Armagedon.'

Bethany leaned back on the cheerful sun-lounger and pulled the huge straw hat over her face.

'Come on, Gem. I was here, and I've got eyes in my head. The ball was out. Now serve again,' the pro coaxed reasonably.

'Bad move,' Paris tut-tutted, *sotto voce*, from the sidelines.

'Like hell it was,' Gemma's voice raised an octave and sounded even more as if it belonged to a querulous child.

Carl Foreman watched as his pupil walked closer, her small but well-shaped breasts jiggling up and down as she trotted angrily to the net. He felt his

111

body stir in an all-too-familiar way, and inwardly groaned.

'What's the big deal?' Carl forced himself to ask in his usual laconic drawl. Gemma Harcourt was not the kind of girl you should show weakness to; she'd eat you alive. 'It's not as if it's a double fault or anything.'

'Obviously he doesn't know her very well yet,' Bethany muttered to her sibling, who yawned audibly.

'Apparently not. He must still be fairly new.'

'What happened to her old coach?' Bethany asked, lazily scratching her leg.

Paris shrugged. 'Perhaps she ate him.'

'That's not the point,' Gemma grated, pointedly ignoring the commentary from her laid-back audience. Her voice dropped to a dangerous octave. 'It was not, NOT not, out.' She stamped her foot for good measure, then abruptly felt foolish.

Carl tapped the base of his tennis shoes with his racket and looked down into the furious face of his pupil. Gemma had huge brown eyes, like velvet pansies, that were fringed with ridiculously long, black lashes. Her face was heart-shaped, her chin pointed and as cute as a button. The same description could also fit her slightly uptilted, three-freckled little nose.

Carl gave another, silent mental groan, and moved his racket in front of his loose white shorts. 'OK, OK, it was in. We'll play a let,' he sighed, backing away.

Gemma smiled – not so much because she had won

the argument, for she'd never had any doubt about that, but because she'd seen the reaction she'd had on Carl's body. Good. If someone as old as Carl fancied her, then surely she could successfully seduce the man she loved?

She was getting tired of being a virgin. Every girlfriend she had had had lost her innocence *years* ago. Gemma hated being the oldest virgin around. It was time she did something about it.

As she walked back to the baseline, she smiled with great satisfaction. And she really didn't mind old Carl so much. At least she'd got a real coach for a change. The last one, gorgeous Felix, had turned out to be gay! Worse, he'd let her walk all over him. How was a girl supposed to improve her game that way?

She served the ball again, this time well in, and for long minutes a baseline volley sent regular 'pops' into the air.

'Looking forward to Oxford?' Paris asked, seeing that the fun was over for the time being, and turning over to give his back a roasting.

'Mm, I am. I can't wait to get there. Mum and Dad both loved it so.' They had, in fact, met and fallen in love there. 'I wonder if it's changed much since they were up?'

Paris snorted. 'I doubt it. Those sorts of places stay the same for centuries, don't they?'

'I hope so,' Bethany said with a beatific smile. 'I can't wait to get my hands on all that culture.'

'Ugh,' Paris said, and gave a long theatrical shudder.

'Speaking of "Ugh",' Bethany riposted, 'have you thought about what college you're going to go to? Always provided you can graduate from our local high, of course.'

Paris groaned again, this time for real. 'Oh, Beth, do I have to? You know I'm no student. Couldn't you wheedle your way around Dad? You know he always listens to you.'

'He always listens to me because I always make sense,' Bethany said, with just a trace of grimness in her tone that her brother, luckily, failed to pick up. 'And you have to get some sort of degree. What do you want to do – bum around doing nothing for the rest of your life?'

'Sounds just great to me,' Paris grinned, then slowly sat up. He looked across the court at his twin's yell of triumph as she shot an ace straight past Carl's tall, swaying figure.

Bethany too sat up. 'I've had enough sun. Fancy a swim?'

Paris always fancied a swim. As they walked across the lawns towards the shaded pool in a stand of lemon trees in the south quarter that was Paris's favourite, they held hands, swinging their arms in time as they walked.

'Really, Beth,' Paris said as he eyed the water eagerly, 'I don't know what I'm going to do. Dad's some role model to measure up to. He's got his own studio, and nine – count them – Oscars for his films. He works like mad for six months then relaxes for three, then he's off again. And he and Mum are as

114

much in love now as ever. You'd think this town and all those groupies would have tempted him, but not Dad. No wonder I feel inadequate.'

Paris executed a perfect dive and proceeded to swim ten laps, so fast that Bethany could only stand and watch in genuine admiration.

'And then there's the rest of you,' Paris added, coming to a rest, and treading water below her. 'You've got a brain the size of Texas. You're off to Oxford in the fall, and you know just what you're going to do with the rest of your life. A BA, then a D.Phil. Then what – a professorial position at Berkeley?'

'Am I that dull?'

This time Paris did catch the undertone in her usually placid voice. 'Hell, no. You're missing the point. You're great – everyone loves you. I just meant that all the rest of my family know just what they're doing and where they're going. Mother's already the greatest fund-raiser of all time, and I don't just mean another Hollywood charity matron. She really gets things done – look at last summer when she went to Sudan. She's really doing something – actually saving lives. You're going to be the academic genius, Dad is and always will be the brightest director in town, and Gemma's going to be a human tornado, break millions of hearts and take the world by the throat. But Paris? What about Paris?'

With that forlorn ending he grinned, realizing how self-pitying he sounded, and so did another twenty laps at breakneck speed. Less enthusiastically, Bethany stripped down to a modest blue bikini and waded into the shallow end. Paris might have finished off his monologue with his usual sod-it-all grin, but she sensed a quiet desperation behind those easygoing brown eyes of his.

She began a slow breaststroke, her shoulder-length blonde hair trailing behind her as she gave it some thought. What exactly could Paris do? He had no favourite subject at school, no hobby save swimming . . . Suddenly, as her brother powered past her, she stopped swimming and stood upright, her face wearing what her father called her 'brainwave' look.

'Hey,' she called, watching as Paris lifted his head from the water, and then obligingly butterflied over to her. 'Why don't you start training seriously?' she asked, her voice all at once excited.

'Huh?'

'Swimming, dummy. For the Olympics, the world games, the state championships or whatever it is swimmers go in for these days?'

Paris stared at her and then threw back his head and laughed. 'Oh, Beth, you take the biscuit. You think you just become an Olympic swimmer just like that? Come on. I'm eighteen already. Most kids start at four.'

'You did start swimming at four,' she said stubbornly. 'You're already super-fit and fast. You've been training all your life, in everything but name. All you need is a coach. You've got rich parents to back you and nothing else to distract you. Why don't you give it a try?'

Paris stared at her, frowned, laughed, then went strangely silent. 'You mean it, don't you?'

he finally said, his voice barely above a whisper.

'Sure I do. Why not?' Her eyes flashed in that determined way that was all Bethany.

'Because chances are I won't make it, that's why,' he snapped back, not sure why he was feeling so angry with her.

'Scared?'

Paris opened his mouth, then closed it again.

'Come on – what have you got to lose? You must know an official swimming coach – you're a member of every club there is on the west coast. What would it hurt just to have someone in the know clock your times for you? If you're not fast enough, they'll tell you and that'll be that.'

Paris trod water thoughtfully, an unfamiliar feeling of excitement beginning to knot in his belly. 'I don't know . . .'

'Of course not. For the first time in your sybaritic life you've been presented with a challenge. The question is – what are you going to do about it?'

Paris met the wide pale blue eyes of his eldest sister, and felt the knot deepen. 'Oh, hell,' he said. She watched him swim to the side and climb out. 'Oh, hell,' he said again, pushing the wet hair off his forehead and shaking out his arms and legs, droplets of water flying everywhere.

Bethany watched him, aware of the tenseness of her own limbs. She raised a challenging eyebrow as Paris turned and pointed an accusing finger at her. 'You're too damned smart for your own good. You know that?'

117

Bethany grinned. 'Good luck with the stopwatch,' she called gaily, and turned away to finish off her laborious length of breaststroke. When she'd reached the other end, her brother had gone. She pulled herself out, dressed and walked back to the house. Passing the tennis courts, she noticed vaguely that they were now empty.

Inside she sat on the third step up in the hall and began to gnaw on her lower lip again. Had she done the right thing? Suppose he wasn't quick enough? There was a world of difference between being a hot-shot swimmer in the eyes of family and friends and impressing a professional, world-weary coach. And what did she know about swimming anyway? Was Paris a sprint swimmer or a long-distance one?

If he came back crushed and humiliated, he'd be even worse off than before. Bethany sighed heavily, then jumped as her father's voice came from her right, where he had been in his study. 'That sounded ominous. What's up?'

She turned, and smiled half-heartedly. 'Paris. I think I may have just done him an injury,' she admitted. Standing up she walked towards him, her eyes troubled.

'Oh?' Kier shoved his hands deep into his pockets as he watched his eldest child rub her damp hair with a fluffy white hand towel. 'Do tell.'

Bethany grinned and did so, Kier listening intently. He had changed little over the years. The hair at his temples was now flecked with grey, the crow's feet at his eyes a little more pronounced, but other than that the years had been kind. Money and success had mellowed him. Bethany knew that her father had come from a very poor farming family. She hoped it didn't still haunt him. She loved her father more than anyone else in the world.

'Hmm. I can't say that I would have thought of swimming as a career,' Kier said, thinking over her words. 'But then, Paris has always been a water baby, right from the word go. I think he could swim before he could walk. Frightened your mother to death!'

'But you've noticed lately how restless he's been, haven't you?' Bethany pressed, needing to be reassured that she'd done the right thing.

'Of course I have,' Kier agreed with a sigh, his eyes looking troubled. 'To tell the truth, I've been feeling damned useless at being able to do nothing for him. When I was his age I had burning ambition to guide me. But Paris . . .' He trailed off helplessly, leaving his daughter to pick up the slack.

'Is like a rudderless ship?' she said, half teasing, half serious. Kier gave her a strong hug.

'Exactly. And you've just given him a rudder. What a princess.' He punched her jaw playfully, and she flushed softly with pleasure, then sighed.

'Or I've just sawed off his anchor,' she said gloomily, then caught her father's eye, and together the two of them burst into laughter.

Gemma paused halfway down the stairs, her heart-shaped face tightening at the happy sound, a harsh stab of pain lancing through her. She had changed into a simple yellow dress that did little to hide the fact that she was wearing no underwear at all beneath it. Her white sandals slapped softly against the steps as she practically ran across the hall, pulled open the doors and then slammed them shut behind her, breathing hard. Bethany had always been her father's favourite.

Her eyes scanned the driveway restlessly, then settled in delight on Simon's broad back as he washed the Rolls. The chauffeur was dark and gorgeous, and the love of her life. Craftily, she sneaked up behind him. Let Bethany be the goody two-shoes. She, Gemma, would have the man she loved.

'Simon,' she purred, and playfully slapped his rump. Simon jumped as if he'd been scalded, and turned around, his grey eyes wary.

'Hello, Gemma.'

Gemma walked two fingers up his chest, as she'd seen an actress do once, in one of her father's films. Simon's grey eyes took on a panic-stricken look. Like everyone else in Hollywood, Simon was a would-be actor. He had taken the job as Kier Harcourt's chauffeur just to be near the great man. But his daughter was smitten with him, and he himself was too young to know how to handle the situation.

'Let's go to lunch. My treat,' she said. 'I've got accounts at Ciro's, Chasens, the Polo Lounge – you name it. Come on, Simon, you know you've got to be seen in all the right places.'

Simon felt torn. She was right – it did pay to be seen at the 'in' places. But . . .

Sensing his hesitation, Gemma wanted to kiss him.

He was so sweet. And so unbelievably good-looking. No wonder it had been love at first sight – for both of them.

'Come on – I'm famished,' she purred, and Simon, knowing when he was beaten, held open the back door of the Rolls for her.

'Oh, let's take the Caddy,' she said, and walked towards the garages. Simon's stomach churned and his brain told him he was a fool to do it. Gemma Harcourt was trouble – with a capital 'T'! Nevertheless, he walked obediently towards the gleaming white Cadillac with black windows and five thousand dollars' worth of extras, and pulled it up beside the waiting girl.

In the back, Gemma was immediately conscious of the smell of expensive leather. As they pulled out on to the country roads – Kier had demanded a home set well away from the Hollywood circus – she pushed a button in the side of her door and slowly a bar swung out in front of her.

'Pull over here for a minute, Simon, and come back here. I want you to have a drink with me.'

Simon reluctantly pulled over on the deserted road, and climbed into the back, his heart pounding. With a sense of the inevitable he saw her press a button, and a tinted partition of black glass cut them off from the front seats. They were now totally hidden from the view of any passer-by.

'That's better. Much more private, don't you think?' Gemma purred, and looked at him from under her lashes. It was now or never. Simon was too much of a gentleman to make the first move.

Simon gasped as she reached across and slipped her hand under the leg of his loose shorts, her fingertips just grazing across his hardening shaft. He jumped again, as if scalded.

'Er, Gemma . . . Miss Harcourt . . . how old did you say you were?'

Gemma laughed. 'Don't worry. I've had plenty of lovers,' she lied airily, then, as if to prove her point, pulled suddenly down on his white shorts, yanking the garment under his buttocks and letting it fall to his feet. Gemma looped her finger under the tighter elastic of his male briefs and wriggled her hand down. Simon gave a weird and wonderful groan, then gritted his teeth. 'I knew . . .' he said, then closed his eyes on another helpless groan as her small hand curled around him.

'You knew what, Simon?' Gemma asked, her heart pounding.

Simon shook his head. All rational thought seemed to desert him, but when she pulled at his briefs he managed to lift his thighs from the seat long enough for her to free him.

Gemma stared down at his beautiful body, her throat clogged with emotion. At last – she had dreamed of Simon for so long. Seeing him every day, and now . . . at last . . .

Before she could get cold feet, she knelt before him and pushed his thighs further apart. She'd heard Cindy Blake telling her best friend all about how to do this properly.

Simon's lips thinned as she began to roll his

member between her two hands and she watched, fascinated and hot-eyed, as the sweat began to break out on his forehead. Tenderly, she reached out to smooth the damp, dark hair off his forehead. Then, without warning, she swung herself across his lap, and lifted up her dress to her waist. Then she let the yellow material settle around them again as she slowly sank back down.

As his eyes flew open she impaled herself on him with a small gasp of pain.

Simon's eyes widened. 'Gemma!' he croaked, his voice shocked.

'Shut up,' she said tightly, and gingerly began to rub herself against him, up and down, slowly at first, cautiously, giving the pain time to fade away. 'Hmmm,' she said, a few minutes later, her breath coming in short jerky pants. 'This is beginning to get . . . interesting.'

Simon's fists clenched and unclenched on the seat beside him as he battled to control himself. He felt a heel because the kid had only been putting on a sophisticated act after all. He swallowed hard, then moaned as she discovered muscles in her body that she'd never even guessed existed before. Her wide red mouth pulled up into an almost feral grin as she watched him begin to thrash his head from side to side against the cream leather backrest. She jerked up and down harder, faster, feeling a tight, relentless tide of tension begin to build deep in her womb. She let her head fall back and began to moan herself as she experienced her first sexual climax, giddy with pleasure at her own audacity, glad to be a woman now, and not a girl any longer. She'd bet everything she owned that Bethany was still a virgin.

Simon watched her face, smiling with satisfaction at the almost animalistic pleasure that contorted her features as she shuddered and shook her way to climax, then collapsed into a still, warm heap on his lap. Then, because he was still hard and strong inside her, he put his hands on her waist and began to move her up and down once more.

Gemma straightened up and smiled ruefully. 'Sorry, lover, I'm still learning,' she apologized. Her knees clamped hard either side of his thighs, her stomach muscles, so young and untried, gaining in strength as she took over the rhythm. Simon's eyes widened as he stared into hers, and for a second he was almost scared of her, scared of the youthful intentness of her expression, scared of the burning determination glowing deep in her dark eyes.

Then, like two children, they began to grin at each other until a second climax overtook them both and she fell on to his chest, her head resting on his shoulder as they dragged in great gulps of air.

Yes, Gemma thought, listening to the sound of Simon's moans and ragged breathing. Let Bethany be the goody two-shoes. She's found a much better way of getting male attention.

Now they'd see who proved to be the more popular Harcourt daughter . . .

CHAPTER 8

Kent, England

Lady Sylvia looked up at the sound of a softly purring car as it turned into the gravel-lined driveway and swept to a halt in front of her thirty-roomed stately mansion. Her long, slender hand tightened on the hand-made rolled gold pen she held, and her hand began to shake over the half-finished letter to her aunt. Nervously she licked her lips and then slowly rose to her feet, her legs shaking precariously underneath her as she walked to the large bay windows and pulled aside the green velvet curtains.

Stepping from a large black Rolls-Royce, her husband straightened his impressive form and slammed the door, the pale but brilliant blue eyes turning to scan the house with brief approval. Sylvia felt her stomach flip and then heard the familiar pounding of her own heart as it thumped faster. She walked quickly across the Oriental rugs to the carved ash door and pulled it open, walking into a light and airy hall where Gainsborough portraits

125

clung to the walls and Venetian mirrors reflected ancient Ming vases and eighteenth-century carriage clocks from all over the world. All were legacies of her seafaring merchant anchestors.

Sylvia paused in front of the nearest mirror and checked her reflection with a mixture of despair and self-directed anger. What looked back at her was the picture of a forty-year-old woman with short, permed brown hair, wide grey eyes, a rather big nose, generous mouth and too-round face. Her skin was clear and flawless, her lashes long and generous, but she was no beauty – passably handsome, as her father had once told her with his usual mixture of blunt honesty and tactlessness. She jumped as she heard the sound of the door opening behind her and something flashed deep in the back of her grey eyes. Fear? Excitement? Hope? Love? Yes, all those and something more. Something that kept her chained to her husband of the last ten years when any other woman would have left him and filed for divorce long ago. It was not that she hadn't thought about it. The first time the idea of divorce had crossed her mind was on her honeymoon. And yet . . .

'Sylvia.'

The sound of his voice sent an icy shaft slicing down her spine, which burned even as it froze, and she spun around. A sickly smile was already on her face as she began to walk towards the tall, towering figure. 'Wayne, this is a surprise. I thought you were going on to London from Paris?'

Wayne D'Arville watched his wife walk up to him,

his nose picking up the scent of her Nina Ricci perfume as he bent down to kiss her. The gesture was automatic rather than affectionate, but as his lips brushed hers he felt her shudder. 'I was, but then I doubted that there'd be anyone around over the weekend, and I wouldn't be able to get anything done, and decided I might as well come home.'

Sylvia felt pain slice through her heart, and bit her lip, calling herself all kinds of a fool as she half turned away.

'Why don't you come into the drawing room? We'll have some coffee and you can tell me about the trip.' She realized she was sounding trite, like some awful character from a bad play, but as usual she felt tongue-tied. Wayne came home so seldom that when he did deign to show up she felt as if she were entertaining a stranger. She walked to the concealed bell-pull that hung by the side of the Turner seascape and pulled it briefly three times. Wayne, watching her, tugged off his tie and dropped his crocodile skin briefcase by the side of his arm-chair, then walked restlessly to the big bay windows that looked out over the acres of landscaped grounds. Nothing changed here, he thought, wondering why he felt so depressed. The fountains always bubbled, the koi-carp always swam among the flowering lilies. The flowers bloomed in strict adherence to the army of gardeners' wishes, and even the birds seemed to sing on cue. Greenway Manor, the ancient stone house set deep in the Kent countryside, looked exactly the same now as it had on the first day he'd set eyes on it, when old man Greenway had invited him down for the weekend, ostensibly to play some golf, in reality to try and sound him out about Platts' threatened takeover bid of his company.

Lord Greenway had not taken the Frenchman's moves seriously. After all, Platts had never been a corporate raider before. When he'd finally realized the danger, his obvious adoption of the old adage, 'Keep your friends close, but your enemies closer,' had amused Wayne. So too had Sylvia Greenway, his only child. Plain, virginal, shy, and smitten with him. It was only after he had added Greenway's to his already enormous empire that Wayne had begun to realize that little Sylvia Greenway was everything he needed in a wife.

Even now, as he watched her motion the maid to set down the silver tray, he realized that she had class stamped all over her. It was a strange thing, class – and nobody had more of it than the British. For years Wayne had tried to pinpoint it, but couldn't. It was not style, that was for sure. Sylvia was a country bird through and through, plain and dowdy. She wore baggy dresses, wellingtons, bulky anoraks, and tramped the countryside looking like a female scarecrow. Yet still she wore that aura of 'quality' about her that was instantly recognizable. It was not beauty either – Sylvia was built like a stick with bumps and had the face of a moonsick cow. Nor was it intelligence. Although his wife had attended Roedean and Girton, she owed her minimal academic sucess to a good memory and ability to retain facts rather than to any ability to think for herself. And yet she was still, and always, Lady Sylvia Greenway. Never Mrs D'Arville. That at first had angered him, then amused him. As the gold-edged wedding invitations had gone out, offering the local gentry the opportunity to attend the wedding in St Paul's of Lady Sylvia Greenway to Wayne D'Arville, he had begun to see the way the English mind worked. Sylvia would always be both a Greenway and a lady. And since there was nothing he could do about that, he'd decided to let it work to his advantage. In the world of finance he was still an upstart foreigner who had gained Platts by nefarious means. The continued and unsuccessful campaign by Sir Mortimer's grandchildren to regain the company had left him with a stigma that was hard to shake. But with a wife called Lady Sylvia, of good English country stock, stately manor and fine guest-list, he was better equipped. Yes, in all ways but one, Sylvia was the perfect wife. Docile, obedient, well-connected.

If only the bitch weren't barren.

Wayne longed for a child of his own. It was the only area where his father still managed to beat him. Wolfgang had managed to sire two sons. So far, Wayne was childless, and it galled him considerably. He had married primarily to produce his own heir. But after ten years – nothing.

'Milk, no sugar, right?' Sylvia asked, then flushed as his lips curled into a sneering smile.

'Well done, darling. You got it right – for once.'

Sylvia's hand shook just a little as she poured the

129

coffee from the silver Spanish coffee urn into the
delicate Royal Worcester cups, but she never spilt a
drop. 'So. How was Paris?' she asked, leaning back
against the Sheraton sofa and taking a deep breath as
she did so, uncomfortably aware of the tightening
sensations in her breasts. Was she always doomed to
be like this? To turn into a quivering, useless mess of
. . . of . . . want whenever he was near? But in all
fairness to herself, nothing in her sheltered life had
prepared her for Wayne. Her mother had died when
she was only seven, leaving her to be brought up by a
succession of nannies who looked after her every
need. No great beauty, and tucked away in the
countryside, Sylvia had seen the tall Frenchman as
like a tiger in a genteel chicken house. She had not
stood a chance. Now she took a deep sip from her
cup, uncaring that the hot liquid scorched her tender
mouth and made her eyes water. How many mistresses did he have tucked away in London? She
knew of at least two, but there were probably more.

'Paris is always the same,' he said crisply, but his
eyes, resting on a jade table lamp, seemed far away
and there was a tenseness in his body that she was
only just beginning to notice. He was excited about
something, but what?

'It must be nice to be so blasé,' she said, her voice
sharper than she'd intended, and she looked down
quickly, her breath coming in rapid jerks as a mixture
of fear and tense excitement knotted her stomach.
Wayne looked at her quickly, a flash of genuine
surprise in his eyes. She was usually such a mouse

that her show of spirit was intriguing. But only for a moment. One glance at her feverish eyes and the way she plucked at her skirt soon provided him with the answer.

'You're feeling neglected, I see,' he said laconically, rising to his feet and shrugging off his jacket to reveal a wide expanse of chest covered by a white silk shirt, the trappings of civilization doing nothing to disguise the emanation of raw masculine virility that oozed from him like hot honey.

Sylvia felt her heart stop and then begin to pound. 'No!' she cried desperately, standing up and looking around her like a trapped rabbit. 'I didn't mean . . .'

Wayne began to unbutton the shirt, his eyes never leaving her face. She was staring at his hands as if fascinated. The years had been kind to Wayne, that much she was at least experienced enough to know. Most men of his immense size ran to fat, the bulk of their body becoming flabby, but Wayne exercised regularly and had zealously avoided this trap. His hair as yet showed no signs of greying, but when it did she knew that the contrast of copper and grey/white would be spectacular. Her lips parted in a soft gasp as he pulled the shirt from his shoulders, revealing lightly tanned skin. She glanced at the door. Wayne wondered idly if she was seriously thinking of running, or was only worried that a servant might come in. She closed her eyes and gave a soft, despairing moan. Why had she been born so weak? And unlucky? If Wayne had not come along she'd be safely married now to some chinless

131

wonder who came home every weekend to make love to her in the dark, in bed, at night.

Instead . . . instead . . . Wayne barely smiled as he reached for her, lifting her cleanly off the floor. She was wearing a summer dress that was at least five years old and of a faded blue colour, dotted with similarly faded red poppies. For a moment, as she was lifted to his chest height, their eyes met, hers a yearning, hating, desperate grey, his a bored, merciless blue, and Sylvia felt her soul shudder deep inside her. Then the moment was past, and she was laid on the floor in front of the empty fireplace. She turned her face away from that of her husband and stared at the large bowl of flowers resting in the recess. Roses, of course, yellow and white, tinged with peach. And there was love-in-the-mist, with its dreamy blue and tiny green fronds. And Ginny had mixed them with columbines. What a strange mixture. She sighed and then stretched.

Wayne splayed his hands across her small breasts, and felt the nipples like tiny pebbles under his fingers. Sylvia's eyes fluttered shut, the long lashes lying across her flawless cheeks like dead insects. Wayne shook his head, aware of the stirrings of his body that seemed totally remote from his brain. He didn't kiss her. He couldn't remember that he ever had kissed her on the mouth when they were making love, for he considered her too ugly to kiss. He realized the dress unzipped at the back, and couldn't be bothered to turn her over. Instead he simply took the dress at the neck in both hands and tore it down.

Sylvia flinched and cried out, the sound quickly strangling in her throat as she began to shiver. Wayne looked down at her body, then dipped his head to take her left nipple into his mouth. Quickly he pulled down her plain Marks and Spencer white pants, at the same time undoing his zip and wriggling out of his clothes. He spread her legs with hands that he pressed imperiously against her thighs.

Sylvia shuddered as she felt her legs opening, and her eyes shot open as she felt his massive organ push inside her. His eyes met hers briefly. They were mocking, still bored, and as hard as cold diamonds, an erotic contrast to his hot member inside her, that quickly began to stroke in a diabolical way that always totally defeated her. She closed her eyes helplessly, her hands coming to cup his hard, muscular shoulders, her fingers digging into him as she began to thrash beneath his large body. The unyielding hard floor made his penetration of her that much deeper, and she wondered grimly if he thought he could make a baby more easily if his sperm had less far to travel.

She smiled suddenly, a triumphant smile that changed into a contortion of ecstasy as the first orgasm hit her. She cried out, then bit down on her own lip in case the servants heard. Wayne glanced over her head at the cool elegance of a Chippendale cabinet as he kept up the smooth, deep rhythm, his body moving like an automaton. Sylvia was sweating hard by the time he finally climaxed, and as she felt his hot rush of semen flood into her belly a second, crowing smile flickered across her face. This time he saw it. Briefly his eyes narrowed, then he rose quickly, zipped up his trousers, and walked bare-chested across the room and through the hall. Sylvia turned her red and wet face just in time to see him almost run up the stairs. She waited a few seconds and then heard the faint sound of the shower running.

She lay still for several minutes, waiting for her breathing to return to normal, and then slowly, painfully sat up, her body aching pleasurably, and pulled the ruined dress over her as best she could. Then she walked unsteadily to the door and looked to her left and right. The house was quiet. Quickly she went to the semi-circular white marble staircase and climbed the stairs, going into the bedroom that adjoined his and using her own shower. When she had towelled herself dry, she moved to her built-in wardrobe and reached for the first thing that came to hand. It was another summer dress, just as old as the last one, that had once been a bright, buttercup yellow, but had now faded to a deep cream. She pulled it over her slender body and slipped on a fresh pair of Marks and Spencer pants. She glanced at the door that separated them and then looked away, instead lying on the bed and burying her round face into the pillow. As she did everything else, she cried quietly.

Gradually the sounds of movement in the other room faded away, and at four o'clock she felt suffi-ciently recovered to go downstairs for tea. Mercifully

Wayne was nowhere in sight. She nibbled her digestives with vague hunger and then brushed the crumbs into her hand and deposited them into a copper wastebin. The afternoon was warm and sunny and she eagerly stepped out into the garden, which always made her feel better. The smell of the earth and flowers, the sight of bees disappearing up foxglove trumpets, the sights of colourful borders and the sounds of birds and water trickling over stones always soothed her. She felt weary but almost content as she walked towards the lily pond, where she watched the lazy, flickering fins of the gold koi-carp as they swam in the cool water. Her favourite black wrought-iron bench was beneath a honeysuckle bower and she sat down and leaned back, feeling the dappled sunlight warm her skin. 'Oh, Wayne,' she said softly, then more sharply, 'Wayne!'

In the study, redolent of leather, books and fine brandy, Wayne unlocked a black leather folder and studied the contents. His father's casino was practically his. All he was waiting for was the final report from his private investigator.

Over the years the documentation he kept on his father, Wolfgang Mueller, had built up into a vast horde that filled two filing cabinets. No less than four private detectives monitored Wolfgang's every move, reporting on his every action. Two more PIs were digging into his past, both in Monte Carlo and Germany. But it was his father's precarious financial situation that was the most fascinating of all. Now, at long last, the Droit de Seigneur was almost his.

Wolfgang had overreached himself. Not content with the casino as it was, he'd made plans to extend and upgrade it, but costs had risen astronomically since he'd first purchased the Seigneur. Consequently, Wolfgang was heavily in debt to the banks and had taken on two partners to help finance his work. One partner had already secretly sold out to him, and Wayne had just finished negotiations with the second. All that was left were the banks – and with his contacts, and the ageing, sightless Wolfgang looking less and less like a wise investment, the Droit de Seigneur would soon be his. Then he could go back, proudly and openly as the conquerer, not the banished, unwanted son. Wayne closed his eyes briefly, feeling the bittersweet pleasure bite deep into his innards.

Over the years he'd prayed constantly that Wolfgang would not die, as had his mother. Her offical death certificate read 'heart attack', but his detectives had discovered it was really liver and kidney failure. Poor Marlene had literally drunk herself to death, but Wolfgang was made of sterner stuff. Wayne didn't know what he'd do if his father died before he could have his final and ultimate victory over him. Wayne hated his father so much, it was a physical pain.

He glanced at his watch and stared at the phone. Pierre Arnot was due to phone at four-thirty and report on this mysterious lead he said he had. Wayne drummed his fingers on the table top, and then reached for the phone. Whatever this lead was, it could hardly be that important. And besides – he needed his fix. The line burred on and off about three times, and then the calm and pleasant tones of Sebastien Teale were at last in his ear.

'Hi. Where are you?'

'Home,' Wayne said, then added, 'Kent. Are you free for Sunday dinner?'

'Love to. What time?'

'Whenever you feel like it. Why don't you come down today, then you can spend the night? We can do some fishing tomorrow.'

'That sounds wonderful!' Sebastien laughed, the sound making Wayne smile. He seemed happy for some reason. 'But not the salmon farm this time. Let's try our luck in the local river.'

'Whatever you like,' Wayne said easily, feeling the muscles in his body begin to unwind at the thought of a quiet day's fishing and talking. 'See you tonight. We'll hold dinner.'

'OK. How's Sylvie?'

'Sylvia? Oh, she's OK. How are things your end?'

'As grim as usual.'

Wayne sighed. He hated the leeches who made such demands on him. Why Sebastien insisted on slogging his guts out for the losers in the hospital he just couldn't understand. 'You shouldn't push yourself so hard. People take advantage of you.'

There was a brief pause at the other end, the quality of silence making Wayne shift on his chair and quickly backtrack. 'When will you be down?'

'Eight OK?'

'Fine. See you then.'

Sebastien slowly hung up and stared for a long while at the receiver before replacing it. Through the open door, Lilas Glendower watched him swinging thoughtfully in his chair. She sensed his tension, and was intrigued.

After the incident in the park, she had taken him to a little pub she knew and insisted on buying him a brandy. There, she had quickly found out that Sebastien Teale really *was* as good a find as she had suspected the moment she'd held his head in her lap.

She'd wangled a dinner invitation from him, and over the candlelit meal had learned all about him, from the disapproval of his parents, who had all but exiled him from his native San Francisco, to his dedicated work at the mental hospital. And, unlike Wayne, Lilas had admired him for not taking the easy and more profitable route into private practice. A little delicate probing had yielded other diamonds – he'd never been married, but wasn't gay. His social life was a big fat zero.

Eventually, Sebastien had caught on, and he'd leaned back in his chair, his eyes twinkling but a little surprised. 'If I didn't know better, I'd say I'd just been given the third degree by an expert,' he'd mused, his voice just a shade worried.

Lilas smiled. 'It makes a change, though, doesn't it?' she'd said softly, understanding him at once. 'Talking to someone else about yourself instead of listening to others.' Her eyes had held his, her gaze level and unthreatening.

And when she'd seen his eyes widen in shock as he realized just how unusual it was for him to relax around someone else, she'd known, in that instant, that she had to save this man. Save him from himself. He was far too precious to be allowed to self-destruct. Besides, she wanted him too much.

After her divorce, Lilas hadn't thought that having a man in her life was an option any more. Now, after just one look from those eyes of his, she knew differently. The thought was an exciting one. A warm and pleasing one. Lilas was too worldly-wise to be afraid. Besides, it was Sebastien who had to look out!

Now, she was at home in his apartment, having all but invited herself back there after that first date, and visiting it regularly since. After that first date, she'd taken him boating on the Thames, and given him his first ride in a hot-air balloon – one of her favourite pastimes. They'd spent a lot of time together in just a few short weeks, Lilas making it obvious, in every way she knew, that she didn't need a shrink. She had no problems. She was single, with a good job and her own place. Her life was one long bed of roses. Sebastien Teale, psychiatrist, was not needed. Sebastien Teale, potential lover, life-partner and soul-mate, however, was definitely on the agenda.

And she was sure that she was succeeding in getting just that message across.

'Who was that on the phone?' she asked now,

139

having sensed something different about him, and – as usual – feeling curious. She saw him stiffen – a sure sign of unease.

'No one. Just a . . .' Sebastien shrugged '. . . private patient.'

'I didn't know you had any.'

Sebastien smiled. It was a strange, weary smile. 'I don't. Wayne is . . . different.'

Lilas, for some reason she didn't then understand, felt a cold shiver travel up her spine. But with her usual common sense she shrugged it off and walked slowly towards him, noting with pleasure how his eyes warmed at the sight of her. 'Why don't we . . . play chess?' she asked, and quickly whipped out Seb's old board from the cabinet.

Sebastien burst out laughing. Lilas was . . . well . . . Lilas. He hadn't been able to figure her out. He knew enough to know when a woman was hunting him. And he had no objection to being hunted. But so far she'd made no move to take him to her bed, and he was far too unsure of himself to try to take her to his. Besides . . . he was intrigued. Lilas was so strong-minded, independent and spontaneous. She was just what he needed.

And he knew it.

She knew it too.

Wayne changed for dinner. It was a habit he'd picked up from Sylvia, who was herself dressed in a navy-blue shapeless gown, and as he sat opposite her he sipped his brandy with quick, uninterested sips. She nervously crossed her legs and checked her watch. She'd be glad when Sebastien arrived, for he was the only person Sylvia knew who had the ability to make her feel totally at ease. He'd also been Wayne's best man and his only guest at their wedding.

She'd seen Wayne's cold nature from the start, of course. Her own father had fallen victim to it, and there were those who thought her marriage to him was the ultimate in bad taste. Especially when her father had died so soon after losing his business. But how could she possibly explain to her peers the power of his dark fascination? How could she say, in polite society, that he totally overwhelmed her? Made her ache to please him, made her burn just at the thought of it?

But Sebastien, she'd felt instinctively, did not judge her, and now she looked forward to his visits every bit as much as Wayne himself, although she had to be careful. Wayne was almost pathologically jealous of his friend, and she'd soon learned to hide her affection for Sebastien, knowing instinctively that if her husband guessed at it, then Sebastien would never come down to Greenway Manor again. She knew that he and Wayne dined often together in London and wondered from time to time if Sebastien wasn't secretly analyzing Wayne. They seemed to talk in intense earnestness, walking in the garden, heads close together, deep in conversation.

Then she smiled. Sebastien probably analyzed her as well. It hadn't taken long before she found herself pouring out her life story into the gentle American's receptive ears. There was something about his soft voice, his instinctive understanding and soothing gentleness that broke down all her English barriers which decreed that troubles should be kept strictly to oneself.

She was even ready to believe that Sebastien knew more about the true state of her marriage than she did.

'What are we having for dinner?' Wayne asked, feeling more restless than usual. The phone call from Arnot after he'd spoken to Sebastien had been something of a surprise. Wolfgang had personally overseen the assassination of a Nazi War Crimes investigation squad, led by Duncan Somerville, ten years ago. That, in itself, was interesting. Although everyone was convinced the car accident was genuine, Wolfgang must still worry about it. What if he dropped a few hints in all the right places that another team was on its way? How would his dear father react to that?

Sylvia watched the vicious smile curl his lips and looked away, murmuring something about roast duck. 'What time did Sebastien say he'd be here?' she added quietly.

'Eightish. Why?' he added sharply. 'Not pining for him, I hope? Sebastien wouldn't look twice at you. No man in his right mind would.'

'Oh? That says a lot about you, then, doesn't it?' she flashed back. 'And it makes me wonder why your best friend is a shrink.'

Wayne felt a brief stab of anger that quickly faded, leaving him only curious. She was very brave all of a sudden. Why? 'You obviously have something to say, darling,' he drawled the last word sardonically. 'Why don't you just come out with it?'

Sylvia's eyes flickered then slid away. 'It doesn't matter,' she mumbled, and nervously sipped her own glass of dry sherry.

But her thoughts winged their way upstairs, to where the precious slip of paper, which had arrived from the hospital only today, rested underneath her blouses and skirts.

Again she smiled secretly. For the first time she could ever remember, she held the upper hand. If only she dared to use it . . .

CHAPTER 9

Unobserved, Wayne watched his wife in the mirror, curious rather than interested. She'd been acting strange for days now, and he was certain it was not just his imagination that she'd suddenly found some spunk.

He shrugged the thought away and turned to more pleasant topics. He could start a two-pronged attack on his father any time he wanted. The casino was practically his already and all that was left was to let the old man know it. And then there was Mossad. The documents his excellent detectives had uncovered about the lorry driver who had murdered their team were bound to convince them of his father's guilt. The thought of Wolfgang being forcibly extradited or kidnapped and standing trial in Israel was so wonderful that it almost gave him a sexual kick, yet he knew he couldn't do it. The newshounds would have him traced as the son of a Nazi within days, and then his own business empire would be in dire jeopardy.

His eyes sharpened as Sylvia paused in front of her

dressing table and stopped humming, her face taking on an expression he'd never seen before. Excitement, certainly, tinged with satisfaction and a touch of sadness. In the doorway he stiffened, instinct alerting him to possible danger. He watched as she opened the second drawer and took out a long white envelope. His first thought was that she had taken a lover, and he smiled savagely.

'I hope that isn't some secret rendezvous you have there, Sylvie.' He used Sebastien's version of her name deliberately, and smiled with satisfaction as she jumped and turned around, looking white and almost ill. She stood paralyzed as he walked towards her and then wordlessly took the envelope from her stiff fingers. He pulled out the sheet, seeing at once that this was no love-note. It was typewritten, and headed 'Hortland Hospital'. His eyes flickered briefly back to her. Was she ill?

Sylvia almost managed to smile, but not quite. She didn't have the heart, nor the cruelty for it. Instead she nibbled on the inside of her lip and turned away to stare blindly out of the window as Wayne read the words, his eyes widening in incredulity.

When he'd finished, he read it again, just to make sure. Sylvia had undergone every test in the book to see whether or not she could conceive, and had passed every one. Wayne licked his lips, forcing his stunned brain to think. All these years he had assumed it was *her* fault they were childless, since he'd had ample proof of his own virility. Veronica Coltrane had been impregnated by him. He'd also given his father's Spanish maid . . . what was her name? . . . a child, too.

But now. Ten years. Ten years they'd been trying for a child, and nothing. And it was not her fault. Wayne slowly folded the paper back into the envelope, glanced once at his wife's stiff back, then threw the paper carelessly on to the top of her dressing table. Without a word he turned and walked away, his legs feeling stiff as he walked down the stairs, across the impressive hall and headed for the garage. He ignored the Bentley and other classic cars and took instead the key for the E-type Jaguar he'd bought new and kept in immaculate condition.

Upstairs Sylvia watched the bottle-green shining car spin out the garage and accelerate up the drive, spewing gravel chips from under its wired silver wheels. Sighing, she wondered when she'd next see him. Or if she'd ever see him again . . .

Wayne drove to London with automatic skill and too much speed. He was stopped once by a speed cop but sweet-talked his way out of it, and arrived at his doctor's office in Harley Street just as they were leaving for the day.

Sir Roger Davenport took one look at the Frenchman's hard face, waved away his receptionist-cum-nurse, and showed him into his plush office. Briefly Wayne told him the facts, keeping his voice curt and making it very clear he didn't want sympathy, platitudes or bullshit. The doctor had him booked into a top clinic the next day for morning and afternoon tests, the results of which came through within two days.

Sir Roger phoned him at his office and asked him to come back to the clinic for a talk, already giving Wayne the answer he'd been dreading. Somehow, somewhere along the way, he'd become impotent. Useless. Incapable of fathering a child. There would never be a legitimate heir, one that he could raise, mould, and use to further the glory of his name.

When he arrived at the Harley Street clinic on a wet Wednesday afternoon, he listened without apparent emotion as the doctor explained the problem. It was so simple. So utterly ordinary. The bout of mumps he'd caught just before his marriage to Sylvia had been the culprit. He'd thought at the time that it was a mere infection of his glands; had not even considered the possibility of a grown man catching such a childish ailment. Sir Roger had to admit there was nothing to be done. He launched into a medical explanation of it, but Wayne was hardly listening. As he stared at the oak-panelled wall behind the doctor's Brylcreemed head, his thoughts were turning savagely to a way out.

He had children – or at least, a child, somewhere in the world. Rosita Alvarez – he had since remembered the Spanish maid's name – must have been Roman Catholic and therefore unlikely to abort her bastard. And a bastard son was better than no son at all.

Sir Roger had stopped speaking for some time before Wayne finally focused his hard blue eyes on him and managed to pull his lips into a semblance of a

147

smile. He rose, shook hands, murmured something adequate, and left, his mind buzzing. He took a taxi to his Mayfair flat, then telephoned the airport. Before it was answered he hung up again, realizing he didn't have the faintest idea where the Alvarez woman was.

Instead he called the detective agency that was handling all his Monte Carlo work, and set them on the trail of his father's one-time maid. He offered an extra five thousand pounds for a quick result and was then forced to wait. He slept only a few hours a night, aware of a pressure building in the back of his head, hearing in the darkest hours a silent scream that seemed trapped in the caves of his brain. He tossed and turned and drank too much, in the vain hope that it would ease the frustration. He neglected his work and forgot to shave.

Even Sebastien, when he called, was put off. The flat became a prison that he could not leave in case he was out when the phone call came. His executives at Platts had a field day, tasting the unusual sweet flavour of delegated power. Wayne had always thought he had so much time and so many opportunities to raise a worthy heir. Now he was obsessed, driven by the need to find his child, a human being that sprang from his seed.

Eventually, five days after his first phone call to the agency, he received a special delivery parcel. Inside was a folder that contained all the information he needed. Feverishly he began to read. Rosita Alvarez had given birth to a baby girl in a Roman Catholic charity home for fallen women in Madrid, and had then gone on to Andalusia where one of the staff had found a job for her with the local grandee of a small peasant village.

Wayne paused and shook his head, the first sentence slowly filtering through to his deepest subconscious. He screwed his eyes up tightly and then covered them with his knuckles. A girl. A *girl*. The insult, the catastrophic injustice of it made a scream rise to his throat, and he had to grit his teeth to stop it from actually escaping. Sweat broke out on his forehead. He knew that if he once started screaming, he'd never be able to stop. He had a sudden hideous vision of himself in a straitjacket, screaming whenever someone took off his gag. Sebastien was there, with his kind, gentle hands and kinder eyes, but this time not even he could stop the screaming. Wayne groaned, took a deep breath, opened his eyes, and then suddenly felt perfectly calm as a cooling wave of certainty washed over him.

Leaving the folder on the cluttered desk, he walked into his kitchen and brewed some coffee, then went into the bathroom to shower and shave. When he came back he was wearing a fresh beige cotton suit and cream shirt. He poured the coffee, picked up the folder and read it through to the end. Rosita Alvarez was dead, and had been for five years. Her death, the detective hinted, was rather mysterious. He'd taken the liberty of investigating the Don, and discovered that no less than six maids, without family and of bad reputation, had worked for him and died within a matter of years. Although unable to get confirmation, there were rumours hinting at sadism, unusual and unlawful sexual practices. But no one had followed it up.

Wayne skipped through this, barely interested, his attention sharpening on the report of his daughter. Rosita had named her Maria, but the detectives had no photographs of her. Her mother had obviously been too poor to have such a thing as a camera, and all her possessions had been burned by the Don. The young woman, in her twenties when her mother had died, had run away. Neither the detective nor Wayne were surprised. Here the trail had become more difficult. The girl could obviously speak English and French, but all her education must have come from her mother, since there was no record of her attending even the local school. Wayne turned the final page and finished his coffee.

Maria Alvarez had been found in Barcelona, working in a sweat shop that churned out cheap T-shirts for the tourist trade. Her hours were 6 a.m. to 9 p.m., with a half-hour lunch break. She lived in a tenement in the slums in the northern part of the city, and rode to work on a stolen bicycle.

Slowly Wayne shut the folder and walked to the telephone, where he booked a ticket on the earliest possible flight, the seven a.m. to Madrid.

Spain, in the height of the tourist season, was as awful as he'd expected. The pavements were crowded with red and peeling English holidaymakers, wearing straw hats and bullfighting-slogan shirts. The Japanese contingent was also in full swing, cameras hanging around their skinny necks, patrolling the bullrings and architecturally interesting sites like squads of schoolchildren. The heat was unbearable.

As he boarded the express train to Barcelona, Wayne squinted in the sun and felt the sweat trickle down his back. The train did nothing to improve his humour, being cramped and stinking of human sweat and stale food. Everywhere he looked, swarthy-skinned and dark-eyed men and women stared at him, his height and colouring attracting attention even to a people grown used to summertime invaders.

Wayne found a first-class carriage and sat down. Even here Spanish businessmen, puffing on nauseating cigars, watched him with interest, and he pulled down the shade to keep the hot sun off him. Over the years, Wayne had become more English than he realized. He'd grown acclimatized to the moderate and wet weather, and had even adopted the reticent nature that made the garrulous Spanish people seem an annoying and intrusive race, better left to themselves.

The journey was tediously long, so monotonous that Wayne felt once again that silent scream migrating dangerously to his throat. He ordered coffee from the lazy steward, and was then unable to drink the lukewarm brew he was given half an hour later.

At Barcelona he checked into the top hotel, took a cold bath, shaved once again and ate a respectable meal. It was seven-thirty, the sun was endurable, and yet he felt strangely reluctant to leave the hotel. Everything about the country nauseated him: the language, the heat, the insects, the people, the dirt, the gaudy lack of order and class. And his daughter had been raised in all this chaos, by a semi-literate Spanish whore who had done who-knew-what with a perverted old man with delusions of grandeur. He sighed deeply, then reluctantly left the hotel. He was unable to find a taxi and was forced to go back in and ask the concierge to telephone for one. He then had to wait half an hour before a battered yellow and grey vehicle of indiscriminate pedigree showed up. He climbed gingerly into the back seat, his nostrils picking up the faint smell of vomit and beer, and gave the address of the sweat shop in terse, clipped Spanish. The driver stared at him the mirror, noting the thousand-dollar suit and gold cufflinks, the perfectly cut hair and handsome face. What would an English turista who looked like this want in that part of town? Surely he wanted a flamenco dancer? All the men did, and with his looks . . .

'Wouldn't you rather go to a nightclub, *señor*? I know all the best . . .'

'Do as you're told,' Wayne snapped back, his hands itching to grab the greasy man's neck and strangle him. The tension was getting the better of him and he was aware of a blind desire to lash out. Without a word the taxi was slammed into first gear and roared away, belching smoke from its dodgy exhaust.

Wayne ignored the furtive looks the driver kept giving him in the rear-view mirror, and watched instead the passing scenery. In this day and age the centre of any big city looked very much the same, whether it was Cairo, London or Istanbul. It was only in the suburbs that a country's true character showed through. And whereas in Cairo or Istanbul there was a certain flavour of dignity or ancient culture, in this part of Barcelona there was only filth and decay. Wayne felt the desperation of the place seep under his skin like a cancer, and he shuffled in his uncomfortable seat. The buildings became pathetic hutches, with tiny windows and crumbling walls. Clothes-lines hung across the narrow streets, getting dusty as the traffic began to trundle over pot-holed roads. Gangs of youths hung out on street corners, looking mean and dangerous, and in doorways to small bars and dirty inns, half-naked women with dead eyes and switchblades touted for business.

The sweat shop he was taken to was five storeys high, had no windows and looked like a big box turned upside down. Wayne got out slowly, looking around at the dustbins being rifled by starving cats, at the interest he was attracting from the women in the streets and the small children who gathered around him and began to beg.

'That'll be five hundred pesos, *señor*.'

'Wait,' Wayne said crisply. The driver opened his mouth, then thought better of it. '*Si, señor*,' he muttered instead, then cuffed one small boy around the ear as he poked at a rusty wing mirror that was half hanging off.

Ploughing his way through the gang of children, Wayne walked towards the large red double doors that led to the sweat shop. A broken-down link fence guarded the grounds, and he noticed that none of the children followed him past the perimeter. No doubt the owners of the building had been more generous with guard dogs than they had with workers' wages. The red doors were rusted and hard to open, but once inside the heat and airlessness hit him like a physical force. He gasped, the smell of cloth, dust and human sweat almost making him retch. The room was lit with bare bulbs that pumped out only forty watts at a time, and the clatter of noise came from armies of sewing machines.

As he became accustomed to the light, heat and noise, his eyes scanned the room, taking in every detail. Large wooden benches lined the room, crammed into the minimum of space needed to allow a person to squeeze between them. Shoulder to shoulder in front of ancient sewing machines were an army of women. Wayne moved closer, still unobserved. The women were practically uniform. All wore sweat-soaked white blouses and long, thin skirts. All wore bandanas that hid their hair, which were also sweat-soaked. The eyes were all black and fixed on the white cottons and coloureds that were flowing under the hammering needles. Some were old, some middle-aged, some looked like only children, but all wore the same expression of hopelessness. As he moved closer he realized none of them was talking. At first he thought it could only be because no one could be heard above the rattle of machines, but then he noticed several men walking around the perimeter of the benches close to the windowless walls. The women's eyes flicked nervously towards them whenever they passed, and Wayne slowly nodded.

Suddenly one of the men noticed him. The sweat-slicked face turned his way, the black eyes briefly flashing in surprise before he came towards him. He was five feet ten, tall for a Spaniard, and as he approached he put his hands on his hips and thrust forward his chin in as threatening a gesture as he could make to a man who was so obviously his physical superior. He said something in harsh, guttural Spanish.

'I want to talk to Maria Alvarez.'

The man did not understand English, but the name was familiar. Julio Corsecia had picked out Maria Alvarez for his own. All the overseers did, for it was the overseers who could protect them, put forward their name for transfers and even bargain for a few more measly pesos. But so far Maria Alvarez was proving difficult, and Julio's eyes narrowed on the handsome stranger. Was this her lover? Was this why she was playing so hard to get? She was by far the most beautiful woman he'd seen, and also the most intelligent.

Then he realized that this *gringo* couldn't possibly be her lover – he was wearing thousands of pesos in jewellery alone. He could afford to keep Maria in downtown luxury if he chose.

Wayne reached into his pocket to withdraw a bunch of notes. He pointed to the women and said again, 'Maria Alvarez.'

Julio took the money quickly and nodded to the fifth bench from the right, then pointed his finger six along. Wayne stepped closer, his eyes searching for the girl in the dim light. She was sandwiched between two other women, and he strained his eyes, hoping to see something different about her, something that would mark her as his. But her head was bowed and all he could see were wisps of black hair on her forehead. At that moment she leaned back slightly, and he could see that her face was sweating and streaked with grease that must have come from her machine, which looked even more dilapidated than the others. Her face was pinched and paler than the others, but the eyes were black.

Wayne felt himself recoil, as if he'd just confronted a snake. There was nothing about her that he wanted. Nothing he could salvage. She was just like all the rest in this dirty stinking country. A sweating peasant, with bovine eyes and a dull brain. What else was she doing here? Suddenly he wished she'd never been born, never been allowed to raise his hopes. The bitch. Trust Rosita to produce this . . . *creature*.

He sneered a smile. He could just imagine springing this peasant on London society as his wrong-side-of-the-blanket daughter. She'd probably go around barefoot and get fat on chocolates. Wayne glanced at

156

the openly curious Julio, nodded curtly, turned and left.

Maria Alvarez did not look up.

Wayne found the taxi driver waiting for him and ordered him back to the hotel. There he repacked his overnight case and called the airport, every action savagely controlled. He was in luck. An eleven o'clock plane had just had two cancellations.

Maria heard the buzzer and almost cried in relief. As if by magic the machines stopped, whether or not a garment was only half done, and the sudden silence almost hurt her ears. Then the gabble of female voices began, along with a general exodus towards the doors, where the usual bottleneck formed. She remained seated. After fifteen hours of being lodged between two sweating bodies, she didn't need another ten minutes of it at the door.

She leaned forward and tugged off the bandana, allowing her wet but lush hair to tumble free over her shoulders. Leaning her elbows on the table, she took deep gulps of stale air. At first, when she'd begun to work here she'd been sure she was going to suffocate. She'd fainted regularly, as did all the newcomers, until she got used to it. The guards and fellow workmates had totally ignored her. She'd been working six months now and it felt like sixty years.

She had to get out. She had to. Even if it meant starving. Even if it meant working the streets. Anything had to be better than this.

'Waiting for me again, I see.' The words were

157

leering and uttered in the thick local dialect. Inwardly, Maria moaned.

'I'm waiting to leave, Julio,' she corrected him wearily. Every night she had to fight him off, and it was getting more and more difficult.

'Aw, come on, Maria. Why don't you come back to my place? I have some wine in the fridge – nice and cold. And if you were more friendly I could get you transferred upstairs.'

'Great,' she sneered. 'They actually have hundred-watt bulbs up there, don't they?' Standing up she found herself trapped against the bench as he pushed against her.

'Ah, you are so ungrateful, little Maria,' Julio chided her. 'They make beautiful dresses up there. Silk and lace. Mmm,' he put his fingers to his lips in a silent kiss, and Maria almost laughed. Almost. This Lothario thought he was God's gift to women because he was not fat and because he earned two hundred pesos more than the women. It was pathetic and strangely sad.

'I must go now,' she said, shoving against him fearlessly, and walking towards the door. Since running away from the Don's villa before her mother's body was even cold, she'd learned quickly how to take care of herself. She'd needed to.

'I hope you don't expect to meet your tall lover-boy,' Julio spat after her, his masculine pride severely knocked. 'Where did you tell him you worked? In some boutique for the *turistas*, huh? Well, I'm afraid, *chiquita*, he's found you out.'

Maria turned around and stared at him. 'What are you gabbling on about, you imbecile?'

Julio laughed spitefully. 'I'm talking about the tall Englishman who came here asking for you, my little *cucuracha*. I suppose I could have let you have a few minutes off, but . . .' He shrugged his shoulders graphically, rejoicing in putting the haughty bitch in her place for once.

'Tall Englishman?' Maria echoed, her heart suddenly diving in her chest. On her deathbed, and in a highly feverish state as she died of untreated syphilis, Rosita had mumbled about her father. About his copper hair and blue eyes.

'What did he look like?' Maria asked sharply, trying to keep her voice neutral. If he guessed how important it was, Julio was likely to clam up.

'Ahh, he thought he was something, because he had the blue eyes and gold hair. But he was nothing,' Julio said, shrugging his shoulders and laughing. 'Not like me. Not even that much taller.'

Her father was French, but Maria doubted if Julio would know the difference. And if it *had* been her father come to find her . . . She glanced at the benches and could easily imagine a rich man's shock and disgust at what he'd seen. A girl, sweating, dirty, a mere peasant . . . Oh, *Madre Mia* . . .

Maria began to run. She ran to the back, where her buckled and tired bicycle was kept, and pedalled furiously up the road a few hundred yards to the nearest phone. There she used up precious pesos phoning all the best hotels. In her fever, Rosita had

159

muttered the name D'Arville over and over again, and as she asked after any guest by that name, using her best and most cultured accent, she could feel her heart hammering in her chest. He had come for her. It had to be that. Who else in the whole stinking world knew or cared where she was? The second hotel she phoned, one of the most luxurious in town, confirmed that they had had an Englishman called D'Arville staying, but that he had just checked out.

'Where? Where did he go?' she all but screamed, and then calmed down, spinning them a tale about finding his wallet. The desk clerk assumed he had gone to the airport and told her so. Maria hung up and almost cried. The small local airport was so far away. She could not possibly bike it. She stashed her battered only means of transport behind a derelict building and ran to the main thoroughfare, where she hailed a taxi. It took up her last pitiful amount of cash.

At the airport she ran into the departure lounge, headed for the nearest free departure desk, and asked if Wayne D'Arville had left yet. The clerk, a middle-aged woman dressed in a red and blue uniform, with perfect make-up, hair and grooming, sniffed politely that they couldn't give out that kind of passenger information. For a second Maria stared at her, wanting to rip her eyes out. What did confidentiality mean, when her whole life had just been flushed down the toilet?

Then she turned away, her shoulders slumped, totally defeated. What did it matter? She already knew, deep in her heart, the answer.

He had come at last to find her, and then decided he did not want her. No doubt she was not good enough for him. No doubt the rich man didn't need a nobody for a daughter. If she'd been beautiful and worked as a shop girl in some fancy jewellery store . . . If only she'd looked different, he would have taken her. All the years of working for a pittance and dodging men who wanted her body had been made bearable only by the thought of being rescued one day. By someone. By anyone.

And although Rosita had taught her to hate the man who had deserted them, leaving them to a life of misery and poverty, the little girl in her, raised fatherless, had nevertheless secretly yearned for her father to come and claim her. To assure her it had all been just a terrible mistake. But now, Maria shared her mother's hatred of the man. D'Arville. What kind of man was he? Knowing that he'd seen her and the kind of life she'd been forced to lead, knowing that he had stood only yards away as she'd sweated and toiled in that awful place, and then just calmly abandoned her for a second time, made the hatred burn, searing down into the very depths of her being.

She stumbled out into the warm night air and dodged the conductor on the airport train back into town. Walking the streets back to the factory, she found that her bicycle was gone. Somebody had stolen it, as she had stolen it in the first place. Slowly she leaned against the wall and began to cry, helpless, hopeless tears of anger, rage, frustration and pain.

Suddenly she heard voices, Julio's and one of the other guards, and watched dully as they began to load the beautiful dresses from the second floor on to vans. Slowly her tears stilled and a hard, cold knot took their place. When they both went inside for the second batch, Maria found herself running. She crouched low, waited for them to reappear, load the next batch and then re-enter the building. Still crouching, she sidled up to the van and looked inside. Quickly sorting through the racks of dresses, she lifted down an evening gown of deep red silk that shimmered in the pale moonlight, the outer covering of plastic crinkling as she folded it over her arm and ran back into the night.

It didn't matter if they found out who had stolen the gown – she already knew that she would never go back to the workshop. She was through with just surviving. She was through with being a good and decent girl, trying to make for herself a decent and honest life.

One thing her father's visit had taught her was that she could rely on no one but herself. From now on, she thought, stumbling through the dark streets with a stolen dress and about ten dollars' worth of pesos to her name, things would be different. She would travel north, to Madrid, where all the rich men were. She'd steal some make-up, do her hair differently, steal some shoes. With her lovely dress she would find a rich man. She would become rich and beautiful and clever, and be all the things a rich man wanted. She would demand jewellery, cars and furs, then sell them for cash.

And then, and only then, would she be ready to find her father.

For leaving her in that awful place, for finding her unworthy to be his daughter, she would destroy him.

She would destroy him if it was the last thing she ever did . . .

CHAPTER 10

Hollywood

Kier frowned as the telephone shrilled loudly and glanced up from the screenplay he was reading to see if anyone else was about to answer it. Apparently nobody was, and after the seventh ring he lifted the receiver and leaned back in his large leather chair. 'Yes?'

'Is this Mr Harcourt?'

'Yes.'

'You are the husband of Oriel Somerville, the daughter of the late Duncan Somerville?'

Kier frowned and sat up straighter. 'Yes.'

'Ah. My name will probably mean nothing to you, but I am Daniel Bernstein. I was a good friend of Duncan Somerville's for many years.'

Kier relaxed again and smiled. 'Yes, I remember Duncan talking of you. You were on the committee in Switzerland, weren't you?'

He rubbed his forehead tiredly, the typed lines of the second-rate screenplay dancing before his bleary eyes. It was three months since he'd finished work on his last film, due out at Christmas, and he was anxious to find another project. He was never easy with his almost mandatory three-month vacation after every film. Hollywood changed constantly and new kids appeared on the block every day, anxious to take his crown of 'top director' away from him.

Sometimes he felt like a hamster in one of those wheels where he had to run harder and faster just to stay in the same place.

'Indeed I was,' the voice on the other end confirmed, warming considerably. 'I was due to go with him on the Monte Carlo expedition but a family crisis at the last minute made it impossible.'

'Then I'm glad you didn't go.'

'Yes. Yes.' The voice hesitated, then coughed. 'Ahem. Mr Harcourt, I am in Los Angeles at the moment. At the Farleys'. Would it be possible to come over and speak to you?'

'Now?' Kier asked, surprised.

'Yes, if it isn't too much of an inconvenience. I . . . have some news that can't be given out over the telephone.'

'All right.' Kier glanced at his watch. 'I'll expect you in half an hour. Do you know the way?'

'I imagine every taxi driver in town knows your address.' The voice laughed warmly, and then, without another word, hung up. For several seconds Kier stared at the receiver, then shrugged and put the phone down, telling himself there was no need to feel so uneasy – Duncan had been dead almost eleven years. Yet he was unable to settle back down to reading the so-called thriller that sat in front of him, and instead he poured himself a weak Scotch and soda, wandering with it into the living room.

The house was deserted. Paris was at the swimming baths, where he seemed to live nowadays, training for the California State Championships next month. Bethany was at a college lecture on the Oxbridge university system, and he never knew where Gemma was. For weeks he'd been meaning to have it out with her, nightmare visions of drug addiction or worse disturbing his dreams, but Oriel was against it.

'If you lay down the law now you'll only make it worse – drive her out even more. Believe me, I know,' Oriel had said, then smiled and took his hand. 'I'll see to it. In my own way. Trust me?'

Of course Kier trusted her. He glanced at his watch and wondered if she'd be back in time from the fund-raiser for the African Famine Disaster to meet their mysterious visitor.

He stretched out on the settee in the main lounge and flipped through the TV channels. Some of his earlier films had been bought by the top channels, and it would be interesting to see them again from a decade's distance. But just then he heard sounds in the hall and looked through in time to see his wife slip off her shoes. Her hair was shoulder-length now and bobbed into a neat curl, but dyed to hide the approach of greying. Her figure, however, was as slender as ever and her face had matured from being girlishly pretty to being maturely beautiful.

'Kier?' she called, the sound of her clear, sweet voice making his toenails curl, as it had always done.

'In here, sweetheart.'

She turned at the sound of his voice and walked in, smiling as she snuggled up against him on the couch, her back pressing against his chest, her hands reaching for his and resting them on her waist. He smelt the fresh rose scent of her hair and leaned forward to kiss her neck.

'Not working?' she asked, pinching his drink and taking a small sip.

He told her about the phone call, and she leaned her head right back to give him a worried, upside-down look. 'Is that all he said?'

'Uh-huh.'

'I wonder what he wants?'

'We'll soon find out. Unless I'm mistaken, that's a car now.' A few moments later the doorbell rang and Jenny, their housekeeper-cum-cook, opened it. Oriel moved to a more modest position on another chair and Kier rose as their visitor was shown in.

He was a small man, about five feet six, with short grey hair, a neat moustache and smiling brown eyes. Dressed in a rumpled blue suit, minus a tie, he walked briskly, like a pedigree dog. 'Mr Harcourt.'

'Mr Bernstein. This is my wife.'

The man turned, and, seeing Oriel for the first time, beamed a smile. Walking over to her, he took her hand and bowed over it in touching old-fashioned courtesy.

167

'Ah, Mrs Harcourt. Your father often spoke of his beautiful daughter, but I must confess I thought that it was a father's exaggeration. I can see now I did Duncan an injustice.'

Oriel almost blushed, then nodded him to a seat. 'Please sit down. What would you like to drink?'

'Oh, a dry sherry if you have it, please.' He took a seat opposite the couch, looking nervous and out of place as Oriel handed him a drink and then once again joined Kier on the couch. The old man took a sip, smiled, sighed and then came straight to the point.

'I imagine my telephone call came rather out of the blue, and you're wondering what all this is about?'

Oriel looked at Kier, who read the silent message in her eyes, and slowly leaned forward to dangle his arms across his knees. 'We are curious, yes. It has something to do with Duncan and his work?'

'Yes. Yes, it does. It has, actually, more to do with his death, and the man in Monte Carlo we suspected of being Wolfgang Mueller. I . . . are you conversant with all the facts?'

'Yes,' Oriel said sharply, feeling a cold chill suddenly snake down her spine. 'You must have learned something else, Mr Bernstein, or else why come here?'

Daniel Bernstein nodded thoughtfully. 'Yes, Mrs Harcourt, we have. Mossad, or rather only a division of it that is attached to the War Crimes Committee, have found several death camp survivors who are willing to testify that D'Arville is in fact Mueller. We

168

are also investigating the possibility that Mueller's lieutenant at the time may have absconded with valuable and irrefutable documentary evidence. Naturally we are searching for that lieutenant now.'

Kier leaned forward and frowned. 'All this has taken rather a long time, hasn't it?'

Daniel Bernstein smiled sadly. 'It always does. If you had seen the chaos, the shock . . .' He shrugged, and as he did so the ill-fitting blue suit rode up his shoulders, and with a cold shock Kier saw the tattooed numbers in faint blue ink on the man's wrist.

'I'm sorry,' he said, knowing that it was totally inadequate but not knowing what else to say. Daniel Bernstein smiled that sad smile again and shook his head.

'We are dedicated to bringing the Nazis to justice, despite the help they receive from the US and Britain, and the other countries as well.'

'The US shelters war criminals?' Oriel echoed, her voice raised several octaves in genuine horror, and watched as again the old man gave that fatalistic shrug.

'To be sure. But that is not why I am here. There has come to light some new evidence about . . . the car crash that killed your father, and all my other good friends. It seems that a . . . friend of mine, living in Monte Carlo, had a tip-off about a private detective investigating Mueller. Naturally, my . . . friend . . . er . . . bribed the man concerned, who then handed over copies of his findings. There is some discrepancy about the legitimate nature of the lorry driver, and other factors that lead us to believe . . .'

'Daddy was murdered,' Oriel interrupted flatly, but her voice was appalled and deadened with shock, and Daniel Bernstein spread his hands helplessly.

'Yes, madam. I'm here to ask you if you know of any of your father's papers that may help us reopen the Mueller case.'

Oriel, pale-faced but composed, shook her head. 'No, I . . . no. My mother probably took care of all that. She's the one you should ask.'

Kier reached across and squeezed her hand, and Oriel closed her eyes briefly. She could see a perfect replica of her father's laughing face on her closed lids. He had been so kind, so gentle. And to be murdered by some Nazi . . . It was almost unbelievable. And yet, here was this little man, with his tattoo and his nightmare memories, drinking dry sherry in her lounge in Bel Air, telling her just that.

'I thought this was the case. Actually I tried to find a Mrs Somerville in Atlanta, but couldn't. I was hoping that you could give me her address?'

Oriel nodded. 'Yes, of course. She remarried several years ago.'

'Ahh, I see.' Daniel waited as Oriel left and rummaged in her handbag for a piece of paper and quickly wrote down the new address where her mother and Kyle had lived for the last eight years.

Oriel had long since overcome her immature attitude towards Kyle. Now they had dinner regularly at Thanksgiving and Christmas, and Kyle was even a favourite with her children, especially Paris, who loved him like an older brother.

In a way, Oriel could even admire her mother for marrying her long-time lover. She had certainly run the gauntlet of Atlanta gossip for marrying a man several years her junior, and a poor one at that. She walked back with the piece of paper, her hand trembling as she handed it over. Daniel rose as he took it, obviously in a hurry to leave. Kier looped his arm comfortingly around her shivering shoulders as they walked the old man to the door.

'You will keep us informed about things, won't you?' Kier prompted, and, assuring them that he would, Daniel Bernstein left.

Thousands of miles away, Wayne D'Arville disembarked at Honolulu airport, where he was given the mandatory *lei* of frangipani flowers. He took a taxi the four miles or so down the strip into Honolulu centre. Everywhere he looked he saw lush tropical flowers, towering white hotels, blue pools and bubbling fountains. Even the trees that lined Tantalus Drive and other famous avenues such as Pali Highway and the beach-fronted Kalakau Avenue were the owners of such exotic names as Hau and Milo, Pandanus, Ohia and Lehua. He vaguely took note of the shower trees, in full colourful bloom as the taxi headed for the famous Pink Palace, or Royal Hawaiian hotel, where film stars and royalty regularly stayed.

The taxi driver obviously had ambitions to be a

tour guide, and gave him an unwanted commentary on the city, the Aloha tower and volcano bowls, going on to wax lyrical about the Hawaiian gods. Wayne would have given him an extra large tip just to shut up, but he was exhausted from the flight and wanted only to rest before seeking out the man he had travelled more than half the world to find.

The streets sped past, packed with gaudily dressed holidaymakers. In that respect the city reminded him of Spain, and he shuddered as he remembered it. He wished he'd never gone.

'Here we are – the Pink Palace. That's twenty dollars.'

Wayne gave him fifty and was too tired to wait for the change. A bellboy grabbed his luggage straight out of the back of the taxi and led him up to the main lobby, through the lush gardens rife with palm trees and fountains. In the high-ceilinged hall, he checked in, ignoring the fountain in the middle of the room and the small, tropical fish that swam in the white marble bowl amongst the flowering water-lilies.

'Would you like to dine downstairs, Mr D'Arville, or would you prefer to be sent up a tray?' the bellboy asked as Wayne walked through the four-roomed suite on the top floor and stepped out on to the balcony. His room overlooked the azure expanse of the ocean, and below him men and women stretched out beside one of the pools, reminding him of fish grilling on a skillet.

'On a tray. Fetch me a menu, will you?'

The bellboy nodded, beaming at the tip Wayne

gave him, and hurried away. A maid entered and began to unpack for him, but he didn't turn around. The hotel was set in a sea of tropical colour – rhododendrons, bougainvillaea, hibiscus and bird-of-paradise flowers. Huge banks of lilies and orchids seemed to grow like weeds, yet Wayne was blind to their beauty, as he was to the sight of that white beach, the most famous in the world – Waikiki.

He turned as the bellboy returned and handed over a heavy leather-bound menu and glanced at it, almost too tired to feel hungry, barely noting that the menu was as exotic as his surroundings; Lomi Salmon, Macademia eggs, Coconut Macademia chicken, Wai-manalo corn, Maui onions, Tropical Salad Platter. He ordered the nutted veal steak and *haupia*, the popular coconut pudding, and a bottle of white wine, saying only that he wanted the best vintage. He couldn't be bothered with a wine list that was probably as long as his arm.

The meal was delivered quickly, and he ate it just as quickly, collapsing on to the bed straight away. When he woke, it was the following afternoon. Evidently he'd remembered to put out the 'Do Not Disturb' notice. He was doing more and more things lately without remembering them later. It was . . . odd. He was also feeling more and more tired. He'd have to ask Sebastien about it. He would know. Sebastien would look after him.

He showered and changed, walking into the main restaurant and ordering coffee and a salad before he saw to hiring a car. For his money he got a chauffeur-driven limousine and a driver who knew the city inside out. The driver was guaranteed to be discreet. Which was just as well.

Reading the address from a notebook the PI agency had sent him, he smiled for the first time that day. He looked around with more interest as he was driven north east out of the city towards Kaneohe Bay, where Lt Friedrich Heinlich now lived a life of mild luxury as Billy Hawker, a retired beer baron from the former Yugoslavia.

Beer baron. Wayne smiled again as his thoughts winged back all those years to that clandestine boat ride across Lake Constance when he and his father, mother and little brother had fled Germany. Heinlich had also been on board, but only Wayne had spotted him. And had kept quiet about it, knowing that his father would have given anything to get his hands on Heinlich. Would the man who had cowered under the tarpaulin, convinced the son of Wolfgang Mueller was about to give him away, remember him?

The car cruised along Route 83, hugging the spectacular coastline, and then turned off, a few minutes later pulling in at a low, large bungalow that boasted a kidney-shaped pool, carefully tended gardens and two guard dogs. Wayne nodded to the chauffeur to stay seated and let himself out.

Heinlich was seated by the pool, a flabby old man. He watched the stranger alight from the impressive car with thoughtful but unworried eyes and slowly sat up as his tall visitor drew to a halt in front of him. As a rich widower, Heinlich was used to being visited by strangers, most of whom came bearing invitations to some social function or another, but this tall individual was obviously nobody's errand boy. He found himself stiffening and straightening even before the man opened his mouth. There was something strangely familiar about him, and something, from a long way off, tugged at his memory.

'Yes? What can I do for you?' he asked, more abruptly than was characteristic of him, and Wayne raised an eyebrow, a little surprised by the broad American accent. Of course, Heinlich had lived on the island for decades. No doubt financed by blackmail in all the right places. He wondered where his father's cronies had all come to rest, and how much they paid this balding, unattractive individual to keep his mouth shut. With the files he had stolen on them, he had been set for life.

'I think it's more a case of what you can do for me . . . Herr Heinlich.'

Billy Hawker, as he'd been known for more years than he cared to count, went as white as a shark's tooth. '*Mein Gott . . .*' he muttered, rising shakily to his feet and staring up into Wayne's blue eyes. 'Come inside,' he said stiffly.

Wayne followed the ex-Nazi into the interior of the impressive bungalow. Inside it was all cool tiling and plain white alcoved walls, each alcove housing original Hawaiian masks. Native instruments, such as guitars and ukeleles, flutes, ipu drums, marimbas and ulivis, stood tall and proud in a dark showcase in one corner. Wayne walked past lush plants climbing

175

rattan screening and down into an ultra-modern room of black smoky glass, chrome and white leather.

'You live well, Herr Heinlich. Much better than a humble lieutenant would, I think,' he commented, selecting a chair and making himself comfortable.

Heinlich took several deep breaths, poured out two neat Scotches, and handed one over. 'Who are you? And what are you doing here?'

For a moment he had visions of kidnapping Israelis or revenge-mad concentration camp survivors, but the man's lack of a weapon and his relative youth calmed him. Heinlich walked stiffly to a chair, but did not sit down.

'Not a very original opening,' Wayne chided, and took a slow sip of his drink. 'Actually I'm very hurt you don't remember me. After all, I did save your life once.'

Heinlich jerked around at that and stared at Wayne. 'Not in the war,' he stated firmly. 'You're too young.'

Wayne smiled and took another sip. 'I was only a boy, I admit. Stood on a boat. Lake Constance . . . ah, now I see it's all coming back.'

Heinlich sank on to the white leather chair, his mouth falling comically open. The English turn of phrase 'like a stunned mullet' had never seemed more appropriate. 'Mueller's son!' he breathed, and Wayne nodded, enjoying himself.

'None other. I've come to collect. For keeping my mouth shut all those years ago.'

Heinlich drained his glass but didn't feel strong

176

enough to get up and pour himself another, although he badly needed one. All these years he'd felt safe, and now . . . 'What exactly do you want?'

'Your documents on my dear father, of course. What else?'

'Ahh. I see. I had heard that Mossad . . . never mind. Forget it. I never said it.'

Wayne smiled, took another sip of his drink, and then crossed his legs at the knee, one black leather shoe swinging absently. 'Well?'

'I don't have them here,' Heinlich said, swallowing nervously, his prominent Adam's apple bobbing up and down on his liver-spotted throat. An old man, Wayne thought, just like his father. And once they were called the master race! He half laughed, and then shook his head. Hell, what a joke that was.

'Then we'll go and get them, shall we? My car's out front.' He stood up and walked to the old man, who tried to shrink back into the chair. Slipping a hand underneath his arm, he all but dragged him to his feet.

'Why now?' Heinlich whinged as they walked out into the hot afternoon sunshine and headed for the black limo. 'Why not before? If you could find me any time . . . It doesn't make sense. Why didn't you turn me over to your father all those years ago?'

'You don't have to understand,' Wayne said softly. 'Just obey.' He looked down into the old, red-rimmed eyes and said with the softness of a snake, 'You were wise enough, all those years ago, to keep out of my father's way. You'd be equally wise to be obey me now.

Believe me, my father is a weak, helpless old fool, and is nothing, *nothing*, compared to me.'

Heinlich listened to the hissed words, his old eyes fixed in fascinated terror at the tight, hate-filled face of Helmut Mueller, and believed him. His lips were as dry as paper as he crawled across the back seat of the limo.

The driver glanced blandly in the mirror. 'Where to, sir?'

Wayne looked at Heinlich, who swallowed hard. 'First National Bank.'

Wayne smiled. 'That's a good boy, lieutenant. And let's not forget. I want all the copies. Yes?' He tweaked the old man's white-whiskered chin and felt him quake. 'No keeping back any photocopies for yourself. If Mossad do track you down,' his voice fell to a tormenting whisper, 'and you spill your guts to save your own neck, and they come for my dear, dear papa before I'm finished with him, I'm going to be most put out. *Most* put out,' he echoed softly, making the blood freeze in the old man's veins.

'I understand,' he said, his voice nothing more than a hoarse rasp. 'Anything you say.'

Wayne laughed. 'It always has been so,' he murmured softly. 'Anything I say, and it's done. You see, I really am one of the master race.'

It was then that Heinlich knew the Mueller whelp was insane.

Sebastien looked straight down, hundreds of feet, across the beautiful Berkshire countryside. He

178

jumped as a loud 'whoosh' sounded just above his head and instinctively looked up. Above him, the flame from the burner gusted into the huge, billowing canopy of the red balloon. Like magic, he felt himself lifted even higher into the air.

'Great, isn't it?' Lilas said, reading the altimeter out of the corner of her eye. It was the first time she'd taken Sebastien up alone. But she'd had a good reason for wanting privacy.

Sebastien looked out at the rolling green hills way below him, and nodded. He sighed deeply, feeling utterly relaxed. It was a new sensation for him. 'It's breathtaking,' he said softly.

There was hardly any wind, just what Lilas had hoped for. She'd planned this day, and this location, carefully. They were too low for planes or gliders to be a problem, too high to worry about electric pylons or cables. And this area of the downs was wild and empty.

'Come here,' she said softly, and Sebastien slowly turned his head. She was wearing a plain white dress that did wonders for her black hair and green eyes. His eyes fell to her beckoning arms. So inviting. . .

His eyes seemed to melt as they looked at her, and Lilas felt her breath catch in her throat. 'Come here,' she said again, soft and imperious.

Sebastien smiled and went to her. How could he not? The 'basket' they were in was five feet high, and huge. He had to move across quite a space to get to her. When he reached her, her arms snaked around his neck.

'Now, kiss me,' Lilas said.

Sebastien kissed her. Her mouth was warm and mobile under his lips, and he felt his whole body shudder in reaction as her tongue darted out to duel with his.

He drew in a deep, shaky breath. Her hands moved from his neck to his shoulders, which were free of their usual tension.

She had started a campaign to take the pressure off of Sebastien Teale, and so far it was working. Now, it was time she gave herself — and him — a little reward!

Her hands dropped to his lower back, then down, to cup his delightful derriere under her palms.

Sebastien gasped. Their kiss deepened.

'Better,' Lilas murmured. 'Much better. Now kiss me again.' She smiled against his lips, and pressed herself harder against him.

Sebastien shuddered. It had been so long since he'd held a woman in his arms. So long since he'd taken something from someone, instead of giving. It was heady stuff.

Lilas felt her nipples tingle against the hard press of his chest. 'Touch me,' she moaned, and gasped as his hands moved between them. His fingers were feather-light on her abdomen, and she threw her head back in joy.

Sebastien kissed her exposed throat as a flock of lapwings broke formation to fly around them. Their wings whirred as they passed by, and Sebastien's hands moved to her breasts, tenderly cupping them in his hands.

Lilas moaned again and feverishly reached for the zip at the back of her dress. With one brief movement, the garment slithered to her feet.

'Lilas!' Sebastien groaned, a little shocked, and totally delighted. For she was naked underneath it. Tenderly, she clasped his head in her hands and lowered him to her breast.

Sebastien felt the nub of her nipple harden against his tongue, and felt his knees weaken. His hands on her bare skin were infinitely gentle as they ran from her breasts, to her ribcage, to her waist, and down over her thighs.

With a quick glance around, making sure the altimeter was still registering a good height, and taking a last check that there were no obstacles for miles around, Lilas gave a low growl, and pushed Sebastien back.

He landed in the bottom of the basket, his face slack with surprise, and looked up at her as she dropped lightly on top of him.

'We can't,' he said, half laughing, half feverish with desire.

For an answer, Lilas's hand went to his trousers and she quickly unzipped them, slipping her hand inside and rubbing hard against him.

Sebastien's head thrashed back, his hips rising off the floor of the basket in instinctive reaction. A low moan groaned from his throat.

Lilas smiled and pushed his shirt from his chest. She had waited for this moment for so long. Slowly, savouring every moment, she lowered her head to nip one of his hard male nipples. He gasped and shuddered, just as she'd always imagined him doing. Slowly, she ran her hands over him, delighting in each gasping sigh.

Then, businesslike, she stripped him naked, but her eyes were glowing like jade as he turned his head to look at her. His own sherry-coloured eyes were aflame with desire.

Eagerly, she lowered herself on to him, her head thrown back in wild abandon as she felt him push deeply inside her. His hands came up to her waist to steady her, his touch still that firm, gentle one that made Lilas want to sing for joy.

She began to ride him, like some fearless bucking bronco. Her face was tight with passion, her eyes glowing like green fire. Sebastien watched her, his body singing her song, his heart so full of gratitude, love and admiration that it felt as if it would outgrow his body and burst out of him.

'Lilas!' he called her name out as the sun began slowly to set, turning the red silk balloon above him into a glowing ball. 'Lilas!' he said again, as she began to moan and thrash above him, her strong thighs holding him a willing prisoner beneath her.

They both cried out together, high above the Berkshire hills, as pleasure overcame them both.

Sebastien lay, naked, satiated and gasping on the basket floor as Lilas rose unsteadily to her feet. Totally and unashamedly naked, she reached up and turned up the burner again.

Like an obedient slave, the hot-air balloon rose on

the thermals. Sebastien watched her, loving the long white lines of her body, the slender arms, loving without any conditions the generous, independent spirit that they housed.

'You're magnificent,' Sebastien said softly.

Lilas looked down at him and smiled sleepily. 'I know.'

CHAPTER 11

Spain

The Villa Fortunata gleamed like a white Imperial palace in the noonday sun. Its red-tiled roofs, black wrought-iron balconies, shaded courtyards with bubbling fountains and imported genuine Greek statues all sat on the crest of a hill overlooking the ancient city of Seville. The whole house, all seventy-three rooms, was eerily quiet, as if the building itself, as well as the army of servants that attended it, was busy sleeping away the siesta.

Inside, lying on a king-sized bed, the pink satin sheets cool to her back, Maria Alvarez stared at the sculpted ceiling. A small Venetian chandelier hung from the exact centre of the ceiling, supported by white plaster cherubs and winged dragons. She looked into the dead plaster eyes and slowly stuck out her tongue.

She could hear, very faintly, the hum of the air-conditioning, and the cool air on her all but naked body made her shiver; but it was a delicious shiver.

The first thing she'd noticed about Carlos's life-style was the cool air in which he travelled. It was with him in his big white limousine, with him in his offices downtown, with him here, in his private home. Cool, fresh, breathable air. Maria slowly lowered her feet to the genuine Roman mosiac floor-ing, the tiny coloured pieces forming flowering patterns in reds and greens. This colour scheme echoed green curtains and red cushions that were scattered liberally over the Gothic Spanish furniture.

She walked slowly to the balcony and stepped out into the sun, looking down on the cobbled courtyard below. Far over to the right, well out of smelling range, were the stables where some of the finest horses in the country were kept. They were all white. When Carlos had first shown them to her she had felt no special interest, and it was only when he talked for hours about dressage, gait, rhythm and breeding that she realized how important they were to him. She was beginning to appreciate the horses a little more, seeing the absurdity of their prancing more in the light of the equestrian ballet that Carlos always saw. She could look at the cups and trophies the Severantes horses had won without thinking, 'So what?'

Now she had Carlos's measure much more fully.

The Villa Fortunata was gabled, like a Gothic piece of history, with belltowers that still rang out the Matins, and ancient fish pools where monks from the sixteenth century had once kept their trout stock. The cellars, deep underground, boasted one of the finest wine collections in the country, and more often than not the luxurious, impeccably appointed rooms received weekend visits from top statesmen, up-and-coming businessmen, the odd movie queen and always a smattering of literary or musical giants.

Maria loved talking to them all. She loved exploring the exotic foods these people ate. Once, bored out of her skull when Carlos had invited over another horse owner, she had wandered down to the kitchens – vast caverns of places – where an army of cooks and helpers prepared sixteen-course meals. The trouble they had gone to! Some of the dishes that only took a moment to eat, a mere nibble from a delicate silver tray, had taken days to prepare. Meat was beaten and pulped for hours. Fruits were slowly simmered and boiled for a whole day. Whole larders were filled with herbs and spices that she had never even heard of.

Carlos, of course, had been miffed when the servants had told her where she'd been. 'My dear girl,' he'd told her patiently, his moustache lifting and falling as his small, somewhat feminine mouth formed the words, 'it's just not the thing to be done. Leave the kitchen to the servants, hmm? All you have to do, that is to say, your part of the job, if you like, is merely to eat the delicacies and smile. Yes?'

Maria turned away from the balcony and shut the windows, feeling the air around her became cool again. She loved the cold. Perhaps she could persuade Carlos to take her to Switzerland, or some other place where there was snow. She needed to be able to ski. She'd overheard a television presenter from Madrid, a stunning and overpoweringly groomed woman, say that skiing was as much of a social skill nowadays as speaking good French.

Maria was now taking French lessons. In fact she was also taking English lessons as well, for although she spoke the language she did not quite have the diction that Carlos required of a first-rate mistress. At first she hadn't understood why it was so important, but now she did. Now she was learning words like 'requisite' 'Bloomsbury' 'neo-classical' and other tongue-twisters that she spent hours practising before nervously joining one of Carlos's famous weekends. She had an instructor in art, an instructor in music who was teaching her the piano, an instructor in fashion, and, of course, an instructor in riding. But still she felt uncomfortable astride a horse, scared either that she would fall or that she would injure the horse. Not that Carlos allowed her to ride any of his prize greys, of course. She could still remember the way he had rocked with laughter when she asked him why he called the horses 'greys' when all of them, without fail, were a brilliant white. How naïve she must have seemed to him then. How pathetic.

Now that she knew the names of the real fashion giants – Dior, Chanel, St Laurent – she wondered why Carlos had bothered with her at all, dressed in her stolen, cheap little red dress.

She did not hear the door open behind her, and did not turn around.

Carlos Severantes closed the door softly behind him and watched her. The curve of her back was delicate and fine, as was the creamy skin that covered her exquisitely shaped calves and shoulders. Her long black hair was lying loose down her back and all she wore was a white silk slip with delicate spaghetti straps and a lace ruffle that just covered her thighs. He smiled slowly, a fond look in his small black eyes.

Carlos was the latest in a long line of Spanish grandees, but, unlike most of his contemporaries who had foundered and sunk in the modern world where peasants could make millions and no one regarded a title seriously, he had had the foresight and ability to survive. He had converted his many thousands of acres into lucrative tourist sites, buying up land on the coast and selling at vast profits to the hotel consortiums. A flair for stocks and bonds coupled with wise investments had quadrupled his fortune until now he was rich enough to do anything he wanted. Anything at all.

The horses had been his last salute to the old world. Their grace and pedigree was ageless. The cost of their enormous upkeep was a mere pittance to his pocket and their beauty made him want to cry.

During his forty-one years, he'd also sponsored a Formula One racing car and driver, a local from Seville with enough talent to make a name for himself, and, by association, for Carlos as well. He had gambled in Las Vegas and won, he had bought a yacht and sailed it around the world. He had bought his own radio station which played only good, classical Spanish music, which had earned him the title of Patron of the Arts. And this girl, this little enigma, was the latest in a long line of experiments.

Carlos had married his father's choice for him at the age of eighteen, the girl and his father both dying within weeks of each other only two years later, leaving Carlos with an infant son and sudden freedom. His son, affectionately known by one and all as Pedro, was currently at the Sorbonne. Carlos had insisted he have a European education, and had in mind Cambridge and then a tour of the United States before Pedro finally came home and got down to the serious business of being a worthwhile Spanish playboy.

Already he could play polo like a prince, and Carlos had a polo pony all lined up. It was still only a foal but Carlos knew a winner when he saw one. It was the same instinct that was the reason why, much to all his friends' amusement and horror, he had taken on the woman who had so openly tried to pick him up one night in a Madrid nightclub.

Carlos's small mouth curled into a wider smile as Maria sighed and stretched, remembering the first time he'd met her . . .

The Flamenco Club was a four-hundred-year-old establishment set deep in the Old Quarter that had a reputation for being ultra-selective. It had taken Carlos all of a month to be granted membership, and even then the cheeky club had asked him for references. Amused rather than insulted by this, and finding himself in Madrid one night on business, he decided to visit the club of which he had been, officially at least, a member for the last six years. It was more or less what he'd expected. The timber itself breathed history, whispering of past Inquisitions, political scandal, and grand love affairs that ended in the public suicides of rich society women and impoverished waiters and *picadors*. The food was good but horrendously expensive, the wine was horrendously good but priced beyond description. The singer, an international star just returned from a mediocre tour of France, had a husky, suggestive voice that bored him, and he spent the entire evening blinking back the Havana cigar smoke from his eyes as his companions, a merchant banker and the son of a prominent minister, had become seriously drunk.

Carlos noticed the girl at once, mostly because she was dodging the men who guarded the front door, but also because of the way she moved. Even in the dim lighting he could see that the dress she wore was tawdry and dotted with too many sequins, but as he watched the silent chase through the oblivious crowd he felt his senses begin to stir.

The girl was lovely, he saw that immediately she stepped in the path of a beam of light from one of the small jade wall-lamps. With one man closing in on her left, the other coming from her right in a pincer movement, the girl had swivelled surprisingly light brown eyes in all directions, reminding Carlos of a panicked filly trying to find a way out of a too-small corral. Perhaps because he was sober, or perhaps because some of his curiosity and sympathy showed in his eyes, the girl selected him, and quickly headed for his table. His two companions rose drunkenly to their feet, their experienced eyes taking in the girl and pigeonholing her in two seconds flat. She had just enough time to say, 'Please, *señor*,' when one of the bouncers grabbed her arm, jerking her upright like a marionette. 'Let go of me, you pig,' she hissed in gutter-perfect Spanish, making Juan, the minister's son, giggle like a girl and wave an admonishing finger at her. 'Can't you see I am with these gentlemen?' The girl nodded her head with imperious arrogance at Carlos, who found his lips curling in silent applause at her bravado.

In spite of her dress, in spite of the way she'd caked make-up on her face, and in spite of her Andalusian accent mixed with ghetto phrases, Carlos noted the fine planes of her cheekbones and the sensitive way her nostrils flared. He also saw in a glance her mixed parentage. Her body was too slender, her skin too light, her eyes too cool to be totally Hispanic. But more than all of these things, Carlos could feel what he always called 'The Tingle'.

The tingle had told him what stocks to buy. The tingle told him what ungainly foal was going to grow to be a champion. The tingle told him this girl was something special.

'That is so, gentlemen,' Carlos said, and rose slowly to his feet. At only five foot seven himself, their eyes were almost level. Almost, but since she was wearing atrocious four-inch heels, he found himself at just a slight disadvantage. The two men looked at one another nervously, then bowed out. At

Flamenco the customer was always right. But as they left, their eyes mocking him, Carlos thought that he wouldn't be at all surprised to find himself soon the recipient of a polite letter informing him that his membership had been cancelled. The Flamenco had turned snobbery into a fine art.

The girl, a comic mixture of satisfaction at besting her pursuers and total incredulity at pulling it off, gave him a huge grin that did nothing for her face. The very first thing, Carlos thought as he pulled out a chair for her and graciously seated her, would be to teach her to smile properly. Carlos had a soul that cringed at anything that was ugly. His two companions watched them with amused, sotten interest.

'What would you like to drink, Miss . . .?'

'Alvarez. Maria Alvarez.'

Carlos was sure that was her real name, for there was something forthright and direct about the way she looked him in the eye as she said it. He had rather expected some exotic *nom de plume*, and was glad that she had resisted the urge. It boded well for her ability to learn.

'I'd like . . . white wine, please.'

Carlos nodded approval at her choice. Soon she'd learn about vintage, vineyards, what was 'in' and what was appropriate. But not a bad choice – simple and safe.

The rest of the evening turned into a subtle game of cat and mouse, with Carlos ferreting out bits of information on her, and Maria probing for some hint about his intentions. She made it clear, much too bluntly, that she was not a one-night stand. He winced at some of her more crude overtures even though his body reacted predictably to the caress of her stockinged foot on his crotch.

'Subtlety, my dear,' he murmured to her on their way out, where his white limousine awaited. 'You must learn subtlety.' The companions they left had passed out at the table. Maria liked the word 'subtlety'. It sounded good.

She half expected him to take her to a hotel. She was after all, resigned to sacrificing her virginity. More than anything else, she was a realist. But instead, after about ten minutes, they pulled up outside a small but luxurious villa on the outskirts of the city that was very obviously a private home. As the car pulled up the cobbled driveway Maria felt the first shiver of apprehension slide up her spine. It was one thing to contemplate bedding a man – but quite another to be so close to having to do it.

Carlos felt the fine tremble with mild concern but much relief. It meant that she was not quite the streetwise, hard-boiled character she was projecting.

'This is nice,' she said, nervously looking around the interior. She was reminded of the Don's villa back in Andalusia, and she shuddered again. She had got away from him just in time. But what was the point if she'd only swapped one dirty old man for another? She glanced at Carlos out of the corner of her eye and smiled weakly. He was small, like the Don, and dressed in the same expensive clothes, yet he was different. Of that much she was sure. As he took her on a brief tour of what he called his town house, she tried to discover where the difference lay. Just then, he turned to hand her a glass of mineral water with a twist of lime, and she caught his eye. In an instant she knew what it was. There was no menace in those coal-black depths. Just . . . what? Amusement. Curiosity. Desire? She wasn't sure.

She drank thirstily, surprised at its non-alcoholic content, and nervously paced the room. What if tonight they . . . did it . . . and then tomorrow he had a servant throw her out? That would hardly fit in with her plans.

As if reading her thoughts, Carlos rose, yawned ostentatiously, and told her he was going to bed. Halfway out in the hall he turned back, and as an afterthought told her that the spare bedroom was the second on the left. Maria watched him go, her mouth hanging open, totally at a loss. She spent ten minutes just wandering about, feeling strangely anticlimatic, then, as her stomach rumbled, found her way to the kitchen and attacked the contents of the refrigerator. It had been three days since she'd last eaten, and as she demolished olives and ham, alternating her mouthfuls with lush tomatoes and a thick chunk of bread smothered in butter, she began to calm down.

Watching her wolfing down the food, for he'd been too curious to stay upstairs and not see what she would do, Carlos shook his head. The second thing he must do was teach her table etiquette.

They had flown back to Seville the next day, and that same afternoon the shopping began. Maria

194

would never forget that day if she lived to be a hundred. They were driven by a chauffeur to the finest stores, where Carlos oversaw the purchases. 'These are just to tide you over, you understand, until we find a designer for you. But you need a few things while we acquire a proper wardrobe for you,' Carlos had explained. The things that 'tided her over' were enough to make her want to yelp and dance in the streets. Dresses of silk, satin, velvet and lace were purchased by the suitcase-full; shoes from Italy and handbags to match were followed by belts, scarves and accessories. Carlos even took her to the finest lingerie boutique in the city, showing no embarrassment whatsoever as he sorted through the lacy underthings that included white silk negligees and see-through baby-doll nighties. The lack of embarrassment was shared by the manageress, who saw only money, vast stacks of it. Furs came next, and then cosmetics, then scent. The day seemed to go on and on forever. Carlos paid by cheque and gave his address as the spot to where it should all be delivered. Maria, who had never even dreamt of such sophistication, wondered how they could be sure that he had the money to pay for it all.

That night, at his permanent home, a villa that made the Don's villa back in Andalusia look like a garden shed, she waited once more for Carlos to come to her bed and once again she was disappointed. If that was the right word. The next day had been punctuated by a visit to the finest hair salon in all Spain, and lessons from a beautician who came every

morning and every evening to 'do' her 'look'. The
following days were taken up with elocution lessons,
visits to the museum and galleries, whilst the eve-
nings were spent at the opera, ballet or theatre. Maria
was delighted. It was what she had always dreamed
of. With every day that passed, the peasent girl
disappeared and a sophisticated European was taking her place.

It was only after almost five weeks that Carlos
finally came to her room. Looking back now, Maria
could see why he had not come before. After five
weeks her new persona had been firmly enough in
place for Carlos's fastidious taste.

Her accent was now pure Seville. Her slender body
now wore the finest designs as if created for it after
the deportment and 'walking' lessons of one Señor
José Curralas. Her hands were now manicured, her
feet pedicured, her make-up, which she had learned
to apply herself, understated and perfect, as was the
cut of her long, heavy hair. Only now was she worthy
of Carlos's king-sized bed.

The first night had, almost of a necessity, been
awkward. But Maria had grown fond of him over the
weeks, and Carlos was as willing to teach her the
manners and techniques of lovemaking as he had
everything else. He had a dry sense of humour and
an old-world courtesy that she'd never before en-
countered. The old books she was now reading, with
their poetry that talked of honour and family pride,
suddenly became reality as Carlos talked of his
illustrious ancestors. She found herself listening to

him because she liked to hear him talk, rather than because she wanted to hoard away knowledge for herself. But most of all, she was hideously grateful to him for introducing her to the world she'd always craved to meet. Now she was getting used to the aeroplane journeys to the Mediterranean and Paris. Now she was getting used to ordering food in the best restaurants and discussing *Carmen* with the country's leading mezzo-soprano. Carlos became brother, father, teacher and friend. And then, as a most natural progression, he became her lover.

In her room, Maria suddenly turned, aware of his presence behind her at last. Carlos smiled. 'Not enjoying the siesta?'

Maria shrugged and turned fully around, watching without embarrassment as his small eyes ran over her breasts. She smiled and held out her hand, nodding to the bed questioningly. Carlos smiled but shook his head.

He had no self-delusions, and knew himself to be a slightly undersexed man. He felt the need for sex only rarely. He had, however, been touched by her gift of innocence, and it had paved the way to her excessive, compulsive buying of jewellery. Carlos knew that the jewellery was her way of providing for the day she would leave him, but he did not begrudge it her, just as she had not begrudged giving him her virginity. In the back of his mind he knew that she would be leaving soon. Already she had learned such a shocking amount. She was like a sponge, learning rapidly everything from French verbs to a witty repartee that would stand her in good stead for any jet-set party anywhere in the world.

'No, not now,' he said smoothly. 'We have a surprise guest. Vincent Marchetti has just arrived. Can you get dressed and come down?'

'Of course,' Maria agreed at once. She was scrupulously honest about keeping up her end of their unspoken bargain. If Carlos wanted her to entertain, she'd entertain. Sometimes, on occasions like this, she almost felt like an employee. 'Who is Vincent Marchetti?'

'He's the man I told you about from the Centre for Paranormal Research. Dr Gottenburg's star pupil. You remember I was talking of him last week?'

Maria smiled. 'I see.' At first she had been shocked that a man of Carlos's education and experience could be fooled by the occult. Silly people looking into crystal balls to cheat people out of their money. How could he? But then he'd brought her some books on the subject, serious scientific research by eminent professors, that had changed her thinking. The tests in ESP in particular had fascinated her, but she'd never quite managed to push away her suspicion about charlatans and fakers. And Vincent Marchetti sounded extremely dubious.

Reading her look, he laughed. 'You'll have that doubting attitude wiped away, my dear, I'm warning you.' Blowing her a kiss, he left her to dress in private. That was Carlos. Sometimes his thoughtfulness brought tears to her eyes. That, and the way he always treated her like a lady. Maria had never felt anything like it before in her life. The doors being opened for her, the chair being pulled out and pushed in for her at dinner and a hundred other little things that Carlos did that made her feel like a real *somebody*.

There was no doubt she would miss Carlos.

She showered quickly and donned a simple white sundress by Valentine. She added only a touch of Fleur de Fleur behind her ears and the lightest dusting of make-up. Adding a garnet bracelet to her wrist and matching red sandals to her feet, she looked spectacular, and knew it.

In the hall, she followed the sound of voices to the main salon, and found herself brought up short by the sight of Vincent Marchetti. She had expected some oily, matinée-idol type, oozing charm and false, trite phrases. Instead she was confronted by the smallest, ugliest little gnome of a man she had ever seen. He was about five foot three, balding, squat, and wearing pebble glasses so thick that his eyes looked huge. In turn, the Italian stared at her, equally entranced for totally the opposite reason. Suddenly, Vincent knew why he had felt the psychic urge to drop in on his old friend, Carlos Severantes.

Maria forced herself to stop staring. Never commit a social gaffe, that was Carlos's golden rule. She quickly forced a smile to her face and walked forward, swaying with unconscious grace. Once she had walked, book on head, for hours to perfect her movements, which had now become automatic.

Vincent swallowed hard, his little Adam's apple bobbing obscenely in his throat. Carlos, eyes twinkling, introduced them and handed round a fine Madeira.

'Mr Marchetti. I've heard a lot about you from Carlos. And about the institute, of course. Tell me, what exactly do you do there?'

Polite curiosity was the mainspring of conversation, Carlos had told her. Even if you were bored out of your skull, you must never show it. Vincent nervously launched into a description of telekinesis, precognitive perception and poltergeist phenomena. He was uncomfortably aware of the closeness of her bare knee against his leg, and he stumbled several times over his words. Maria nodded encouragingly, only vaguely interested, her mind on the dossier she kept upstairs. She had needed to ask for Carlos's help in compiling it, although she had not wanted to do so. But how else could she find out about Wayne D'Arville without Carlos's help?

Typically, he'd asked no questions, but had put the best detectives on to it. Consequently, she now knew every detail of her father's life. The early years in America before he moved to Monte Carlo, her grandfather's casino and the fact that they were estranged. His years at the Sorbonne, his aborted engagement, and then his career in England. She had studied the book he wrote, grudgingly admitting it to be a work of genius. She had pored eagerly over the pictures of his wife, the Lady Sylvia, and had been rather surprised at her father's choice. But by now she was reading between the dry typewritten lines, and gaining a good impression of the way her father's mind worked. His acquisition of Platts had been almost diabolically clever and manipulative. In the light of his social climbing and ambition, Lady Sylvia made more sense than some outrageously lovely but socially unacceptable beauty. Oh, yes, she was beginning to know her father very well. She knew about his upcoming takeover bid of his own father's casino, and felt, instinctively, that this was his most vulnerable spot.

It was rather ironic. He was going after *his* father, whilst he himself was being hunted by *her*. Perhaps it was a family trait. But knowing all about him and finding a way to defeat him were two different things, and she knew she couldn't involve Carlos in this. For one thing she was not stupid, and knew that his Professor Higgins to her Eliza Doolittle act was, and always had been, the main attraction for him; now that he had all but succeeded, she sensed a waning of his interest.

Besides, she was too fond of Carlos and owed him too much to get him involved with a monster like her father. He would gobble Carlos up for breakfast as he had Sir Mortimer Platt.

'Perhaps Maria needs a demonstration to make a believer of her, Vincent,' Carlos said softly, snapping Maria back to the present. She forced herself to watch, contemptuously amused, as the little man fairly leapt up, his ugly round face alight with excitement.

'Yes, indeed. Yes, yes, a demonstration,' he said,

looking at Carlos like a beseeching puppy as his host searched out a pack of playing cards.

Maria watched indulgently as the man removed the cards, and then obeyed as the little gnome asked her to shuffle. She did so, and then raised her eyebrow questioningly. 'Place the pack face-down on the table, please . . . Maria,' he added her name shyly, the blush creeping up from his cheeks to cover the bald head. Maria smiled. Really, the man was sweet, in a dorky kind of way.

'The first card is . . . the six of spades,' Vincent said. Maria turned the top card over. It was the six of spades. Her eyes sharpened on the little man with genuine interest now, and he fairly bristled in pleasure, sensing that he had at last commanded her whole attention. With a faster-beating heart she turned the next card over, which was, as Vincent had predicted, the jack of hearts. On and on they went, right through the pack, going faster and faster, and when the last card had been turned over, Vincent had got only three wrong. It was amazing. Stupendous. Fantastic . . . Wonderful.

Maria moved closer to the little man, her eyes alight. Carlos watched her, just a little sadly. So, he'd lost her at last. Well it was inevitable. But why to Vincent? What use could she possibly have for him? And if he knew Maria – and he did – he had no doubt at all that she must have something in mind.

Maria had.

Just like the man in the song, she was going to break the bank at Monte Carlo.

CHAPTER 12

New York

Wayne looked out of the window, the world-famous panorama of the Big Apple slowly sliping by beneath him as the plane continued on to the airport. Unlike most of New York's visitors, he found nothing exciting and certainly nothing beautiful in the city. He'd never had to come to the States before, and as he hailed a taxi, giving the gum-chewing driver the name of the Plaza hotel, he looked out of the window with sharp eyes.

It was just approaching the rush hour, and traffic lined the roads to make one long caterpillar that stretched for miles. The driver took the scenic route, passing Regine's and Club A, giving him a slow tour past Bloomingdale's and Maud Frizon, the famous shoe shop. Wayne glanced at the ticking meter with a bare twist of his lips, but made no demur. He didn't mind the extra time which allowed him to school his thoughts and calm the rough pounding of his heart. The noise of the city was immense, and in a different kind of man the towering skyscrapers might have produced the cloying anxiety of claustrophobia; but Wayne barely glanced up at the huge monoliths of chrome, glass and steel.

Big Apple or not, he was used to taking bites out of what he wanted. On the streets, pedestrians lined the sidewalks as thickly and with as much congestion as traffic lined the roads. There was the usual mix – winos and drunks begging for dollars, women in Russian lynx jackets carrying Tiffany Peretti-designed evening purses, no doubt on their way to an early dinner with some up-and-coming lover. Men and women with tired faces and simple suits poured out of offices and headed for the subway trains, buses and taxis. Wayne could smell above the carbon monoxide the scent of frying onions from a street vendor, reminding him of his own hunger.

'Where can I get a decent meal in this city?'

'Huh? What kinda money you got?' The accent was broad and drawling, and although Wayne didn't know the difference between downtown Manhattan and the Bronx, he instinctively placed the man's origins as being firmly from the latter.

'Plenty,' he said shortly.

The driver snorted. 'There's three places in here for you lot.' He offered the knowledge grudgingly. 'There'ss Delmonico's, the Carlyle and Le Crenouille.' Wayne winced over the pronunciation of the names, and then nodded. The cab smelt of vomit and cheap vinyl. He would be glad to get to the hotel but the tour seemed interminable, up

Fifth Avenue, on to Park Avenue, then Madison Avenue, giving him a wonderful tourist-style look at Central Park, Times Square and Broadway. The driver certainly knew how to push his luck. Eventually, when the meter seemed in danger of running out of clicks, they pulled up at the Plaza, and he paid the cab fare in exact money.

'Hey, whattabout a tip?'

'Forget it.'

He followed the bellboy into the hotel's interior, oblivious to the colourful language coming from the taxi behind him. He checked into the best suite available, took a quick shower and changed into a white suit with a blue shirt that matched exactly the colour of his eyes. He combed his hair, added a gold Cartier watch to his wrist, and slipped his crocodile wallet, thick with credit cards, into his inner jacket pocket. He needed, for a reason he couldn't quite identify, to look his very best. When he re-entered the lobby, every pair of feminine eyes watched him leave. The desk clerk looked down and memorized the name – Wayne D'Arville. Sure enough, five minutes later the first woman came and asked after him: Mrs De Winter, the steel tycoon's widow from Alabama. The desk clerk elegantly accepted the hundred-dollar bill and gave out the man's name and room number, knowing others would soon follow.

Veronica was curled up on the settee, reading a chatty letter from an old friend, when the doorbell rang. It surprised her, for usually the doorman screened all visitors and always buzzed through before allowing anyone up. She uncurled her legs and walked barefoot to the door. She was wearing a long turquoise kaftan of cool cotton with embroidered peacocks that curled exotic feathers over her thighs and across her back. As she walked to the door and opened it, there was no warning sensation to prepare her for the shock that was to come. Her first impression was of something solid, massive and white, and then, as she looked up into the blue eyes, her face drained slowly of all colour. Her mouth went dry as sand, and she gasped as her breathing abruptly stopped, trapping air in her lungs. Aware of a fine trembling breaking out in every part of her body, she took an involuntary step backwards.

'Hello, Veronica.'

She blinked. The voice was different. Every other thing about him seemed the same – the overpowering height, the gut-wrenching good looks, the aura of power, of tight, dangerous energy. But the voice was different. It took her a second or two to realize that he had lost the French accent. Wayne moved forward and she was too slow to stop him. Shock held her immobilized for the few seconds he needed to step around her and into the room, and immediately the place felt violated.

'What are you doing here?' she finally managed to croak, her voice sounding pitifully weak and ineffectual even to her own ears. Wayne, who was looking around the apartment with assessing eyes, turned back and glanced at her.

'You might as well shut the door. I'm not leaving until I've got what I came for. And while I personally couldn't care less if it's advertised to all your neighbours, unless you've changed radically in the last seventeen or so years, you will.'

Veronica felt her fingers release the door practically before her brain had given the orders. Dimly she heard the door click shut over the roaring of the blood in her ears. 'Of course I've changed,' she managed to say, her voice coming out hard now, almost sneering. 'I went to prison because of you, or had you forgotten?'

Wayne shrugged, unmoved. 'I had, as it happens. You were never particularly memorable, Veronica.'

She dragged in a harsh breath, hate and venom rising from out of nowhere. 'You filthy bastard. You stole my book, you stole two years of my life! How could you forget something like that?'

Wayne moved towards a picture, studying the brilliance of a Dali with an experienced eye. 'That's good,' he said, his attention captivated by the melting clocks. 'Melting time,' he murmured. 'Have you ever noticed how true that is?'

Veronica blinked nervously as some of the protecting numbness began to wear off. 'If you don't leave,' she said, every word coming out crisply and clearly, 'I'm going to kill you. I've got a gun – hell, every New Yorker has a gun.'

Wayne turned, looking her over without fear. Her hair was shorter than he remembered, and she had a patina of sophistication that had been missing before.

'Oh, come now.' He shook his head mockingly, feeling almost pleasantly content at the confrontation. 'You should really thank me for what I did.' As her mouth fell open in stupefaction, he suddenly smiled, and Veronica felt a gut reaction deep inside her that made her want to vomit. 'If it hadn't been for me, you would never have come to this fine city and then you'd never have been a world-famous model, and never have overseen such a large business empire. Just think.' He moved to a low white leather couch and sat down with all the lithe grace she remembered so well. 'You'd be a bored English spinster by now, writing cookery books in Cheltenham, if it weren't for me. Now, be honest. You wouldn't have had the guts for all this otherwise, would you? Hmm?' The soft encouraging voice was a parody of gentleness as he waved a hand to encompass her flat with its view of the huge city, and she felt bile rise to her throat.

'You're sick,' she hissed, her hands clenching and unclenching by her side. 'You have no idea what you did to me, have you? *Have you?*' she all but screamed, her breaths coming in short, sharp gasps. She walked unsteadily to the drinks tray and poured herself a brandy with hands that shook so much she nearly dropped the decanter.

'I don't care what I did to you,' Wayne said bluntly, sounding suddenly bored.

Veronica took a deep gulp of the Napoleon brandy, feeling it erupt hotly in her stomach before spreading out in a slow burn, deep in her veins. The hatred must have been inside her all along, maturing like the brandy. It gave her a sense of strength at last, and drove out all fear, all self-doubt. When she turned to face him, her mouth was smiling, but Wayne saw that her eyes were like jets: hard, brilliant and sharp. He leaned back, resting his arms straight out along the back of the sofa, and crossed his legs elegantly at the ankle.

'You don't, hmm?' she repeated mockingly. 'For a man who couldn't care less, it seems to me that you're pretty up to date on all my comings and goings,' she pointed out, gently swirling the amber liquid in its huge bulbous glass. 'I'll bet you've got a dossier on me this thick.' She held out her thumb and finger about two inches apart. 'That doesn't sound like a disinterested man to me.'

Wayne slowly grinned. 'Oh, I have. You and your Valentine.' He saw her stiffen at the mention of her husband's name, and slowly smiled. 'I even bought one or two of his designs for my wife,' he lied, watching her eyes narrow, and anticipated her next words.

'So, you actually found someone stupid enough to marry you, did you?'

'Oh, yes. There are plenty of women – just like you – around. This one, however, happened to have a title and an estate the size of this city.'

She blanched at the mention of how she too had once yearned to marry him, and looked down into her glass. She felt a familiar sense of helplessness begin to impinge on her hatred and grimly tried to fight it off.

209

'That was a long time ago. A lot has happened since. I've found a real man, for a start.'

Wayne leaned back his head, blue eyes watching her closely. 'A lot *has* happened,' he agreed, his voice losing its mocking edge, and she glanced at him sharply, scenting danger. Suddenly she asked the question that should have been asked immediately, if she hadn't allowed shock, anger and fear to get the better of her.

'What do you want, Wayne? Why are you here?'

Wayne smiled a smile that made her blood freeze. 'I'm here for my son, of course. What else?'

For a second, a wild, wild second, the room seemed to angle away from her. Then it rushed back, making her head spin, and without conscious effort she found herself beginning to laugh. 'Your son?' Her voice was hoarse and ugly before she turned her laugh into a broad grin. 'Your files must be out of date, Wayne. The only son I have is Travis – Valentine's son.'

Wayne never moved but he was aware of a shifting of power – in her favour. 'Is he?' He kept his voice neutral, aware that they had come to the crux of the whole matter much faster than he'd intended.

Veronica forced herself to stare at him, hoping she was a good enough actress to bring it off. 'Didn't my father tell you? Our baby died. I asked him to inform you.'

'Naturally he told me. But just because I get a phone call telling me my child died at birth, you don't seriously expect me to believe it, do you?'

Veronica prayed her shock looked real, then forced

a slow, bitter-sweet smile to her lips. 'He told you that, did he?' she asked meditatively, watching for his reaction out of the corner of her eye.

Wayne's heart did a quick flip, but only his blue eyes wavered for the merest moment. 'Are you admitting it isn't true?' he asked eventually.

'Of course it isn't,' Veronica said. 'I had your child aborted. Scraped out of me, like the unwanted . . . thing! . . .' she hissed the word with all the disgust and venom she could muster '. . . it was. Trust Daddy to lie that way. He's hopelessly old-fashioned.'

Wayne stared at her, feeling as if he'd wandered on to quicksand. 'My people didn't find any record of an abortion,' he said suspiciously, and Veronica felt a moment of panic. Fool, she cursed herself. Why did you tell him something that could so easily be checked out? But in the next instant she was rallying.

'Were they looking for it?' she challenged, her voice laconic.

Wayne slowly uncrossed his legs and leaned forward. No, they hadn't been. He'd had them looking for a death certificate for Veronica Coltrane's baby. They hadn't found it, which had been good enough to have him on the next plane to New York, convinced that his baby lived, that the Spanish whore who was his daughter was not the only child he had fathered. But now . . . Wayne felt a deep, dark hand clutch his guts. He had been so sure of victory. So sure of the outcome. He felt a horrifying wave of defeat slowly creep up his throat, strangling his vocal cords, filling his head like gas filling a balloon. No – it was not possible. It wasn't. Travis Coltrane Copeland *must* be his. He *must*!

Veronica sensed the silent desperation behind the blue eyes, and relaxed for the briefest moment before an overwhelming urge to twist the knife made her smile. At last, after all these years, she had her revenge. Unexpected, unasked for revenge. It was like having champagne injected straight into her veins. 'What's the matter, Wayne?' she asked softly, allowing a hateful parody of concern to soften her voice. 'Why this sudden urge for a son? Is your lady wife incapable? Or is it you . . .?' She broke off with a small cry as Wayne suddenly lunged to his feet, and in spite of herself she quickly backed away. Violence filled the room like a tangible force, and for one moment, one truly terrifying moment, she was certain he was going to kill her.

Wayne thought he was too. He took a step towards her, and then stopped, his brain throwing the cold water of logic into his consciousness just in time to prevent him pouncing on her. He had no alibi if he killed her now. Besides, she was not important – she was a nothing that had just managed to hit him on a raw spot, that was all. Slowly he relaxed, even managed to smile.

'Travis is with his . . . with Valentine, I suppose?' he probed softly. 'At the – let me see – Warehouse 15, isn't it?'

Veronica released a long sigh of relief, then managed a cool shrug and was amazed when her voice was just as cool. 'I expect so. Why?'

Wayne didn't bother to reply, but instead walked quickly to the door and opened it. He had to see the boy. He had to see his face. He would know if Travis was his or not. He would just know.

Veronica followed him silently at a safe distance, and the moment he was gone she threw herself against the door and locked it. Her hands were shaking so much that it took her almost a minute to perform the simple task, and then she slowly leaned back against the wall and hugged her arms around her waist. 'Oh, God,' she whispered, over and over again, tears squeezing past her closed lashes as reaction began to set in.

A dull but persistent question prodded at her, denying her desire to just collapse on to the bed and crawl under the blankets and forget the whole nightmare had ever happened. She stumbled into the living room, spotted her still half-full glass of brandy and reached for it, gulping it down in one go. As the alcohol exploded in her belly, the truth exploded in her brain. He was going to the warehouse. To see Travis. Blue-eyed, square-faced Travis!

She ran to the phone, in her panic misdialling the number. She slammed the receiver down, and forced herself to breathe deeply. It would take Wayne at least half an hour to get to the warehouse. She dialled again, this time correctly, and got through to Stan, the security guard, and asked for Val.

'Come on, come on. Oh, Val, come *on*!' She took the phone to the settee in front of the coffee table and collapsed back against the orange cushions.

'Yeah?' The voice sounded preoccupied but so fantastically dear that for a few moments she could say nothing but his name.

'Val! Oh, Val!'

Ten miles away, Val frowned, his skin beginning to prickle. 'Veronica? You OK? What's up?'

Veronica took a deep, shaky breath, clearly audible to her now thoroughly worried husband, and launched into speech. 'Listen. There's a man on his way over, right now. You've got to get Travis away. Hide him somewhere. Anywhere. Only do it now.'

'Hey, hold on, luv. What man are yer talking about?'

Veronica groaned. 'Don't argue with me! For pity's sake, just trust me. Val, please!' She was screaming now, her voice coming out in a tangle of sobs and high-squeaking, panicky demands.

Val glanced over his shoulder. The workers had gone home half an hour ago, leaving only a few lights burning. Vast benches of half-finished garments cluttered the acres of floor, and Travis, walking around with a clipboard, was taking stock. Val's eyes narrowed on the boy who would always be his son, and looked back at the blank brick wall on which the telephone was hung.

'This man,' he said quietly. 'It's Travis's . . . other father, ain't it?' He couldn't bring himself to say 'real' father, and something strong in his quiet, composed tone got through to her and calmed her down as nothing else could.

214

'Yes,' she said dully. 'Yes, it is. And he's dangerous.'

'Dangerous?' Val ran his hand through his over-
long hair and sighed. The day had been a normal one
up to now. He was silent for a long, long second, and
then began to think quickly as Veronica's voice,
panicking again, said urgently,

'Val. Val, are you still there?'

''Course I am. Where d'ya think I'd got to?'

Veronica managed a real laugh this time, then said
once again, 'Val, you've got to hide Travis. Quickly.
He'll be there in a few minutes.'

'Wait a minute. Just wait. You think he's coming
here to take Travis?'

'Yes. Maybe. Oh, you just don't understand.
You're not dealing with a normal man. He's
warped, twisted. He's power-hungry. Valentine,
he's a . . . monster! I told him I had an abortion,
but when he sees Travis he's going to know. His eyes,
the shape of his face . . . He'll know I was lying.'

'If I hide Travis we'll never get rid of him,' Val
pointed out with cold logic. 'We've got to convince
him, now, that Travis is mine.'

He turned, suddenly aware that Travis, made
curious by the sound of his own name, was stood
right behind him. Val glanced at his son, meeting the
concerned, puzzled blue eyes, and reached out his
hand to his shoulder and squeezed tightly.

'What do you mean?' Veronica asked, but already
she was beginning to understand what he was getting
at. All the paraphernalia of his last fashion show was

215

stored at the warehouse, and since Valentine Inc. had gone unisex there would be men's wigs and make-up there as well.

'Leave it to me,' Val said abruptly, and rung off, leaving Veronica to wait through the worst hour of her life.

'What's going on, Dad?' Travis asked, looking troubled.

'Listen, Trav . . .' Val put his other hand on the side of the boy's other shoulder, and leaned forward so that their faces were barely inches apart. 'We never thought we'd have to tell you this . . .' He paused, searching for the right words but coming up with only blank air.

'Tell me what?' Travis prompted.

Aware of time ticking away, Val shook his head, then looked Travis straight in the eye. 'We don't have any time,' he said, his voice regretful. 'You're gonna have to take it straight. Veronica had you before she met me. You're not mine . . . hell, that's not right. You *are* mine . . . just . . . not physically mine. You understand?'

Travis managed a weak grin. 'Hell, is that all? I thought something terrible had happened. I was old enough to remember you at the start, actually. I was six when we first met, remember?'

Val stared at him, and then began to laugh. Abruptly, however, he sobered. 'Your . . . biological father is on his way here now. From what your mother said, I think he's gonna try and take you away.'

216

'What?' Travis yelped. 'Dad, I'm hardly a kid any more. I'll soon be voting.'

Valentine grinned. 'I know. But your mum's in one lulu of a flap. According to your mum, he's rich as Midas, as powerful as a Kennedy, and has the mentality of Attila the Hun. And she should know.'

Travis shook his head, grappling to come to terms with it all. 'So what are we going to do?'

Val smiled grimly. 'Trust me,' he said, and, grabbing him by the arm, led him to the changing rooms. 'I have no idea what he looks like,' Val muttered, searching out a wig that was the exact shade of his own hair, 'but the idea is to make you look as much like me as possible.' He fitted the wig over Travis's natural hair, who grinned at his reflection in the mirror. Val then selected a tiny box. Travis watched, fascinated, as the lid was lifted to reveal sets of coloured contact lenses. 'Sometimes,' Val muttered, selecting a brown pair and reaching for the cleaning fluid, 'I need a model to have eyes to match the dress . . .'

Travis tensed, his eyes doing strange gymnastics as Val put them in, and then blinked rapidly. 'Hell, they feel funny,' he complained, and then blinked some more as he stared at his image in the glass. It felt distinctly weird to meet brown eyes instead of the blue ones that had always been his.

'At least there isn't anything you can do to change the shape of my face.'

'Oh, ye innocent,' Val muttered, and reached for some cotton wool padding. 'Open up.'

217

Travis had just enough time to moan, then gagged on cotton wool that seemed to fill his cheeks. 'I feel like a chipmunk,' he mumbled, swallowing hard, and fighting the urge to retch.

'Shut up,' Val muttered, reaching for the make-up case. Travis groaned again and closed his eyes.

Outside, Wayne told the taxi driver to wait and walked around the building, finding a side door open that creaked loudly.

Inside Travis and Wayne glanced at each other at the sound, and quickly left the dressing room. Wayne walked into the interior of the huge building, his footsteps echoing on the concrete floor with a hollow, echoing sound. He looked around vaguely then turned to the right and began to walk past the racks and racks of plastic-wrapped clothes, following the sound of human voices.

'Silk?' The man who asked the question was tall, very slender, and was dressed in scruffy jeans and a loose wool cardigan that fitted about as well as a sack would fit a parking meter. It could only be Valentine Copeland, fashion guru.

'Sixteen tonnes.' Wayne's head shot around, seeking out the owner of that young voice. It took him a second or two to locate the boy by a far wall.

'Hello. Can I 'elp yer?'

Wayne turned, the cockney voice taking him slightly by surprise, and found Valentine, approaching him. Instinctively Wayne felt the hackles rise on his back. It was a strange

218

sensation, one he hadn't experienced before, and it unnerved him.

Val approached the man responsible for Veronica's imprisonment, and felt the insane urge to thump the bastard in the stomach, just for the pleasure of seeing his huge frame double over. As he got closer the blue eyes came as something of a shock. They were Travis's eyes, but deep-frozen. He sensed no warmth, not even anything remotely human, in their depths. He could almost have been a robot – a well-dressed, too-handsome robot. Valentine hated him on sight.

'I'm looking for Travis Coltrane,' Wayne said, deliberately omitting this man's surname. Val had no doubts now that this man was all that Veronica had said he was and more.

'Nobody here by that name, Sonny Jim,' Val said with painful bonhomie. 'Only my lad over there – Trav Copeland. Trav, come over 'ere a minnit, will ya?'

Travis moved closer, feeling his limbs move stiffly. He left the darkness reluctantly and stepped into the circle of light, forcing his lips open. 'Yeah?' He half turned towards Val, not intending even to glance at the tall stranger who was supposed to be his real father. But, before he knew what was happening, he was looking full face at the stranger. He saw his own blue eyes staring back, and felt a sudden, terrible fear. He could not explain it, and had never felt anything like it before, but it made him almost faint.

Val stepped closer so that Wayne could compare

219

them. Exact same shade of hair, exact same shade of eyes. Even Travis's naturally pale skin had been darkened to Val's own more swarthy shade by the make-up he had applied.

Wayne stared at the boy, and felt suddenly cold. He glanced briefly back at Val, feeling again an almost animalistic surge of violence, but pulled his lips into a snarl that was supposed to pass for a smile. 'My mistake,' he said simply.

Val nodded and gave his best cockney grin. 'We all make 'em, mate.'

Wayne nodded, turned and walked away. He did not look back. Travis waited until he was gone and then said quietly, 'I think I'm going to be sick.'

'Well, do it in the lav,' Val said, not unkindly, giving him a gentle push. 'I have to phone your mum. Was she ever right about that bloke.'

Travis *was* sick. That . . . that . . . creature with the snake-like eyes and unmoving face was his father?

Back at the hotel, Wayne walked to the window and stared out at the bright lights of New York. Another dead end. Another defeat. But she would pay. The bitch Coltrane would pay. And her husband. He walked to the phone, dialled a number, and waited for it to be answered. 'Sutter? It's me. I want you to dig around and find out the date of an abortion. Yeah, that's right, the Coltrane woman. It would have been done in the prison hospital, I imagine. I want to know the time, as well as the date, if you can.' He listened for a few seconds and then hung up.

Slowly he walked back to the window. She had robbed him of his heir, but she would pay.

Once he knew when the abortion had taken place he would make his plans. At exactly the same time, on exactly the same date that she had killed his baby, Veronica Coltrane herself would die.

CHAPTER 13

Sebastien depressed the switch on the tape recorder and leaned back in his chair. 'Wednesday 25th. Wayne D'Arville. Personal case, continuing notes. I have recently become concerned at this subject's NUC during our sessions. His recent trip to New York has agitated him considerably, and I am more and more convinced that secondary crisis oscillation has occurred. Concurrently, I believe his achievement motivation has been severely disrupted, and will attempt to carry out a thematic aperception test on the subject at the first opportunity.'

Sebastien paused for a moment. He thought he'd heard the door open, but there was no other sound. He shrugged, and continued. 'I am more than ever convinced that there was sustained physical abuse by the father during the patient's infancy, as well as maternal deprivation. The combination, mixed with the obsessive compulsion to succeed shown continually by the patient, is, I believe . . .'

In the hall, Lilas listened to his tones, a happy smile on her face. She hadn't intended to eavesdrop, but she'd been surprised by the sound of his voice. At first, she'd thought he'd had a visitor, but . . .

She jumped as someone knocked on the outside door. Feeling suddenly guilty – she knew how fierce Seb was about confidentiality – she quickly nipped into a closet, stifling a giggle. Really, a middle-aged woman should have outgrown this kind of thing!

Sebastien put the small recorder into the top drawer of his desk and walked to the door. Wayne pushed past him without waiting for an invitation, and through the crack in the closet Lilas felt every hair on her body quiver. A cold hand seemed to catch her heart. She knew instantly who the man was – Wayne D'Arville. Seb's only 'private' patient. She couldn't have said why, but she knew he was dangerous. Or, to be more specific, a danger to Sebastien.

Sebastien led him to the living room, alarms going off in his head. 'Hi. Sit down. Want any coffee?'

Wayne shook his head, then, unusually, changed his mind. 'Yes, OK. Black.'

Sebastien made it quickly, all the time watching his guest. He looked fit and healthy, but there was a tightness to his face that Sebastien had never seen before, and his eyes, always a bright, brilliant blue, seemed to be actually glowing.

Wayne glanced at him, his lips tight. In the hall, Lilas very carefully crept from the closet and hovered, torn with indecision, by the closed door.

Inside, Wayne reached for his cup, Sebastien noticing how the fine shaking of his hand made the black liquid shimmer.

'I'm going to Monte Carlo on Friday,' Wayne said abruptly, his loud voice carrying clearly to the woman outside.

'Oh. You're not a secret gambler, I hope?' Seb teased.

It was a joke, but not funny enough to warrant the great burst of laughter that made the tall Frenchman nearly double over. Outside, Lilas jumped in alarm. The man was coming unravelled! It was the kind of situation where she knew Sebastien excelled. And normally she didn't worry about her lover – didn't give his rather depressing and potentially dangerous job a thought. After all, Seb had been working in hospitals for the insane long before she met him. And doing very nicely, too. But something about this man . . . Lilas just *knew* there was something about this man . . . She wanted to march in there and put her arms defensively around Sebastien, and tell Wayne D'Arville that he was hers and she'd guard him to the death! Ridiculous, she knew. So she just hovered, unsure of what to do. It was not very Lilas-like.

Inside, oblivious to her plight, Sebastien watched Wayne in silent alarm, making sure that his eyes were carefully neutral when Wayne looked his way.

'In a way, it is a gambling expedition,' he admitted softly. Then, like a tap being turned off, all expression left his face. Sebastien had seen this phenomenon in him before, but never to such an extent as this. 'I have business there,' Wayne said, his voice as flat as the top of Sebastien's desk. Only the glow in the back of his eyes, a demented and, to Sebastien, tormented glow, begged for help and understanding.

'It has to do with bad debts,' Wayne corrected himself, his lips twisting briefly. He finished his coffee and slowly stood up. Staring down at Sebastien, his eyes seemed to focus on him properly for the first time. He opened his mouth, closed it again, and gave a brief nod. 'I thought I'd drop in and tell you I wouldn't be here for dinner on Saturday.'

'OK. Thanks.'

Sebastien watched him walk to the door, unaware that outside Lilas was just darting back into the closet. Seb gave a brief smile as the copper-coloured head turned to glance at him, then stared thoughtfully at the door as Wayne closed it behind him. They had made no arrangement for dinner on Saturday, but Sebastien doubted that Wayne was aware of it.

He also doubted if the Frenchman knew the real reason why he had called in. But Sebastien knew. He reached for the phone and dialled the home number of Clive Jamison, the chairman of a conference team due to fly out to Monte Carlo in the morning for a three-day conference on the causes of socio-psychological voting patterns. He'd just secured himself a place on it when the door opened.

But it was Lilas who entered. 'Hello,' she said cheerfully. 'Who was the big guy who just left?' she asked innocently.

Seb glanced at her sharply. 'No one,' he said sharply. 'No one for you to worry about, that is,' he added, aware that he had surprised her. But he didn't want Wayne to know about Lilas. If Wayne became aware that he, Sebastien, had a lover . . . Well, Wayne was capable of anything.

Lilas nodded. Just as she'd thought. Seb was well aware of how dangerous the man was, but was trying to help him all the same. Typical of him, of course. It was one of the reasons she loved him so much. Well, she was not about to just sit back and let Sebastien fall prey to his own goodness. No way!

Two days later, Wayne stepped out on to the balcony of a Monte Carlo hotel and glanced across the harbour. He reached for the *Nice-Matin* and unfolded the paper, ignoring the croissants that cooled on his breakfast tray. The news was full of a *monte-en-l'air*, a daring cat burglar currently prowling the ripe villas and relieving inhabitants of jewels and fine art. The Marine Cup de Monaco was due to start next week, and the sports section was full of news of the speedboat trials. The event fought for supremacy with the Monaco Grand Prix, but Wayne ignored both, turning to the financial pages instead with steady hands but a heart that was doing strange gymnastics in his chest.

It was there in black and white, sensational news only to those interested in the financial life of the Principality – which was practically everybody. Marcus D'Arville had lost the Droit de Seigneur to an unknown company called Helm Enterprises. The paper speculated on the ethics of the takeover, and a final editorial asked for news of the mysterious Helm Enterprises, making veiled and empty threats against the corporation that had so scurrilously

226

attacked one of the country's finest citizens, a tragically blinded American émigré. Slowly, Wayne returned to the bedroom where a maid, ostensibly retrieving damp towels and replacing them with dry fresh ones, glanced his way, and smiled shyly.

She was small, with a cap of dark hair and huge dark eyes. Her eyes flitted from his bare legs to the deep V of chest visible under the robe. 'Is there anything else I can do for you, sir?' she asked in perfect French, her voice reminding him of a five-year-old's. Wayne smiled and nodded.

'As a matter of fact, there is,' he said and the dark eyes lit up. Wayne walked to his suitcase and extracted a hefty envelope, which contained copies of all of Lt Heinlich's documents. 'I want you to post these – post them, mind, not send a messenger – to Marcus D'Arville, at his home address. Not his office. Can you do that?'

As he turned around, the girl managed a disappointed smile, but nodded as he approached with the envelope in his hand. 'Of course, sir. Anything else?'

Wayne handed over the envelope and then slowly raised his hand to rest under the girl's chin. He could feel a pulse hammer at the base of her neck and heard the soft catch of her breath as she gasped. 'Yes,' he murmured. 'You can come back again.' Slowly, curious to see if she would react, he lowered his hand across the prim black dress that she wore and splayed his long fingers around her right breast. 'I think you can do much more for me than post a letter. What's your name?'

'Odette,' the girl said on a slowly exhaled breath. 'Odette. Will you come back?'

'Yes, sir.'

Wayne watched her leave, his eyes on the envelope. Wolfgang would get it later today. Following the blow of losing the casino, it might even finish him off.

Wayne wandered around the room feeling strangely lost. He had enough money to do anything, but he couldn't think of a single thing he wanted to do. It was like being in the eye of a hurricane, waiting for the storm to hit. Restlessly he wandered to the balcony once more. Below was the usual pool, the usual topless bathers, the usual mobile bar dispensing cocktails at an absurdly high price. Wayne was about to turn back when the sight of a familiar face stopped him. Even though he was five floors up, he knew he couldn't mistake that certain turn of the head, coloured a deep chestnut.

His heart lurched and then settled down. *Sebastien*. Sebastien was here. He felt a moment of uncontrolled joy and relief, then almost cried aloud as it fizzled and burst. Wayne's first instinct was to go down and demand to know what he was doing. But he wasn't sure he could withstand those sherry-coloured eyes just yet.

A few minutes later, the maid returned. As she walked towards him she began to strip. Wayne watched her, unimpressed but able to admit that she had a good body, young and slim, and tanned a not-too-dark brown. She was quickly out of her clothes and entirely naked when she reached his position just inside the balcony. Wayne glanced back over his shoulder. Sebastien was still there, waiting for him. It felt good.

He turned as a small hand curled against his chest, the fingers tugging at his left nipple. The girl murmured something in French, something seductive and suggestive, and Wayne closed his eyes. 'Shut up,' he said in English, and kissed her hard. The girl reacted eagerly, clutching his shoulders and swinging her legs around him to lock behind his waist. Wayne gasped, then laughed as they staggered towards the bed. He threw her down, falling with her as her legs clung to him tenaciously. He was naked beneath his robe, and it had fallen open enough to allow his member to rear up, strong and hard, through the navy silk. The girl, feeling the hot shaft touch her thigh, released her leglock, but Wayne shook his head as she wriggled under him. The girl frowned, then gave a gasp of surprise as Wayne flipped her over, his impressive strength easily turning her. The girl gasped as she found her face stuffed into the pillow, and then moaned in desire as Wayne's hands slipped around her stomach and lifted her half off the bed. He closed his eyes as he parted her thighs and pushed deeply into her.

Sebastien ordered a Coke with ice, and waited under the shade of the sun umbrella. He would wait all day if he had to.

The postal service in Monaco was excellent. With the principality being so small, there was no reason why it shouldn't be, and within five hours of the letter

229

being posted it was delivered to Wolfgang Mueller's home. His secretary, Vince Perroit, glanced at it curiously, but did not interrupt his employer's lunch. Actually, Wolfgang was not eating. He knew the meal was there, for he had heard it being delivered and could smell the scent of herbs and the appetizing aroma of cooked meat, but the news that had arrived yesterday was still robbing him of any appetite.

Vince, as usual, had shared the breakfast table with him, reading the morning's correspondence over the toast and coffee. The first inkling Wolfgang had had of impending disaster was when the voice of his secretary faltered and then stopped. He had been reading a letter from a company called Helm Enterprises, one that Wolfgang had never heard of. Vince had got as far as, 'Dear sir, this is to inform you that the casino known as the Droit de Signeur is . . .' and then had choked to a stop.

'Vince?' He remembered he had been impatient, his blinded eyes imagining the little man to have stopped for a drink of coffee or bite of toast, and he'd been annoyed at the man's impertinence. But it had not been hunger but stunned surprise that had stayed the secretary's voice. Shakily he'd read the letter through, a letter that informed Wolfgang that he was no longer owner of the casino, and then glanced at the blind old man, his anxious green eyes taking in the sudden pallor, noting the way the old man's body went rigid in shock. The same shock that was only now just beginning to fade.

Wolfgang reached forward, his fingers 'reading' the table, and pushed the plate of food away. He rose slowly to his feet and picked up the cane that went everywhere with him, and tapped his way into the foyer. 'Perroit. Perroit, where the devil are you?'

He swung to his right, towards the sound of the man's reply. 'I'm here, sir. The mail has just arrived.'

Wolfgang grunted, and Vince tensed. He had always been in awe of his employer. He was not so stupid as to underestimate the old man, as so many did. To their cost.

Wolfgang made his way to his favourite chair and sat down. He was used to relying on Vince to be his eyes. Wolfgang trusted him implicity because he knew that he could destroy him if ever the need arose. 'Has Ariche come up with anything more yet on Helm's identity?'

Ariche, one of Wolfgang's lawyers, had been assigned immediately to check the claim from Helm Enterprises that the casino was now legally theirs. Five hours after being given the assignment, the confirmation had come. Helm had done all that Helm had claimed. It did indeed have the banks and two of his partners in the corporate back pocket.

Wolfgang shuddered now as he remembered the frustration that had hit him and kept him awake all night. How could the faceless Helm have done it? How? Wolfgang was sure he'd been so careful. Hell, he *knew* he'd been careful. Who knew him this well? Who had betrayed him?

'I haven't heard from Ariche yet, sir, but he must

have arrived in Geneva by now.' Helm Enterprises had been registered in Switzerland.

'This smacks of Swiss expertise, all right,' Wolfgang murmured. 'But why the Droit de Seigneur? It doesn't make sense.' The secretary kept quiet, but cringed under the viciousness of the cracked and ancient voice. Wolfgang cursed silently, feeling like a rat in a maze. Someone had taken away the cheese, and he could not even see who, or why, or when. The helpless sensation of having been successfully stalked was a new one, and one that he hated.

The phone rang half an hour later. Vince had read through the other mail, consisting mainly of invitations from friends and the odd letter from disgruntled casino punters. He left the large envelope till last, some instinct making him avoid it. Its padded bulkiness gave Vince a strange feeling of *déjà vu*.

The secretary lifted the phone, spoke briefly, and then took Wolfgang's hand and placed the receiver carefully into it. 'It's Ariche.'

Wolfgang lifted the receiver, banging it against his ear. Normally his co-ordination was good, but his nerves had been impossibly strained over the last twenty-four hours. 'Yes, Philippe. What have you got?'

'Nothing,' Philippe Ariche said, his voice clipped and angry. 'The offices here are nothing but a rented shell. There's one girl who sits behind an impressive desk and does nothing but read romances all day long. She knows nothing, not even the name of her employer. She get's a regular pay cheque from the bank. It's just a front.'

'Shit!' Wolfgang said, then let loose a long list of expletives in German, making Vince glance at him in puzzled surprise. 'The bank?' Wolfgang asked briefly.

'As close-mouthed as a duck's arse.'

Wolfgang almost cried. He felt the absurd desire to stamp his feet and scream, and he swallowed it back. 'Any ideas?' he asked, but without hope.

'No. Not at the moment. But . . . there was a message waiting for me.'

'Message? What do you mean?'

'A letter. The girl gave it to me. She said that she'd been told someone would come and that she was to give it to whoever it was.'

'And?'

'And it says that you're to clear out your desk. Today.'

'The hell I should!' Wolfgang shouted, getting to his feet. 'They can't insist. Can they?' he added, his voice suddenly sounding small and old in the vast recesses of the enormous and empty villa. Ariche confirmed his worst fears. Wolfgang listened, slowly slumping back down into his chair. His legs and back ached, but he refused to give in to arthritis. Ariche was talking about possible moves, but the fancy talk was more jargon than substance, and they both knew it. Wolfgang hung up a few minutes later, and Vince nervously smoothed the big envelope that rested on his knees, still unopened. 'I have to go to the casino,' Wolfgang said, his voice flat. 'Have Finalle bring the car round.'

'Yes, sir. There's one more letter we haven't dealt with.'

'Leave it.'

'It's a bulky one, sir. It looks . . . important.'

'Then bring it. You can read it to me in the car.'

Miles away, Wayne stared at the ceiling, a sheet hanging loosely across his loins, even though the girl had been gone for hours. He watched the patterns of light on the ceiling, letting no particular thought stay in his mind for longer than the briefest second. The buzz of the phone made him frown, but its persistence made him leave the bed and pad naked to the *bergère* on which it rested. 'Yes?' he barked, then stiffened, listening to the voice on the other end, a slow smile crawling across his face.

'Good. I'll be right there. And Ariche . . . you'll be getting a nice fat bonus.'

Wayne walked to the shower and turned it on to the cold setting before standing beneath it. Five minutes later, as he left the hotel and hailed a cab, he forgot, or would later suppose he did, that Sebastien Teale had been waiting for him.

Wolfgang's car, a large black American Cadillac, pulled to a halt in front of the casino. Raymond Galvalais, the manager, watched it and waited, but to his surprise the old man did not immediately emerge. Everyone had read the papers, of course, but still everyone hoped the takeover was just rumour. The papers had been wrong before.

When Marcus D'Arville finally emerged, he looked . . . ancient. But Raymond's hazel eyes were

234

not the only ones that watched the old man's approach. Wayne had arrived at the casino five minutes earlier, having driven like a madman. It had felt strange to walk into the crimson and gold cocoon of the casino again. He had felt oddly nervous, as if expecting someone to stop him, someone to point at him and shout, 'There he is. There's the old man's son. He blinded his own father. Get him!'

But no one had, of course. Everyone was too busy staring at the roulette wheels spinning the magical white ball that could either bankrupt them or award them a fortune.

It was as if he had never existed. This strange sensation of being a non-person was still with him when he saw his father again for the first time in almost twenty years. He had moved to the doorway, his breath trapped in his lungs, his big body shaking so much that he felt, for a moment or two, as if he was going to pass out.

Sebastien had followed him, and now his eyes narrowed on Wayne sharply, as he too moved to a side door, curious to see what had prompted the reaction. But, looking out, he saw only an old man, carrying a white stick, and a tall, thin young man, obviously an employee of some kind. He turned and watched Wayne again. His face was still; too still. Only his eyes burned. Sebastien could feel an awful, creeping, dark hatred filter into the room, the sensation becoming overpowering as the old man with the stooped shoulders and black glasses entered. He watched Wayne follow them like a stalking hunter, walking parallel with them as they moved through the gaming rooms, through the smoke and rolling dice.

Wayne saw the man with his father shift something to his other hand and stared at the envelope. It was open, and slowly he smiled. So, his father had had his present. He glanced at the thin white face of the secretary and wondered how he had taken the news that his employer was actually a Nazi criminal, responsible for the death of thousands.

Not well, apparently.

Wolfgang paused. He felt terribly cold. His blind eyes swivelled uselessly, trying to pinpoint the location of something that instinct told him was in the room. He could smell it. It was a familiar smell. The smell of an old enemy.

'Is there anyone not playing the tables, Vince?' Wolfgang hissed, almost sniffing the air.

'Only a man in the corner. Over six feet tall, with reddish hair, and . . . blue eyes,' Vince said, his voice wavering. He felt badly rattled. The contents of the envelope were obviously forgeries, designed to smear Marcus D'Arville's name, but even so . . .

Wolfgang shook his head. He was sure he could feel danger . . . It felt, in some way, familiar. He dismissed the hovering manager, and then Vince, who protested mildly. 'I can find my own way to the office,' barked Wolfgang, but the energy it took to be angry was too expensive and he finished in a quieter tone, 'I want to be alone for a while.' Relieved, Vince backed away, anxious now to go.

Wayne watched the old man push aside the heavy

velvet curtains and disappear. Quickly, he followed. He walked to the end office and slowly pushed open the door, careful to be quiet. Even so, Wolfgang's sensitive ears heard the faint noise, but he felt, more than heard, the presence of another man. And not just another man. The enemy.

'Who are you?' His voice sounded loud in the room, and for a moment he wondered if anyone would answer him. He flinched when someone did.

'I own Helm Enterprises.' The voice was English.

Wolfgang's lips twisted into a bitter smile. 'Just making sure that I cleared my desk, eh? Scared I might refuse to leave?'

'No. You'll leave,' the voice said confidently. 'If you have to be dragged out kicking and screaming. The sight might make your customers look up from their cards for a second, but only for a second. Then you'll be forgotten.'

Wolfgang snarled, showing yellowed teeth. 'You think so?'

'I know so.'

Wolfgang frowned. It was not the words, which he knew to be perfectly accurate, but the voice itself that troubled him. 'I know your voice,' Wolfgang said, then stiffened. He thought he heard someone else in the corridor.

'I imagine you do. You've heard it often enough in the past.'

Wolfgang slowly shook his head. He shifted, aware of a pain in his chest, but not giving it a second thought. Indigestion from eating still-warm croissants hardly seemed important at this moment. 'I don't . . . remember.' Wolfgang said. The coldness was back with a vengeance, and he could hear the ticking of an ormulu clock not five feet away. 'Who are you?' Wolfgang demanded finally, his fingers tightening around the top of his cane.

'I told you. I'm Helm Enterprises. I'm also the one who sent you that little parcel your secretary was holding just now. Read it to you, has he?'

Wolgang felt an explosion of rage detonate inside him. 'Where did you get those documents?' For a split-second all the old authority was back, the voice, the anger, the familiar demand that he bend to his will, and Wayne was a small boy again, crying in the dark. Then his father stumbled against the table, and the moment was gone. Wayne relaxed, unaware that Sebastien, standing just behind him, had seen him tense in terrified reaction.

'From your old friend, Lieutenant Heinlich, of course,' Wayne said. 'What's the matter, Herr Mueller? Did you really think your days as Commandant of a death camp were forgotten?'

Sebastien shuddered, but made not a sound.

'Who are you?' Wolfgang asked, but his voice was nothing more than a whisper now.

'Doesn't the name Helm mean anything to you?' the English voice goaded, sounding almost amused. 'It should. It's short for Helmut.'

'Helmut?' muttered Wolfgang, then shook his head, totally dazed. 'Helmut?'

'You remember Helmut, surely?' the voice

mocked. 'Your first-born. The best of them all?'

'Helmut,' Wolfgang said, and sat down abruptly into the chair. The indigestion was worse now, spreading to his left arm, making breathing difficult, but he barely noticed. 'You,' he finally said, without heat. There was no strength in the word, just a defeated, helpless acknowledgement.

'Of course it's me, Father. Who else?' Wayne moved closer, close enough to lean his knuckles on the table-top.

Wolfgang reared back in his chair. 'You killed your own brother,' Wolfgang said, uncaring that he was crying, beyond caring if he looked foolish. 'Hans. Hans.'

'You killed me first,' Wayne replied. 'Or have you forgetten the whippings and the beatings?'

'You blinded me,' Wolfgang accused, and Sebastien felt the floor tilt underneath him. Was that possible? Was Wayne capable of that too?

'You were trying to strangle me at the time, if you remember,' said Wayne laconically, sounding as if he were discussing old times with a schoolfriend.

Suddenly Wolfgang launched himself forward, taking both Sebastien and Wayne by complete surprise. The old clawing fingers were on his throat for the second time in his life, but this time he dragged his father's weak fingers away easily before stepping back and testing his neck for bruises. Wolfgang fell across the desk, his breath rasping horribly. He felt his face pull into a grimace, his left cheek and eye seeming to fall from his face. The pain in his chest tightened into a screaming agony.

Above it all, he heard the voice again. 'I told you I was the best, but you wouldn't listen. Now you have to. Now I have your precious bloody casino. Now I have the evidence that'll send you to Israel, to die for what you did . . .'

They were the last words Wolfgang Mueller ever heard.

Slowly he slid sideways, falling off the side of the desk and on to the floor with a heavy thud. Wayne stared at him, then looked blankly as Sebastien appeared and knelt by the old man's body, turning him over, checking his heartbeat. Slowly, from his kneeling position he looked up, his expression unreadable. 'He's dead,' Sebastien said.

Wayne didn't look back at the old man's body. Instead his eyes remained locked on Sebastien. He could feel insanity open its jaws and yawn around him. He could feel himself falling, and was terrified. He swallowed hard, unaware that he was as white as snow and trembling uncontrollably.

'Sebastien!' he said. Just that, but it was enough. He fell forward slowly on to his knees, but Sebastien was there to catch him. He buried his face against the white cotton shirt, feeling Sebastien's skin warm his cold cheek. Slowly he closed his eyes, aware of fingers gently brushing the hair from his temple, aware of a voice, soothing, warm, and kind, washing over him in anaesthetizing waves. Then he said the words Sebastien had been waiting for years to hear.

'Sebastien. Help me. Please.'

CHAPTER 14

Sebastien watched from the windows of what had once been Wolfgang Mueller's villa as Wayne began to stir on the lounger. Putting down his half-full coffee cup, he opened the French windows and stepped out on to the patio. It was just after seven, and the day had that mild feeling of approaching evening. A blackbird sang sweetly amidst the branches of a magnificent magnolia tree as the sun began a slow descent out at sea. He could hear the drone of bees in the honeysuckle bowers as he sat down on the lounger's matching chair. Wayne opened his eyes, aware of his presence. 'Hello.'

'Hi.'

'What time is it?'

'Just after seven. You've been asleep for a few hours.'

Wayne nodded and slowly sat up. His face was gaunt and pale, and he pulled a green and white robe further across his chest. He sat forward, putting his hands over his eyes, and took a deep breath. 'Is everything sorted out?' he finally asked. Sebastien said nothing, forcing him to take his hands away and look at him. Only when he did so did he answer.

'Yes. The body's in the morgue. There's going to be an autopsy, but that's nothing to fear. He almost certainly died of a heart attack.'

Wayne glanced at the psychiatrist, his gaze skidding off the familiar face and across to the gardens. 'What happened . . . just after? I can't quite seem to piece it all together.'

Sebastien felt totally exhausted himself, his body aching dully. He wanted Lilas, and the thought, coming from nowhere, made him frown, then smile. But he quickly turned his thoughts to the matter in hand. 'I fetched the manager. I told him I'd heard a sound from behind the curtain. When I looked, I found the old man dead, and you, an old friend, in a state of shock. He called the ambulance and police. I gave my statement, insisted as a doctor that you were in no fit shape to be questioned until morning, and had your father's chauffeur bring us here. I thought it was better than a hotel. More private.' In fact Sebastien had wanted to bring Wayne back to what had once been his home in the hope of triggering off more memories, striking while he was still vulnerable. Sebastien felt the cold-blooded ruthlessness of it and hated it; yet at the same time he wasn't going to let it stop him. He was not sure how much those final words of Wayne actually meant. The cry for help in times of stress was not always a reliable indicator.

'You'll have to talk to the police tomorrow, but by

242

then they'll be sure it's natural causes. They'll probably only want to know the details.'

Wayne tried to smile but found his stiff face uncooperative. 'It won't matter. I'll just say the shock of meeting his long-lost son was too much for him. It's no more than the truth, after all.' This time he did manage a twisted travesty of a smile, but still couldn't look the American in the eye.

Sebastien shifted on the chair, sensing the approaching crisis. If he could get him to talk now – freely and without lies before giving his damned barrier a chance to get back in place – he might stand a chance. 'You've spent a long time planning this, haven't you?' he asked quietly.

Wayne stared down at the patio tiles beneath his feet. 'I suppose. Since I was five.'

'Five?'

'Yes. Five. It was in Berlin, and he'd just come back from a party. One of those Nazi parties – he was full of talk of Goebbels, I remember. I heard him out of the window. I wasn't supposed to listen out the window . . .' Once the words came he found them unstoppable, like a dam that had burst with an unending supply of dirty water. He went on to relate the fiasco with Heinlich on the boat, still not knowing, after all those years, the motivation and instinct behind that defiant gesture. Sebastien listened, appalled and yet elated. So many things began to explain themselves. The need for revenge, his strange, ambiguous nature with women. No wonder he associated sex with them as something shameful or

243

wrong. No wonder he treated them, and everyone else, as no more than pawns in a game.

'Tell me about Hans,' he urged softly when Wayne's voice began to falter and fade away.

Wayne ran his hand through his hair and turned to face the sea. 'I don't . . . I can't.'

'Did he hate you? Is that why you killed him?'

'No!' Wayne turned to him, his eyes blazing. 'He loved me, the poor little bastard. He only did the dive to try and show me . . .' He got to his feet in a quick, jerking movement and walked several paces across the well-tended lawn, knowing that Sebastien was only a step behind him. He was always just a step behind him, like a bloodhound. A very subtle, very clever bloodhound, pinching little drops of his blood here and there, over weeks that turned to months, that turned to years. Like a parasite, like a leech. A leech that he needed. A leech that gave his whole stinking life some kind of relief. 'You're a ruthless bastard, Sebastien Teale,' he said, not sure how he wanted his voice to sound. It came out flat and hopeless.

Sebastien smiled gently. 'I know. With you, how could I be anything else?'

Wayne felt a kick of reaction in his gut, and took a deep breath. 'What do I have to do to make you give up?'

'Tell me about Hans.'

Wayne gave a harsh bark of laughter. 'That will only make you dig into me more.'

'I know. So do you,' Sebastien said simply, his eyes

level and facing the blue glare head on. Slowly, the pale lips tugged up at the corners.

'I could still destroy you, Sebastien.'

'Tell me about Hans.'

Wayne looked out to the flat blue line of the sea, his shoulders suddenly relaxing. 'He was . . .'

'Mr D'Arville, sir. Telephone.' Sebastien turned abruptly, glaring at the poor servant in a moment of blind frustration. He could cheerfully have throttled the inconspicuous little man at that point. By his side he heard Wayne heave a great sigh. Was it anger, despair or relief?

'All right.' Wayne did not look at Sebastien as he turned and followed the man into the house. Once there, he picked up the phone. 'Yes?'

'Johnson, sir.'

Craig Johnson was one of Wayne's army. Over the years he'd acquired men at regular intervals, poaching them from security firms, police forces, even catching some of them from the fallout of the armed services. For three years now he'd had a team on his father, another team on the Platt offspring, still trying to make trouble all these years later, and another team to look after his private security. Johnson was on the Mueller team.

'Yes?'

'Trouble, sir. The family of Duncan Somerville, the man your father . . . entertained . . . a few years ago?'

'I remember.'

'His family, that is, his daughter and her husband,

245

are on their way to Monaco tomorrow. They were recently visited by our old friend Daniel Bernstein.'

'Bernstein,' Wayne repeated slowly, having difficulty dragging his mind back to reality. Those few wonderful minutes talking to Sebastien had been a catharsis, hurting like hell but feeling wonderful. Now reality was back, and with it, all of life's landmines just waiting for him to step on one. 'They could be trouble,' Wayne said grimly, speaking his thoughts aloud, giving himself a few more seconds to get his brain back to proper working order. 'If they have information, they could expose me.'

'Yes, sir.'

Wayne knew that no mention had yet been made of Wolfgang's death to the press. Damn, why couldn't they have waited a few more days? He hung up and turned around just as Sebastien stepped into the doorway.

Sebastien took just one look at Wayne's face and knew that the barriers were back. Wayne smiled slowly. 'It seems that "saved by the bell" isn't just a cliché after all.'

Sebastien leaned against the door-jamb, feeling ready to just lie down and die. 'You weren't saved, Wayne,' he said tiredly, but his voice held the ring of defeat. For a long, long second the two men just stared at one another. Wayne swallowed hard. He had a strong, almost overwhelming desire to walk across the few feet separating them and . . .

He turned away quickly, but not before Sebastien had time to see the overpowering look of pain and desperation that flitted across his face. Wordlessly, Sebastien watched him walk away.

He wanted Lilas.

As a Louis XIV clock began to strike the half-hour, he suddenly shuddered. He didn't believe in prophecies, but for a wild, ugly moment he had the unshakeable feeling that it was all too late.

Too late for Wayne, and too late for himself.

It was approaching four o'clock in the afternoon when the plane that had stopped over at New York touched down at Nice. 'It looks hot out there,' Kier said, and lifted Oriel's hand to kiss it. She was dressed in a yellow summer dress by Valentine and her hair hung loose across her shoulders. She smiled and squeezed his hand in reply, but her face wore a pinched, tight look.

'It's Nice, isn't it? If it had been raining I'd have asked the pilot to turn around and go back!'

Kier grinned. That was his Oriel. His one constant rock in a sea of Hollywood junk. Slowly he stretched then stood up to retrieve his jacket from the overhead rack. Oriel took a deep breath and slowly rose to her feet. Her legs felt shaky, and it was not just because of the long flight they'd made. They were to meet an associate of Dan Bernstein's at the airport, and although Dan hadn't been very forthcoming on the phone she knew that to ask them to come to Monte Carlo he must have something very definite.

For the thousandth time she found herself

remembering her father, his voice, his smile. Duncan had been so supportive.

'Come on.' Kier gently took her hand and together they followed the queue of passengers off the plane and out through the concrete and glass tunnel to Customs, where their luggage awaited them. As Kier lifted the heaviest suitcase, Oriel took the smaller one, both their minds on the forthcoming interview and the consequences to them both of trying to prosecute Duncan's killer.

'I'm feeing really dry,' Oriel said wryly. 'Let's stop off and have a cup of coffee.'

Kier smiled. 'You must be feeling really parched if you want airport coffee!' But he was already leading the way to the functional coffee lounge. Once there, he queued up for the usual brew and took them back to their table. Oriel took a sip and sighed. On the coffee table in front of her she noticed a copy of a recent *Nice-Matin*, and began to look away. Suddenly a picture of half a face caught her attention, and she leaned forward and opened it up.

'Kier!' she gasped, looking up as her husband leaned over her. 'Isn't that . . .?'

'Mueller,' he said with conviction. The man was older, but they both remembered seeing his pictures in Duncan's files, when they'd gone over his things after his death. The headline confirmed the name.

'*Marcus D'Arville Mort*,' Oriel read aloud. 'He's dead, Kier!' Oriel slowly shook her head. 'This doesn't make sense. We've come all this way only to find . . .'

Kier frowned. 'It does seem rather . . . convenient, doesn't it?' he murmured.

Oriel looked at him. 'You think something . . . funny's going on?'

Kier shrugged. 'I think, now that we're here, we should have a nose around. What could it hurt?'

Back at the Harcourt mansion, Gemma was reading *Nice-Matin*. She'd ordered it, ever since her parents had sat down and told their children what was going on, and why they were flying to France. It was thrilling, in a way, to have a grandfather who might have been murdered by Nazis. Sad too. She'd noticed how pale and angry her mother had looked.

Now, the notice of Mueller's death was splashed across the front pages! Damn! She'd just been in the middle of planning a wild party, with Paris's grinning help, and now this.

'What are you scowling at,' Paris said, wandering in after doing his usual two hours' practice in the pool.

'He's dead,' Gemma said succinctly.

Paris gave a double-take. 'Who's dead?' he demanded.

'Mueller. Here, have some breakfast.' Gemma pushed a plate of toast his way. She could see her wild party disappearing in smoke. And she'd told Matty Haines it was definitely on!

'Well, if Mueller's dead, I expect Mom and Dad will be back soon.'

Gemma sighed petulantly. But, no sooner was the

249

sigh echoing around the room when the phone rang. 'Well, that's our party gone down the tubes,' she muttered as she lifted the receiver. 'Hello? Oh, hi, Mom . . .'

Paris listened to her giving a lot of 'uh-huh's and 'oh?'s before she hung up. When she turned back, she was wearing a very strange expression.

'Mom and Dad are staying on in France for a while,' she said slowly, and Paris threw a cushion at her. She fielded it expertly.

'So, let's party on!' he yelled exuberantly, then settled down as he realized that Gemma was hardly enthusiastic. 'What's up?'

'They think there's something odd about Mueller's death,' she mused, her eyes taking on a bright gleam that had Paris instantly on the alert. He knew that look. It meant trouble.

'Gem?'

'What if it was murder?' she breathed, her face taking on an excited look. 'Mom and Dad could be mixed up in this great Nazi murder mystery, and we're stuck over here in boring LA.'

'Gem!' Paris groaned, but could already see where she was heading. And, in spite of himself, he could feel himself becoming intrigued. 'Perhaps it was his son,' Paris mused, and, finding his sister's glowing eyes fixed on him, quickly grabbed one of his sporting magazines and began to hunt through the pages.

'What are you talking about, rodent-breath?' Gemma asked, craning her head to look over her brother's shoulder as he found the page he was looking for.

'Here,' Paris handed it over. 'Wayne D'Arville. I thought I knew that name. Some English financial firm that he owns is sponsoring the open golf classic at Gleneagles next year.'

'The son!' Gemma breathed. 'Daddy said something a long time ago about Mueller's having a family.'

'It makes sense,' Paris said, turning the page to be confronted by a full-page colour picture of a smiling, red-headed man. 'He can't want the whole world finding out his father was a Nazi.'

Gemma squealed and grabbed the magazine. 'What a hunk!'

Paris watched her with smiling eyes. 'First he's a killer, now he's a hunk.'

But Gemma wasn't listening. She turned the magazine so that the picture of Wayne D'Arville stared straight at her, the blue eyes seeming to bore deep into her head, making her blink. She felt her breath flutter in her throat as her breasts tingled and her nipples tightened into hard nubs. Slowly she began to read the article.

'*The imposing figure of the six-foot-four entrepreneur with the copper hair and sky-blue eyes has set more hearts fluttering than any other man of his generation, but for widely differing reasons. Though the ladies have fallen in droves for the man with the looks of a movie star, their husbands react to his shark-like presence on the stock exchange with deep shivers of foreboding. So far in his impressive career . . .*'

When she'd finished the article – written by a

woman, she noticed – her eyes were glowing. 'So that's the son of the man who murdered Grandad,' she said quietly, but her voice was excited rather than disgusted, and Paris, in the act of buttering his toast, glanced at her worriedly.

'You know, Paris,' she said, reaching forward to filch the toast from his hand, 'I don't think he should get away with this. Why should Mom and Dad have all the fun? Bethany's off in Oxford, living it up. Why shouldn't we see Europe too?'

'Huh?' Paris said, around a mouthful of toast.

Slowly she stood up, and stared down at the magazine. The blue eyes seemed to laugh at her, mocking her, challenging her . . . 'I think it's about time he was taught a lesson.'

Paris, his voice doubtful, asked nervously, 'What are you going to do?'

Gemma looked at him. Her eyes were bright, her face flushed, and her red-painted, beautiful mouth was forming a cocky grin. She was wearing a pair of cyclamen-pink shorts and a white lace top, and with her short cap of dark hair she reminded him of an all-too-beautiful, mischievous pixie.

'Fly to Monte Carlo, of course,' she said. 'Mom and Dad need never know we're there.'

'Gemma!' Paris wailed. 'You can't just . . .' He waved a hand vaguely in the air, feeling his stomach turn over. 'Gem, you can't be serious.'

'Why not?' She looked incredibly young, incredibly stubborn, and Paris was suddenly terrified for her.

'He's a Nazi, for Pete's sake,' he yelped. 'He moves money around as if . . . He probably has an army of men . . .'

Gemma let him splutter and flounder, still wearing that aggravatingly confident smile. 'He's used to dealing with the most powerful men in the world!' Paris finally exploded.

'He hasn't dealt with me before,' Gemma pointed out softly, with the supreme confidence of youth, and the utter certainty that only the truly spoiled could generate. She simply could not conceive of not getting what she wanted.

'Look, Gem, I know about you . . . I have friends at school too, you know. I'm not deaf. You've got a reputation that would curdle Mum's blood if she ever heard about it, but this is different. He . . .' he tapped the photo of Wayne D'Arville with a jabbing finger '. . . is not some high school kid or college jock that you can just wrap around your little finger. He's bloody dangerous.'

Paris got to his feet as he realized he was not getting through to her, looking alternately angry and alarmed. 'Gem, you can't!'

Gemma looked up at him, put her hands on her hips, cocked her elfin face to one side and smiled beguilingly. 'If you're so worried about me, big brother,' she purred, 'why don't you come with me?'

CHAPTER 15

Wayne stared at the photographs in front of him, as unmoving as a chameleon. Reluctantly he dragged his eyes from those of a blue-eyed boy and re-read the report from his team investigating Veronica Copeland, which had come in only half an hour ago. 'The subject's birth certificate was registered under the grandmother's name, not that of Coltrane. This is what led to the initial delay in double-checking the certificate.' Wayne gave a brief snarl, and skipped the page. He wasn't interested in why Veronica had registered the birth under her mother's maiden name. No doubt she wanted all traces of the child's being born in prison to a jailbird mother covered up. Perhaps, even then, she'd subconsciously been afraid he would take the child away. Again his eyes wandered to the photographs. Immediately on finding the birth certificate that had 'Father Unknown' written in the appropriate section, the team had staked out the Copeland boy. The resulting pictures bore hardly any resemblance at all to the boy he'd seen in the warehouse that night in New York. The photographs, hundreds of them, had been taken over a series of days, and caught the boy in every daily ritual possible: leaving for his summer job, on the bus, carrying trays of coffee to the newspaper journalists he worked for, talking to a pretty blonde-haired girl, and eating a hamburger. And always the same face stared back at him.

His hair was as dark as Veronica's, not the mousy brown hair of that bastard Valentine. That had been the first thing that had struck him. As Wayne had turned over the photographs for the first time, a full-face shot had had his heart stopping in his chest. The boy's eyes were blue – as blue as his own. The face, too, looked different from the one he remembered. The colour shots were of the highest quality, and Wayne found himself looking down at a skin as fair as his own. And the shape of the face . . . How the hell had Valentine managed to change the boy's face? It had taken only seconds for Wayne to piece it all together. The bitch had phoned her husband the moment he was out of the door. He should have realized that the dressmaker was a make-up artist too.

Wayne glanced at his watch. He had another four hours before his commercial flight was due, and made a mental note to purchase a private jet at the first opportunity. He paced the villa, now legally his, unable to stay still. 'Travis,' he said his son's name, over and over again. The boy in the photographs looked incredibly young. Just seventeen. Wayne could remember well what it was to be seventeen.

'Travis,' he said again, savouring the two syllables. 'You're going to love Monte Carlo.'

He put in a call to his man in Monaco. 'Fletcher? I want you to buy an oceangoing yacht. I'll have the bank transfer the funds. No, I'm going to New York. Hire a crew and have the boat meet me there. What? I don't care about that, or the paperwork. Just rush it through, will you? And Fletcher – I want a discreet crew. Find as many of your men with seagoing experience as possible. I want it there within the fortnight. And Fletcher – I want the boat named the *Travis Helm*.' If he was going to kidnap his own son – and he was – he could hardly take the boy bound and gagged on to a jumbo jet.

Travis was up to his neck in files. Jake Conran, the features editor, had asked him to research a series of murders several years ago of five drug pushers. Jake was sure that the death of a pusher downtown was the work of the same killer. 'The MO boy.' He had tapped his nose. 'Always look out for the MO.' Travis had spent four hours going through old editions, ferreting out the relevant stuff from all the dross. Now he glanced at his watch. It was getting late; he'd have to call home and tell them not to hold dinner.

'Hey, kid, how's it going?' Travis turned to see the sweating, grinning face of Andy McCall, the baseball and associated sports writer, block the doorway.

'How does it look like it's coming?' he shot back, grinning as the man began to wheeze in laugher.

'Welcome to Grub Street, kid.' And with that cryptic comment the big man lumbered off, leaving Travis grinning. He turned, and glanced at the towering piles of old editions and files stacked around him.

'Hell, I love this job,' he said softly as, high in the air, a Boeing jet from Nice began its descent to New York airport.

'Get the phone, Val,' Veronica called, lifting one suds-covered leg as she lay back in the bath. She had the Mancini buyout to oversee tomorrow. The thought of dealing with all those accoutants was enough to send her barmy. 'Aaarrghhhh,' she groaned, as Val stuck his head around the door.

'Dying?' he asked, going down on to his knees beside the bathtub.

'At least,' she sighed. 'It's a rare disease called Chronic Accountant Dyspepsia.'

'Sounds painful,' Val said, and slipped a hand into the water, uncaring that the hot soapy water drenched his sleeve.

'Hmmm,' she sighed as his hand curled around one calf and began to stroke higher. 'Who was that on the phone?'

'Travis. He'll be late. He's researching a gory story for the feature creature.'

'You're a poet and you don't know it.'

'I do my best. You do the rest.'

'I think you're a . . . oh, Val!' Water sloshed over the side of the bathtub, but neither of them noticed for quite some time. Fully dressed, he joined her in the tub, his jeans soaking into a darker blue as he lay between her parted legs.

Downtown, Wayne listened to Cyril Francis and Frank Parton as they brought him up to date. Cyril, an ex-Marine who'd been dishonourably discharged, was a tall man, about six foot one, with a mean face that would have sent a Hollywood director into fits of rapture; dark, saturnine features were offset by a vivid white scar on his cheek. In direct contrast, Frank Parton looked like the ex-FBI man that he was. He wore a powder-blue suit, which offset the careful cut of his pale hair and watery blue eyes. Frank was the electronics and surveillance export, Cyril the brain and muscle.

'You have his school records?'

Frank handed them over and watched as his employer read through the ten years' worth of essay reports and exam results. Frank was openly intrigued by his employer. He paid top dollar, spoke like an Englishman, had the manners of a Frenchman and the square features of a German. He had money, but hardly any of the trappings he'd expected. Cyril's eyes were unreadable as the tall man paced and read. But then Cyril's eyes were always unreadable.

'What else?' Wayne demanded, spending the next few hours going through the bulk of material that had not been included in the preliminary report. By the time dawn pushed away the night's darkness, Wayne had read every medical report on the boy, read details of every place the boy had ever lived, every school, every teacher, every friend. Frank wondered how he'd been so careless as to misplace a son in the first place.

'Where's the boy now?'

Frank lifted a small box to his mouth and spoke quietly into it. Wayne heard a crackle of static and a tinny voice answering.

'The boy's home, sir. The complex on . . .'

'I know where it is. Has there been any unusual activity since my last visit?'

'No, sir. The boy is still working at the paper. He worked late last night. School's out for summer, but I've got prior notification of his results. He graduated third in his class.'

Wayne nodded. 'College?'

'He has a place at the local Uni, sir. He could have gone to one of the top places, with his result and financial backing from his . . . mother. Obviously he wants to stay local.'

Wayne walked to the window and looked out over the city. It never stopped. He thought of all the racial unrest, the drug pushers, the street gangs, and shuddered. What a place to live. Travis could have been killed by this place. Or had that been Veronica's intention? The bitch. And Valentine. An image of the cockney man grinning at him suddenly super-imposed itself over the city landscape, and Wayne felt that familiar hot spear of antagonism. All these years, that . . . that . . . dressmaking nancy-pancy bastard had been raising his son. Who knew what harm he'd done? What if . . .?

259

Wayne turned so suddenly that both men tensed. 'Girlfriends?' Wayne snapped out, almost wilting in relief as Frank Parton began to read a list of names. He finished up with Gayle Granger, the blonde girl in the set of photographs Wayne had left behind in Monaco.

Wayne said softly, 'I want them dead.'

The two men remained silent. Slowly he turned around, expecting them to look shocked, or at least uneasy. Neither did. Frank Parton merely wanted clarification. 'The Copelands, sir?'

'Yes.'

'Both?' It was Cyril who spoke, for the first time since Wayne had entered the room.

'Yes,' Wayne said again, his voice firm.

'You want it to look like an accident?' Parton again.

'Of course.'

'Car crash?'

Wayne looked down into the street below. 'No. They might not die. I want to be sure they're dead. I want them . . .' He paused, then enunciated the next word with grim relish. 'Eradicated. I want them . . .' He blinked as the sun emerged between two high-rise towers, throwing a deep orange light into his eyes. Slowly Wayne began to smile. 'I want them burned.'

'Burned?' Frank repeated, puzzled. He thought they'd already established that he wanted them dead.

'A warehouse fire happens nearly every day in this city,' Cyril mused, having caught on at once. His voice was surprisingly soft coming from a face like his.

'Oh. You mean *burned*,' Frank repeated. 'That warehouse is full of flammable material. Solvent, too. And all that make-up. Did you know almost ninety-nine per cent of make-up is based on flammable substances?' Frank asked of nobody in particular.

Slowly Wayne turned back from the window and stared at him. Something in the quality of those blue eyes made Frank go cold. Cyril smiled. 'I want it done now,' Wayne said, successfully wiping the smile off the older man's face.

'You mean this week?'

'I mean this day. Now. This afternoon.'

'But Mr D'Arville! These things take planning. They take time. We have to be careful . . .' Frank began, his voice rising an octave.

'Are you saying you can't do it?' Wayne asked, mildly enough, but again Frank felt a cold chill climb up his spine.

'We'll do it,' Cyril said, his eyes meeting those of his partner, a silent message passing between them.

Wayne nodded. 'Good. I'm going to get some sleep. Wake me when it's all set up. I want to watch.'

Both men were silent as he kicked off his shoes and walked towards the bed. Equally silent, they then left. Frank closed the door after him, and turned to his partner. 'I don't know about you,' he said, as he pressed the button for the elevator, 'but I think we're working for a nut.'

'A clever nut,' Cyril corrected with what seemed pedantic nitpicking.

'Yeah,' Frank agreed heavily. 'They're the worst kind.'

Val was just about to take a Budweiser from the fridge when the phone rang. He glanced through the alcove to where Veronica lay on the settee, poring over her latest business scoop. She got up and walked to the old fashioned white and gold telephone. 'Hello.'

'Is that Mrs Copeland?'

'Yes.'

'Oh, thank heavens. This is Phelps here – I'm the watchman at Warehouse 6.'

'Yes?' Her voice sharpened. The man sounded distinctly panicky.

'A few minutes ago your son came in. He said he had to check something to do with shipment of Bruges lace that came in last night.'

'What? Travis? But he's at the paper.'

'No, ma'am. That's what I'm trying to tell you: he's here. And there's been an accident, ma'am.'

'Accident?' She heard her voice yelp out the word, and glanced up as Val sprinted closer and jammed his ear against the outside of the phone. 'What do you mean? What's happened?' Her voice was sharp with anxiety, and to Val she mouthed the word, 'Travis.'

'Well, ma'am, somehow one of the stacks of bales came loose. I ain't sure how it happened. I heard him call out, and when I found him his legs were pinned under the bales. It's the Thai silk shipment, I think.'

Quickly Val snatched the phone away from her.

'Have you called the ambulance, man? Good. Can you get the bales off him?' Veronica waited, scanning her husband's face for any expression. 'OK. We'll be right there.'

Val drove to the warehouse with grim speed. Veronica could feel a tremor in the pit of her stomach, making her breathe in small gasps. What if his legs were crushed? What if he could never walk again? When they arrived, the warehouse looked deserted.

'Why aren't the ambulances here yet?' Veronica asked, getting out of the car without bothering to lock it.

'I dunno,' Val admitted, looking around. 'Where's the watchman?'

'He must be with Travis,' Veronica said, her voice wobbling as tears filled her eyes. 'Val, he must be so damned scared!'

Val took her hand, pulling her inside. 'Come on.'

The place was deserted. 'The silks are over here,' Val said, and set off deep into the heart of the warehouse. Veronica looked around her at towering bales of beige sacking. They both jumped as a hollow 'clang' echoed through the building. 'Well, somebody's about,' Val said. 'That was the outer door.'

By now Veronica was hopelessly lost. Since giving up modelling she hardly ever came to the warehouses any more. 'Travis?' she called, making Val jump. Nobody answered.

'Perhaps they've already got him out,' Val whispered, and for a few seconds they ran through the maze of bales, eyes swivelling. Suddenly Val slowed down to a stop, staring straight ahead, then began looking around, his face puzzled.

'What is it?' Veronica whispered.

'This is the place,' Val answered, waving a vague hand around at the bales clearly labelled as Thai silk. 'But there's nothing here.'

'I don't get it,' Veronica said. 'Where's Travis?'

Val began to speak, then stopped as a sound came from behind them. It was an odd sound – a sort of small 'whump' that echoed in the big room. 'What was that?' Veronica demanded, her voice strangled.

'I don't know. It sounded like . . .' He broke off as Veronica clutched his arm.

'Look!' She pointed to the top of a pile of satin from Vienna where a plume of smoke curled high into the air.

For a second they both stood and stared, then Val grabbed her arm, his voice terse as he ordered gruffly, 'Come on.'

They began running in the opposite direction, Val sure of the layout. They ran a few yards, turned down an aisle stretching to the right, and skidded to a halt. A wall of flame blocked their exit a few yards away.

'But the fire's back there,' Veronica panted, jerking her head in the direction behind them and beginning to panic for the first time. She looked sideways and up at Val, and saw his jaw clenched so tight that the whole bottom half of his face was white. 'Val?' she said in a small voice, like that of a terrified child. Val looked down, opened his mouth, shook his head, and dragged her back. They ran to the left, but again, only a few yards away, there was a third fire. Veronica felt tears on her cheeks which were dried in seconds by the hot air surrounding them. 'We've got to find Travis,' she cried. 'He'll burn to death!'

'I don't think Travis was ever here!' Val had to shout now to be heard over the rising roar of the fire. The materials were burning much too fast – they had to be covered with petrol or something like it. Quickly he looked around. The windows were situated almost at the roof, a good thirty feet above them. 'Quick. Help me stack these bales.'

Veronica began to cough and choke as the smoke attacked her lungs, and behind her she could feel the hot lick of air that was becoming super-heated by the flames. She could feel the oxygen being burnt off, and her lungs were already beginning to labour.

Within five minutes they had built a rickety stairway of bales, but she could hardly see it as her eyes began to water from the smoke. She could feel death all around her and clung grimly to Val's hand as he began to climb. 'Watch where I put my feet and . . .'

'What?' she screamed. All around was a loud roar of crackling flames. Val pointed at his feet, then the bales. Veronica nodded. Outside they could hear the wail of sirens. 'Oh, thank God,' Veronica said, but Val never heard her. They were already four bales up, and the whole structure began to wobble precariously. He looked down ten feet or so, and saw the flames slowly creeping towards the bottom of their makeshift ladder.

Veronica took off her shoes, but forgot that she was wearing stockings, which were hardly designed for traction. Above him Val could see the thin line of windows. They had to be wide enough to allow them out. They *had* to be. He glanced down and saw the top of Veronica's dark head.

'I've got to let go of your hand for the next bale, OK?' He choked on the smoke, but Veronica nodded and let go of his hand, clinging to the next bale with two white-knuckled hands. Her heart was thumping so loud in her chest that she thought it was going to burst. She just couldn't get enough air into her lungs. She could feel herself begin to pass out. She wanted to be sick, and scream, and cry, all at the same time.

The bales wobbled as Val pulled himself up to the next one and she clung on grimly. Below her she could not even see the ground, only the orangey-yellow flames that glowed beneath the thick black smoke. She looked up and saw Val beckoning her. Taking a deep breath, she choked and retched, then reached up. Her hands grasped the red string that bound the bales together and, feeling with her feet, she found a foothold. Hoisting herself up, she balanced precariously between the two bales, like a fly on a wall.

Suddenly and without warning her foot slipped and she fell forward, banging her chin on the bale and biting her tongue, filling her mouth with the iron taste of her own blood. She lost traction and scrabbled desperately with her hands. She glanced up just in time to see Val lunge forward, desperately trying to grab her hand. For a second it looked as if she must fall. For a second, a horrible second in time she seemed to hang suspended in mid-air, and then she screamed.

But Val, with a superhuman effort, just managed to grab her. Her weight threatened to pull him down, and he rocked precariously on the bale. But he did not let her go. If she died, he was going to die with her.

He grunted as he pulled her up. She hung limp in his arms, and he realized she'd finally succumbed to the smoke.

'Veronica!' he screamed her name, and began to haul her up to him, calling on every ounce of his strength. Once there, he held her in his arms, gasping and choking himself. He looked up at the window. It seemed so far away.

In the newsroom, Travis had just placed a cup of coffee on the desk of Owen Twinsmith, one of the top 'hot shot' boys, when the desk phone rang. Travis would have moved on except that the mention of Rineway Street caught his attention. Sharply his eyes focused on the young reporter who was busy scribbling down in shorthand. 'Is it worth covering? Really? Shit! Have they saved the other buildings yet? OK.' He hung up and grabbed his jacket.

'Hey what's going on?' Travis called after him.

'Fire at the warehouses,' Owen mumbled, already running and shouting for his photographer and back-up man. Travis stared after him, an ugly feeling uncoiling itself in the pit of his stomach. There had to be hundreds of warehouses on Rineway Street. Even so . . . He reached for the phone, punching out his own numbers.

'Hello. Valentine's,' said the chirpy voice of their cleaning lady.

'Glenny? It's Travis. Listen, is Dad there?'

'Nope. He and your ma left for the warehouses about half an hour ago.'

Travis hung up and left at a dead run. It took him only ten minutes to get to the site, but he had to abandon his taxi at the top of the road and run the rest of the way, as fire trucks and police blocked the road. He dodged a policeman keeping away spectators, his eyes fixed on the sky ahead where black smoke choked the air. He was gasping and totally out of breath when he reached the first engine, his agonized gaze confirming what his heart already knew. Warehouse 6 was just a wall of orange flame. Travis pushed past the people who had also got around the cordon, uncaring of the disgruntled yelps coming his way.

'Is anyone in there?' he yelled, grabbing the first fireman he found. The heavy-set man of about forty-five with a sweat-soaked, soot-blackened face shook him off angrily. 'Outta the way,' he snapped. Travis let him go, and walked to the nearest engine where a driver sat in the front, controlling the pressure gauge on the hoses. 'Is anyone in there?' he yelled through the window. The man never took his eyes off the instruments. 'Please! My father owns the warehouse. For God's sake . . .'

The man glanced up at him. 'They got two people out about ten minutes ago.'

Travis stared at him. 'Alive?' he croaked the word, barely managing to get it past his tight throat.

The fireman shrugged. 'The ambulance took off fast, so I guess so. But . . .'

'But what?' Travis all but screamed.

The fireman looked at him with sympathy. 'They were in there a long time, by all accounts.'

Travis turned to the burning building, his face a sickly white. 'You mean . . . they got burned?'

The fireman sighed. He felt sorry for the kid. But it was best to know the worst. You had time to prepare that way. 'It's not just the flames, kid,' he said gruffly. 'It's the smoke. Smoke burns off the oxygen, see? And if your brain is robbed of oxygen for any amount of time . . .' He trailed off.

Travis stared at him blankly for a few seconds, then swallowed. 'What hospital will they have taken them to?'

But at that moment, a part of the warehouse started to collapse, and the fire chief ordered his men back. Travis stumbled away, his head reeling.

A firecrew rushed past him, knocking him to the ground. He barely felt it. But, just as Travis straightened, the sight of a copper-coloured head, standing head and shoulders above the rest of the crowd, caught his eye.

Travis went cold. Since Wayne D'Arville's last visit, Val and Veronica had researched the man thoroughly, coming up with some startling and ugly

269

facts that had made them all feel sick. Now Travis froze as the head turned his way. He expected the blue gaze to keep moving, not expecting to be recognized as the same boy he had seen just over a month ago, but instead the blue eyes sharpened and remained fixed on him.

Travis began to shake. As he looked deep into those blue eyes, he suddenly knew. He'd started the fire. He glanced at the burning building, then looked back to the space where Wayne D'Arville had stood, only to find his biological father bearing down on him, shouldering his way through the crowd with arrogant ease. Travis looked once more into that face, then turned and fled.

He knew the district well, and dodged down the narrow, twisting alleys at random, pausing every now and then to look over his shoulder. He walked for miles, in no particular direction, feeling dazed and totally disorientated. Val and Veronica might both be dead – or worse – but his other father, the man called Wayne D'Arville, was very much alive, and coming after him.

Travis stumbled into a café and ordered a coffee. His legs felt like rubber. He tried to lift the cup to his mouth, but it shook so hard that the coffee fell to the table-top.

'Hey, you! Junkie. Get outta here.' The man who served him the coffee was scowling at him. Travis blinked then he looked blankly down at the coffee cup. 'Bloody junkie. Do the world a favour, kid, and go top yourself.'

Travis stumbled to his feet and lurched out the door. He looked left and right, not sure where he was. He had to go home. He had to get safe. He found himself at a bus stop. Swaying on the bus, he felt curiously light-headed. He knew it was shock, and got off at the nearest stop to his apartment building. He staggered to the nearest wall and leant his hand against the solid concrete. The few minutes it took him to walk a block and a half seemed to take forever. But eventually he found himself staring at the blue and white awning that was the entrance to his building.

Through his misery, Travis felt a slow prickling start low down on the back of his neck. Quickly he swung around. A few yards away a man was walking towards him wearing a fancy blue suit, his blond hair neatly trimmed. He was smiling. Travis stared at him for less than a second, and then inexplicably found himself running. He was not sure why, but at the corner he half turned, and almost cried out loud. The man was almost on top of him. He dodged, cannoning into a tall black youth, who was carrying a ghetto-blaster that screetched forth a Jimi Hendrix classic.

'Hey, man, watch what you're doing,' he snapped. Travis saw the blond man's hand reaching out for him, and without thinking he gave the stranger a vicious shove that sent him flying into the blond man behind him. Both went down. Ignoring the swearing and shouts, he carried on running, dodging in and out of stores, side-streets and back alleys. Finally he ducked behind a set of garbage cans outside a

Chinese restaurant, panting hard. He felt tears in his eyes and brushed them away.

After a while he began to breathe normally again He had to go to the police. Why should he run from his real father? With his testimony and an arson expert's evidence, he would make sure D'Arville stood trial for attempted murder.

Travis began to sob quietly. 'I'll see you in hell,' he sobbed, his eyes fixed unseeingly on a big black rat that was investigating a neighbouring garbage can. He had to think! He needed an ally to fight Wayne D'Arville.

Half an hour later he was back on the street. He couldn't go home, but the paper would help him. They'd do anything for a story. Crusading journalism was what won papers the Pulitzer Prize. A block from the paper, he slowed down and began inspecting every parked car. He glanced continuously over his shoulder. He stopped at a payphone to get through to Owen's desk. 'Owen, it's Travis. Listen, about that fire.'

'Fire? Oh, the warehouse. Forget it. The cops have already got the dope from the watchman.'

Travis went cold. 'What?'

'The owner started the blaze. You know, for the insurance. Incompetent bastard got himself and his wife caught up in it instead. Look, kid, I gotta go.'

Travis heard the dialling tone buzz in his ear, and for a long moment stared stupidly down at the receiver still clutched in his hand. His brain seemed sluggish, incapable of thought. Slowly he hung up, and as he did so he saw a man turn the corner and look around. He was tall and lean, and as he turned his head and spotted him in the booth, Travis saw a vivid white scar slashed across his right cheek.

The blue eyes of the frightened boy in old jeans and windcheater met the steely brown eyes of the man in the brown suit, and a silent message that Travis understood only instinctively passed between them.

Then, once again, he began running.

CHAPTER 16

Monte Carlo

The moment Maria stepped out of the taxi, she felt a great wave of happiness wash over her. Facing her was the Beach Plaza Tower, built in front of a small, curving white-sanded beach. Once this whole scenario would have overwhelmed her: the white city that was Monte Carlo, the plethora of yachts, the smell of money. She could almost have wished she had come straight to this place from Andalusia, just for the thrill of the total contrast. Then Vincent was by her side, his head just reaching her shoulder, and she forced a smile to her face. 'Well, this is it. What do you think?' she asked gaily.

Vincent Marchetti glanced up at the building and shrugged. 'It is all right. Let's get out of the sun.' Maria watched him walk ahead, a small smile on her painted lips. She watched the bellboys collect her mountain of luggage, for she had taken everything with her from Carlos's villa. The jewellery she had halved, keeping the very finest pieces to wear and selling the rest. Now her bank balance practically dazzled her with all the zeros.

The hotel room boasted air-conditioning, a queen-sized bed, private bathroom, colour television, mini-bar and telephone, but the first thing she did was check that her adjoining room with Vincent Marchetti was locked. It was, and the key was on her side. Not that he was in any way threatening, and she knew she had to keep him sweet. So far she had succeeded in bringing him to Monte Carlo, but already he was making noises about rejoining the institute and continuing with his proper scientific work.

But she was confident she could handle him, without having to go as far as sleeping with him. After all, who really cared about science when there was life to be lived, and all the treasures it held to be explored? Treasures like parties, new places, love. And revenge. Oh, yes, she was looking forward to revenge.

A sea breeze feathered across her skin, cooling her arms and making her shiver. Somewhere in that jungle of white-painted buildings, hotels, casinos, shopping malls and royal palaces was the lair of Wayne D'Arville, her not-so-beloved father.

Ironically enough, she had arrived in Monte Carlo almost five weeks to the day after her grandfather's funeral. She wondered what he had been like as she walked to her cases and began to unpack. She had worked hard for all those magic labels – Valentine, Dior, St Laurent, even a few classics from Balmain and Chanel – and she didn't want some maid creasing

275

them. She had just put away the last of her things and was holding her jewellery case in her hand, ready to take it down to the hotel safe, when a soft knock came on the door connecting the two rooms. She walked towards it, but made no move to turn the key. 'Yes?'

'You hungry?' The voice was muffled but she was relieved to notice he made no move to turn the door handle. In his own way, Vincent was a sweetie.

'Starving,' she admitted. 'Meet me in the restaurant in ten minutes.' She changed quickly into a summer dress of dramatic ruby-red, which was practically nothing more than a poncho that flowed and rippled whenever she moved, leaving a long length of leg bare. Watching with eagle eyes as they put her jewels into the safe, she asked for directions to the restaurant, which turned out to be practically empty. They ordered *poulet sauté aux olives de Provence*, followed by raspberries in a rich cream, enjoying the meal after the short flight. Maria drank sparingly of the white wine. She had to remain clear and level-headed for later on tonight. Later on, she would face her father not as a dirty, sweating peasant working in a sweat-shop clothes factory but as a wealthy, beautiful woman who was taking his money.

'Shall we take a walk on the beach?' Vincent asked, his voice hesitant and containing his usual hopeful squeak.

Briefly she shook her head. 'No. I want to check out the equipment.'

Vincent's face fell, but he rose obediently when she did, leaving his dessert unfinished to follow her to the

276

lifts. Upstairs, Maria unlocked a black leather briefcase from which she extracted a small box. Inside was a small pink, oddly shaped disc, designed to fit snugly into her ear. She carefully inserted the plastic mould into her right ear then walked to the mirror to check it was invisible under her dark curtain of her hair. It was. 'OK. Try your end. No – not here,' she murmured as Vincent retrieved a small microphone from the same briefcase and held it up to his hand. 'Go outside – by the pool – and then try it. If it'll work from that distance we'll have no trouble at the casino.'

Vincent flushed with anticipatory pleasure. He was looking forward to tonight, too, though for different reasons of course. Maria smiled indulgently. She was getting fond of little Vincent. 'And, *caro*, try practising a little more discretion, yes? My . . . Mr D'Arville will have security men scattered all around the place on the lookout for cheaters with angles. You can't just lift up your hand and talk into it. Pretend to be scratching your cheek or something. You can do that for me, can't you, darling?'

'Of course. I'll practise in front of the mirror tonight. Before we leave.' His face wreathed in a smile. He was having more fun in one day than a whole year at the institute!

Maria wandered around the room restlessly, occasionally touching her ear to make sure the disc had not fallen out. It felt strange at first, but the plastic had been moulded especially for the purpose of fitting snugly into a human ear, and she suspected that after several nights of wearing it she would hardly notice its existence. How or where Carlos had found such state-of-the-art listening and transmitting devices she didn't know or care. Even the microphone of Vincent's was barely bigger than a thimble.

She jumped, then smiled broadly as she heard a small, tinny but unmistakable voice deep in her ear. 'Maria. Can you hear me? I hope so. I'm by the pool now. I'm coming back. We'll talk in a minute, OK?'

Vincent felt as if he'd just stepped into a James Bond movie. He only hoped he wouldn't let her down, but he wasn't really worried about his 'gift' failing him. He had a ninety-nine per cent success rate that sent the professors and occasional visiting experts from other countries into fits of rapture.

He returned to Maria's room and knocked timidly. He knew he was making a fool of himself with Maria, but she was so lovely, how could he deny her? The door was flung open and he saw instantly that her face was glowing; her eyes were shining like stars, and her cherry-red mouth was wide and laughing. 'It worked, Vincent! It worked.' She reached out and pulled him inside, dancing with him around and around the room.

Eventually she danced to a halt, and then impatiently tugged out the pink plastic from her ear. 'Come on. Let's tour this little city of his, and see some sights!'

Vincent wanted badly to ask exactly who Wayne D'Arville was and why she wanted so desperately to take his money, but he was scared of spoiling her mood. So they rented an English Jaguar and got lost in the maze of streets that bore exotic names like the Boulevard des Moulins, Avenue de la Costa, Rue Princesse Florestine and Boulevard Albert-Premier. They drove to the Port de Monaco and watched the yachts as the sun slowly set, then drove past the Cathédrale, the high arched windows aglow with colour. As night slowly approached, the lights came on – thousands, millions of twinkling lights. She could feel the pulse of the city begin to stir and hum, like blood in invisible veins.

'Let's get back. I want to change,' she said, her voice suddenly lower and colder. She had work to do.

Back in her room, Maria stared at her wardrobe carefully. She wanted this first meeting to be something special – something he would never forget. She thought of white first, for dramatic contrast with her hair and eyes, but then decided against it. White was the colour of a victim, and tonight it was Wayne D'Arville who was going to bleed. Red, then. She pulled out a sequined gown by Régis, then shook her head. Too bold – she was not a whore, but a sophisticated woman. Her eye ran along the rails of clothes and stopped at a deep orange velvet gown, cut with a narrow but plunging V at both neck and back. Thoughtfully she pulled it on and checked her reflection in the mirror. The orange velvet, as rich and luxurious as any material could be, glowed softly against her creamily tanned skin, turning her hair into a midnight-black and making her light brown eyes look intriguingly tawny. Slowly she smiled. After adding a golden brown shadow to her eyelids and burnt orange lipstick to her mouth, she donned a tiger's eye necklace that consisted of a single stone on a delicate gold chain, the gem nestling between the braless valley of her breasts, drawing all eyes to that point. To complete the outfit she stepped into three-inch-high gold shoes that glittered as she walked, and took out a matching clutch-purse.

She slipped in her earplug and brushed out her hair, as a final touch spraying gold glitter sparingly over her ebony locks. She walked a few steps, turned her head, and saw how the glittery drops flashed in the light as she moved. Perfect. She knocked on the adjoining door, rechecked her appearance and turned as the door opened and Vincent walked in.

He was dressed in a dinner jacket. 'Vincent, darling, you look very debonair,' she said, trying to be kind.

Vincent said nothing – his mouth was open, his eyes almost standing out on stalks. 'Maria,' he said hoarsely. 'You're . . . beautiful isn't enough. There must be a better word. You're . . . everything!' He shrugged helplessly. Maria felt tears come to her eyes and she swallowed hard. Vincent went hot, then cold as she ran a few steps towards him then leaned down to kiss his cheek, but when she straightened up again, her eyes and voice were hard. 'Right. Are you ready?'

At the Droit de Seigneur, Paris stood behind the roulette wheel. His mother and father, he'd managed to find out, were following up a lead on Hans Mueller, the son who had drowned, and had travelled up the coast to interview the fisherman who had pulled the young lad from the water.

Unlike Vincent, Paris's tuxedo fitted him perfectly, accenting his lean, tall body, deepening his brown hair and eyes and giving him an added maturity that belied his tender years. At the moment his gaze was fixed on the small white ball bouncing around like a thing demented before settling into the black sixteen spot. He groaned silently and looked across at his sister.

Gemma was wearing shimmering black in a fourteen-tiered dress that glittered with her slightest movement. Her short cap of hair had been teased by a top hairdresser to curl to a point at each cheek and in the middle of her forehead. Her make-up was dramatic, all deep red lips and heavy dark eyes. She looked young, and at the moment impossibly alive. Paris felt a stab of panic as she eagerly thrust out a stack of chips on to the red two spot. Don't get the bug, sis, he prayed silently. Dad'll kill me!

They had arrived yesterday and checked into the best hotel, Paris learning only an hour later that they they were relying on one of Gemma's credit cards. He himself had all but emptied his bank account and had a fistful of traveller's cheques, but he hoped that their money would run out soon and force them to leave. Monaco, and the casino in particular, made him nervous.

At first it had been intriguing. They'd toured the

281

harbour on one of the tourist trips, tried out French croissants and coffee, listened with wide eyes to the gabble of languages around them – French, Portuguese, German and Italian – and dressed up for gourmet meals at the best and priciest place in town. Used to the Hollywood syndrome, where everybody was involved in 'the business' to some degree, as producer, agent, starlet or whatever, Paris found the cosmopolitan sophistication of Monte Carlo an eye-opener. In fact, with all the water-skiing, powerboat-racing and topless beaches, Paris might never have wanted to leave.

Except that tonight they had come to D'Arville's casino.

Paris had not known quite what to suspect. Certainly there was no sign of the man himself. Gemma had insisted they go to the bar first, where she'd ordered a Bloody Mary. 'The colour will go with my lipstick, stupid,' she'd hissed when Paris had raised one dark brow at her. He himself ordered a beer, both of them turning to look around. The sight of the world's wealthiest people, all competing to lose their money faster than anybody else, was an awesome sight, but Gemma's head had swivelled ceaselessly. 'I don't see him,' she'd hissed after ten minutes, and Paris, bored and nervous, had shrugged and turned to pump the barman. 'Hey, who owns this place?'

The barman obliged, not only with the owner's name, but also with the information that Monsieur D'Arville was in New York. Whilst Gemma fumed, Paris had to bite back the laughter.

They'd travelled the ocean to come here, even stopping off in New York, and found they needn't have bothered. It was hilarious. Gemma, however, didn't appreciate the irony, and to prevent the evening becoming an entire waste had promptly stalked to the nearest roulette table, with Paris following more cautiously.

At first she had won – almost ten thousand dollars – and her youthful delight had even made the world-weary oil sheiks and professional gamblers raise a smile. But then came the losing streak. The ten thousand dwindled and went, and she was back to using her own money. As the total of losses mounted up, Paris began to fidget, at one point even shouldering his way around the table, leaning over her shoulder and whispering in her ear that perhaps it was time to quit.

For his brotherly concern and trouble she had given him a vicious fulminating stare that had sent him away, smiling ruefully. 'OK. But you're the one who's gonna have to face Dad,' he'd warned her. Now, ten minutes later, she had lost another two thousand dollars.

Paris sighed and moved away. Hell, he didn't have to watch! Suddenly he stopped, jerking like a marionette whose strings had just been pulled. Not ten feet away, dressed in flame orange, was the most beautiful woman in the world. Paris swallowed hard, ridiculously unable to move. The girl turned and pulled off a gold lace shawl and handed it to a small, ugly man by her side. The contrast between the two

283

was comical. Paris found himself moving towards her, but was not aware of his feet supporting his weight.

Sensing a tall presence moving in on her, Maria Alvarez spun around, expecting her father. Her mouth opened ready to spit venom, then, as her head completed the ninety-degree turn, her eyes froze in shock as they met those of the handsome young boy who was staring at her with an absorbed, almost stunned expression. For a long, long moment, Paris Harcourt and Maria Alvarez did nothing but stare at one another. Then Paris managed a smile, nothing more than a bare movement of his lips. 'Hello,' he whispered.

Maria blinked, her mind grappling for a hold on reality. Something had happened. She was sure of it. But what? 'Hello,' she whispered back.

Vincent turned and looked up at the handsome face, frowning deeply. His small pudgy hand tugged at her dress as a child might tug on his mother's apron strings.

Maria looked down, focusing her eyes on Vincent with some difficulty. But the sight of his jealous face snapped her back to reality. She had a job to do, and she needed Vincent.

'*Señor*.' She nodded coolly at Paris, smiled brilliantly down at Vincent and then moved away, as regal as a queen.

Paris turned and stared after her, his eyes wide and pained, his thoughts chaotic. As he watched, her ugly companion condescendingly patted her hand, and he saw her smile at him vaguely, the meaning seemingly unmistakable.

Just another beautiful woman with another rich but ugly man.

Paris's young face suddenly tightened, and the eyes that followed her progress around the room were suddenly those of an adult. In a city like Monte Carlo, there were probably many such sights. It meant nothing. It was just a chance meeting – a little unpleasant, certainly disappointing, but nothing to get het up about.

He should just forget her. He knew that.

But he also knew that he wouldn't be able to.

CHAPTER 17

New York

Yesterday's copy of the *New York Sentinel* fluttered in the breeze blowing down a cramped and filthy alley, its slight rustle waking the boy whose torso it covered.

Travis blinked and stared at the garbage can next to him, which was buzzing loudly. The sound puzzled him, reminding him of the weird sound-effects in science-fiction movies. Too tired to be curious, he lay back again on the cracked concrete and rubbed his eyes with a hand grown unbelievably dirty. He hadn't realized just how dirty you could get when you didn't wash. Just a week ago, he'd have been getting out of a warm bed and taking a shower with hot water and soap and shampoo.

He closed his eyes, but only for a moment. It was a luxury to do something so rash – that much he had already learnt. Instead he tucked himself into a foetal position and licked his dry lips.

Even something as simple as finding a drink of

water had been an obstacle at first. Public toilets were the only answer, and their squalor and chlorine-filled water often made him vomit.

But after only a week on the streets he now knew which train-station toilets had the best water. Much good that that would do him now. Only an unlocked staff door had saved him last night at Grand Central, when one of his biological father's lackeys had been waiting for him. How they knew he was there, he was not sure. He supposed Wayne had enough money to pay untold numbers of derelicts to spy on him and report his every movement.

Travis glanced up as the buzzing in the can seemed to rise in pitch, making the battered galvanized can vibrate. Still he was too tired to be curious.

Besides, he had more pressing matters on his mind. Like – what was he going to do for water now? He'd already learned that café and bar owners weren't too happy about kids wandering in and using their facilities without buying a drink.

Buying a drink!

Travis grinned in the cold early morning dawn, a wide grin which barely hid the desperation that clawed continually at his innards. He was not cut out for this, he thought, without a trace of self-pity – he was beyond that now. He was merely thinking straight. All his life he'd been able to rely on two rich and successful parents.

He'd read in yesterday's paper, gleaned from a city wastebin, that the famous Valentine Copeland, and his ex-model wife, were still in the intensive care unit at City Memorial, suffering from smoke inhalation. At first he'd been elated just to know they were still alive. Not that he could visit them – his father would have the hospital staked out.

But after the first euphoria he began to worry. Why were they still in intensive care? *Had* there been brain damage?

The thought of Val and Veronica, so near yet so far, made him want to weep. But he knew that if he gave in to that impulse he was lost.

But Travis was coming to the end of his tether. While Val and his mother hadn't exactly spoiled him, they certainly hadn't been stingy with him either. His schools had all been civilized, fee-paying schools, the kind where pupils still opened doors for their teachers. His job had been in a rough-and-tumble world, but one with its own camaraderie. And even at work he had so far merely watched as others reported what had happened, hoping one day to do the same. He'd never personally been present just after a woman took a butcher's knife to her husband, or when a fifteen-year-old girl had been gang raped.

Nothing in his life before had prepared him for the cut-throat world that existed on New York's streets.

Travis frowned and then tensed as he heard a sound. A human sound. He'd been quick to learn the difference between the sound of a cat or ferreting rat and that made by a man or woman. Cats and rats weren't dangerous.

Cautiously, as the shuffling noise came closer, he lifted his head from where it was resting on his arm

288

and peered around the noisy garbage can, slowly releasing his breath when he saw who it was.

An old man was slowly working the alley, poking in the litter and dumped waste and checking the garbage cans. Travis had seen him around before.

Bill, or Will, something like that. He looked black, but Travis knew that it was only years of accumulated dirt that made him appear so. He'd made that mistake before, his first night out.

Travis glanced up as the old man reached the buzzing garbage can and lifted the lid.

Immediately a swarm of flies, like a black mass of smoke, rose into the air, and the stench of rotting meat fouled the breeze. Travis gritted his teeth to stop from retching. He had managed to find a half-eaten Chinese meal yesterday, and he couldn't afford to throw it up now. Already his legs were weak, and whenever he moved he felt light-headed. Starvation was setting in.

'Hey!' the old man yelped, the word a bark of alarm as he spotted Travis. Travis jumped and looked up just in time to see the old man relax. 'Oh, it's only you.'

Travis wasn't sure whether to laugh or cry. In this town, where practically anybody would slip a knife between your ribs to steal your booze, he wasn't sure that it was a good thing for this old man to consider him harmless.

'Nothing much up here, is there?' the old man grumbled. 'Why'd you sleep up here, kid?'

Travis slowly sat up. There was not much point

289

staying down – he would certainly never sleep. In fact, he supposed he slept on average three hours a night, if that, and lord, he was tired. 'There's nobody around here,' he explained wearily. The old man snorted derisively.

'Tha's a fac'. Too windy, boy. See – it's open down that end. There's plenty of streets round here that ain't. You're still green, boy – that's all. You'll learn. If'n you live long enough.'

Travis smiled weakly. 'I dare say.'

His companion grunted and then moved to the wall opposite the young boy. The space was so narrow that barely four feet seperated them. Travis watched the old man burrow his butt into the wall and slowly slide down, one hand on the booze in his charity overcoat, the other on whatever was in his second pocket. A knife, probably.

The old man's eyes, a washed-out grey, stayed fixed on him as his backside settled on to the concrete with a bump. Perhaps, Travis thought with another wide smile, he looked a little bit dangerous after all.

'Wha's funny, kid?'

Travis's grin faded quickly as he settled himself more comfortably against his own wall and pulled the insulating newspapers more firmly over his chest. Nevertheless, he still shivered in the five o'clock chill. He was acquiring a cough and wondered, bleakly, how far away pneumonia was. Probably not that far. 'Nothing's funny,' he finally answered, his voice perfectly flat. 'Nothing at all.'

'Ain't that the truth.' The old eyes watched him, taking in the thin, useless windcheater and the haphazard way he'd pulled the papers around him. Seventeen, no older, the old man thought. Well-spoken, gentle, useless. He'd not last a month.

Travis looked up as the old man sighed, extracted a bottle of meths from one pocket and took a swig. Travis stared. So it was true – they really *did* drink meths! He'd always thought that that was just typical TV bullshit. He shuddered as he wondered what the liquid was doing to the old man's insides.

'Look, kid, if you're gonna rely on newspaper to keep warm, you gotta do it right. Look.' The old man got painfully to his knees and crawled over to Travis, who had tensed automatically at the old man's approach. 'The idea is to take off your coat. . . this thing –' he nudged the windcheater with a contemptuous finger '– and then your shirt. You wrap the paper over your bare chest, see, then put on your shirt.' The faded grey eyes glanced up into blue ones to see if he was making any impression. Satisfied by the boy's alert and interested look, he nodded, mumbled something, wiped his nose on his sleeve, then sat back on his heels. 'Then you put on another layer of paper, then your coat. See, to get it in layers. It's layers an' stuff that keeps you warm. Then, finally, you pull papers over you, but you gotta roll into 'em, so that the wind can't blow up 'em and get at yer kidneys. Got it?'

Travis nodded, and then blinked, feeling absurd tears begin to make his vision waver. It was stupid, but he had to swallow hard before he could speak. This old man, with his rank body odour and breath that could make him feel ill from a hundred paces, was the first person to do anything for him that could even remotely be called a kindness.

'Thanks,' he said gruffly.

The old man grunted, then lifted off a few pages of the newspaper still covering Travis's legs. 'OK boy. Any time. Course, the best thing you can do is find a coat like this 'un.' He plucked at his own heavy serge khaki coat, but was too busy reading his paper to tell Travis how to go about getting one.

'Hmm, not much going on in the world, is there?' the old man muttered, crossing his legs at his ankles and turning a page. He looked so dignified that Travis had to fight the absurd desire to just laugh and laugh until he died.

A cop car crawled past the entrance to the alley a hundred yards away but didn't stop. Nevertheless, Travis tensed, his eyes on the blue and white vehicle until it had totally disappeared. When he glanced back at his companion, the grey eyes on him wore a knowing look.

'Look, kid, lemme give you some advice that'll really do you some good. Go home – no matter what the old gal or old man has done to yer, it can't be worse than this.'

Travis glanced away. 'It's not like that.'

The old man shrugged. 'Suit yourself.'

Travis wanted to explain, feeling a very human gratitude to this old man for sharing just these few minutes with him. Loneliness was another thing he'd never had to deal with before. But before he could speak he began to cough, then couldn't stop. For long minutes he struggled to catch his breath, and when he did, he didn't dare say anything in case it provoked another attack.

It was mid-July, and during the day he sweated, but at night . . .

Instead of talking, he glanced down and leaned forward into his chest, trying to keep warm. As he did so, his eyes met the headlines on the fourth page of the newspaper. It was a story about his parents. The reporter, like himself, had come to the conclusion that the Copelands' chances of survival did not look good. A doctor at the hospital had given some meaningless quotes.

There was no mention of him, listing him as missing or otherwise. His father's influence must be even stronger than he'd thought.

Travis gave a small moan and turned his head, the rough brick of the wall scraping his cheek. The old man looked up, his gaze skidding off the young boy's look of utter despair, and went back to reading his paper. He wanted nothing to do with despair. 'Here, you oughta read the personals. That's always good for a laugh.' The gruff voice dragged him back from the dark yawning pit, and Travis grabbed the lifeline eagerly.

'Yeah?' He tried to inject at least a particle of interest in his voice.

'Yeah.' The old man grinned, revealing rotting

teeth and an oddly blue tongue. 'Listen to this. "Rosy-face, your loving Dido needs you. Come home. Kissy-Sue." Ain't that hilarious?'

Travis began to laugh. He was not sure why – he didn't find it particularly funny, but for a short while the red-brick alley with wall-to-wall rats, flies and despair was filled with the laughter of an old man and a half-dead young kid.

Then, somewhere in the distance a clock chimed, and the old man sighed, getting stiffly to his feet. 'Gotta go, kid. Here.' He threw the personal column page at him. 'Have a laugh on me. You need it. And take care of that cough, kid.'

Travis blinked, feeling more alone now than he had last night. 'OK. I will. Mind how you go, won't you?'

The old man held up a hand and shuffled off. Travis shook his head, then looked up quickly as the old man turned back.

'There's a hot-dog man over on Fifth and Main, usually sets up about seven o'clock. If he has any left-overs from last night, he's good for a touch-up.'

Travis smiled with lips that wobbled. 'Thanks. I'll be there.'

'Be early. There's always a lot of people waiting to give him the touch-up, son.'

Travis watched the old man turn the corner, the wind blowing the long, matted grey hair back from his face for just a few seconds. Travis wondered if the man was even forty.

The flies settled back to their garbage can. Travis

wondered idly where they got in. Another cop car crawled by and ignored him. He was sure that his father had several cops on his payroll, for once or twice he'd had to dodge cops who'd seemed to be coming specifically after him. Of necessity, he'd become a master at finding escape holes – down storage drains, through the air-conditioning tunnels in stores, out of skylights and up tenement fire-escape ladders.

But the constant need for vigilance was wearing him down. He could feel it, actually sapping his vital energy. He didn't mind the hunger so much – after a while you got used to the gnawing, empty pain. He didn't even mind sleeping rough; you could get used to the cold too. Keeping out of the way of the street gangs, the perverts, the men in fancy cars looking for a boy for the night, and keeping your head down twenty-four hours a day was wearing on the nerves, but Travis could live with it. The loneliness, the constant draining despair of feeling unwell but needing to keep moving, moving all the time, also took its toll, but they were not in any immediate danger of hammering the final nail in his coffin.

No, it was the bone-numbing weariness, and the certain knowledge that the hounds were closing in, that made Travis want to weep. He could trust no one. Even now, he knew, that old man might be holding out his dirty mittened hand for a pay-off to the man in the blue suit, or the scarred man, or any other of the many minions in his father's pay. Any second the handsome blond man, or the ape with the scar, could walk down the alley from either end, sandwiching him in, closing in like the pair of jackals they were.

Travis shook his head in silent negation as his hands fell limply on to the newspaper. He looked down and read the first message. 'Lost – beige pekinese, answers to the name of Jenkins. $500 reward.'

Five hundred dollars, Travis slowly repeated aloud. What would he give for five hundred dollars?

The day of the fire, after finally losing the ape with the scar after a prolonged and bitter chase, he had discovered he had exactly thirteen dollars and fifty-seven cents on him. That had gone within a day. Stupid – stupid, stupid, stupid! If only he'd known seven days ago what he knew now.

No – no, he couldn't give in to despair. He couldn't. His father's army of cops, informers and paid narks had slowly moved him down, down from suburb to suburb, down from where the rich folk lived to where the wealthy folk lived, to where the workers lived, to finally this place – not Brooklyn, not the Bronx, but somewhere close.

How long before they had him cornered to just a few blocks? It was hard to say just how they had done it. There was no one thing Travis could remember, for the past week had gone by like a nightmarish blur.

At first he had tried the charity shelters. The first night he had even settled down for the night, when whispers in the corridor had alerted him. Only by squeezing through a narrow window in the back of the soup kitchen had he escaped the elegant blond man, who had been busy searching the beds with a small flashlight. Travis had just caught a glimpse of the priest counting a wad of notes as he crawled past the window.

After that, he had tried bus stations, train stations, anywhere where it was warm, but always there was someone waiting for him. Only his paranoia and the fact that shock and grief had made him gaunt and pale and unlike the smiling, healthy boy in the photographs his father's army carried of him had allowed him to escape. That, and the fact that so far he had been extraordinarily lucky.

But Travis knew luck couldn't last for ever.

He glanced down at the paper again, seeking a distraction from his grim thoughts, and his own name leapt up off the page. He blinked, pulled the paper closer to him, and read the ad.

'Travis. You are tired. You are hungry. By now you are probably ill. You can stop all that by going to Bloomingdale's. I have a man waiting for you there, twenty-four hours a day. Father.'

Travis stared at it, shook his head, looked up and down the alley, at the buzzing garbage can, then back at the paper. He read it again, each word hammering cruelly into his head. 'Ill. Tired. Hungry. You can stop it . . .'

Travis threw the paper away and got to his feet quickly. Too quickly, as it turned out.

He groaned, leaned against the wall and waited for the alley to stop spinning around him. Staggering along against the wall, he began to search for other, older papers. He found Wednesday's. Feverishly he looked through the papers, grimacing at the vomit and tomato ketchup stains caking the pages together, and found the personal ads. There it was.

'Travis. You can't go to the shelters. You can't go to the cops. You can't go to the paper. You can't go to friends. You can only come to me. Father.'

Travis looked up from the paper, his gaze meeting an advertising billboard for Marlboro cigarettes.

Slowly the paper slid from his nerveless fingers. He moved, staggering slightly as his weakened knees gave out periodically. In the trash from an apartment building he found Tuesday's edition.

'Travis. I have a yacht waiting for you. Champagane. French food. A Queen Anne bed. Beautiful girls. Anything you want, Travis. Anything. Father.'

He dug deeper into the bins, coming up with Monday's. It was as far back as he could go. The weekend *Sentinel* didn't carry personal ads. As he searched through the paper, wet from the rain, the words kept swimming around inside him, conjuring up cruel hallucinations of a warm bed with real sheets, food that was hot and properly cooked, nourishing and appetising.

He was almost crying by the time he found the right page and his father's first message.

'Travis. Don't run. Please don't make me hunt you down. Father.'

Travis slowly sat down on the concrete steps, ignoring the grafitti that covered the walls around him, and began to laugh.

A roadsweeper began to whistle, a tune from one of the current Broadway hits, and Travis found the laughter turning to a fit of coughing. Without the protection of his paper blankets he was shivering hard, and he hugged himself with his arms as he waited for the coughing fit to pass.

The roadsweeper, a middle-aged man with a beer-belly and nicotine-yellowed hands, stopped whistling and leaned on his broom to stare at him with mildly curious eyes. Travis glanced at him, then away again. It must be approaching seven. He would find the old man's hot-dog stand, then rustle up a copy of today's paper. He stood up and carefully negotiated the concrete steps, ignoring the sweeper who began to whistle again. He didn't notice the man extract from his yellow cart a walkie-talkie, and thought nothing of it when the whistling behind him suddenly stopped.

At Fifth and Main, Travis found himself across the street, staring at a sea of derelicts. Bag ladies shoved elbows with children of no more than ten or twelve. He could not even see the street vendor, who must surely be somewhere in the middle.

For a long, helpless moment he stared at them, wondering if he felt strong enough to try and fight his way through. Then he remembered reading about a wino getting knifed for doing just such a thing. His body had lain on the sidewalk for hours, people just stepping over him, before a coroner's van had finally arrived.

Travis turned and walked away. He walked slowly because his chest felt congested and every few minutes he had to stop and gasp for air, but he knew just where he was going. Across the street, parked in a green sedan, Cyril Francis had a good idea too. He glanced at his watch, put the car into first, and idled along, ten yards behind the boy, talking into a radio.

Travis paused on one corner, scanning the newspaper stall for the right customer. He ignored the secretaries on the way to work, and the cab drivers picking up their six or seven papers for the day's reading between fares. He made his move only when a man in a thousand-dollar suit and crocodile briefcase purchased a copy of the *Sentinel*. Quickly, Travis followed him, praying he didn't hail a cab before checking the stock exchange and business section. He didn't.

Turning the pages as he walked, somehow managing to read and not cannon into people as he went, the tall, ginger-haired man who was his 'mark' finished the pink-sheeted 'city news' section, and, leaving the rest of the paper unglanced at, dumped it straight on to the side of the street before hailing a cab. Travis, a few steps behind, picked it up and walked to the nearest wall, out of the way and out of the wind.

It made a wonderful change to handle a clean newspaper, still smelling of printer's ink and cheap paper.

He managed to find the personal column at the first try.

'Travis. There is not a place that you can hide where I won't find you. Don't drag this thing out. You know it's only a matter of time. Father.'

Slowly Travis let the paper fall out of his hands. As he did so, a green car suddenly swerved across the traffic, the squeal of other cars' brakes and the honking of horns making him look up.

Through the windscreen, he saw the lean dark face with its white scar, and for a brief moment in time he couldn't move. Then he swivelled, moving a step forward, only to find the blond with the suit not ten feet away, shaking his head with a sad smile.

Travis swallowed hard, feeling his stomach lurch and the pavement do the same beneath his feet. He turned around. He didn't recognize the men waiting behind him, but he picked them out from the gathering crowd of early-morning New Yorkers with ease. He glanced back at the car. The man with the scar was out of it now, but only leaning against the bonnet, totally at ease.

Puzzled, Travis, still with his back against the wall, began a crab-like walk sideways, away from the blondman to where a narrow loading alley ran alongside a huge department store. He kept a wary eye on the two, heavy-set men to his right, but they did nothing but watch him with bland, merciless eyes.

Travis glanced back at the blond man as, with his hands flat against the bricks, he groped for the opening. The man hadn't moved.

Travis frowned. What the hell was going on? Why didn't they jump him, for Pete's sake? Tension

301

throbbed at his temple, but suddenly his hand found open air, and with one last look he slipped into the alley and began to run, his breath coming in short, laboured gulps.

The alley curled around, narrowing as the huge bulk of the department store gave way to pitiful offices. A few yards on Travis found himself facing a twenty-foot wall. He stopped and stared at it. It was perfectly smooth and without any footholds or crumbling brick. Similiar walls boxed him in at his left and right. No fire escapes. No boxes or garbage cans to climb up – nothing.

He turned, expecting them to be right behind him, but the way back was clear. Except he could not go back; belatedly he realized that he had done just what they wanted him to do. Slowly, he began to back up, closing his eyes as the wall behind him stopped his despairing retreat. He was trapped.

He half turned into the wall, fighting the cowardly desire to cry, and waited in the darkness of his closed eyes, coughing occasionally, shivering in the shadows where the rising sun could not reach him.

He was almost asleep on his feet when he heard the first sound, but he didn't open his eyes. He didn't want to see. He didn't want to know. He was tired – oh, dear God, he was so tired. He felt ill – not in pain, but ill in a sapping, relentless way that made breathing hard, standing difficult, and fighting impossible.

He should have known he couldn't fight a man like Wayne D'Arville. He should have known!

He could feel a presence close by – and suddenly

302

knew why the others had waited. He could smell the expensive aftershave, could hear the soft, regular breathing, could almost feel the heat from his father's skin warming him.

He flinched when he felt a hand on his face, but the touch was surprisingly gentle. Fingers curled around his chin, forcing him to face forward. A silent but irresistible command had his eyes opening.

As he looked into eyes as blue as his own, he cringed back and made one small sound, too low to be a groan, too weak to be a moan.

Wayne was leaning down to his son's slightly lesser height, his eyes searching Travis's face with an intense power and concentration that made him shake in the deepest recesses of his soul.

Wayne saw at a glance the boy's pallor, the thinness of his shivering body and the bruised, defeated defiance in his eyes. Grimly he shook his head, his hand still curled possessively around his son's face. 'Travis,' he said softly, chidingly. 'Travis. You're going to have to learn to obey me.'

CHAPTER 18

Monte Carlo

'Sir, I think you should see this.'

Wayne looked up from the ledgers in front of him, meeting the worried eyes of Antoine Dorlhac, the newest manager of the Droit de Seigneur. He was a small man with snapping brown eyes, a voice to match and a brain composed like a steel trap. At the moment he was hopping nervously from foot to foot. 'What is it?'

'A winner. A big winner. Every night for a week now.'

'Claude?'

Antoine Dorlhac shrugged. 'He says he cannot see how they are cheating.'

'What are they playing?'

'*Vingt-et-un.*'

Wayne shut the ledger with a snap. His mind was not really on the work anyway, but on the boy safely tucked away in his newly purchased residence at La Turbie. Since it appeared his son was determined to be difficult, his father's old villa had not been nearly secure enough, and the events of the last week were never far from Wayne's mind.

He wished Sebastien were there to help, and then was glad he wasn't. His manager said that Sebastien had received a call from a woman, and had returned to London. Probably a secretary at one of the mental hospitals. It was for the best. He couldn't explain it, but Wayne was sure that if Sebastien ever turned against him, it would mean the end.

Almost a week ago to the day, a team of doctors had been waiting for them on board the *Travis Helm*. Strangely quiet though he was, the boy had let his eyes sharpen curiously on the huge, luxurious yacht. It had been a strange meeting of man and machine; the yacht, gleaming, white and impressive, bore no affinity to the dirty, ill and struggling boy after which it had been named.

Travis had let himself be led from the alley in New York without a word, his body leaning heavily against that of his father. He had barely glanced at Frank Parton or the two others, but as he moved past Cyril Francis, who was holding open the green sedan's door, a long, level look had passed between them. Wayne had felt insanely jealous for a moment, but had shrugged it off. He had no more use for Cyril, and Travis would never see him again.

Travis had not been able to remain immune to the luxury of the yacht – how could he? The previous owner had been one of the growing number of Arab sheiks, grown bored with his new toy. Everywhere was the gleam of real brass polished to a high sheen by a loving crew, and fire-resistant mahogany, teak, English walnut and pale ash had been lavished in all of the twelve state rooms. The medical equipment had been set up in the best of the suites. Travis found himself being bathed in a claw-toed bathtub with real gold taps, passive and pale as two male nurses stripped off his stained and filthy clothes. He'd barely glanced at Wayne, who'd watched the procedure with careful eyes.

Slowly, as the dirt washed off, Wayne had begun to relax. The boy was handsome, lean, strong, intelligent – a worthy son. Hadn't his ingenuity at avoiding his men for as long as he had proved it? Dr Lomax, whom he'd poached from a top Paris clinic, completed the initial examination. There had been no surprises; exhaustion, the early stages of malnutrition, and bronchial trouble that might have become pneumonia if it had been left untreated a day or two longer. Travis was not awake to hear the verdict. The moment he had found himself between cool white sheets and warming blankets, he was asleep. He had, in fact, slept for most of the ocean voyage back to Europe.

Only for short periods during the last two days had he been allowed up. It had been the first time they had sat down to breakfast together. The meal had consisted of scrambled eggs, crisp bacon, French toast, grapefruit, muesli, coffee and biscuits.

For a long while Travis had just stared at the food

set out on warmed Wedgwood china, silently finger
ing the stiff white linen tablecloth and napkins. Then
he had looked up and across, meeting Wayne's gaze
head-on for the first time.

The eyes were hooded and bland, but Wayne was
not fooled. He could easily sense the waves of
antipathy shimmering across the laden table. But
Travis had eaten – slowly at first, then ravenously.
Neither had spoken, but the moment the male nurse
came to take him back to his bed Wayne had gone to
the radio room and ordered his team in Monaco to
find him a house high in the hills with an outstanding
security system. What kept people out would keep
people in.

Wayne had had to pay almost double what the Villa
du Soleil was worth, but didn't care. His team had
done wonders in the three days they had been allotted
before Wayne took up residence, putting new,
electrified gates into the twenty-five-foot wall and
chopping down any trees that grew too near the walls
and might be used in an escape bid. Wayne had
approved the extra security cameras and doubled
the guards patrolling the house.

Travis, wrapped in a quilt and seated in the back of
the black limousine with his father, had watched the
sliding electronic gates open in silence, his eyes
seeking out and finding the cameras, the Dober-
mann dogs, the polite but armed guards. Wayne
had expected him to say something sarcastic, but
the boy had merely leaned back against the seat
and closed his eyes. Wayne hoped the defeat that

307

it signified was real, but he was not counting on it. He had the strongest feeling that Travis was only waiting to rebuild his strength before trying once again to escape him.

The boy couldn't seem to understand that he was *his*, Wayne's; that he had been stolen from him, his *true* father, by a lying bitch and her male whore. He had spent hours trying to tell him he wanted only the best for him, and was interested only in improving the standard of his life, but the boy was stubbornly silent, refusing even to talk except for a few truculent syllables . . .

'We're down twenty thousand and still losing,' Antoine Dorlhac said now as he followed the towering figure down the white-washed corridor, dragging Wayne's impatient thoughts back to the present.

'How long has it been going on?'

'An hour. Maybe a few minutes more.'

'What's the average size of his bet?'

'*Her* bet,' Antoine corrected grimly. 'A hundred to two hundred francs. Petty stuff. If she wasn't winning so consistently I'd swear she was an amateur. She doesn't have the confidence or the familiarity with the chips and cards of a true professional.' The little man shrugged. 'I cannot figure it out.'

'Her accomplice?'

Antoine snorted. 'Must be seen to be believed.' The low hum of voices, the clacking of dice and the whine of roulette wheels that percolated through the casino twenty-four hours a day became louder as Wayne stepped behind the curtain. 'Room four,'

Antoine murmured, glancing around to make sure everything was in perfect order. It was. Managing the Droit de Seigneur was Antoine's biggest break to date, and he was determined not to blow it. Besides, there was something about his good-looking employer that scared him witless.

Wayne moved quickly but with unconscious grace through the rooms, his eyes scanning and taking in every detail around him. He saw but paid no particular attention to a fresh-faced young man, obviously an American, nor the girl with him, though she was startlingly pretty, with an elfin face, wide dark eyes and clinging silver dress.

Gemma nudged Paris in the ribs, making him spill his drink, but her eyes never left those of the man making his way through the room, stopping to chat here and there to a particularly favoured customer. His progression through the room made her think of a king and a receiving line. 'There he is,' she hissed unnecessarily, for his towering figure and copper hair were hardly inconspicuous. Paris looked at the hooded blue eyes and saw the cold ruthlessness.

Gemma looked and saw something she wanted. His height, the way he moved and wore the expensive white St Laurent suit as if born to it, made her palms itch. The blue eyes, meeting hers briefly and then moving on with just a flicker of sexual interest, was a challenge that made her mouth water. Even his age, the same experienced age as her father, made her vagina contract and flood. She wondered what he looked like stripped, imagining him walking towards

309

her, slowly removing the jacket, the shirt, bearing down on her . . . Gemma took a deep, shaky breath.

'I know what you mean,' Paris said, with a cold shiver. Suddenly he felt scared. Before, when D'Arville been safely in New York, it had all seemed like a game. An exciting but hardly dangerous game. Now Paris felt outmatched, outclassed and outrageously nervous. 'Gem, let's go home, huh? Or let Mum and Dad know we're in town.'

'You can go home if you like,' Gemma said scornfully, giving him a long, level look. 'But I'm staying right here. I wonder where he's going.'

Paris watched her as she moved away, following in the wake of that leonine head. The silver lamé dress she wore was cut low at the back, and he could see her young spine swaying subtly as she moved. Paris sighed, and quickly followed her, his interest quickly veering away from that of his sister's impetuosity the moment he spied the woman at the blackjack table.

Paris felt the breath being squeezed out of him as he moved closer. There was quite a crowd around the table now, but Paris elbowed his way in without a qualm. He could hear the excited whispers around him only vaguely and guessed there must be a big winner at the table, but couldn't have cared less about the gambling that lured so many people into a life of debt and ruin.

Instead his eyes were on her. She wore green tonight, a deep jade green that made her hair look as blue-green and glossy as a raven's wing. Green shadowed her lids, and picked up the tints in the emerald and diamond necklace she wore like a spider's web around her creamy throat. She looked up barely a moment later, her eyes finding his in the crowd, and he saw a flicker of expression shimmer in the tawny brown irises, making his spirits soar. He had not been imagining it! That tight sensation of awareness was the same as the night he had first seen her, over a week ago.

He had come back to the casino every night since, but always she evaded him. He'd been in a state of moody despair for days, convinced he'd never see her again. Gemma had given up on him in disgust, exploring the town on her own, getting invited to an inordinate number of parties. Some feat, since she was still a stranger in town.

Maria Alvarez felt her stomach begin to quiver as the boy called Paris Harcourt continued to stare at her; she'd found out his name and where he was staying the very next day after their first meeting. She'd been ready to scream in sheer frustration that first night, on learning that Wayne D'Arville was not even in the country, and she'd needed to do something to stop herself going mad. At least, that was the excuse she had given herself to justify her sleuthing spree.

She had even found out something about Paris's background. His father was a big-time hot-shot in Hollywood; she was sure she had even seen one of his films once. The girl by his side was beautiful, and if she had not known that she was his twin sister, Maria knew that jealousy would be eating into her even now.

'The next card's a two. Take it. We'll try for a five-card trick.'

The tiny voice in her ear snapped her thoughts back to the table, and reluctantly, feeling it to be an almost physical wrench, she tore her eyes away from the handsome face and indicated to the croupier to turn her another card over.

'Two of diamonds to *mademoiselle*, possible five-card trick. Dealer stands.' The two players on the right folded; an old colonel-type man opposite her took an eight and busted. 'The next card's a five. Take it.' Vincent's voice hissed in her ear. She took it and completed her trick. A small murmur of delight and admiration for her luck and daring rippled around the gathered crowd.

Her nails, painted a pearly pink, stacked her growing pile of chips. Paris stared at them, then looked back at her, realizing she was the one drawing the crowd.

Beauty and luck too. He felt a powerful punch of sexual awareness deep in his loins, and took a steadying breath. He had lost his virginity at fourteen to his mother's masseuse, a tall Swedish girl with kind eyes and knowing hands. Since then he'd had a few steady girlfriends, but nothing had prepared him for this.

Maria glanced up, feeling his eyes burning into her, and her hands trembled in front of her on the green baize.

'There he is – behind the tall brunette with the fake pearls. See him?' Antoine whispered in Wayne's ear, and Wayne found himself looking at a tiny, ugly man, with quick nervous eyes and an immobile expression that only came with intense concentration.

'What signal are they using?' he asked.

'We can't tell. Hand signals certainly – see how he keeps scratching his cheek? But no one can get near enough to him. Watch.' Antoine signalled René, one of the casino's 'watchers', dressed in a waiter's suit and carrying an empty tray. As he moved around, working his way behind the small man, Wayne saw the ugly creature spot him and slowly move around the table. René followed, a silent game of chase being played out in front of the unsuspecting crowd until Antoine ordered René off with the merest lift of his eyebrow.

'Interesting,' Wayne said, feeling the first stirrings of anger in his gut.

'It is more than that, Monsieur D'Arville. It is dangerous. I – none of us – can see how it is being done.'

Wayne moved closer, still standing at the back, watching the dwarfish man in his overlarge tuxedo. He'd already made up his mind the girl was just the mule, doing the work whilst the man was the brains behind it. Concentrating on the little man, trying to figure out how the scratching fingers conveyed to the girl whether to pass or not, it took a few seconds for the warning alarms to sound in his head, but slowly his skin began to crawl, telling him that he was being watched.

Wayne let his eyes wander around the room. All eyes were on the game, except for those of the young American girl, whose dark eyes met his boldly. Wayne's eyes narrowed on her, then passed on, recognizing the hot look, but also knowing it was not the one making his spine shiver.

Gemma's heart began to thump with a painful, wonderful power.

Finally Wayne looked to the table, confident that no one in the audience was giving him the trouble. Maria Alvarez felt the exact moment the eyes dropped on to her face, like vampirish worms burrowing into her soul, and she forced herself not to shiver. This man, this . . . monster was her father. The thought was so repellent that it made her feel nauseous, and her chin came up as she stared him down. Wayne was mildly surprised by the force of the venom in the eyes, but Maria was aware that there was not even a flicker of recognition in the assessing gaze he gave her.

'Monsieur?' Antoine prompted.

'Give Jean-Luc the nod.'

Antoine smiled happily and met the eyes of the croupier, not even needing to move his head. Jean-Luc, sociology student by day, croupier and ladies' man by night, palmed the cards expertly. Maria saw the queen of hearts that Vincent promised her turn into a five of diamonds, and frowned. In her ear, she heard Vincent swear. 'It was the queen. I know it was.'

She lost the hand, and three thousand francs. She

314

lost the next hand too, but by then she knew what was going on. Her eyes shot daggers at the handsome croupier, who gazed back at her with placid, innocent eyes.

Slowly she rose to her feet, collected her chips and turned away, ignoring the disappointed murmurs all around her, not feeling sufficiently in charge of her emotions to meet her father's no doubt crowing and triumphant gaze. She made her way slowly to the grille, where she exchanged her chips for cash.

'I don't understand what went wrong,' Vincent's whining voice complained in her ear, and she turned, looking around to find him. He was standing behind a huge umbrella plant, and she moved slowly past it, not looking at him but murmuring loud enough for him to hear her.

'I do. He ordered the damned croupier to deal from the bottom of the pack.'

Vincent watched her walk away towards the cloakroom with sad eyes. He had done his best. He could not be expected to deal with cheats, after all. They never cheated at the institute. Suddenly Vincent felt very homesick. He turned away sadly, knowing they would meet back at the hotel and discuss strategy. But Vincent, much as he admired and feared her determination and intelligence, could not see how even she could do anything about this.

Maria didn't see how she could either. As she handed over her ticket and waited impatiently for her stole, she fought against the urge to go back, march into his

315

office and claw his eyes out. The bastard had not even recognized her – his own daughter. She would make him pay. Oh, he would squirm . . .

'You're not thinking of going out alone with all that cash, I hope?'

She spun around at the sound of the voice, looking up into caressing dark eyes, for the first time in her young life knowing what it was to actually *want* a man. Not need a man. Not be grateful to a man. But *want* a man. Panicking just a little, she managed a cool shrug. 'I can take a taxi.'

'So can I. Why don't we share one?' Paris smoothly took the mink stole from the checkout woman, who nodded and turned discreetly away. He settled it lovingly across her shoulders with hands that shook, not sure what he'd do if she said no.

Maria did not say no.

In the taxi she sat nervously pleating her dress with her fingers, aware of their arms pressed together, their mutual body heat warming them, speaking all the words they could not say themselves.

At the hotel Paris watched her hand over the cash to go in the safe and then turned and walked with her to the lift. Maria did not know what to say. For the first time ever, she was not with a man for what she could get out of it.

At the door, Paris took the key from her unresisting fingers and followed her inside the dark room, locking the door behind him. She made no move to put on the light, but after a few moments their eyes became accustomed to the dark.

'What's your name?' Paris whispered.

'Maria. Maria Alvarez.'

Paris reached for her, drawing her into his arms where she fitted snugly against him. 'I love you, Maria Alvarez,' he murmured, then lowered his head to kiss her. It should have sounded ridiculous, of course – he was a young man, and, since they'd hardly met, the line was corny.

But it was not ridiculous, because Paris meant it.

And Maria knew he meant it.

Her lips were like padded, perfumed velvet under his mouth, and his arms tightened compulsively around her. Maria forgot the frustration of the night and determindly pushed aside thoughts of what she was going to do next. She felt herself moving backwards and gasped as Paris lowered his head and sucked her nipple through the green silk of her dress. Her knees threatened to buckle and she gulped in a great gasp of air.

Paris lifted her, moving to the bed and falling across it with Maria beneath him, taking his weight on his elbows. Maria arched her back, feeling the strong pressure of his thighs against hers, and felt her vagina begin to throb and itch, her thoughts becoming hazy. So this was desire. Real, honest desire.

Paris began to undress her, clumsy in his urgency, but Maria did not care, not even when she heard the expensive gown tear as the zip got stuck. Paris kissed her exposed neck, throat, shoulders and ears, working his way down her sternum to her bare breasts, where the rosy nipples stood straining to attention,

317

eagerly awaiting his smooth, warm, wet tongue. Maria buried her hands in his clean, silky hair, her neck falling back, her eyes staring at the blank ceiling. Only her occasional gasp or moan and Paris's muffled words of encouragement and adoration filled the room with sound.

Her legs jerked in helpless reaction as his fingers curled around her calves before pulling off her shoes and panties. Impatiently he shrugged out of the tuxedo, letting the expensive clothes lie where they fell.

Maria felt the soft hairs on his chest scrape across her belly as he moved lower down her body, dipping his tongue into her navel, making her knees jack-knife in reaction. Her arms came above her head and grasped the antique wooden headpiece as he firmly pushed her thighs apart and nibbled on her engorged clitoris.

Carlos had never done anything remotely like this to her. His caresses had been practised, carried out expertly under the covers, and were always over in minutes.

Already she felt as if this slow, painstaking exploration of her body had been going on for torment-ing hours. She jerked and thrashed on the bed as the first climax of her life hit her, rippling weakening waves through her belly, turning her knees, her arms, her brain to water. She was gasping, almost sobbing as Paris moved gently to lie atop her, taking her chin in his hand and kissing her deeply.

As his tongue delved deep into her mouth, so he

thrust deeply inside her, feeling her body convulse around him. Maria almost screamed. Carlos's skinny and short penis had felt nothing like this inside her. Paris seemed to invade all the way to her womb, his hot velvet shaft spearing deep into her, thrusting, plunging, making her want to buck off the bed. Instead she wrapped her legs around his hips, her heels digging into the whiter flesh of his buttocks, her actions allowing him an even deeper penetration into her body. He took advantage of it immediately, of course, their young, sweating bodies beginning to strain and buck in a wild, seemingly uncoordinated rhythm that brought ecstasy crashing through their veins minutes later, flashing light across their vision, their fused mouths filling with the silent crescendo of each other's cries.

Beyond a sensation of almost tormenting ecstasy, Maria was aware of his collapsing weight pinning her to the bed with satisfactory heaviness, and above the sound of her own laboured breathing and happy sobs she heard him moan. It was a long, long time later that they began to talk.

'You were doing well at the casino tonight,' Paris complimented her, feeling a little shy now, and choosing what he thought was a neutral subject. 'Are you always that lucky?' He was lying beside her, running his finger lightly over her forehead, down her nose and then outlining the shape of her lips.

'I wish!' she sighed, her eyelids fluttering closed as his fingers travelled on past her neck and began to

319

turn in ever decreasing circles around her breasts until they were gently nipping her nipples. 'Vincent was telling me what to do.'

'Vincent?'

'Mm. The little man I was with. He's a psychic. You know? He could tell which cards were going to come out before the croupier turned them over.'

Paris stopped his caresses and stared at her. 'Are you kidding me?'

Maria smiled. 'No. How else do you think I won?'

'What went wrong towards the end?' he asked, not sure yet whether he believed the outrageous story. Briefly Maria told him her theories and Paris shrugged. 'That's easily solved. Just go to another casino.'

'Uh-uh.' She shook her head so hard that her hair splayed across his cheek, and a firm scowl settled across her satiated, softened face. 'It has to be the Droit de Seigneur. I want to break *him*, not the casino.'

'Him?'

'Wayne D'Arville.'

Paris looked away quickly, his eyes thoughtful. His voice was almost a whisper when he said, 'What do you have against him?'

Maria slowly expelled her breath, fighting a brief battle inside herself. On the one hand it was crazy to give away her plans to a stranger. But on the other hand, with the afterglow of her climax still rippling in her body, the comfort and closeness of lying in his arms gave her a nagging urge to tell him everything.

Trust won out over cynicism. 'He's my father,' she said simply, and turned to find the dark, caressing eyes looking at her oddly. Suprisingly they were not accusatory, just puzzled and questioning.

'What did he do to you?'

It took her an hour to relate her life history, and she found it both therapeutic and cleansing to talk, glorying at the intimacy possible only between lovers. She had a man of her own now – a real lover to talk to in the early-morning hours, to love and lie beside for the rest of her life. The thought made her glow deep inside.

When she had finished he was silent for a long while. Finally, she turned to him and said, a question in her voice, 'You don't seem surprised.'

Paris took only a few minutes to explain the reason they were there. Maria gasped as she heard about her grandfather – a concentration camp *commandant*. It left her feeling oddly disorientated. She hadn't thought *anybody* could be worse than Wayne. Now she knew where her father had inherited his treachery and cruelty.

It was four o'clock in the morning before they were talked out, both knowing every intimate detail their partner could think of about childhood, home life, country, customs, personal favourites and ideals. Knowing her favourite colour was pink, his orange, they were free to discuss less interesting topics. Such as what Maria could do about her plan now.

She sighed dejectedly in the darkness. 'I don't see

what we can do. Vince can't help if they change the cards at the last second.'

Paris looked up at the ceiling, a thought formulating in his brain, and he slowly began to smile. 'You're wrong, you know,' he said softly. 'There *is* something we can do. Or rather, something the Gaming Commission can do.'

The next night they were back. Antoine called in Wayne immediately. The scene was almost an exact repeat of the night before, with the same crowd clustering around the same table. Except that now there was an extra spectator at the forefront, dressed inconspicuously in a dark suit. Only Antoine and the croupiers noticed him, and it was Antoine's dubious privilege to point him out to Wayne and explain the trouble the man's presence was causing them.

Wayne listened in tight-lipped frustration to Antoine's words, then glanced at the Gaming Commission agent and frowned. The girl was winning heavily, and there was not a damned thing he could do about it. Any misdeal by the croupier would be spotted immediately by the Gaming Commission expert, resulting in a heavy fine, maybe even a revoked licence.

Monte Carlo was proud of its 'honest' games. It gave Wayne no satisfaction at all to realize that the Commission's man could no more make out how the girl was winning than he could. 'When she's finished, have her come to my office. Keep closing the tables, and limit the bets to a hundred francs,' he ordered, leaving abruptly.

Antoine bowed and watched the tall Frenchman leave. He didn't blame him. It was a painful thing to watch.

By one-thirty Maria was willing to call it a night. She knew it would take her a week at least to break the casino, but so long as the Commission agent stayed with her she was safe from Wayne's cheating. She knew the tall pock-marked man was itching to find out how she was doing it, and knew that that alone would have him coming back tomorrow, allowing her to win another six hundred thousand dollars, unimpeded by her father's cheating dealers.

She walked to the barred grille to cash in her chips, stiffening as two men materialized either side of her. Paris, waiting by the door, quickly walked forward, but Maria herself waved him away. He watched, feeling cold and scared, as she disappeared behind a curtain that led to the offices.

Wayne looked up at the knock, nodded to the two security men to leave, and waved a hand at a chair. 'Sit down, Miss . . .?'

Maria sat. She was wearing burgundy tonight, shot through with silver. Platinum and diamonds sparkled at her wrist and throat. Wayne looked her over, a disinterested part of his brain telling him that she was truly beautiful, while another part wondered how much he'd have to pay her off.

'Cigarette?'

She shook her head, her eyes glittering with

satisfaction as he leaned back in his chair. She had him! She had him now! The glory of it made her want to leap up and dance around the room.

Wayne saw the glow banked deep in the eyes and slowly straightened. This was personal. Suddenly he knew it, though he couldn't see how, and on top of that thought came another realization. He had seen her before. He knew he had. He frowned, scraping through his memory without success. 'Tell me, Miss . . .' Again Maria remained stubbornly mute. 'Just how much is it going to cost me to have you go elsewhere?'

He reached into his desk where he withdrew a small strongbox. He opened it up with quick, precise movements, and turned it around, so that she could see the notes stacked inside.

Maria slowly leaned back and allowed herself a brief, ironic laugh. 'There's not enough money in this world that'll make me back off,' she warned him, slowly straightening her spine so that she was ram-rod-straight in the chair, her face pinched into a tight, vengeful mask. Even so, she realized that he looked more amused and curious than worried.

'I intend to come back . . .' she said softly '. . . night after night . . .' she enunciated each word clearly '. . . until I've broken this bank . . .' she slowly stood up '. . . this casino . . .' she leaned across the desk, her breasts rising and falling with every panting breath she took '. . . and you . . . Father.'

Wayne's face froze into immobility at that last

324

word. In a tidal wave, memory returned. 'Maria,' he said softly.

Maria tossed back her waving mane of black hair and walked to the door where she paused with her hand on the door handle, staring at the handsome man as still as a statue behind the imposing desk.

'See you tomorrow night for another half-million, Daddy dearest!'

CHAPTER 19

Gemma checked her appearance as she passed the seven-foot mirror that graced the reception hall of the Chemin de Fer, the hottest restaurant in town. Then she glanced into the dimly lit interior, where candles and ornate silver wall-lamps were the only providers of light. She ignored the elegant man standing behind a podium, checking her reservation. Instead her eyes turned again to the huge mirror, just to make sure she looked perfect. Tonight was the night – she could feel it in her bones. She'd dined at the restaurant three times so far, knowing that sooner or later he'd come. Everyone came to the Chemin de Fer eventually.

Her reflection reassured her that she did indeed look perfect. The dress was strapless, sleeveless, backless and almost frontless. Only two scarlet diagonal swathes cut across her breasts, revealing the sides of two perfect white orbs before meeting in a diamond cut at her tiny waist. From there, accordion pleats fell to the ground with seemingly out-of-place-modesty, the cleverness of the design only becoming apparent when she walked, for then side splits at both thighs revealed practically all of her legs. The dress came with matching scarlet panties, and was one of Valentine's latest designs. She hoped the man recovered soon – no one could design drop-dead-gorgeous gowns like Valentine. The last she'd heard, he and his wife were 'improving' in hospital, so it looked hopeful. To do the gown justice, she wore three-inch-high silver shoes, and silver and rubies glittered in her ears and in a choker at her throat. Silver eyeshadow and evening bag completed the look, along with deep ruby-red lips and dark, penetrating eyes. Yes. Tonight had to be the night.

'You have your . . . usual table, *mademoiselle*.' The concièrge finally condescended to admit her, and Gemma almost laughed aloud, so obvious was his disapproval of a lady dining alone. Well, to hell with him, and to all the rest of the sheep. She was her own woman, and if she wanted to eat alone she would. Besides, Paris was too busy with his latest little pet to accompany her. Gemma frowned as she walked into the room. There was something about this Spanish girl that was different. She could sense it when she saw them together. Paris had introduced her yesterday morning, and Gemma detected a nervousness in the girl that was unexpected. She was overly anxious to be friendly, needing too much for Gemma to like her. And as for Paris . . . He looked as if he'd been hit by an express train. Could it be love?

Her thoughts suddenly jerked to a halt, her body almost following suit. There, at the best table of the house, Wayne D'Arville was reading a menu. Her eyes made a quick inventory of the woman sitting next to him. Tall, blonde, slender. Gemma smiled. The hair was bleached, the nails and breasts were false and the body was like a beanpole. No match for her.

'*Mademoiselle*?' the waiter prompted her. Gemma gave him a short, sharp look, then left the man open-mouthed as she moved away from her paltry table tucked into a dark corner near the kitchen, and headed for the centre table stood on a small dais. Wayne caught a glimpse of dazzling scarlet out of the corner of his eye and looked around. Gemma felt the blue irises contract slightly, and shivered as he watched her approach. His hair, in the candle and lamplight, gleamed like copper, and the dark shadows deepened his cheeks and the planes of his face. Only his eyes glittered.

'Mr D'Arville,' Gemma said, ignoring the blonde completely, and holding out her hand. Wayne rose, Gemma's head falling back and back until he'd reached his full height. Wayne took her hand, kissing it continental-style. Gemma's lips parted to allow her to hiss in a harsh breath. Wayne felt her hand tremble and, still bending over her fingers, lifted his eyes to hers. He was amused by her boldness, intrigued by her dark, youthful beauty, and knew she'd probably had the restaurant staked out for weeks. 'Enchanted, Miss . . .?'

'Harcourt,' Gemma said, her left eyebrow raising in a challenging stare. 'Gemma Harcourt.'

Wayne recognized the name immediately, of course, as she knew he would, and his own eyes became less bland and much, much more interested. Gemma saw his lips twitch with something that could have been amusement or annoyance, she couldn't decide which.

'Ah,' he said softly, straightening again, not taking his eyes off her for a moment. 'I see.'

Gemma gave a delicious shudder. 'Aren't you going to invite me to join you for dinner?'

Wayne glanced at the blonde . . . what was her name . . . Frida, Frederika? She was glowering like a bad actress and Wayne gave a Gallic shrug and turned back to Gemma. 'Alas, as you can see, I am already entertaining.'

Gemma turned to glance at the blonde woman dressed in powder-blue. Insipid. Unimportant. The words were in her eyes as she turned back to Wayne, who had to agree with her. This firebrand of an American was distracting, if nothing else. 'Tell her to go,' Gemma said simply.

Wayne slowly smiled, turned to the blonde and said, 'Frida. Would you like to go?' The blonde blushed an ugly red, picked up her silk evening purse and stalked off without another word.

'Well?' Gemma prompted.

Wayne held out the chair for her, giving the waiter a brief, dismissive nod. Gemma held the menu in front of her face and took several deep gulps. She stared at the white card for a long, long while, making him wait, and only when she sensed a waiter's renewed presence did she lower it. 'I'll have the *focaccia di fiori de sambuco*, the *fermière*, followed by the *carré d'agneau de sisteron*.'

The waiter inclined his head and glanced at Wayne. 'I'll have the same.'

The waiter left. 'We're being stared at,' Gemma said.

'I'm not surprised,' he agreed mildly, his face deadpan. Gemma began to laugh, slowly at first, and then threw her head back and laughed in earnest. Wayne watched her, his eyes hooded. How young. How beautiful. How naïve. How sure of herself. How stupid.

Wayne said nothing as the food approached, his eyes glancing towards the clock. It was nearly ten. It should be happening any minute now. He turned his eyes back towards Gemma Harcourt, the irony of the situation amusing him enormously. That he should be sitting here, pursued by one Harcourt twin, while, miles away, his long arm was reaching out for her brother . . .

As Gemma flirted and tantalized, he began to smile.

Paris was whistling as he made his way to the exit of his hotel. He had wanted to move to the Beach Plaza Tower to be nearer to her, but Maria was against it. She was touchingly old-fashioned in many of her ways. He'd promised her faithfully that he'd introduce her to his parents the very next day after Wayne D'Arville disappeared down the drain of bankruptcy.

He knew they were staying just down the coast, and were doing their own research into Wayne's background. He could imagine the telegram he'd soon send them. '*Dear folks stop have met the girl I'm going to marry stop bringing her home soonest stop her name's Maria stop she's Spanish stop you'd better love her or else stop Paris.*' His daydreams were so pleasant, he didn't realize he was being watched.

Outside two men waited in a car, a third beside the hotel door. Seeing Paris in the foyer walking towards the swing doors, the third man nodded briefly at the parked car. The driver remained where he was, but the passenger, a big, heavy-set man with hooded grey eyes and hands like melons, left the car and began to stagger towards the door. He was singing something in French. Paris stepped on to the pavement and looked around for a cab, grinning as a drunk stumbled against the kerb. He couldn't understand the words of the song, but the jaunty tune and some of the man's hand gestures made guessing easy. The drunk tripped over his own feet and lurched towards Paris, who caught him, more to save himself from being knocked down than anything else. 'Hey, buddy. Take more water with it next time, huh?'

The big man gazed up at him, bleary-eyed. Just then a car pulled in across the street, and the driver leaned out, calling out, 'Claude,' and waving his hand. Paris glanced at the car, and shook his head.

'Come on, buddy. Over here. I hope your friend's in a better state to drive than you are.'

Behind him the third man left the shadows and

walked up behind Paris. The driver opened the back-seat door, still gabbling in French and wearing a helpless grin. Paris manoeuvred the drunk with surprising ease, considering his weight and state. Suddenly, just as he was pushing the man on to the back seat, he felt a shove in the middle of his own back. He grunted, falling forward into the car, where the drunk suddenly straightened, clamping a firm hand over Paris's startled face, cutting off his shout of surprise. Off balance and off guard, Paris found himself falling over the man's lap. Behind him a third man got in, shoved his legs aside and slammed the door as the car accelerated away with a squeal of tyres.

Gemma felt her tongue and cheeks turn icy cold as the lemon sorbet she had ordered numbed her face. It was delicious – tangy, freezing and refreshing. Wayne poured her her fourth glass of wine. 'Brandy?' he asked, and Gemma leaned back in her chair, twirling her long-stemmed black champagne glass.

'I'd love some.' She waited until he'd imperiously flicked his hand for a waiter and then added, 'At your place.'

He smiled and rose. 'Whatever you say.' He didn't bother to pay the bill. He had an accountant who paid his bar and restaurant bills at the end of every month, including generous tips. Gemma gave him her hand, which he held with ironic patience as she stepped down off the dais. She could hear the whispers behind her as every table they passed began to hum with yet another discussion of the spectacle.

Gemma felt as if she were walking on air.

Outside, the bus boy drove up in Wayne's Ferrari, which was midnight-blue. Wayne seated her in the bucket seat of cream leather and tipped the boy. His own seat had been modified to accommodate his height, she noticed. The engine started with a powerful roar and then softened to an idle, almost contemptuous purr. Wayne glanced at her, then at his watch. 'I have to make a stop at the casino. If I give you ten thousand pounds' worth of chips, do you think you could entertain yourself for a few minutes?'

Gemma gave him a sharp glance. 'Oh, I can do a lot of things by myself,' she assured him. 'But it's more fun with two.' This time she had succeeded in shocking him, she realized with a great wave of delight as he turned his head quickly towards her, the blue eyes wide and surprised. Then it was his turn to throw back his head and laugh.

At the casino, Maria looked around, even as she played her hand and won another four thousand. Where was he? Paris was supposed to meet her before they began playing. Only Vincent, anxious to get on with it, had insisted they start without him. 'The lady wins. *Mesdames, messieurs, faites vos jeux.*'

Maria glanced at the Commission man, who was wearing his usual puzzled, frustrated frown, and then at her watch. Paris was over an hour late. It was not like him. She stiffened as she saw her father walk in. Her eyes flew to Gemma by his side, her eyes questioning. Was Paris's sister pursuing some private idea for revenge on her own? Perhaps she was out to avenge her grandfather, Duncan Somerville. Perhaps Paris was helping *her* tonight? Yes, that must be it. Maria slowly relaxed, only to stiffen again as she found her father making his way purposefully towards her. Gemma watched, only vaguely interested, and placed her first bet. Wayne leaned forward and whispered into Maria's ear. She glanced at him, then gave a short nod to the Commission man and left the table.

Vincent, from his position behind a Grecian column, hopped nervously from foot to foot.

'Make it quick, Daddy dearest,' Maria said a few moments later, leaning against the door to his office, watching warily as he walked across the room to sit behind his desk and lift the phone. Quickly he punched out the numbers.

'Is it done?' he asked. He listened for a brief moment, then hung up. Slowly he leaned back in his chair and looked at her. She was dressed in white tonight, shot through with silver. The contrast with her long dark hair and red lips was stunning. 'I made a mistake about you,' Wayne murmured thoughtfully. 'When I saw you in that sweat shop, I thought . . .'

Maria smiled grimly. 'I know what you thought,' she spat out, the old familiar pain of rejection making her eyes fill with tears and glitter.

'Not that it matters,' he carried on, his tone still conversational. 'But how did you manage the transformation?'

'I thought you had something important to say,'

she snapped. She was in no mood for a trip down Memory Lane. 'I wish you'd hurry. I still have a hundred and fifty thousand more francs to win before calling it a night.'

Wayne leaned further back in his chair and folded his hands behind his head. 'That's what we need to talk about. You've done well, Maria, I'll grant you that. I'm impressed, and I apologize for not seeing your potential before. And if you want to, you can stay on in Monte Carlo and we can get to know one another better. But the time has come for you to take your little man and whatever extraordinary system you have, and inflict it on someone else.'

Maria sneered out a laugh. 'Save your phony apologies,' she scoffed. 'You think I'm going to let you off the hook just because you're suddenly so magnanimous? Hah!' She tossed her head, standing with her hands on her hips. 'I'm staying, and I'm bleeding you dry.'

Wayne watched her, almost smiling. She was magnificent. A pity her mother had not had more of the same spirit. Yes, things were looking up. Not only did he have a worthy son, but also a daughter worth acknowledging.

'I'm going to destroy you, Father,' Maria said, her hand on the door handle.

'I don't think so, Maria,' Wayne said softly, almost regretfully.

'Nothing will make me stop,' she warned him, but her voice did not hold quite the same conviction as it had before.

335

'Won't it?' he queried softly. 'Not even the life of Paris Harcourt, Maria. Won't that stop you?'

Maria went white, her eyes rounding into dark pools of pain. She sagged against the door as Wayne slowly walked towards her. She began to shake her head. 'No. No.'

Wayne slowly reached out and brushed a few strands of raven black hair from her face, his voice still the same gentle, regretful tone of before. 'I have your American lover,' he said softly, looking down into her dazed brown eyes. 'I'll kill him, Maria,' he continued, sounding almost friendly now. Maria moaned, and turned her face into the door, her bare shoulders shaking uncontrollably. Satisfied, Wayne turned and walked back to his desk.

'Send your little man packing,' he ordered, his voice crisp and businesslike now. Maria slowly turned around and stared at him, defeat in the slump of her shoulders. 'And return all the money you've won to me. Will you be broke then?' Numbly she shook her head. 'It wouldn't matter if you were. I'll buy you a villa here in town – or would you prefer an apartment? Never mind.' He jotted something down on a notepad as Maria continued to stare at him speechlessly. Wayne glanced up, and slowly smiled. When would his children ever learn that they couldn't fight him and win? Travis was still being difficult. Only last night he'd tried to escape the villa by hiding in the back of a laundry truck.

'Get to it, Maria,' he prompted softly. 'I want the little man gone by tomorrow – Daughter dearest.' He saw her back stiffen at his final parting shot, but she never turned around. Instead she walked stiffly out of the door like a disjointed doll, and closed the door quietly behind her.

Gemma looked up from the bouncing white ball, on which rode the last of her chips, and promptly forgot about the roulette wheel. Maria looked awful – dazed even. She left the table and intercepted the Spanish girl, who let herself be led to a quiet corner. 'What's wrong? You look like death warmed over.' Gemma stared at her. She was shaking and breathing in short, sharp jerks. 'You're not going to faint, are you?'

Maria shook her head. 'No. No . . . I . . . have things to do. Oh, God, he wouldn't really kill Paris, would he?'

Gemma's mouth fell open. 'Kill Paris? Who? What are you talking about?' Her voice was sharp, and she had to resist the urge to shake the Spanish girl by the shoulders.

'My father,' Maria said listlessly. 'He says he has Paris. And I believe him. I have to stop winning or he says he'll kill him.'

Gemma frowned. 'Who's your father? And what has your winning streak got to do with anything?'

Maria slowly raised her head and looked at Gemma with hopeless eyes, crammed with terror. 'He –' she tossed her head in the direction of the offices – 'is my father. I came here to deliberately break the bank. Oh, it's too complicated to explain now. Paris was helping me. He says he's got Paris. He'll kill him if I don't stop. I must stop. I must find Vincent and tell him to leave. Excuse me.'

Gemma watched the girl get up and walk across to where an ugly little man awaited her approach nervously. They talked for several minutes, but Gemma was already on her way to the payphone, where she rang the hotel. The clerk told her Paris had left two hours ago for the casino. Gemma hung up and looked around, but already knew that her brother wasn't there. She quickly marched towards the offices. A man moved to block her path, took one look at her face, grinned and let her pass. He had noticed his boss enter the room with her earlier, and as he heard her clacking heels recede down the corridor, he vaguely wondered what was eating her.

Wayne looked up as the door was flung open, then smiled as she slammed the door behind her.

'Where's my brother, you bastard!'

Wayne spread his hands as he got up. 'I assure you I'm not a bastard. My parents were legally married.'

'If you don't tell me, right now,' she gritted, her cheeks high with furious colour, 'I'm going to call the cops.'

'And tell them what? That I . . .' he spread his hands with innocent shock '. . . a wealthy and re-spected businessman, have kidnapped some upstart little American?' He laughed and shook his head. 'I don't think so, do you? Now . . .' His face changed in a shocking instant from laughing mockery to savage coldness. 'How about that brandy you wanted?'

'Brandy?' Gemma echoed, then gave a brief cry as

he suddenly lunged for her. She staggered backwards, falling on to the huge, overstuffed black settee behind her. Her eyes were wide and disbelieving as he stood over her, his hands already shrugging off his jacket and undoing the buttons of his shirt.

'No!' she screamed, struggling to sit up, but with one hand on her sternum he easily pushed her back, his hand fumbling now with the zip to his trousers. His eyes were like blue diamonds – hard and without feeling – and Gemma felt the first waves of numbing shock begin to wash over her. This wasn't true. It couldn't be happening. Not to her! 'I'll scream,' she whispered as he knelt over her, but he only shrugged, fumbling to free himself from the trousers.

'Scream all you like,' he offered carelessly. 'No one will hear you out there. And no one will be allowed to interfere with us even if they do.'

Gemma rammed her hand upwards, trying to hit his face, but her reach was too short. She gasped, and then began to struggle furiously as his hands pulled down the scarlet silk of her panties. 'No. *No!*'

She felt her legs being pulled apart, and struck out wildly, her clenched fists glancing a harmless blow off the solid muscle of his shoulder. He leaned over her, yanking her hands together and holding them in a tight, numbing grip. She was going to be raped! The thought hit her like a cold tidal wave of drowning water. The fear, the revulsion was something she had never felt before.

With a cry of utter panic, she raised her knee. Luck was on her side. Her timing turned out to be perfect.

Wayne grunted and turned red in the face as her knee connected with her groin. Still panicking, Gemma shoved him aside, but he was too big to move. Scrabbling frantically, she wriggled under him, biting his hand hard as he reached for her.

Then she was sprinting for the door, pulling her panties back up into place. She rushed from the casino, uncaring of the spectacle she must have made. She hailed the first taxi she could find, and only then, in the back seat, did the numbing fear begin to recede. But she knew the memory of it would stay with her forever.

Back in the casino, Wayne slowly recovered and straightened his own clothing. So the bitch had been lucky. He shrugged. He had more important things to think about. He wanted to get back to Travis. They were going to reach an understanding sooner or later, even if it killed them both.

Safe in her hotel room, Gemma nevertheless checked the lock. She had to think. Paris was in danger. No matter about her, she was all right. She'd nearly been raped, but she was alive. It was Paris who needed her. She went straight for the phone, asking for the number of the hotel where she'd discovered her parents were staying and asked to be put through to their room number.

'Hello?'

'Daddy.'

'Gemma?'

'Daddy.' She was crying uncontrollably now, the sound of his voice breaking down her precarious calm.

'Gemma! Gemma, what is it? What's going on?' He was shouting now. Suddenly her mother's voice came over the line. The sound of the soft, drawling southern accent, so soothing and familiar, calmed her once more.

'Gemma, honey,' Oriel coaxed. 'What is it? Tell us, honey.'

'P-P-Paris,' she stammered, wiping her eyes furiously with her fingers. 'Paris,' she said again. 'Something t-terrible's happened.'

'Oh, God.' That was her father's voice again. 'There's been an accident? Swimming, or something else?' For a moment Gemma was totally confused, and then remembered that her parents still thought they were at home.

'No. We're here in M-Monte Carlo.'

'What are you doing here? No, never mind. Just tell us what's happened to Paris?' Kier sounded grim and angry, and Gemma began to shake.

'He's g-gone.'

'Gone?' The word came from her mother, whispered in a tone of such utter despair that Gemma realized immediately that Oriel had misunderstood.

'No, not d-dead,' she almost screamed. 'Gone. Kidnapped. By Wayne D'Arville.' Haltingly, she managed to get out the whole story and give them the name of their hotel.

'Gemma, honey, listen to me.' Her mother's voice came back a few moments later and she knew that her parents had been discussing strategy away from the phone. 'I want you to stay where you are. We'll come over to you. Understand?'

'Yes.'

'Good. Lock yourself in. Your father and I will be there as soon as we can. We're leaving now, right now. Do you understand me, Gem?'

'Yes,' Gemma said again and hung up abruptly. She must have a bath. She felt so dirty.

CHAPTER 20

Sebastien looked up, his eyes softening as Lilas walked towards him, wrapped only in a very see-through white peignoir. 'Here you go.' She put down a cup of steaming coffee in front of him. 'Don't say I don't know how to treat you right first thing in the morning.' She winked at him as she turned and headed for the bathroom. Seb laughed softly and sipped his coffee, his eye straying to the big brown envelope that had arrived with the morning post. He opened his other correspondence first. He knew what was in the big envelope, and felt oddly reluctant to open it. His other mail consisted of two invitations to speak at functions, one an offer to become chairman of a fund-raising committee to finance a new wing to a mental hospital. There was a sad letter from an ex-patient, a few hate letters threatening to kill him in any number of ways, a letter from his mother and the telephone bill.

He stacked them in order, and finished his coffee. Only then did he finally reach for the hefty envelope and slit it open, pulling out week-old copies of New

York papers, ignoring all but the reports on the Valentine story.

What he read did not make sense.

He had never met Valentine Copeland in person, but Veronica had written every now and then, and through those letters Sebastien felt he knew nearly as much about Valentine Copeland as he would if he'd actually been treating the man in person.

The story about attempted arson in order to defraud the insurance companies had finally been dropped due to lack of evidence. Valentine Inc. had no financial worries – it was, in fact, a very profitable company. Which meant someone else had to have set the fires – since the fire department was sure that the fire *had* been deliberately set.

Sebastien began to frown, and search through the papers more rapidly. They made absolutely no mention of Travis. How was he coping with all this? Why had the boy not replied to his letters, offering help? Sebastien had even suggested Travis come to London and stay with him for a few weeks or months, until things had settled down. It was possible, he supposed, that the boy had gone into hiding to escape the press, but surely someone would have forwarded his letters to him?

Sebastien sighed and leaned back in his chair. Something was wrong. He could feel it. And as usual he knew its source. Sebastien ran his hand across his forehead, feeling suddenly tired. He was not yet forty-five, but he felt ancient. In the doorway, Lilas stopped, her cheery words drying on her lips.

344

She saw the newspapers, and knew they had something to do with Wayne D'Arville. Whenever Seb got that strange, suffering look, it had to do with D'Arville.

Her lips thinned.

Sebastien knew that over the years he had helped many people, perhaps more than most psychiatrists had managed, but it was not enough. Not enough to stop feeling guilty himself for all the ones that got away. And all his failures in his never-ending battle against pain and suffering seemed to personify into one man – Wayne D'Arville.

His recent failure in Monte Carlo nearly a month ago, which had so nearly been the triumphant breakthrough he'd been waiting for all these years, had only added to the growing feeling of hopelessness.

And now this. The fire. Travis missing. Veronica – that lovely, loving, warm girl, still in hospital, along with her husband. They were out of intensive care now, but still not up to receiving the press or any other visitors. And he knew who was responsible.

'Wayne,' Sebastien said, the word a cry of pain, of pity, of anger. 'Wayne, what have you done?'

In the doorway, Lilas made a sound, and he looked up. He forced a smile to his face. 'Hi, darling. Just in time to make me some toast,' he teased.

Lilas nodded. 'Sure thing, honeybunch.' And after she'd made his toast, she was going to arrange a flight to Monte Carlo. It was time she had a word with the man who was making her lover's life a misery.

It was a long day. Sebastien knew he had to go back to Monte Carlo. He could sense that things were coming to a head. But he had a crisis in the mid-afternoon with one of his paranoid schizophrenics threatening imminent suicide, and he was not sure he would make the airport on time. He did so, but with only minutes to spare.

The girl at the BA flight desk was annoyed, but only for a few seconds. His totally sincere apology, gentle smile and sherry eyes crinkled at the corners had her practically escorting him on to the plane.

Sebastien shook his head to the stewardess's offer of a meal, but accepted a tiny bottle of Scotch, which he sipped neat. Something was troubling him, and for a while he couldn't pin it down. All around him were chattering and excited holiday-makers or bored businessmen. The aircraft was soon descending again. His ears popped, the Scotch warmed him but he had a strange feeling of displacement. If he'd believed in that sort of thing, he might think that he was having a premonition of doom. He felt cold, but he knew it was not a physical thing – he wasn't catching a chill. He just knew, in his gut, that something awful was going to happen. And he was scared. He was also almost asleep. Fear and sleep didn't mix. Or it shouldn't.

Sebastien shook his head. He was in trouble. Wayne was in trouble. And the closer he got to Monaco, the more uneasy he felt.

'We're landing, sir. Please do up your seatbelt.'

Sebastien glanced at the stewardess and realized

he'd missed the announcement. 'Sorry. Sleeping,' he mumbled, and did up the belt with a smile. The girl passed on, checking for other slackers. The huge jet touched down safely at Nice, and he was through Customs quickly, since he'd packed only a small suitcase and wasn't stopped for a baggage check. He took a bus to Monte Carlo, and tried without success to settle his nerves. But it was hard, much harder than he was used to, and when he stepped off the bus into a town coloured red by a sinking sun he stood on the pavement for long, long minutes before getting his bearings and heading for the casino.

He was still carrying his suitcase when he walked through the door of the Droit de Seigneur. He had not had time to change, and his beige jacket and trousers were crumpled, his white shirt a little travel-grubby. Slowly he looked around.

Sebastien had been reluctant to leave Monaco before, but Wayne had reverted to his hard-eyed, locked-in self. To be locked in with constant pain was something Sebastien feared more than anything else. If he was tired after years of seeing other people's pain, then how much more tired must Wayne be after an entire lifetime of living with it?

'Can I help you, sir?'

Sebastien turned to see a small, dapper man dressed in a dinner jacket looking at him with polite curiosity, tinged with contempt. This was not the same manager he'd dealt with over a month ago, and the new man no doubt thought he was panting to lose his money – so much so that he had not even bothered to check into a hotel. Sebastien grinned, in spite of it all.

'Yes. I'd like to see Wayne. Mr D'Arville. Is he here, or at home?'

The man's eyes flickered, and Sebastien could almost hear the wheels turning. No doubt others had tried to bluff their way into the inner sanctum. 'Tell him Sebastien is here to see him. I think you'll find he'll want to see me.'

Antoine Dorlhac nodded. The man seemed very sure of himself, and there was something particularly unthreatening about him. 'Very well, Mr . . .?'

'Teale.'

'Mr Teale. If you'll wait here a moment . . .' He left the sentence to hang in mid-air as he left the room, nodding to one of the security men to keep an eye on him.

Sebastien looked slowly around the room. At one table, a beautiful young girl with black hair had attracted a crowd. At first he thought it meant she was winning, but as he moved closer he could see that that was not the case. She was losing quite spectacularly, thousands of francs at a time.

Antoine knocked on the office door and walked in. 'I'm sorry to disturb you, sir, but there is a man here to see you.'

'A loser?'

'No, sir. I haven't seen him in before. He arrived with a suitcase.'

Wayne looked up from the documents in front of him. 'Is Maria still losing?'

'Yes, sir.' Antoine smiled, the first genuine smile Wayne had ever seen him give. Wayne had insisted that Maria pay back the money in the same way that she had won it. It pleased him and re-emphasized the change in their positions. When she was humbled enough, Wayne would pick her up, brush her down and think of some use for her. He was currently chasing a Brazilian lumber lord for the paper rights to his timber, but he was proving to be difficult. The man was unmarried and had a weakness for beautiful women, as Wayne knew from the dossier he'd had compiled on him. And in Brazil, as in old Spain, arranged marriages were still more or less the norm.

'What shall I do about the man, sir?' Antoine prompted him from his thoughts.

'Did he give a name?' Wayne asked, sounding as bored as he looked.

'Sebastien Teale, sir.'

'Seb?' Wayne stood up, his eyes and face lighting up so obviously that Antoine felt his mouth drop open. 'Well, bring him in,' Wayne snapped, suddenly angry. 'At once. And in future, don't ever keep Dr Teale waiting again. Is that clear?'

'Yes, sir. Of course.' Antoine backed hastily out of the room and all but ran down the corridor. Only as he approached the gaming rooms did he slow down to a more dignified walk, and stepped behind the curtains. 'Mr – I mean Dr Teale. Won't you please come this way? Guy!' He snapped his fingers at a man lounging by the cashier's window. 'Guy will take care of your suitcase, sir.'

'Thanks,' Sebastien said, but was already moving towards the offices. He remembered its location easily enough. He still had nightmares about it. He hadn't even reached the office when the door opened and Wayne's tall figure filled the opening.

'Seb! What on earth are you doing here?'

Sebastien reached forward to take the hand, the familiar handshake doing nothing to calm his nerves. As he was ushered inside he shrugged his shoulders. 'I just needed a break, that's all. And I thought of sun and sand, and Monte Carlo.'

'And me,' Wayne said softly.

'And you.' Sebastien sat down in the chair facing the huge desk, Wayne moving quickly to its other side. As he did so, Sebastien stared at him, hard. There was something different . . . something had changed since that last grim day over a month ago. 'You look . . . contented,' Sebastien offered the opening gambit, and Wayne grinned.

'Why not? I've just gained a child. The casino is mine. My father is no longer around to haunt me and I'm finally free.'

'A child?' Sebastien said, his voice sharper than he meant it to be. Could it be that he knew about Travis? Sebastien's mouth went dry when he thought of another, more sinister explanation behind Travis's disappearance. Wayne watched him intently.

'That's right. You must have seen her outside?'

Sebastien blinked. 'Her?'

'Mmm.' Wayne grinned. 'In my younger days, there was a maid at my father's villa . . .' Wayne broke off with a grin and a shrug. 'She left the same summer and I never even guessed she was pregnant. Then, a few weeks ago –' he spread his hands wide – 'in she walked – Maria, her daughter. My *daughter*.'

Sebastien felt his whole body wilt in relief. Wayne's blue eyes crinkled at the corners as he watched it. Wonderful Sebastien. He never changed. 'Isn't she beautiful?'

'I'm not sure I . . .'

'The last I heard,' Wayne interrupted, 'she was losing quite a lot of my money. Luckily for me, this is my casino, so I get it all back again!'

'Oh – oh, yes. Yes, you're right. She is lovely. You must be proud of her.' Sebastien smiled, bringing the girl's face into mind.

'Oh, I am,' Wayne nodded, a strange smile on his face. 'Yes, I really am.'

'What does Sylvie think of her?' Sebastien asked curiously.

'Sylvie?' For a second there was a totally blank expression on his face and Seb felt a sudden tension tighten his insides. Incredible as it seemed, he knew that this man had forgotten he had a wife. 'Oh, Sylvia. They haven't met yet.' Wayne leaned back in his chair, just glad to be alive again. Sometimes it was easier to forget that only Sebastien could accomplish this. 'I'm glad you're here, Seb,' he said softly. 'I need you.'

Sebastien's eyes sharpened, as Wayne had known they would. 'Oh?'

'Relax. I didn't mean . . . that.' Wayne picked up a

pen and fiddled with it. Sebastien knew it meant that he would get nothing more productive out of him that night. Unless he could catch him unawares . . .

'Did you hear about the fire in New York?' he asked abruptly. Wayne froze for a fraction of a second and then threw down the pen and looked up. Sebastien looked pale, on edge, and for a second Wayne was swamped with a feeling approaching painful tenderness. Then he shrugged.

'New York? I don't think I've ever been there.'

'Veronica and her husband were nearly killed in a fire there a few weeks back,' he said, watching Wayne's face for any tiny clue to emotion.

Wayne shook his head slowly. 'That's a pity.' He'd assumed they'd perished. Oh, well. He could live with them being just badly burned. Unless they tried to get Travis back. Then he'd have to make sure that his people did the job properly.

Sebastien nodded thoughtfully. 'Funny, isn't it, that you can forget you have a wife, but remember immediately the name of a lover from nearly twenty years ago?'

The voice was soft and speculative, but Wayne was not fooled. Clever Sebastien. Clever, clever Sebastien. Slowly he lifted his eyes from the top of the desk and looked the American straight in the eye. 'Memory's forever playing tricks like that,' he agreed softly.

Sebastien decided to take a chance. 'Apparently their son is still missing.'

Wayne slowly stood up. 'You haven't booked into a hotel yet, I trust?'

Sebastien rose in response, but more stiffly, feeling the weariness deep in his bones. 'No. I was hoping . . .'

'You didn't have to hope, Sebastien,' Wayne said softly. 'You know damned well you'll be staying with me.'

Sebastien ignored the jibe. 'You still have the old villa?'

'Still?' He inclined his head with familiar mockery.

'I'm surprised you haven't sold it. Surely it has bad memories for you?'

'It has good ones too. I conceived a daughter there, remember?' They were in the outer corridor now, and as Wayne pushed aside the curtain Sebastien found himself searching out the beautiful brunette, who was just rising from the table. Out of the corner of his eye he saw Wayne beckon her. The girl paused and then turned reluctantly. She was wearing a pale lilac that did wonders for her raven hair and creamy skin, but there were dark smudges beneath her eyes.

'She is lovely, Wayne,' Sebastien said softly as Maria walked towards them. He searched her face carefully, noting instantly the tight, pinched mouth, but it was the girl's eyes that fascinated him the most. They looked at her father and then away again in a confusing battery of emotions. Hate, fear, despair. Sebastien almost cried out loud. He looked at Wayne sharply, just one thought clearly ringing in his mind, and so well did they know each other that he might just as well have spoken it out loud. Wayne, what have you done now?

Wayne smiled, feeling deep in his soul the unique power that he had over this man alone, and yet also aware of the equally exquisite pain of being dependent on him. 'Sebastien Teale, this is my daughter, Maria Alvarez. Maria, Sebastien.'

Maria glanced at the man by her father's side. Any friend of his was her enemy. Her eyes were black and scornful, spitting hate and contempt. 'Señor Teale.' She made his name sound like a poison.

'Sebastien is a doctor, Maria. I want you to be nice to him. In fact, I insist on it,' Wayne said softly, but with an edge to his voice. Sebastien glanced quickly between Wayne and the highly strung girl in front of him, sensing a hidden message in those few, bland, ordinary words. Maria went a shade whiter, her lips pulling up into a fiasco of a smile as she tried once again. 'Dr Teale. I'm so pleased to meet you.'

Sebastien reached out his hand, taking hers in a firm grip when she would have pulled away. 'Hello, Maria,' he said softly, feeling the exact moment when the girl looked at him properly. He smiled slowly. 'I look forward to getting to know you better. You're staying at the villa?'

'*Si*.'

'Wonderful. So am I. Perhaps we can have breakfast tomorrow?'

'You should be careful of talking too much in front of Sebastien, Maria,' Wayne said with a warning smile. 'He's a psychiatrist.'

Maria Alvarez looked once more into those warm, sherry-coloured eyes, and Sebastien saw a flash of

354

understanding followed by desperate hope suddenly flood her eyes. 'I look forward to it, *señor*,' she said, her voice husky now.

Sebastien squeezed her hand, passing on to her his own hidden message to bear up, and then released her. Beside him Wayne said restlessly, 'Shall we go?'

Sebastien saw the silent plea in the Spanish girl's eyes, and thought quickly. 'If you don't mind, I'd like to stay here for a few minutes. For all the times I've been in Monaco, I don't think I've actually placed a bet.'

Wayne smiled, not fooled, but feeling too magnanimous to spoil their fun. 'Why not? How much money have you got?'

Sebastien laughed. 'Precious little.' He reached into his pocket and extracted all the notes he had – not quite thirty pounds. Wayne slowly reached forward and took them out of his hand.

As he did so, Maria noticed a strange, long, level look pass between them, and her heart began to pound. There was something . . . odd going on. It was almost as if . . . 'Excuse me a moment, please,' she murmured, making up her mind with an impetuosity that was second nature to her, and headed for the ladies' room, where she quickly used the phone.

'Gemma? It's me. Listen, something's happened. There's a man here, a friend of my father's called Sebastien Teale. I'm not sure, but I think he could be helpful. He's . . . I don't know. I can't explain it. He's a head-doctor . . . you know . . . what's the word? A shrink! Yes, a shrink, so he obviously knows all about Father.' She paused and listened for a few seconds, then shrugged. 'I don't know exactly. I want you to talk to him. I'll separate them somehow. Gemma, you must come here and talk to this man . . . I know.' Her voice lowered to a sympathetic murmur. 'You're so brave. So very brave. Good. Give me half an hour to think of something, then come. You can't mistake him. He's American, I think, like you. Not too tall, nice hair – like cara-mel, and eyes like sherry. Oh, you won't be able to miss him. There's something . . . oh, I don't know. Something . . . kind about him. Yes. All right. Your parents arrived all right? Oh. But I don't think the police will be much help. My father's such a powerful man, but perhaps it's worth a try. OK. I'll see you later. And try not to worry,' she added foolishly. She hung up, took a deep breath, and went back to the craps table, where Sebastien was rolling the dice.

His eyes met hers briefly, and she smiled. He threw a neat seven. Maria glanced at her watch, then watched her father's face. He, in turn, was watching Sebastien with all the concentration of a cat at a mousehole. It made her shiver. Twenty minutes later, Sebastien's thirty pounds had become two hundred and twenty.

'Are these dice loaded?' Sebastien asked quietly as he straightened up and jiggled the dice in his hand. Wayne looked down at him, leaned a heavy hand on the younger man's shoulder and smiled grimly.

'The dice are always loaded, Sebastien,' he said.

Maria put her hand to her head and sighed. It was Sebastien who noticed. 'You all right?'

'Just a headache. Daddy, could we go home now?'

'Sure.'

'Oh, please, Dr Teale, you don't have to come as well,' Maria said, catching Sebastien's sleeve in an excruciatingly tight grip. Startled, Sebastien nevertheless caught on quickly. Before Wayne could object, he turned and rattled the dice once more and rolled them. 'OK. Thanks.'

Wayne hesitated for a long moment and Maria moved closer, almost bumping into him. 'See you in the morning, Dr Teale,' she murmured, and Sebastien nodded. Only when they'd gone did he slowly straighten up, a small frown tugging at his brows. He cashed in the chips, pocketed the notes and wandered to the bar, settling down to wait.

He fully expected Maria to come back. He was drinking his third soda when he became aware of a young girl hovering nervously a few feet away. He turned, but knew at once that he'd never seen her before in his life. She was young, no more than eighteen, he guessed, despite the sophisticated, high-necked navy-blue gown she wore. She smiled nervously. Sebastien smiled back. Maria was right, Gemma thought, her raw nerves reacting immediately to the gentle eyes. He does look kind. It had taken a great deal for her to leave her room, after her parents had told her to stay put. They had arrived late last night, and she had told them the whole story. Oriel had slept with her daughter in her arms, and this morning her father had been making phone calls to everyone he knew, calling in favours, and getting the names of the top men in Monaco. When they had left just a few hours ago to try and persuade the police to act, they'd told her to wait for them, and not to leave the hotel room in any circumstances. But now she was glad that she had. She sensed this man could help. 'Dr Teale?' she asked nervously.

Sebastien, surprised by her American accent, half turned. 'Yes?'

'I'm Gemma Harcourt. You don't know me. Maria sent me. She seems to think you might be able to help us.'

Sebastien left his drink at the bar. 'Is there anywhere we can talk in private?'

Gemma went white, her whole body tensing. Automatically she took a step away. Sebastien froze for a second, then said softly, 'Some café somewhere, where we can find a quiet corner, away from prying eyes?'

Gemma nearly wilted in relief. 'Of course. There's one just over the road.' Sebastien followed her in silence, noting the way she looked around nervously. It was not until they were out in the street and crossing the busy road that she relaxed. The café was quiet, only a few couples holding hands and slowly dancing by the juke box. Sebastien steered them to a dark corner and purchased two coffees at the counter. He watched her add sugar and milk to hers, then said softly, 'How long ago was it that you were raped, Gemma?'

Gemma's spoon clattered in her cup, and she gnawed on her lower lip, taking several deep breaths before she could speak. 'I d-don't . . .' She lowered her head, unable to meet his eyes. 'I wish my father were here,' she said, irrelevantly.

Sebastien said nothing for a moment, but deliberately stirred his coffee. Watching the spoon go around and around, Gemma sighed and slowly relaxed. Then she reached for her own cup, taking it to her lips with shaking hands.

'It was recently, wasn't it?' Sebastien tried again.

The quiet words, soft, like raw silk on an open wound, made her wince. 'Please,' she said.

Seb caressed her hand gently. 'You can tell me, Gemma.'

'You're his friend!' she suddenly hissed, her pale cheeks flooding with colour. 'How can I tell you?'

Sebastien stared at her, then closed his eyes briefly. 'Oh, God. It was Wayne, wasn't it?'

Gemma looked away. 'It was last night,' she confirmed briefly. 'But he didn't actually . . . I got away, just in time,' she mumbled. Sebastien shook his head. He knew about Wayne's distaste and distrust of women, and while in some men fear of women resulted in a need to rape, he'd never seen any signs of it in Wayne before.

'He did it because . . . Oh, it's not important,' Gemma finally said, and Sebastien looked up at her quickly, his expression stunned.

'Not important! Gemma – Gemma listen to me.' His hands reached out for hers, but surprisingly she felt no urge to pull them away. 'You must get professional help – believe me, I know. You have to work this through with a professional doctor, one who knows how to help you. Here.' He reached into his pocket, and on the back of his card wrote out a number. 'This is the number of a rape crisis centre in England. They can put you in touch with an American doctor. Promise me you'll talk to them?'

Gemma took the card, but barely glanced at it, though she did slip it absently into her purse. 'You puzzle me,' she said at last. 'How can you . . . someone like you . . . be his friend?'

'You say that as if he were a monster . . .'

Gemma smiled grimly. 'He is a monster.'

'Rape is a terrible crime,' Sebastien said, and meant it. 'But there are . . .'

Gemma was already shaking her head. 'I told you, that's not important. It's my brother who's in danger. It's him we have to save.'

'Your brother?'

'Paris. Wayne's kidnapped him. Yes, I know.' She laughed harshly as he reared back. 'It sounds ridiculously dramatic, doesn't it? But it's true. Oh, God, I wish Daddy were here. He'd know what to do.'

Sebastien briefly rubbed his tired eyes with his fingers, then said softly, 'I want you to tell me everything. Right from the beginning.'

Half an hour later, Gemma had done so. She felt talked out, washed out, wrung out. She was beyond tears now, almost beyond feeling at all. 'So when Maria phoned, she just had this hunch that you would help,' she finished the story, and looked at him, her dull voice trailing away. 'You look like I feel,' she said with another harsh laugh.

Sebastien, who sat with his head in his hands, slowly straightened up to stare for a moment out of the window. 'I knew something was wrong,' he said. 'But not this. I never suspected this.'

'It's a mess, isn't it?' Gemma said, watching as the older man nodded his head. 'So you see, he *is* a monster after all. He's crushing all the life and spirit out of Maria, just because she dared to defy him. He seems to enjoy . . .' Gemma grappled for the words that would help her understand '. . . actually *need* to hurt those who are nearest to him. I'm only surprised he hasn't done the same to you. Can you help us?'

Sebastien thought of all the years of his life boiling down to this one moment. Alone, sick to his soul, in a café in a town he didn't know, with a girl who was just one more victim of the man he'd tried to call a friend.

And Lilas – the one good thing in his life. His one chance of love and happiness, so far away. But he mustn't think of her now. He didn't know that, at that moment, Lilas was flying across the Channel to join him.

He had to concentrate on one thing only. It had gone too far now. He would have to have Wayne committed, and take the chance that he'd succeed first time. But he was in Monaco – Wayne's home territory. He'd have to be careful . . .

'Yes,' he said finally, his voice no more than a whisper, but nevertheless, containing something hard. 'I can help.'

CHAPTER 21

Kier Harcourt looked across at Max Dupont and said crisply, 'Well?'

Max Dupont, now sixty-five, had at one time been a hero of the French Résistance. He was a big man, heavy-set, with iron-grey hair and big bushy eyebrows. 'Getting into D'Arville's villa without getting spotted is, as I see it, the greatest problem. Once inside, my men can take out the security guards. How sure are you of your intelligence?'

Kier smiled grimly. 'Sure enough. D'Arville's daughter herself has been compiling the information for us.' Kier, who'd never had much faith in the police, had quickly formed a back-up plan. It was a desperate plan – but he and Oriel were equally desperate.

'Ah, here's Pierre.' In the small, discreet hotel room, both men looked around as a tall lanky youth with bad teeth and a wide smile walked into the room, an envelope in his hand. 'Anything?' Max asked with a short grunt.

Pierre spilled the photographs on to the table. Kier

slowly spread them, picking out one of a pale-faced but wonderfully alive boy looking pensively out of a top-floor window. 'That's him,' Kier said softly, wilting in relief. 'That's Paris.'

Max took the photograph and looked across at the American speculatively. Max had met Duncan Somerville only twice, but he was an ardent admirer of the Somerville Commission. So when he had had been awoken at one o'clock this morning, and found himself confronted by this man and his pale-faced but enraged wife, he had reacted immediately to Oriel Harcourt's maiden name. For three hours he had sat in the chilly barn of his kitchen, brewing innumerable cups of coffee and listening tight-lipped to their story.

He had agreed to help at once, and the speed in which he had everything organized took Kier's breath away. 'I'm just going to go and show these to Oriel,' Kier said, taking the photos. Max didn't bother looking up as the American rose and walked to a connecting door.

Oriel was standing at the window, looking out at the beaches of Ste. Maxime. Silently Kier walked beside her and handed over the photos. 'He's alive. That was taken just a few hours ago.'

Oriel took the photographs with shaking hands, tears flooding her eyes. 'Oh, thank God,' she whispered.

Kier looked across to the second single bed and glanced at his daughter's sleeping face. 'How is she?'

Oriel continued to stare at the photos of her son. 'She's not too good.'

Kier sighed. But he knew he could count on Oriel to look after Gemma. At first she had insisted on coming to the villa with them, but Kier had made her see that she would only be a hindrance, and therefore a liability to Paris. Now she was resigned to staying behind.

'What does Max say?' she asked quietly.

'Nothing yet.'

Oriel turned into Kier's arms, burying her face into his hard, comforting chest. Kier hugged her briefly, silently, then went back to the other room.

Max had the photographs separated into piles. There were four more shots of Paris, a whole pile of the grounds and every room of the villa, and three more of an unknown boy, about Paris's age. He too was dark-haired, but his eyes were blue. 'Do you know him?' Max asked, nodding his head at the pictures.

Kier lifted one and stared at it. 'No.'

'Pierre got the impression that he's also a prisoner at the villa. Apparently they're together quite a lot, and whenever they walk in the grounds, the guards follow both of them.'

Kier sat down heavily on the edge of the bed. 'I don't . . . want to sound hard-hearted,' he began, his voice as strained as his face. 'But . . .'

'But you want your son rescued come what may, and we'll worry about this other boy second, hmm?'

Kier grimaced. 'Life's strange,' he said quietly. 'Until a few days ago, I thought I knew myself pretty

365

well . . .' He broke off the train of thought, and stared thoughtfully at the unknown boy's face. 'You know, he looks a lot like D'Arville. The eyes, especially. And the shape of the face.'

Max nodded. 'You noticed that too, huh? Well, we won't have time to find out anything more concrete. We move tonight.'

Kier's head reared up. 'Tonight?'

Just a few miles away, Travis glanced at Paris nervously. 'Are you ready?'

Paris managed a half-laugh, half-shrug. 'No. Are you?'

Travis grinned back. 'Nope.' He glanced over the side of the balcony that seemed to hang over a sheer thirty-foot drop.

'You know, don't you, if those creeper cords don't hold, we'll probably break our necks?' Paris said, almost conversationally, as Travis leaned down and pulled on a fibrous, twisted cord of a green-leafed creeper, no thicker than his thumb. Travis slowly straightened and looked out over the grounds. They were beautiful – full of lily-choked ponds and fish, iron and white marble gazebos, lawns mowed in criss-cross patterns, flower borders, rose arbours, honeysuckle bowers, trees, even a bridged stream. How he hated it. He hated the house too, with its priceless *objets d'art*, Regency furniture, Oriental carpets, modern stereo and entertainment centres and indoor swimming pool.

'Yeah,' Travis said heavily. 'I know. But personally I think I'd rather have a broken neck than stay here another day with that maniac.'

Paris glanced across at the boy who, in only twenty-four hours, had become the greatest friend of his life. 'He's mad, you know. Not screaming, lock-me-up mad, but . . . twisted.' He looked down the vertical wall, and his thoughts drifted back. He had not known what to say in the car on his way to this place two nights ago. He had looked first at the drunk who was not a drunk, at the back of the driver's head and finally at the tight-lipped man who had sneaked up behind him. He knew he was not being mugged, unless the French had a very strange way of going about it. His heart had pounded uncomfortably, but he firmly kept his fear under control. He was damned if he'd panic and make an ass of himself. He kept telling himself over and over that so far they had not even hurt him. For all of that long, long drive, he'd kept up a wait-and-see policy that had allowed him to walk with dignity from the car when it was parked in front of the impressive villa, and not disgrace himself.

Paris had not expected the villa, which had the white-washed beauty of a truly luxurious residence. The driver left in the car, leaving the two others to 'escort' him upstairs. There, a large room that could have looked like a luxurious guest room except for the bars over the windows, awaited him. Without a word the two men had turned and left. Paris had tried the door, of course. It was locked. Then he'd walked to the windows. After making sure the bars were solid, he'd noted that they were newly installed. By then, of course, he had figured out that D'Arville was behind it all. Who else could it have been?

That first night he'd waited for hours, finally rushing to the window at the sound of a car arriving. There, in the light from the vestibule, he saw Wayne D'Arville get out and nod to the chauffeur. His height and the colour of his hair was unmistakable. It was almost unbelievable. Why had he done something so stupid? Surely not even Wayne D'Arville thought he could get away with kidnapping? And why? Why? He'd been nervous and uptight waiting for D'Arville to come to him, but as the hours passed, and it slowly dawned on him that he would have no visitors that night, he paced the room, ignoring the comfortable Queen Anne bed with white satin sheets, and forced his over-active mind and imagination to calm down and start thinking logically. When he'd done so, the answer was obvious, and came to him easily. He'd been snatched to put a halt to Maria's 'lucky' streak. For just a single fleeting moment, Paris wondered what would happen if Maria refused to comply. A little demon, twisting deep in his brain, reminded him of how obsessed she was with revenge. Then he shook his head. Maria would not let her desire for revenge outweigh the thing they had going between them. No way.

'You ready?'

Paris blinked, Travis's words bringing him back to the present. He managed a cocky grin. 'After you.'

368

Travis grinned back. 'Thanks a bunch.' It was a game between them, of course, all this grinning, all this wry laughter. It was supposed to cover up the fear and keep their spirits up. To a certain extent it worked. Only at times like this did the fear become a solid reality, sitting like a rock in the middle of their stomachs.

Paris had finally given in to mild shock that first night and lain fully clothed on the bed. About eight-thirty the next morning, he'd been woken by the door opening, his disorientated mind snapping to attention at the sight of the tall, red-headed Frenchman. Wayne had been mercifully brief and straight to the point. Even now, as Paris swung his body over the stone balustrade, the dizzying pull of gravity making him grapple for vines and stone ledges, he could remember Wayne's words verbatim.

'Maria has agreed to give back the money, you'll be pleased to hear. It will take her a few nights to lose it all at the tables, however.' Seeing his surprised look, Wayne had smiled. 'I insisted she lose it the same way she won it. Once that's done, you'll be released.' Paris must have given himself away then, because the handsome face had looked more amused than ever. 'You think I'm going to kill you? You fool; I have no reason to. If you went to the police and told them I'd held you here, they'd laugh in your face.' Wayne had become impatient then, flicking his hand in a typical, Gallic gesture. 'Think it through yourself,' he finished shortly. 'I have things to do.'

Paris had never been so relieved in all his life

before. But as he'd groped his way to the bed, he'd felt someone else in the room. It had not been the Frenchman returning, but instead a boy about his own age, with distrustful eyes, and hands dug deep into his trouser pockets. 'Who the hell are you?' he'd demanded.

'You OK?' a voice said now.

Paris looked across and down to Travis, who was ramming his instep tightly against a knotted branch. 'So far. Hell, the ground seems a long way down.'

'Don't it, though?' Travis muttered grimly.

The two boys only took a minute or so to reach the paved patio. Nervously they looked around. They had spent a day watching the guards patrolling the grounds, and worked out their timetable. Now, as they looked around, the evening shadows were just beginning to throw elongated shadows across the lawns, and by their reckoning the fifth guard, whose sector this was, wasn't due for another ten minutes. Paris gave Travis a victorious punch to the top of his arm, and together they ran at a low crouch towards the trees. Once out of sight of the main house, they followed the line of trees to their end, and then crouched down behind the last trunks. Ahead of them stretched the open ground of the kitchen garden. Rows of radishes, lettuce and carrots competed with beans and peas climbing up wigwam-shaped sticks. 'Great,' Paris muttered angrily. Beyond them was the huge wall. 'There has to be a gap in that bloody thing,' he muttered, but Travis was already shaking his head.

'There isn't. I've been here longer than you have, remember?' He shook his head again. 'Believe me, it just goes on and on and on.'

Paris wiped his sweating forehead with his sleeve. 'What now?'

Both boys stared gloomily at the high red-brick wall with its topping of barbed wire. 'You gotta hand it to my old man,' Travis said, with a sarcasm made bitter by the taste of defeat. 'He sure knows how to build a prison.'

Paris looked back at the wall, his mind winging back to yesterday morning. At first, both boys had suspected some kind of trick. Travis wasn't sure that Paris was not some lackey of his father's, sent in to try and win his confidence and spy on him. Paris had similar thoughts about Travis, but a few minutes of crisp, suspicious questioning on both sides had gradually given way to a growing trust. Paris had been particularly appalled to learn of the fire in New York, and Travis's life on the streets. And he'd thought his own genteel kidnapping had been an ordeal!

'Can we use those sticks in any way?' Travis asked with a hopeless kind of desperation as he pointed at the thin beanpoles, and Paris shook his head. 'I doubt it. Unless you want to try and pole-vault that thing!' Travis half turned, another grin on his face. Paris tensed as his blue eyes slewed over his shoulder. Paris felt his own shoulderblades tighten, and slowly looked around. A few feet away, two uniformed and armed guards watched them. Paris glanced back

371

at Travis, who slowly stood up. Wordlessly both boys followed the guards back to the house. There was nothing else to be done.

Walking around the side of the house, they both saw the midnight-blue Ferrari parked out front. Now they knew how they had been found missing so quickly – Wayne was home.

The room they were taken to was hexagonal, the floor tiled in black and white patterns. It was obviously a music room. Sitting at a piano, picking out a tune, Wayne looked up at them. The energy in his blue eyes made Paris take a quick, involuntary step backwards. Travis, who'd had more practice at withstanding the icy blast than his friend, held his ground.

Slowly Wayne arose to his full height and approached them, but it was to Travis that he walked. When he was only a few inches away, father and son stared at one another, and Paris knew that this confrontational scene had been played out before. The room was deathly silent. 'Where did you get out?' Wayne asked. Paris was surprised at the soft tone.

Travis, who was not at all surprised, said nothing. Wayne turned and nodded at one of the guards. Paris had just enough time to yelp as the guard behind him grabbed his arms and then the other guard punched him solidly in the stomach. Paris had never felt anything like it before. Dimly he was aware of Travis shouting something, and guessed that he was telling Wayne what he wanted to know. Pain radiated from the explosion in his stomach, making him feel viciously sick. He bent double, but was prevented from falling on to the floor by the guard still holding him. He gasped, and gasped again, his eyes watering.

Travis watched him helplessly. Unseen by either of them, a third guard had been in the room, and was now holding Travis in a similar but more gentle stranglehold. Slowly, painfully, Paris straightened up. Travis saw the beads of sweat pop out on his forehead, but his eyes, looking at Wayne, were dark with hate.

'That's better.' Wayne said. 'Now.' He turned once more to Travis. 'You checked out the patrol times of the guards?'

'No. We just took pot luck,' Paris said, one part of his brain telling him he was an idiot to goad him, while another part told him that if he let fear of pain rule him, he'd never be much of a man.

The guard in front of Paris swung his fist again, this time into Paris's face. His head exploded in pain, bright lights flashing across his closed lids. He felt something on his lip, and when he grunted in pain he felt the taste of his own blood in his mouth.

'Where were you planning on going, if you got out?' Wayne asked, once again looking to his struggling son. Travis was twisting and turning, desperate to free himself, wanting only to launch himself at his father and tear out his heart. 'Save your breath, Travis,' Wayne advised softly. 'Where were you going to go?'

'Don't tell him,' Paris found the words came out of his mouth in a lisp because of a loose tooth.

Travis looked at him with agonized eyes. '*No!*' he screamed, but too late.

This time Paris blacked out for a few moments. When he opened his eyes he realized he was lying on the floor. He tried to sit up, and moaned before he could stop the sound escaping his lips. The guard had punched him viciously in the back, and his kidneys felt like aching rocks in his body.

'The American embassy,' Travis screamed. 'Stop it! All right? Just stop it! I'll tell you whatever you want to know, but leave him alone!'

It was dark outside now, and as a catering truck approached the city limits, Kier Harcourt felt his heart pounding inside his chest like a jack-hammer out of control.

'We're nearly there,' Max said, watching as the American stiffened. But he was confident about Harcourt. Then he turned and looked at the other American, a frown of unease appearing between his bushy, iron-grey caterpillar eyebrows. Max wasn't so sure quite what to make of Sebastien Teale.

When Maria Alvarez had brought the American to them just an hour before the assault would begin, Max had been adamant that he was not to come along. He found the psychiatrist's innate gentleness worrisome. Kier, too, had been against it. He didn't know Teale, and didn't trust Teale, and didn't want the plan put in any kind of danger.

It was Sebastien himself who had argued both of them around, with a logic that was infallible. 'If things go wrong – and they might – you're going to need someone there who knows how to deal with D'Arville,' he'd pointed out simply. 'And if you don't take me, I'll simply call a cab and go in on my own.'

Still Kier had not liked it. Sebastien had looked at him steadily. 'What do you do if Wayne gets a knife to Paris's throat? What do you say, when one wrong word or expression could mean death for your son? This man has no sense of right or wrong – none. He has no friends, no loyalties, no allegiances, only different grades of enemy. Right now, I'm the least of his enemies. He already hates you.' He turned to Kier, who said nothing. 'And will have only contempt for you.' He turned to Max. 'Remember, this man was raised by Wolfgang Mueller.'

Finally, with time becoming pressing, both men had been forced to concede that Sebastien might come in handy.

'Teale comes,' Kier had finally said, his voice brooking no argument.

Now, as the van approached La Turbie, Sebastien, much to Max's relief, showed no signs of cracking up. Rather, he was grimly quiet, with a determination that Max recognized from the old days before a raid against the occupying Germans. It made him feel better about having the shrink along.

In a taxi, barely a mile behind them, Lilas Glendower stared resolutely ahead. It hadn't been hard to track down Wayne D'Arville's villa. Now, all she had to do was rehearse what she'd say to him when she got there.

Max glanced at his watch, then looked around at the six silent men, all blacked up and swaying easily in motion with the van. All were the sons of ex-Résistance fighters. All had been in the army. Max Dupont was still enough of a national hero to assemble such a team at short notice.

The van pulled up in a narrow lane, several hundred yards from the only entrance to the villa. 'Here we go,' Max said, and checked his gun. Sebastien had no weapon, and had declined Max's offer to provide him with one.

The night was cloudy and moonless. Sebastien and Kier took up the rear, watching in silent admiration as two of Max's men efficiently cut the wires to the alarm system and knocked out the video cameras. One man fiddled at the gateposts. It seemed like hours, but was in reality only a few minutes, before the gates slid silently open.

Everyone knew the plan down to the last detail.

Paris was almost sleeping, aware of a dull continual pain all over his body. His face was stiff with caked blood. He had not been allowed to wash after a guard had carried him to his room, nor had he seen Travis for several hours.

Dimly he heard a scraping noise coming from behind him, but couldn't be bothered to look around. The scraping persisted, and Paris frowned. But he was too sore to get up and investigate.

Outside, the first two bars had been removed. Kier was already halfway up the ladder. The one called Jacques, who had been removing the bars with acid and a lever, was the first one in, moving so silently that Paris was not aware of another presence in his room. Kier, however, was not quite so silent. Paris turned slowly on the bed, careful to keep his cut and misshapen lips firmly shut.

He would not moan again. If D'Arville had come for him again, then . . . A flashlight dazzled him, making his blink. Then he heard his name, spoken in a voice he knew so well that, for a second, he could not believe it could be true.

'Paris. Is that you? God, son, what have they done to you?' Kier's face was barely visible in the dark, but Paris somehow managed to launch himself towards it. Kier, coming to kneel on the side of the bed, caught him, hearing the harsh breath of pain Paris gave at being held. 'Easy, son, easy,' Kier murmured, brushing back the sweat-damp hair from his face. Outside, they could clearly hear the sound of a car.

In the taxi, Lilas got out and paid the driver. She was surprised to see the gates standing open, but shrugged, straightened her shoulders, and walked determinedly up the path to the front door.

Upstairs, Kier lowered his son back on to the bed, staring grimly at the boy's bruises. Jacques whispered in French into his walkie-talkie, informing

377

Max that they'd located the boy, and giving a run-down on his injuries.

Downstairs, Max had picked the lock of the front door and waved Sebastien inside. He too had heard a car out on the road, but doubted it was coming here. The rest of his men waited in the garden to deal with any guards. Wordlessly he motioned Sebastien upstairs, himself on the alert for individual internal alarms.

'Paris, listen,' Kier whispered. 'We're going to get you out of here now. These are friends. OK?'

Paris glanced briefly at the faces around him. 'OK. But we have to get Travis as well.'

'Travis?' Kier glanced up as Max joined them.

Behind him, Sebastien Teale said softly, 'Travis Coltrane. He's Wayne's son.'

Kier looked down as he felt his hand being held tightly. Paris's one good eye gleamed brightly. 'You have to get him out, Dad. I won't go without him. I mean it!'

Kier nodded. 'We'll get him. But you're leaving now.' As he'd talked, two of Max's men had tied a sheet into a hammock, and one of them put a gentle but firm hand over Paris's mouth as they lifted him. Paris's moan of pain as they moved him was a barely muffled sob. They walked with him out into the corridor. There Kier watched at the top of the stairs as the men silently carried his son out of the hall and into the dark night air. Back to the van, where he'd be safe.

They missed bumping into Lilas by moments.

'Pierre said the other one was kept in the room next to D'Arville himself,' Max whispered. 'This way.'

Wayne had just put the finishing touches to his letter to the Brazilian timber man, and enclosed a stunning, full-length photograph of Maria in a clinging silver lamé evening gown. He sealed the envelope, addressed it, and stood up, stretching hard. Suddenly he froze. From Travis's room he heard a small sound. Instinct had the hairs on the back of his neck standing on end. He turned, glanced at the connecting door, took two quick steps towards it, then stopped. He walked the rest of the way quietly, and put his ear to the door.

Inside, Max Dupont had his hand firmly over Travis's mouth, and was looking down into the wide, startled blue eyes, which shifted to Kier as he came into view.

'Don't be afraid.' It was Kier who spoke, in no more than a whisper. 'I'm Paris's father. We've got him out, and he asked us to come for you. Do you want to leave?'

Under his hand, Max felt the boy's lips try to curve into a smile, and slowly withdrew his huge palm from the boy's face. 'God, yes!' Travis breathed, swinging his legs to the side of the bed, trying not to let the mattress squeak. He was wearing only his jeans.

Sebastien moved to the window to check that all was well outside. Travis and Kier were nearly at the door when the lights suddenly blazed on. Only Max responded immediately, spinning and crouching, his

379

gun-hand coming up, whilst Kier, Sebastien and Travis blinked in the sudden brightness, disorientated and confused.

Below, Lilas saw a light go on upstairs. She stared at the open door, feeling suddenly afraid. But she had come this far, and for Sebastien's sake she would do almost anything. Grimly, she walked into the hall.

Upstairs, Sebastien jumped and went ice-cold as a small, silent 'pop' sounded in the room, and Max staggered back through the open door. His hand on his shoulder was red with blood. Even so, Max reacted quickly and ducked out of the door in the dimness of the corridor beyond.

In the hall, Lilas heard the sound and began to mount the stairs. Max disappeared into Paris's bedroom and made for the ladder. He had to get the rest of his men back in here, fast!

'Shut the door,' Wayne ordered grimly, looking at Kier. Kier glanced down at the level, deadly gun in the German's hand, and did as he asked.

'Dad, give it up.' It was Travis who was the first of them to speak. Sebastien knew that Wayne had not yet seen him. Long velvet draperies half covered him, and all of Wayne's attention was focused on the door area. In profile, Wayne's face looked tense and white, but for once Sebastien knew that others needed him more.

On the landing, Lilas moved cautiously towards the sound of voices. She hesitated outside the door, her hand going slowly to the handle.

On the other side of the door, Sebastien's thoughts

were racing. He knew that Wayne would kill Kier Harcourt without a moment's hesitation, but Travis, he knew, was perfectly safe. Wayne would never kill his own son. He gauged the distance between Wayne and himself and realized that he could never cross it without being seen. The question was – would Wayne kill him also? Would he?

Sebastien tried to think it through like an analyst, but found he couldn't. This was personal. This was so very, very personal.

'Father, please,' Travis said, taking a few steps forward, deliberately putting his own body between the gun and Kier Harcourt. Kier knew what he was doing, and hesitated, unsure what to do next.

Nobody heard the door open silently. The first person Lilas saw was Sebastien. She was about to push the door open and call his name happily. Although she was surprised to see him, she was also glad. She'd been feeling rather scared and out of her depth. Then, just in time, she noticed something strange. Sebastien was moving, very very slowly, away from the window. He was almost tiptoeing. What . . .?

'Travis, move out of the way,' Wayne said, his voice cold and imperious. Lilas froze.

'No!' Travis gritted back. 'Kier, get out now. Quick!'

'Don't move!' Wayne's voice rapped out harshly, but it held no confidence. Travis's body blocked that of Kier's, and he moved a pace to the right. Travis immediately followed suit. It took them all further from the door, and Lilas, her breath locked in her throat, slowly pushed it open. Thankfully, everybody was too engrossed to notice.

Kier didn't move. 'I'm not leaving . . .'

'Go!' Travis hissed. 'He won't shoot me!'

'He won't shoot me, either,' Sebastien finally spoke for the first time. In the doorway, Lilas watched as Wayne's body seemed to jerk like a puppet whose strings had just been cut. He spun around, his incredulous eyes searching out the source of that voice he knew so well, his brain, which a moment before had been so crisp and clear, suddenly turning into a confused maze of emotion and confusion.

'Sebastien!' The name leapt from his mouth, even as he lowered his hand. Wayne stared at him, the shocked, confused blue eyes finally coming to rest in the two sherry pools of Sebastien's own eyes. He took a few steps towards him, taking him closer to the open French windows, and the small balcony beyond. 'Keep back!' Wayne said sharply, his voice high and unnatural, the gun levelling once more to point squarely at Sebastien's heart.

Lilas moved quickly into the room. She had no idea what tragedy was being played out here, but she knew a maniac was pointing a gun at Sebastien. And that was all she needed to know.

Sebastien never stopped in his slow, deliberate approach across the room, and Wayne retreated further back, out on to the concrete balcony.

Travis glanced over his shoulder at Kier, who had

moved up behind him. Then, out of nowhere, a woman was in the room. A woman neither had ever seen before. She silently crept up behind Sebastien.

Kier grabbed Travis, who made an instinctive movement to stop her. Neither Sebastien nor Wayne noticed the newcomer. They were too intent on each other.

Before their very eyes, the tall, powerful figure of Wayne D'Arville seemed to crumble, as the gentle, humane man whose voice and eyes were as soft as that of a deer seemed to grow in size and stature.

'Take my hand, Wayne,' Sebastien said softly, holding out his hand. 'You know I'm the only one who can help you.'

Behind him, Lilas wanted to sob out loud. Even now, with his life in peril, he was trying to help the maniac! She crept closer, keeping her slight figure hidden from view behind Sebastien's own body. She was close enough now to touch him. She didn't have the faintest idea what she was going to do. She only knew, somehow, that she must save him.

'Sebastien!' Wayne said again, his voice a strangled plea as he shook his handsome head from side to side. 'Don't make me kill you. Please!'

Sebastien shook his head, a gentle smile on his face. 'It's time, Wayne,' he said softly. 'Time to let go of all the pain. I'll help you. I promise you.' Overhead, the balcony light illuminated the two men, locked in their own private world. 'You have to choose. Now, Wayne. Now. I won't wait for you any longer.'

'I can't . . .' Wayne screamed, the words torn out of him like thorns that had been buried in his flesh.

Sebastien slowly reached forward, his hand coming out to take the gun.

Travis felt Kier's hand digging hard into his shoulder. They both breathed a massive, joint sigh of relief as the American reached forward and took the gun from Wayne's lifeless fingers and tossed it harmlessly back into the room. It nearly hit Lilas, who was standing so close behind. She saw the gun land on the carpet, and nearly melted with relief. She started to straighten up from her couch as Kier reached forward and picked the gun up.

The movement distracted Wayne. Seeing the American with the gun, a sudden image flashed through his mind – an image of a media circus, crucifying him, branding him the criminal son of a Nazi. Looking into Kier Harcourt's eyes, he saw a prison sentence, exile, disgrace. He snarled, his arm pushing against Sebastien's chest as he tried to launch himself across the room. But Sebastien was too quick. Without thinking, he grabbed Wayne's arm, the sudden jolt making him stagger back. He felt his legs hit the back of the balustrade, and he gave a brief cry. Wayne was swung around by the unexpected force of the backlash, and felt himself begin to topple forward.

'*No*!' Wayne and Lilas screamed together. Lilas flung herself forward, and just managed to catch one of Sebastien's windmilling arms in a fierce grip. But the sudden movement, and Wayne's sheer size, worked against him.

Sebastien's eyes met his for just a second. He tightened his own hold on Wayne's arm, but already the huge Frenchman was falling over the balustrade. 'Wayne!' he screamed helplessly, as the man's weight dragged him nearer the edge.

Lilas hung on to Sebastien for grim death. She knew only one thing. If Sebastien was going over, then so was she.

Wayne's blue eyes widened on Sebastien's eyes for just a moment. He knew Sebastien would not let him go. He also knew that, unless he did, Sebastien too would plummet to his death.

With a sudden yank, Wayne tore his grip loose and fell into the darkness below. The last thing he heard was Sebastien's agonized voice, screaming his name.

When Travis and Kier ran to the balcony and looked down, Wayne was sprawled across the rock garden like a broken doll.

On the balcony, Sebastien fell to his knees and stared at Lilas. He didn't know how she came to be there. It seemed like a miracle. One moment he was about to die, the next she was holding on to him, her grip as strong and sure as her love.

He stared at her, speechless with gratitude. Then, as if drawn by a magnet, he glanced down at the body sprawled below. 'He let go of me,' Sebastien said shakily. 'He knew he was going to die – that we were both going to die and he . . . let go . . . He wasn't all bad, Lilas,' he said urgently, turning back to her, taking her cold, shaking hands in his own. His eyes beseeched her. He wanted to tell her how much he loved her. Needed her. He also wanted her to understand. About Wayne.

Lilas already understood. She held him tightly.

'No,' she agreed softly, looking down at the body below. 'He wasn't *all* bad.'

CHAPTER 22

One week later, Travis walked into the hospital and caught his mother throwing a pillow at Val.

'Ow!' Val hollered. 'That 'urt!'

'Baby!' Veronica poked her tongue out at him, then caught sight of her son. 'Travis! About time too. I was beginning to get a craving for more grapes.'

Travis laughed and put the bag of mixed fruit on the side of the table. Val promptly leaned across and nicked the grapes.

'Hey!' Veronica yelled.

Travis laughed again, and silently thought what a good thing it was that his parents were in a private room, far away from the other patients. Now that they were almost fully recovered, and tests had proved there was no brain damage to either of them, they were becoming a handful.

'Now behave,' Travis scolded. 'Dad, give Mum her grapes back.'

Val scowled. 'She hit me. With a blunt instrument.'

'He called me baldy!' Veronica retorted.

Indeed, Veronica still had little hair on her head – but then neither had Val. The fire had singed it so badly, the hospital staff had shaved both their heads for them. Now, though, Veronica's skull was covered with downy-soft dark tufts, and it would soon grow back into its usual raven-dark cap.

Travis was only relieved that they hadn't suffered any serious burns. Just a few to the hands; Val's in particular were still bandaged. He'd burnt them trying to open the windows – the steel had been red-hot.

He'd learned, over the past week, how Val had carried Veronica, unconscious from the flames. And he couldn't have asked for a better tonic, after all he'd been through, than to find his parents back to their usual, squabbling, loving selves.

But he wouldn't dwell on the past. Nor would he think of Wayne D'Arville. He'd told Val and Veronica everything, of course, but since that first visit they had never mentioned it again.

Now he pulled a large, square envelope from his breast pocket, like a magician producing a rabbit from a hat.

'What yer got there?' Val asked, munching a grape with a hearty appetite.

'A wedding invitation,' Travis said. 'To Sebastien's and Lilas's wedding.'

Veronica squealed in delight. 'Give it to me!' She scanned the details of the invitation, and sighed. 'April in England. How wonderful. I'm looking forward to meeting this Lilas. She'd better be good enough for Sebastien! Val, you'll have to design me an outfit especially for the occasion.'

Val groaned around a grape. 'Slave driver.'

'And,' Travis pulled out another square envelope, 'we also have a second invitation. To Paris and Maria's wedding. Don't worry – it's not till June. We can make it to both.'

Veronica, her eyes sparkling, turned to Val.

Val tossed the bunch of grapes disgustedly her way, and she caught them neatly. 'I know, don't tell me,' he grumbled. 'You'll want *another* outfit for that do.'

'Well, it will be a big Hollywood society wedding,' Veronica said, selecting a juicy berry. 'And you know what they're like.'

Val groaned, and ducked his head under the sheet. 'Wake me up next Christmas.'

Travis grinned at him, then reached across and took his mother's hand and squeezed it in sheer happiness.

Veronica looked at him steadily. 'So, how's Gemma?' she asked quietly.

Travis shrugged nonchalantly, looked at her as she rather comically raised one burned eyebrow high on her forehead, and laughed. 'She's fine. She's set up a rape-crisis centre in downtown LA.'

Veronica nodded. 'Good for her.' She squeezed her son's hand. 'You like her, don't you?'

Travis grinned. 'Yep. And in a few years . . . who knows? You might even get an invite to *my* wedding.'

Val gave a disbelieving snort from beneath the sheet.

Travis grinned, leaned back against his mother's headboard and pinched one of her grapes.

THE EXCITING NEW NAME
IN WOMEN'S FICTION!

PLEASE HELP ME TO HELP YOU!

Dear *Scarlet* Reader,

As Editor of *Scarlet* Books I want to make sure that the
books I offer you every month are up to the high standards
Scarlet readers expect. And to do that I need to know a
little more about you and your reading likes and dislikes. So
please spare a few minutes to fill in the short questionnaire
on the following pages and send it to me.

Looking forward to hearing from you,

Sally Cooper

Editor-in-Chief, *Scarlet*

P.S. Make sure you look at these end pages in your *Scarlet*
books each month! We hope to have some exciting news for
you very soon.

QUESTIONNAIRE

Please tick the appropriate boxes to indicate your answers

1 Where did you get this Scarlet title?
Bought in supermarket ☐
Bought at my local bookstore ☐ Bought at chain bookstore ☐
Bought at book exchange or used bookstore ☐
Borrowed from a friend ☐
Other (please indicate) _____

2 Did you enjoy reading it?
A lot ☐   A little ☐   Not at all ☐

3 What did you particularly like about this book?
Believable characters ☐   Easy to read ☐
Good value for money ☐   Enjoyable locations ☐
Interesting story ☐   Modern setting ☐
Other _____

4 What did you particularly dislike about this book?
_____

5 Would you buy another Scarlet book?
Yes ☐   No ☐

6 What other kinds of book do you enjoy reading?
Horror ☐   Puzzle books ☐   Historical fiction ☐
General fiction ☐   Crime/Detective ☐   Cookery ☐
Other (please indicate) _____

7 Which magazines do you enjoy reading?
1. _____
2. _____
3. _____

And now a little about you –
8 How old are you?
Under 25 ☐   25–34 ☐   35–44 ☐
45–54 ☐   55–64 ☐   over 65 ☐

cont.

9 What is your marital status?
   Single ☐   Married/living with partner ☐
   Widowed ☐   Separated/divorced ☐

10 What is your current occupation?
   Employed full-time ☐   Employed part-time ☐
   Student ☐   Housewife full-time ☐
   Unemployed ☐   Retired ☐

11 Do you have children? If so, how many and how old are they?
   _____
   _____

12 What is your annual household income?
   under $15,000 ☐   or £10,000 ☐
   $15–25,000 ☐   or £10–20,000 ☐
   $25–35,000 ☐   or £20–30,000 ☐
   $35–50,000 ☐   or £30–40,000 ☐
   over $50,000 ☐   or £40,000 ☐

Miss/Mrs/Ms _____
Address _____
_____
_____

Thank you for completing this questionnaire. Now tear it out – put
it in an envelope and send it before 31 August, 1997, to:

Sally Cooper, Editor-in-Chief

USA/Can. address
SCARLET c/o London Bridge
85 River Rock Drive
Suite 202
Buffalo
NY 14207
USA

UK address/No stamp required
SCARLET
FREEPOST LON 3335
LONDON W8 4BR
*Please use block capitals for
address*

RESOL/2/97

Scarlet **titles coming next month:**

TIME TO TRUST   Jill Sheldon

Cord isn't impressed by the female of the species! And he certainly doesn't have 'time to trust' one of them! It's just as well, then, that Emily is equally reluctant to let a man into *her* life – even one as irresistible as Cord. But maybe the decision isn't theirs to make – for someone else has a deadly interest in their relationship!

THE PATH TO LOVE   Chrissie Loveday

Kerrien has decided that a new life in Australia is just what she needs. So she takes a job with Dr Ashton Philips and is soon hoping there can be more between them than a working relationship. Then Ashton's sister, Kate, and his glamorous colleague, Martine, decide to announce his forthcoming marriage!

LOVERS AND LIARS   Sally Steward

Eliot Kane is Leanne Warner's dream man, and she finds herself falling deeper and deeper in love with him. When Eliot confesses to having memory lapses and, even worse, dreams which feature . . . murder, Leanne begins to wonder if she's involved with a man who could be a very, very dangerous lover indeed.

LOVE BEYOND DESIRE   Jessica Marchant

Amy is a thoroughly modern woman. She doesn't want marriage and isn't interested in commitment. Robert seems as happy as she is to keep their relationship casual. And what about Paul – does he want more from Amy than just friendship? Then Amy's safe and secure world is suddenly shrouded in darkness and she has to decide which of these two men she can trust with her heart . . . and her future happiness.